SUNDAY BEST

ROBBI NEAL

SUNDAY BEST

A Memoir

HARPER PERENNIAL

HarperPerennial
An imprint of HarperCollins*Publishers*, Australia

First published in 2004
by HarperCollins*Publishers* Pty Limited
ABN 36 009 913 517
A member of the HarperCollins*Publishers* (Australia) Pty Limited Group
www.harpercollins.com.au

HarperCollins*Publishers*
25 Ryde Road, Pymble, Sydney NSW 2073, Australia
31 View Road, Glenfield, Auckland 10, New Zealand
77–85 Fulham Palace Road, London W6 8JB, United Kingdom
2 Bloor Street East, 20th floor, Toronto, Ontario M4W 1A8, Canada
10 East 53rd Street, New York NY 10022, USA

National Library of Australia Cataloguing-in-Publication data:

Neal, Robbi.
Sunday best.
ISBN 0 7322 8059 1.
1. Neal, Robbi. 2. Breast - Cancer - Patients - Biography.
3. Artists - Biography. I. Title.
362.196994490092

Cover design: Ellie Exarchos, Scooter Design
Cover photo of author and internal illustrations: Robbi Neal
Typeset in 10.5/13 Sabon by HarperCollins Design Studio
Printed and bound in Australia by Griffin Press on 50gsm Bulky News

5 4 3 2 1 04 05 06 07

Dedicated to my two grandmothers Hilda and Lyne,
both pure pearls.

And to my husband Peter and my children
Asher, Seth, Indea, Zane and Maia
who are my angels and bring me messages
of hope.

Author's Note

In the beginning I never expected this book to be read by anyone but my children. I started to write because I thought I was going to die and I wanted them to know who I was. You cannot possibly put a whole life into one book; you can only focus on some aspects and the story determines what they will be. I set myself rules when I started. One was that I would not write anyone else's story or assume to know their feelings or thoughts. Consequently this narrative is from my perspective only and someone else would probably write about the same events and paint a picture unrecognisable from this one. This is the truth about what happened to me. Some of the names have been changed.

Contents

Prologue

'There are three things that remain —
faith, hope and love — and the greatest
of these is love.'

I Coe. 13:13
Living Bible Version

1

What I am most afraid of is fear. Fear is so debilitating.

The fear I have at this moment is that I might die.

Soon.

Really soon.

Like maybe in three short months.

It's not death itself I'm afraid of. I mean, well, everybody has to die.

Death happens to all of us. And once it happens there isn't much you can do about it. Either you will be happily in the ever after waiting for your loved ones or you will simply cease to exist and you won't know you're dead.

What I am afraid of is not death but the lack of control I may have over my death and the thought that it could happen to me way before I'm ready for it. Death seems such an awful anticlimax to a life.

My baby is only three years old. She is my angel, the child that I linger over, that I am never too busy to hold and always regret letting go of. She sleeps next to me so close and tight that we almost become one. In the night when I am racked with fright and panic I get up and pad quietly to her room. I lift her sleeping body out of her warm bed, she half wakes, murmurs contentedly and folds herself into my body as I carry her to my bed, where I can now sleep because she is wrapped up in my arms. I pretend I can hold her safe forever. I don't want to leave her.

I am also in love with my other four children, each one an endless source of joy and pride. And there is my husband, who snores blissfully next to me, while I fret and weep beside him. I am in love with my husband. I know he doesn't realise it, but I adore him. I even have a stepson who I cannot help but love. He is so like my husband, in him I see glimpses of my husband's youth.

At two in the morning the fear makes me tremble and I cry silently as I lie there with my snoring husband, envying his dreams. Eventually I cry myself back to sleep.

When I wake I wonder how soon my family will be at my funeral.

I imagine my children there and my heart breaks, not for myself but for them. I can see them distraught because I have left them. I see them afraid, disillusioned as their safe world is torn apart. I see them inconsolable as adults hover close by trying to comfort them.

Children expect their mother to be there for them always, anticipating their needs even before they are aware of them.

I do not want to die and destroy my children's faith.

I shake myself from the torture of imagining my children without me. I remember the first funeral I ever went to, my grandfathers, and the family photograph taken there.

I hope there will be no such photographs at mine.

In it my mother and her five brothers and two sisters are gathered around my grandmother, smiling into the camera. An outsider might look at the photo and think — 'well he must have been a right old bastard — they're happy to be rid of him.' This wasn't the case. My grandfather was respected and loved and my family's happiness comes from knowing that within their heads they held the truth and within their souls they drank a spiritual cocktail of joy and security because my grandfather has not died, but has gone to join the Lord. His funeral is a time of celebration because he has attained the perfect state of being by the Lord's side. Now he will be forever happy and healthy and will sing praises to God.

I am eleven at his funeral and I am supposed to rejoice that my grandfather has gone to join the Lord.

2

I miss my grandfather. His name was Joseph, such a soft name. When I grow up I want to name one of my sons Joseph. My grandfather was the tallest man I have ever seen. He could hold me in his arms and I would be safe forever. He had an English accent and the biggest nose you ever saw. My mother says his nose was big because his mother was a Jew, one of the Lord's chosen people.

My grandfather spoiled me so I look sad at his funeral.

He walked me to the corner milk bar, which is not on a corner at all but is sandwiched in the middle of the block between two houses; still, everyone calls it the corner milk bar. It is only half a block away. My grandfather walked me out the front gate, past the Hampton Baptist Church right next door to his house where he was the minister, and down Thomas Street to the milk bar. I skipped all the way because I knew he was going to spoil me with a bag of lollies. He gave me threepence to spend, which would fill a white lolly bag right up. It would be so stuffed with clinkers and mates and jersey caramels that it was hard to balance it in one hand, eat with the other and walk home all at the same time. My grandfather was the only person in my whole life who bought me lollies.

When the currency changed he gave me five cents. I was a

bit worried about the new coins, but he assured me that in fact I was better off.

'Five cents is more than threepence, my popsy,' my grandfather told me.

He loved fishing, like the disciples, Peter and John. Mostly my grandfather was a fisher of men, but he loved fishing for fish too. My grandfather sent me jewellery when he went away fishing on his holiday from doing the Lord's work. My necklace and bracelet arrived in a little brown box. On the outside was my name and address in his scrawly, old-fashioned writing. I opened it as fast as I could, tearing at the brown string tied around the parcel. Inside, the white pearly stones appeared so precious and fragile lying there in their bed of tissue paper. I dared not touch them for fear of spoiling their purity. There was a note for me. 'A good woman is a pearl among swine,' it said.

Even though I am a child I sense the finality of his death. He will slip away from me and be gone forever. So I am failing to be a pearl because I am miserable that he has died, when I am supposed to rejoice that he has joined the Lord in heaven and will suffer pain no more.

'Stop looking so sad,' says my mother.

She has her good wig on for the funeral. It looks like a coconut stuck on her head. When she was getting dressed I said, 'Why do you wear a wig? What's wrong with your own hair?'

'Wigs,' she said, 'are the height of fashion. And besides, the Lord's chosen people, the Jews, wear wigs in public.'

And now she says to me, 'Do you think the Lord wants to see that unhappy face?'

She is exasperated.

My mother, grandmother and uncle are standing over me. I feel as small and insignificant as a mouse. It would be okay if I felt like a sparrow, because I know the Lord takes note even when the tiniest sparrow falls. I've heard that in children's talk lots of times. But I don't think the Bible says anything about mice.

I glance over at my brother, Wayne. He is in his Sunday-best suit, standing by the trestle table covered with my grandmother's best damask cloth, stuffing lamingtons and hedgehog into his mouth at a rate that would make my mother say, 'You'd think we never fed him.'

'It is a blasphemy,' my uncle says to me, 'not to praise the Lord. You should be rejoicing that Granddad is at his side. It is selfish of you to think only of yourself. You should be glad for him.'

I love my grandmother more than anyone in the world and she looks at me and explains, 'You must bear good witness to unbelievers. You are letting the Lord down with your gloomy face. The unbelievers will look at you and think, "See? They are no different from us. They are sad when someone dies. They do not really believe in the resurrection of the saved." You must bear good witness to the Lord. It is a sin to be ruled by your own selfish feelings.'

I scratch at my neck, fighting back my tears. I am sad about my grandfather and I am letting the Lord down with my misery.

I too am in my Sunday best. Sunday best can only be worn to funerals, weddings and church. We have our weekday clothes, Sunday best and Saturday clothes.

'If you were asked to present yourself before Queen Elizabeth,' says my grandmother, 'you would put on your Sunday best. So you must wear your Sunday best when you are visiting the house of the king of kings.'

I do not know anything about Queen Elizabeth except that her face is on a four-cent stamp and she doesn't look very friendly. You would think that if your face was going to be on everybody in the whole world's letters you could at least smile. So I don't know if I really would put on my Sunday best for her or not.

My weekday clothes are a discarded private school uniform that my mother got at an opportunity shop. I have to wear to school, every day of the week, a white shirt with a Peter Pan collar, a grey tunic with a matching grey belt and a grey blazer. It is all very grey and proper. I am the only person in my whole school wearing anything like it. My mother has taken off the private school emblem on the blazer and sewn my initials over the tiny holes it leaves. Frankly, I know I look stupid traipsing off to the state school in my uniform every day of the week. The other kids wear jeans, but I am not allowed to. Jeans are modern and sinful. You can see the outline of a girl's bottom in them. I hate my school uniform. I like my Saturday clothes. I haven't got jeans, which I really want, but at least I can wear trousers and a jumper on Saturdays.

My Sunday clothes I also hate. My Sunday best is a grey checked gingham dress. It has a netting petticoat attached at the waist. The netting makes the dress stick out like a tutu and itches like nothing else where it is sewn on at the waist. The dress has a fake pink apron with lace edging sewn over the top and a big pink bow at the back. It is the daggiest dress I have ever seen in my life and I dread someone from school walking past the church one Sunday morning and seeing me in it, shaking hands with the pastor. My mother tries to assure me that pink and grey together are the height of chic, but I suspect that it was the best offering in my size at the opportunity shop.

I put my hand up under my skirt and scratch at the waist, completely ruining, I suppose, my mother's chic effect.

My brother has started on the butterfly cakes now and has whipped cream spread from ear to ear. I wish I could stuff my face like he does, but I do not like food very much. I always have this slightly sick feeling in my stomach, as if the ocean is stuck in there constantly swooshing from side to side. My brother did not care for my grandfather anyway, so he can eat and rejoice in the Lord. I know that my brother is not saved and never will be.

Every Sunday morning when he is supposed to be learning about God in Sunday school, which he really needs to do, he sneaks down the road to the milk bar, spends the collection money our mother gives us and stuffs his face with ten cents' worth of musk sticks when that money is supposed to go towards spreading the word of the Lord among the unsaved. And now some hungry child in Ethiopia is going to die unsaved and go to hell, when they could die and go to be with the Lord. And worse than that, it is a sin to go to the shops on the Lord's Day.

My grandmother asks my brother to say grace at meal times because he is a boy.

'God likes to hear a boy's voice,' she says, 'because boys are created in His image.'

I feel cheated because I love the Lord and I love the chance to pray and show publicly my love and devotion to Him in prayer, but I am not made in the Lord's image. So my voice is not pleasing to Him and my grandmother does not realise that my brother is not saved. In fact he is on the slippery wide road to hell. At the very least he has a spirit of gluttony upon him.

My grandfather was the tallest man I have ever seen and my grandmother is the smallest woman I have ever seen. She is tiny, but she always stands tall and proud with her head held high and she always dresses smartly, ready for the Lord should he come back. She has tight curls on her head and doesn't need to perm, which is lucky because only unbelievers perm and use make-up or nail polish.

Now this is what my mother and grandmother have told me about themselves and our family.

My grandmother was old when she met my grandfather. She was twenty-eight and had already been engaged. She broke it off when her fiancé tried to exercise his rights as her spiritual head.

'I don't care if the Lord did make women to be submissive,' she told him. 'I answer to no man. I am accountable only to the Lord!'

I admire my grandmother. Soon after that she met my grandfather. She thought he was the ugliest man she had ever seen, but she heard the Lord tell her in her heart that she was to marry him.

'Well, Lord,' she answered, 'if he's the man that you've chosen for me, then I trust that you will make me love him.'

Three months after they met they were married.

She also had to love his five children.

Their mother had recently committed suicide. No one knows why. Maybe my grandfather drove her to it. Maybe he was harsher with her than my mother says he was to his children. Maybe she was mad, but she drowned herself in the river while he was busy preaching the Lord's word on a Sunday morning. The children were aged between three and sixteen.

In three months my grandparents married and she became a mother of five. In another nine months it was six, but my grandmother didn't even know she was pregnant until she went into labour with my mother. My uncles and aunt came home from school for lunch and there she was.

'Fancy,' said my grandmother, 'last night I was playing the church organ, singing praise to the Lord, and now you have a new sister. It just goes to show what praising the Lord can do.'

My mother was called Hilda Rowena. My grandmother says that having a girl was a bit of a mixed blessing. Boys might be better because boys are created in God's image, but at least with a girl there are no messy corners to navigate when changing their nappies.

Then there was another girl, Mabel Prestonia, named like my grandmother after the town of Preston, because my grandmother was born when my great-grandfather was its mayor so they passed the name on. Then at last came the boy, made in the image of our Lord.

All up there were eight of them.

My grandmother told her new children to call her 'Matey'. She thought it would be too cruel to make them call her 'Mum' when their own mother had only just died and they were so little. 'Matey' very quickly became 'Mato'; it stuck and everyone who loved her called her that ever after. Except, of course, my father, who calls her Tomato.

Six of the children are saved. The older two? No one is quite sure if we will see them in the New Jerusalem or not. My mother's older sister ran off when she was sixteen and came back later with an adopted child plus two of her own and a husband. My mother's oldest brother ran off to war and then went to live in Tasmania. My grandmother sends him lots of tracts to try and bring him to the Lord, but I don't think they've worked. The favourite tract is a little pamphlet entitled *God's Four Laws*. I know this tract off by heart. I can also recite all the names of the books of the Bible in order, Old and New Testament, plus Psalms 23, 121 and all the New Testament verses that relate to salvation. The most important is John 3:16:

> *For God so loved the world that he gave his only begotten son/that who so ever believeth in him should not perish but have everlasting life.*

But the first Bible verse I was ever taught is from Numbers. Numbers 32:23:

Be sure your sins will find you out!

Of my mother's other brothers and sister, Dan became a missionary and worked in Kashmir for twenty-five years, George sold Electrolux vacuum cleaners and Claude ran a farm in Tasmania. Next was my mother, a secretary, then Tonia, an art teacher, and finally William, who started his career with Johns & Waygood lifts and ended up a state manager and the pride of the family when you had to go through sixteen secretaries to get him on the phone. I have fourteen aunts and uncles and that is just on my mother's side and doesn't include my great-aunts.

My mother is saved, but this didn't stop her from falling by the wayside or backsliding when she was young.

My mother and her five brothers sinned and their sins found them out.

They tried to make alcoholic ginger beer in the far corner of the shed at the end of the yard. They made their brew amongst the tools, boxes and cobwebs. But none of them managed to get the slightest bit intoxicated on it. They didn't even get to taste one alcoholic drop. They let it ferment for too long, it exploded all over my grandfather's tools and they all got the strap.

When my mother was about thirteen the family moved to Dawson Street Baptist Church in Ballarat where my grandfather was the new minister. The Catholic Church was over the road. My mother and her brothers snuck out of church and let the frogs they had collected loose during mass. As my grandfather was shaking hands with his flock and hearing how the Lord had really spoken to them this week through his sermon, he saw the angry priest stomping over the road towards him. After a brief word with the priest and when the flock had gone home to Sunday roast, my mother and her brothers all got the strap.

My mother told me these stories to show me how your sins always find you out.

My mother was the tallest girl in high school on both her first and last days at school. She was five foot, eleven inches and everyone always thought she was older than she was. She fell in love with a boy named Peter. My grandparents approved of him because he was from a good Christian family. His family was Exclusive Brethren. If we hadn't already been Baptists we'd have been Brethren. Brethren are okay.

No one else is okay. Catholics are the antichrist. They have a Pope who they say is the head of the church, but all good Christians know that only Christ himself is head of the church. They also have priests who are middle men, like untrustworthy salesmen. They come between God and the chosen. Catholics even confess their sins to the priests, when only God has the power to forgive. Besides the scripture says that every saved person is a priest of the Lord; somehow I think this must be a mistranslation, because even in the Baptist Church only men are pastors. So I can't see how the priesthood of all believers, that gets preached about nearly every Sunday morning, can mean me.

Anglicans are not true Christians. They only go to worship the Lord at Christmas and Easter and don't understand that they need to be saved to be a real Christian and go to heaven. Besides, Anglicans are almost Catholics. The Methodists, Presbyterians and Congregationalists aren't real Christians either because, my mother says, if they were real Christians they'd hear the Lord speaking to them and telling them to become Baptists. They are closed to God's voice and, besides, they baptise babies who are unsaved and haven't yet accepted the Lord as their Saviour. Church of Christ are Christians — just. They baptise adults, but they don't celebrate the Lord's Holy Communion often enough, so they are like watered-down Baptists. The Brethren, though — they have our respect because they might be even more strict than we are.

My mother fell in love with one and when she wanted to marry him, my grandmother and grandfather made her write to him and tell him that she would be unable to do so. My grandparents wrote the letter. They wrote that she was unworthy of him and they confessed all her past sins so that he would know what he was wanting to marry. My mother signed that letter as though it was from her, but she was devastated. She decided that she would never have and didn't deserve a good husband and that my father would be the best she could get.

My mother had known my father since childhood; my grandparents had watched him grow up and they weren't impressed with the way he had turned out. But after going out together for three months my parents got engaged on my mother's twenty-first birthday. An occasion on which she was also given the strap by my grandfather for answering him back. My mother always tells me how she was strapped on her twenty-first to remind me that you are never too old to be disciplined by your parents.

My father led a Bible study and my mother, his fiancée, went along. An old lady who liked my mother was at the Bible study and asked my mother to sit with her, so she did. But my father wanted my mother to sit next to *him*, now that they were engaged. My mother chose to stay next to the old lady and my father was furious and lost his temper in front of everyone. My grandparents saw this as a warning sign and did not want my mother to marry my father, but she was determined and they held their peace. My parents were married a year later when she was twenty-two.

Then my father applied to be a candidate for the Baptist ministry. When he was rejected he fumed and he left the church and God. My mother and he were already married and now my Christian mother and my backslidden father were unevenly yoked. Two years later I was born, but unfortunately I was not made in our Lord's image. I was a girl.

Part One

Hope

3

My mother wants me to go to the shop. I don't want to go. I am scared of crossing the big road and try to look hopeless so she will change her mind.

'Don't be so selfish,' she says. 'You have to go for me; I can't go, with your brother and sister to look after. For goodness sakes, Robbi, it's only around the corner. I need some milk for cooking.' So she puts down her wooden mixing spoon and reaches in beside the refrigerator for the milk bottle holder. She passes it to me. It is made of wire and has a handle and a place for four milk bottles to sit so they don't crash against each other and break. Every night my mother puts it out for the milkman, sometimes with paper money curled up in the neck of one of the bottles. Obviously she hasn't asked him for enough milk and that's why I have to go to the milk bar.

'I need two bottles,' she says and she gives me a two-pound note.

The new money is coming in soon. Everyone is talking about the new money. My brother and I hang over the front gate and people walking down the street say, 'Not long now, kids, and it'll all be different. We'll all be richer. Ha, Ha, Ha!'

'Now this is a lot of money,' says my mother sternly, 'and there will be plenty of change. You make sure to take care of it.'

So I hold the note tightly in my hand and walk past my brother, who is squatting on the floor playing with his Meccano. He doesn't do much but squat on the floor. My sister is having her afternoon nap.

I walk down our street, Lantana Street, and cross the road several times to avoid the houses that have the frightening dogs scrambling at their gate to get out and tear you to shreds. We don't have a dog anymore. He kept picking my brother up like a pup and carrying him by the seat of his rompers. So my mother and father said they were sending him to a farmer to round up the sheep. I cried when my dad put him in the back of the station wagon and drove him away, because I loved him. It can't have been far to the farm, because my dad was back before morning tea. Our dog was a cocker spaniel. I should be happy that he is running around big paddocks with the sheep. That's what my mother says anyway.

I get to the big street that I have to cross and I don't know what to do. The traffic is whizzing past and never seems to stop. I wait and wait for a safe time to cross, but no time seems safe to me, so I stand and wait. The cars keep rushing past and I keep waiting.

A lady crosses the road from the other side and I am amazed that nothing runs her over.

'Now, dear,' she says when she reaches me, 'I have been watching you from my lounge-room window. You're having trouble crossing the road, aren't you, dear?'

'Yes,' I say.

She takes my hand and as we cross the road she says, 'Does your mother know you are out alone?'

'Yes, she's sent me to get milk, see.' And I open my palm to show her the two-pound note.

The lady looks at me; she doesn't believe a little kid like me would have paper money. I can see she thinks I am lying so I say quickly, to explain, 'I am the biggest, I am nearly six and a half.'

‘All right, dear. Well, you’re right now,’ she says when we are safely on the other side of the road. She turns on her stiletto heels and walks into her own driveway.

I skip off to the milk bar. I like to skip, you almost feel like you are flying, and at the milk bar I ask for two bottles of milk. I hope my mother will let me have the cream off the top for getting the milk, but usually she gives it to my brother. ‘He needs it,’ she says.

I stand outside the milk bar and wait for a space in the traffic so I can cross again. The traffic noise rings in my ears and blurs around my brain and the man from the milk bar, in a white doctor’s coat, comes out and he helps me to cross. It takes two hands to manage the holder with full bottles, so I have shoved the change into the pocket of my shift.

‘Off you go,’ he says. He gives me a little push and I run across the road.

I am tired because going to the milk bar has taken a long time with all the waiting to cross the road and I think I will take a shortcut across the empty block. The grass is really long and there might be snakes so I sing:

Jesus bids us shine with a pure clear light,
Like a little candle burning in the night,
In this world of darkness so let us shine,
You in your small corner and I in mine.

I sing in a big loud voice so the serpents can hear me coming and know that the Lord is protecting me and that he is more powerful than the devil whom they belong to.

Finally I am home with the milk. I walk into the kitchen where my mother has an apron on and is still cooking. I hope she is cooking pancakes because I love her pancakes. I give her the milk, hoping she will see that I really want the cream off the top and I deserve it for being so good and getting the milk for her.

'What took you so long?' she says crossly, wiping her doughy hands on a tea towel. She puts the milk in the fridge door and stands up. I look at her. My mother is even taller than the refrigerator. 'I needed this milk half an hour ago. I can't trust you to do anything, can I? Goodness, you're a dreamy girl!' she snaps.

Then she holds out her hand and says, 'Change?' And I fish in the pocket of my shift for the coins and note, but I suddenly feel sick. The sickness hits my stomach like when you know you are going to crash into a tree on your bike because you are going too fast down a hill. There is no change in my pocket. I look at my mother. She is staring hard at me. Waiting.

'I've lost it,' I say nervously.

She growls at me, 'Well, you'd better go back and find it, young lady!' She puts her hands on her hips. 'You'd just better hope you do find it, too, or I will be dealing with you!'

So I walk back to the vacant lot where the grass is long and there might be snakes. My stomach feels like it has worms slithering around inside, I feel sick with worry about the trouble I will be in if I don't find that change and I ask the Lord to help me find it. I search and search in the long grass and I am so tired and even though it is summer I am starting to get cold and I am alone here in the empty paddock. It is starting to get that eerie night-time feel. My skin is getting prickly and everyone says that strange men wait for little girls in empty paddocks. So I go home to face my mother rather than wait for a strange man to get me.

'Did you find it?' she says, putting her hands on her hips.

I shake my head to say no. I am trying to stop my eyes from crying.

'I can't afford to lose two pounds,' she says in her most furious voice. 'Really, Robbi, you are so irresponsible! You may as well have stolen that money, you are so careless. It's just plain thievery to be so careless with something that isn't yours!'

Her voice is getting louder now. It's a tidal wave coming to knock me over with its force.

'I don't know what to do with you sometimes,' she growls. 'Well, you can just make up for that lost money, young lady. There will be no lunch for you for two weeks!'

Then she sits on a stool, muttering to herself, picks up the phone and arranges for me to go and stay with my grandparents. I love them so much, I hope she doesn't tell them that I am a thief. I don't want them to know how bad and careless I am. I run straight to my bedroom, because I am going to cry with shame.

When my father gets home from work I rush out to meet him because everyone else just ignores him, but he pushes me away and yells at my mother, 'Get this bloody kid off me, Ena!'

'Leave your father alone,' says my mother, putting her head into the entrance way. 'Can't you scc he's tired from working all day?'

And he turns on the telly and watches that new show 'McHale's Navy'. I don't like it. That show is full of men with wicked, sickly smiles that make their teeth look like little white demons.

Two days later, on Monday, Mato, my grandmother, and my grandfather who are my mother's parents come and pick me up and take me to their house. I live with them a lot. I don't know why, but my mother is always sending me to their house, but I'm very glad because they are so kind to me.

They set up a camp bed for me right beside their bed. It is made of hessian and has little wooden legs and I imagine that my grandfather used it during the wars when he was a padre. Before going to sleep at night I crawl into bed with them and we all say our prayers. First my grandfather, then my Mato, I take special note of her 'Thees' and 'Thous' and her 'beseeches' and then it is my turn to say:

Now I lay me down to sleep,
I pray the Lord my soul to keep,
If I should die before I wake,
I pray the Lord my soul to take.

To tell you the truth, this prayer always makes me shiver a little bit. It's the line about dying in the night that scares me. I wonder, as I go to sleep, whether that could really happen. Could I just die in the night? Would I go to hell?

In the morning I crawl into my grandparents' bed again and cuddle with Mato while Granddad makes us all a cup of tea. Then after the tea he reads from the Lord's word, we say our morning prayers and then the best bit, Granddad shaves with his electric razor. When he's finished he cleans it onto a sheet of newspaper that he keeps over his enamel potty under the bed. All those little shavings of hair are the softest things I ever touched, yet they were so prickly on his face. Then he tips his shavings into the wee in his potty and they dissolve into nothing.

We have to be out of bed in time for the next cup of tea and the eight o'clock ABC news on the wireless.

This morning I need to go and have a wee before I can say my morning prayers.

'Can I go to the toilet?' I ask Mato.

'Of course, but be sure not to dawdle. We must make time to spend with the Lord,' she tells me. I hurry to the toilet and on my way back I notice the bowl of nuts from last night on the dining table. I haven't had any breakfast and I am hungry from missing out on my lunches, so I take a few and go on to my grandparents' room, ready to climb back into bed with them. When I get there Mato is standing in her nightie with her hands on her hips. I know that when women put their hands on their hips they are really angry and her face is dark and heated.

I feel the sickness that is always waiting, clawing at my insides.

'What did you do?' she asks.

I say nothing because I don't know. It can't be that I went to the toilet, but I say that anyway. 'I went to the toilet.'

'Yes, and on your way back from the toilet?'

'I ate a few nuts.'

'That's right,' says Mato. 'You stole those nuts. No one offered them to you. Those nuts did not belong to you. You stole them and stealing is a sin. You must ask the Lord for forgiveness,' she says.

So during prayers I have to ask, 'Please, Lord, forgive me for stealing from my grandparents and for sinning against you. I repent and I will endeavour not to commit this sin again.'

I love my grandparents more than anyone in the whole world and I am so happy when I live with them but now they think that I am a thief.

Sometimes my grandparents take me to Hepburn Springs where my grandfather is the interim pastor and I love it. I sit quietly while he preaches, then I have lunch with him and my grandmother in the manse next door and I help collect mineral water in glass bottles from the pumps on the reserve. My grandparents live in Hampton next door to the Baptist Church where my grandfather was the minister and still preaches a lot. My grandparents treat me as though I am special.

If I am sick my grandmother makes a bed for me in the lounge room and I get to watch TV. All day. I watch 'Peyton Place' and 'Days of Our Lives' and then in the afternoon 'Robin Hood' is on and he is so handsome that I want to marry him when I grow up, provided the actor is a born-again Christian, of course.

I will eat up big this week at breakfast because I am not allowed to have lunch as punishment for my irresponsibility. My mother can't afford to lose two pounds and I may as well have stolen it! So when Mato puts on her blue floral housecoat and makes my Vegemite toast, I ask for an extra slice. She puts on just the amount I like and then cuts the toast into eight little triangles. It always tastes best when Mato makes it.

Then lunchtime comes and I feel sick with worry, wondering if they have heard what I did and whether they know I am not allowed to have lunch. I sit at the table with my grandfather while my grandmother makes him a sandwich.

She gives him looks but I can't quite catch what they mean. Then she says, 'Fancy not giving a young girl lunch.'

He looks over his round spectacles at her and nods in my direction. This means that she must not question my mother's God-given authority in my presence.

I want to die because now I know that my mother has told them.

Mato mutters to herself and makes me eggnog that I hate but she says, 'I'm not giving you anything to eat, popsy. Just something to drink and goodness to help you grow, so I'm not usurping your mother's authority. I'm sure she knows what she is doing.'

So this week I am not a pearl, I am a thief — a double thief — and my beloved grandparents know it. And I can't tell Mato that having no lunch is better than having eggnog.

4

We have moved.

One weekend my mother and father just packed everything onto the back of the trailer and after several loads we had moved. We hardly took anything with us: just our beds and clothes and kitchen things. They left all the furniture behind, but I don't know why.

My father hasn't got a job anymore and my mother cries all the time. Then through her tears she says, 'We must trust in the Lord. God always has a plan and a purpose.'

'Why hasn't Dad got a job anymore?' I ask when he is not around.

'Because he had a fight with his boss,' she answers.

'Why?'

'Because Daddy's boss didn't know how to run his business properly and Daddy had to tell him how to do it and his boss didn't like that,' she explains. 'Your daddy is a very clever man. Far more clever than his boss.'

So we have moved from the house in Lantana Street, North Blackburn, that my mother loved and was proud of and we are living with Grandmother Lyne and Great-Grandmother Lucy, who are my father's mother and grandmother.

This is what my mother has told me about my father's family. Great-Grandma Lucy's husband was a surveyor and moved from Kangaroo Island to survey the land around Sandringham when it was full of gypsies and Aborigines. They had four children and Grandma Lyne was one of them. She says her name is spelt 'Lyne' after her ancestors. She says her name shouldn't be pronounced 'Lin' but 'Line' and that she is the only person she knows with that name.

Grandma Lyne always says she could have been rich, because her ancestors owned Lea & Perrin sauces. But the money wasn't handed down correctly. She and her brother married a brother and sister, so Gran says that Auntie Margaret, who married Gran's brother and was her husband's sister, is her in-law twice. But Grandma Lyne's husband ran off with another woman after the war. It was a good thing too, says my mother, because he beat my father up all the time, even though my father was so sick with polio. And that, says my mother, is why my father does it to us.

Grandma Lyne's brother ran off with his wife's niece, who was only a young student, so I reckon that means Auntie Margaret is not a relative twice over now.

Sometimes we go and visit my father's father and his new wife. We have to keep it a secret from Grandma Lyne because she likes to pretend he is dead and tells everyone she is a widow. I don't like him. He just sits in his chair and watches the television and yells if we are too loud, even though we have to drive all the way to Rosebud to see him. His wife is lovely and very pretty. She was a hairdresser, so she cuts our hair. She smiles and sings and dances when she walks and she wears make-up.

'She danced with Sir Robert Helpmann,' says my mother. I don't know who he is but he sounds important.

They have two daughters. My father's half-sisters have beads and scarves all over their bedroom walls and boyfriends with long hair and beards. Even though I am young I can see they are afraid of their father, so he probably does to them what he did to my father and what my father does to us. When Grandma Lyne tells everyone her husband died in the war I bet she wishes he did. The bad thing about living with her is that when my mother disciplines my brothers, Grandma Lyne sneaks them lollies to make up for the trouble they have got into, but if my sister and I get into trouble, we get nothing because we are only girls.

The good thing about living with Grandma Lyne and Grandma Lucy is that they live just near Mato and Granddad, so I am living with Mato and Granddad almost half the time. My school is in between both houses, so I can walk from one house to the other. I spend Wednesday to Monday with Mato and Granddad and the rest of the week with my parents and my other grandmothers.

It is Sunday and I am staying with Mato and Granddad. Sunday is the Lord's day of rest, and is a real pain, not only because I have to wear my Sunday best, but because it means that Saturday is a day of work. On Saturdays the females of the family clean and cook; no work is to be done on a Sunday. The potatoes are prepared and soaked in water so they won't go grey, the roast is cooked and after a while the potatoes are thrown in and Mato runs a broom around the cornices to get rid of any cobwebs.

'We must be ready,' she says, 'in case the Lord comes back.' It is obvious a clean house is very important to Jesus.

On Sunday I have breakfast, then I go to Sunday school where I always win a prize for being a good student because I know that no matter what question the teacher asks the answer will be God, Jesus or Sin.

'Who wrote the Bible?' the teacher asks.

I throw my hand up in the air. 'God,' I say.

'Who died to save us?'

‘Jesus,’ I answer before anyone else gets a chance.

‘Why did Jesus die?’

‘Sin,’ I say solemnly. The way I see it, you have a one in three chance of always being right.

After Sunday school comes church, which always starts at eleven and finishes at precisely twelve-fifteen, unless of course we are celebrating the Lord’s Supper. We have to sit in the last row and I want to sit up the front, near my grandfather in the pulpit, but Mato says, ‘No. We must practise humility and let others sit up the front.’

Once the children’s talk is over I fidget all the way through the sermon and play with Mato’s kid gloves that are lined with soft white fur. I watch the clock on the side wall work its way through the time. By twelve I am so hungry that I am dying to put that little square of white communion bread in my mouth and drink the little cup of grape juice that represents the Lord’s blood. But I am not yet saved, so my mother will not let me.

I listen to the minister, who is sometimes my grandfather, as he says the words that are said before communion. ‘We invite all who know the Lord Jesus Christ as their personal saviour and who wish to serve him to partake in this, the Lord’s Supper.’

Then he says, ‘This bread is the symbol of our saviour’s body, broken on the cross that we might be saved.’ And he tears a piece of Tip Top white sliced in half.

‘This wine is the symbol of his blood, shed for the forgiveness of our sins,’ says my grandfather, holding a little cup of grape juice high in the air.

I have heard that Catholics think the bread and grape juice really do change to our Lord’s body and blood, but my mother says it is a sin to crucify the Lord over and over and that we are not cannibals. And, even worse, I have heard that they use real wine, which Mato says can turn followers away from the Lord and into alcoholics.

After church I feel ashamed. I am always sure everyone will have noticed that I did not have communion and am not saved. When the deacons walk past with the little cubes of bread and the little glasses, I put my head down to hide my red cheeks. I am sure everyone is looking and whispering, 'See, she is not saved. She does not partake in our Lord's Supper.'

I must get saved soon, because once I have been born again I think my mother will let me have communion.

We file out into the sunlight and I stand around bored, moving my weight from leg to leg, while the grown-ups talk to each other.

Mrs Alley is talking to my grandmother and I dream of marrying her son, who is my Sunday school teacher. He looks like an angel of the Lord. He has straight blond hair that goes all the way to his shoulders and blue eyes and his name is Grant. It is the most beautiful name in the world and I want to name my son Grant when I grow up. I hope he will wait for me to grow older. I think he must be twenty. Suddenly Mrs Alley shifts her handbag to the other arm and says, 'What do you want to be when you grow up, dear?'

'I want to be a minister and spread the Lord's word,' I answer proudly.

'Oh well, perhaps you'll marry one, dear,' she says and ruffles my hair.

No, I think, I don't want to marry a minister. I want to *be* a minister of the Lord. I am going to be the first woman minister, but I wonder if God is going to punish me because I obviously have a problem with being submissive like a woman who is a pearl.

The grown-ups say goodbye and we go next door through our special gate that leads from the Hampton Baptist Church to my grandparents' house, where we all have a cup of tea. The grown-up women, my aunts, get lunch ready and the men have their cup of tea sitting in the living room. I love this bit of Sunday because my grandmother reaches up to the highest shelf in the kitchen and brings down the tin of Arnott's cream biscuits. I am allowed two — even just before lunch.

Sunday lunch is a banquet and the best part is that I am allowed to wind out the big dining table so we can put the extra leaves in. When I go back to the kitchen the women are fussing because my grandmother has run out of butter.

'Oh well,' she says cheerily. 'There'll be no butter now till Monday. We will have to make do with lard; after all, it was good enough during the war.'

We are most definitely not allowed to go to the milk bar for anything on the Lord's Day.

After lunch there is rest time, which is boring. We are not allowed to watch television or listen to the wireless or read, unless they are Christian books.

I amuse myself by singing, 'Yeah baby yeah yeah, I love you baby', which is the only modern song I know and the only bit of it I know. I have heard it on transistor radios as people walk past me in the street.

I sing as I dance around the house, but my dancing is brought to an abrupt halt by my grandfather standing before me. His face warns me.

'That song does not give praise to the Lord,' he says, 'On the Lord's Day we sing only songs that give praise to Him!'

So I have to sing, 'When the road is rough and steep turn your eyes upon Jesus'. It's not half as intriguing or as fun to dance to as 'She loves you', which makes me feel grown-up when I sing it.

At two o'clock I go to Christian Endeavour, where I am winning lots of stickers because I have memorised all the names of the books of the Bible in order and because I know Psalms 23 and 12 off by heart. I also know that if you open your Bible in the middle you will open it at the Psalms and if you open it a quarter of the way through you will open it at

Judges and three-quarters of the way through you will open it at the New Testament. This makes everything easier to find and I always get an A+ when I sit for my Sunday school exam and whenever Mrs Black, our Christian Endeavour teacher, wants someone to volunteer to pray I always offer. I stand up and remember to speak clearly and loudly so everyone can hear and I try to pray just like my grandmother and remember to say 'thee' and 'thou' and 'beseech' as often as I can.

'Oh gracious Lord, we beseech thee. Thou art merciful indeed. We pray that thou wouldst lookest upon us and hearest our prayers.

'We prayest that thou word wouldst be spread amongst the earth and that many souls wouldst be ledst to thee.

'We ask that thou wouldst bless our ministry . . .'

Then I pray for everyone I can think of who is sick and for my father, who desperately needs to be saved and never ever comes to church to hear the Lord's word.

After Christian Endeavour there is more rest, then tea, which is leftover lunch — except we get to have jam and whipped cream on bread for dessert and it is the eating highlight of the week. Mato lets me eat as much as I want. My grandparents are so kind to me.

At seven it's off to evening service, which is modern and up to date, and I know I am supposed to enjoy it more. Because in this service for us younger ones we use the *Sankey Sacred Songs and Solos*; it is the same book that my grandmother sang out of when she was a teenager. My grandmother's favourite song is 'Blessed assurance Jesus is mine' and she whistles it endlessly when she is doing the housework.

I know I am reaching the age for salvation. I am nearly eight and, although we are all born into sin and depravity, eight years is long enough for anyone to spend in sin. I have nightmares that the tribulation has come, that all the Lord's children have been taken up in the rapture and I am left alone in a world ruled by the antichrist, which is probably the Catholic Church. I will have to have the number 666 stamped on my forehead and then I will be the devil's own and nothing will save me from the depths of hell. Of course my father will be left behind too, even though everyone is praying for his salvation. I don't care if he gets left behind and I will have to ask for forgiveness for such wicked thoughts.

But everyone I love will be in heaven with the Lord, so I want to be there too.

Another reason I must be saved is that it will make my grandparents proud of me and so happy. If I die unsaved I will never see them again, because they will be in heaven and I won't be with them. If I get saved I can have communion and not feel like I stand out as a sinner, but mostly I want to get saved because the grown-ups talk as if it is the most wonderful thing in the world. They say that when Jesus comes into your heart you are never lonely again, and you have no more problems because Jesus is going through everything with you. I have a lot of problems and would like to have Jesus in my heart. And I would like to never feel alone or frightened or sad again.

So one night, when I am staying with my parents and my mother says goodnight to me and my father is watching telly and cannot hear us, I ask my mother to lead me to the Lord and to salvation. I tell her I want Jesus in my heart. My mother is really happy with me, smiles and gets out her Bible. She tells me that in Revelation it says Jesus is standing at the door of my heart, knocking to be let in. Jesus wants to come into my heart, but I have to ask him in. She tells me Jesus has been knocking all my life, waiting, and I cry, thinking how awful I am to have left Him standing alone outside, in all sorts of weather, endlessly waiting to come in.

She explains that I am standing on the edge of a great precipice called sin. It is not only the wrongful thoughts and deeds I have done, but the fact that I was born sinful and separated from God. She tells me God is on the other side of this canyon and at the moment there is no way for me to cross it and reach Him because I am not saved. I cry some more when I hear this, for I am filled with such a sense of desolation at the vision of myself standing there so small, ready to topple into the canyon.

Jesus is the only bridge across it. So I ask Jesus to forgive all my sins and I give my heart to him and I am saved. Now I will go to heaven.

'Now,' I ask my mother, 'can I have communion?'

'I will wait,' she says, 'and see how committed to the Lord you are.'

My grandparents are so thrilled that I am saved and that I will be in heaven with them that they give me a Bible of my own. The pictures are so beautiful I am sure they have been painted by an important artist who must have really loved the Lord. Inside there is an inscription:

To dearest Robbi,
Praying that the Lord will bless her always,
Love, Mato and Granddad.

I am very committed to the Lord. I have my quiet time with Him almost every day, when I read my Bible and pray so that I will continue to grow in the Lord. Sometimes when I have been bad my mother says to me, 'Have you been having your quiet time with the Lord lately?' And I say, 'Yes', whether I have or not.

When I forget to have my quiet time I feel so guilty that I pray to the Lord for forgiveness, but I forget a lot and need a lot of forgiveness.

I try to convert the other children at school. I tell them they are lost in sin and are going to hell and that they need salvation, which is found through our Lord Jesus Christ. I especially try to convert my best friend Karen, who is a Catholic. And that is why, says my mother to my father, her parents keep having babies. My father, who is not even a Christian now that he has backslid into the devil's clutches, agrees with her.

It's a shame to have so many babies, I think to myself, when they are probably all going to hell.

Finally, one day in church my mother looks over at me and says I can have communion. I hear my grandfather say, 'This table is to be shared by all who love the Lord with all their heart and serve him.'

I don't know if I love the Lord enough. Maybe I want communion more than I love the Lord. I am so nervous that I change my mind, and when the bread that symbolises the broken body of our Lord and the cups that symbolise his blood shed for us on the cross go past, I don't take them.

On the way out of church my mother looks down at me and says, 'I thought you loved the Lord.' I don't answer; I can't tell her why I didn't take communion, because I don't really know. I know, though, that I have to give a testimony at Sunday night service and maybe then I can prove my love for the Lord.

Giving a testimony for the Lord is a wonderful thing to do. When I tell Mato that I want to give a testimony in church she is proud of me. I have listened to lots of testimonies and some of them are very exciting; some of the people who have turned to the Lord did terrible things before they were converted. As they talk about their life of sin, you can hear a pin drop in the church and just when you can imagine them sinking no lower they meet the Lord and say life has been wonderful ever since. Though, of course, not as exciting.

I am worried about my testimony because I am eight and

don't really have any exciting stories of a sinful life of free sex and drugs.

When you give your testimony you must try to get along as many of your unsaved friends as possible. They will see how much happier you are now that you know the Lord and they will be saved too. So I ask my father to come and hear my testimony and I dream that when he hears it he falls on his knees before the Lord and comes to the front of the church while we all sing, 'Just as I am without one plea but that Thy blood was shed for me'. Then he gives his heart to the Lord and is saved.

But my father refuses to come.

I ask him one night during the ad breaks in 'Young Talent Time'.

He yells, 'I am not going anywhere near those bloody wowser in-laws of mine!'

Then he gets up out of his chair and starts pacing like a lion looking for food. 'They've sucked you in, have they?' he shouts at me.

I start to shake.

'Got you too, have they? I've got a bloody Christian daughter, have I? Nero had it right,' he screams. 'Should've fed the bloody lotta ya to the lions!' And I know that if I hang around he won't just be yelling at me, so I run to my bedroom, crouch down in the corner and cry. I have set him off now and I can still hear him yelling at my mother.

'Look at that Jamie Redfern!' he yells. 'Now why can't I have children like that? What's wrong with my kids? Why aren't they on "Young Talent Time"?'

Then my parents are both screaming and all I can hear are words like 'bloody' and 'Jesus! Jesus! Jesus!' It will go all night and start again in the morning.

Every night and every morning they scream and yell. I don't even know what they scream and yell about. If someone asked me I would just say 'everything'. We go to sleep at night to their screaming and it wakes us in the morning, but nothing makes my father yell like something to do with the church or God or my mother's family.

I think I am the only kid I know who likes going to school. When the bell goes in the afternoon and it's time to go home, I feel so ill in my stomach that I think I will never be able to eat a morsel of food again. I walk home slowly, trying not to think about the sort of mood my father will be in when I get there.

My father does most of the yelling, then he starts to throw furniture around the house and after it he throws us. He can hit us so hard that we fly from one side of the room to the other. I feel like I hate him. I can't forgive him for what he does to us and I know that my attitude is unChristian. But I get to live with my Mato and Granddad a lot and they never even so much as raise their voices.

My brother Wayne is two years younger than me, and then there is my sister Karyn and another brother Davie. My brother Wayne is very sick and he can hardly walk more than a few steps before he is exhausted and has to rest. Everyone says my sister Karyn is sweet and cute. My brother Davie doesn't say much to anyone except his invisible friend, Robert. We are all about two years apart. My mother is proud of this and I often hear her tell people, 'Oh, we did very well. We managed girl, boy, girl, boy.' I know she really wanted a boy first. Maybe this is why my name could easily be a boy's name and she keeps my hair really short. I hate my short hair. I hate my name. I entered a colouring competition and won, but they sent me a boy's prize, and when I was walking to school some council workers yelled out to me, 'How yer doin, son?'

When I am grown-up and can decide for myself, I am never going to have short hair. I will grow my hair as long as I can and everyone will know I am a girl.

One birthday my mother and father gave me a microscope with a picture of a boy on the box, when I really wanted a soft baby doll that cried or wet. My sister has lovely dolls and she doesn't even like them.

Auntie Margaret, who is huge in all directions and wears bright floral dresses and is not really an aunt, laughs so loudly that my Grandma Lyne's Royal Albert teacups rattle in their saucers. Then Grandma Lyne whispers to my mother, 'Well, she's not really a relative, is she?'

Auntie Margaret says to my sister, 'Oh, aren't you cute and sweet.' Then she looks over at me and says, 'Yes, well, you're certainly going to be tall and lanky — just like your mother.' She is not the first one to say this to me, she just says it a lot louder, and I know that being like my mother is not a good thing. I wish I was my sister.

It is because my brother Wayne is sick that I have to live with Mato and Granddad so much. That's what my mother says anyway. She says Wayne's illness is taking up all her time and he is very needy. I don't mind because I love Mato more than anyone in the world. My mother says the reason my father hits my brother Wayne the most is that he is sick, but this seems stupid to me and I say, 'Why?'

'Well,' she says, 'he feels angry that he has a child who is so sick.'

'Why?'

'Because your father was sick when he was a child with the polio, and *his* father hit *him*.'

'Why?'

'Because his father wasn't saved. A good Christian man doesn't hit his children, except to discipline them. You have to hit children sometimes. For their own good,' she adds. 'The Lord's word says to spare the rod is to spoil the child.'

'Well, why can't we all leave him?' I ask.

'Because I am his wife and a Christian wife must submit to her husband, no matter what he does. It is what the Lord requires of me,' she says.

But it seems to me that we only get the rod and none of the spoiling and when I am grown-up and have my own children I will never let anyone hurt them — even if it means I am disobeying the Lord and not submitting to my husband. Sometimes I hate my mother almost as much as my father, because she never stops him belting us.

I don't think I want to be a wife when I grow up. I would much prefer to be a husband.

I have a fight with my only friend at school, Sally Cole. She is my only friend at school because my other best friend, Karen, will only be my best friend at home. She says she has to act like she doesn't know me at school because I am so unpopular. Sally Cole has stopped playing horses with the other girls and is leaning against the fence to catch her breath. She says parents always love you; that is what parents do — love you. I know better and give her the hard cold facts.

'Parents,' I say, 'only love you when they feel like it.' She stomps off, so I don't get to tell her that grandparents are a different matter altogether — not to mention the Lord.

I wish I was Sally Cole. She is beautiful with blonde hair in pigtails. I dream of having hair long enough to put in pigtails. Her mother even puts ribbons in her pigtails, red tartan ones. Sally Cole wants to join the circus when she grows up. She wins all the art prizes and I would give anything to win one. I love drawing and painting almost as much as I love the Lord.

Of course, I win the prize for religious instruction, which is like wearing a huge sign that says 'Dag Here'. But at least I win a hard copy of *Prince Caspian*.

* * *

With my short hair, my school uniform, my name that is not exotic and feminine like Monica or Felicity, my award for religious instruction, my distrust of my parents and my desire to bring the other kids to the Lord, I don't exactly have the easiest time at school. I spend every lunchtime alone and get teased because I always eat my cake before I eat my sandwich. Mind you, the other kids don't have to eat my mother's sandwiches. They get things like Vegemite or ham or peanut butter; I get Milo and sugar, which goes all syrupy. Yuk! Even though Sally Cole is my friend, I understand that it is embarrassing for her to be seen with me and at lunchtime she cannot play with me if she is to play with the other kids.

5

There is only one time I ever lie and when I do I always ask the Lord for forgiveness. It is when my mother says to me, 'Have you done a big job today?'

Every day she asks me this. I used to tell the truth and say no and then she said, 'I'll give you to dinner time.'

When dinner time came and I still hadn't she made me lie on her big bed, face down on the floral quilt that was scratchy and crisp, and she pulled down my pants and put bits of Velvet soap up my bottom. It stung and I felt so ashamed and filthy it made me cry.

So now, although I am sinning and breaking the Lord's commandment, I always say yes when she asks. And when I am at Mato's and she asks me if I have done my big job I say yes to her too because if I don't she will ring up my mother and she will come with the Velvet soap. I hate lying to my grandmother because I love her so much and I wonder if she can tell. I ask the Lord to forgive me for lying and to give me the courage to tell the truth. He hasn't given it to me yet.

My mother has bought Colgate toothpaste instead of Ipana and I am brushing my teeth. I've been brushing for hours — brushing and smiling, brushing and smiling — and my gums are sore. I brush and brush, round and round, like you are supposed to and then I smile into the bathroom mirror with the chipped sides and nothing happens. I still can't get it.

'Robbi, what on earth are you doing in there?' my mother yells through the door.

'I'm trying to get the ring of confidence.'

'What on earth are you talking about, child? You're going to be late for school!'

'You know the ring of confidence, the one that flashes around your head if you use Colgate,' I say to her.

She walks in from the kitchen and pushes me towards the front door. I quickly wipe the toothpaste on my sleeve and I am on my way to school without the Colgate ring.

I don't always walk to school like the other kids. When my brother Wayne is well enough I have special permission to ride him to school on a tricycle. He sits in the back, in the paddy seat. My mother ties a piece of metal, like a slice out of a rubbish bin, to his chest each day with leather straps. It's to protect him in case another boy punches him in the chest, because he has a hole in his heart and my mother says that his valves are letting the blood rush the wrong way around his body. I try to imagine what a heart looks like with a big gaping hole in it and the blood rushing the wrong way, like riding your bike into oncoming traffic, and it seems a miracle to me that he is alive at all.

The Catholics walk one way, down one side of the street, and we ride up the other side in the opposite direction. We yell at them, across the street, 'Catholic dogs stink like frogs!' They yell back, 'Proddy frogs stink like dogs!' I don't know why they yell that because I'm not a proddy, I'm a Baptist.

This year I have a lovely teacher, Mr Bleeser. I am in love with him and want to marry a man just like him but it can't actually be him because he is not a Christian and we would be unevenly yoked. That would lead to all kinds of trouble — just look at my mother.

He reads 'The Loaded Dog' to us. We all laugh in class and he grins with pleasure at having made us so happy. At night the story gives me nightmares, but I still think he is wonderful.

The big goal in grade three is to get your ink pen, which is the new sort with a cartridge instead of a bladder. I am the only person in class still using a pencil. My writing is so bad, though I can't work out what is wrong with it, and eventually Mr Bleeser says, 'Oh, here. Have it.' And he tosses an ink pen onto my desk. 'You're never going to get it if I wait for your writing to improve,' he says.

My pen is a lovely shiny blue one with a gold ring around it. Blue is my favourite colour because it is the colour of heaven. Mr Bleeser considers me for a moment and I wonder if I am in trouble. Maybe he has changed his mind and will take the pen back. Then he walks away and I assume he has decided I can keep it. I sigh with relief and I am still admiring my pen when he announces, 'I'm making some seating changes.'

My heart starts thumping because I hate it when teachers change the seating. You never know who you will end up next to. Will he put me next to someone who hates me? Will he put me next to a boy? I hope he puts me next to Sally Cole.

'Monica will move and sit next to Helen,' he says. If she sits next to Helen, where is Duncan going to sit? He is the worst kid in our class, perhaps in the whole school. He answers the teacher back and doesn't care if he's given the cuts. He gets in heaps of fights with other boys. He has a crew cut, which my brothers really want but my mother will only let them ask the barber for short back and sides please, and I am petrified of Duncan.

'Duncan will sit next to Robbi,' Mr Bleeser says. 'Because

Duncan is the worst behaved in the class and Robbi is the best. So,' he says, looking down at me, 'perhaps you can be a good influence on him.'

I just about wet myself, I am so scared.

'The new seating will start tomorrow,' says Mr Bleeser. How can Mr Bleeser blithely do something that is going to ruin my entire life?

The whole way through dinner all I can think about is that I have to sit next to Duncan the following day at school. I push the pinwheels of carrot around the plate and get into trouble for playing with my mother's food. My father wallops me over the head.

'Don't be so bloody ungrateful!' he yells at me. 'Your mother's cooked you a meal. You be bloody grateful and eat it!'

I pray, *Lord, please make Mr Bleeser move Duncan to another desk*, as I try to swallow my mother's lumpy sago pudding. I have learnt an important lesson. It does not pay to be good. If I hadn't been good I would never have had to sit next to Duncan. *Please, Lord, make Mr Bleeser put Sally Cole next to me*, I pray in bed.

I go to school trying to have faith that my prayer will be answered, but obviously I did not have enough faith because Duncan sits next to me all day and copies my work, even though I try to hide it with my arm. He just leans right over and copies anyway. At home time I get my satchel and hurry out of school to get away from him.

I am always scared going home because we have to cross the big paddock opposite the school and sometimes the big kids trap the smaller kids and pull their underpants down. I scurry home across the paddock, but someone is following me. I am sure it is a big kid and my stomach is churning as if there is a Ferris wheel stuck inside it. I am frightened. I am going to have my pants pulled down. I quickly glance behind me and it is worse than a big kid. It is Duncan. He follows me all the way home, but I pretend he is not there till I am safely through our back door.

I pray to the Lord again, but my faith is still lacking the day after, because Duncan sits next to me all day, copies my work and follows me home. I beseech the Lord again that night and every night as the week goes by. But Duncan is still there, copying, borrowing my work, my ruler, pen and rubber and following me home. Strangely, though, I am starting to feel safer crossing the paddock with Duncan right behind me because I know no one will pick a fight with him.

Finally Friday afternoon arrives. No school — no Duncan — for two whole days. I walk home with my head down, pretending that Duncan is not there.

And he speaks to me — for the first time. I am so stunned that I stop.

'Robbi,' he says, 'I love you.' And he gives me a macaroni necklace he has made for me.

'Thank you,' I say as I take the necklace and, because I have been taught to be polite when people give you gifts, I put the necklace around my neck and Duncan walks me home, swinging his tattered satchel around his legs as he goes.

'Will you come to my house for the weekend?' he says. 'My parents won't mind and I have a bedroom.'

'I don't think my parents will let me,' I say.

'Who is this boy?' yells my father, throwing his arms about. 'Asking my daughter home for the weekend when she is only eight years old!'

'Vic,' says my mother, 'he's only eight years old as well!'

'Doesn't matter!' he yells. 'Boys are boys and I know what boys want!'

Then he changes tack. 'What sort of daughter have I got?' he yells, thumping his arm against his leg. 'That gets asked home by a boy when she is only eight years old!' Then he starts to move in on me. But my mother sends me to bed with a meaningful look and a flick of her arm and they keep yelling. I don't get any dinner and this time I don't pray for Duncan to be moved.

All weekend I am itching to get to school on Monday. I have a friend. A real friend, even if it is a boy.

Because it is Monday morning there is assembly and the principal is saying good-bye to Mrs Crabbe, who is retiring. I hate Mrs Crabbe. I had her in prep and grade one and she gave me bruises all down my back where she punched me with her knuckles. It really hurt. My mother, who is not shy about using the big copper stick on my brother, was furious.

If you wet your pants in Mrs Crabbe's class she made you put on a pair of huge old-fashioned bloomers that hung down below your dress and everyone knew you had wet your pants and laughed at you. She never let you out to the toilet no matter how badly you had to go. Once I had to wear the bloomers and my mother washed them and sent them back in a brown paper bag. But now Mrs Crabbe is going and the principal is making a speech about how much we will all miss her and he gives her a going-away present of a green tartan suitcase.

Mrs Crabbe steps up to the microphone to make a speech but I am not listening to her. I can hear the mothers, standing at the back of assembly. I listen to them instead.

'Well, that's certainly tactful,' a mother says.

'Sending her on a *long* holiday, are we?' I hear another voice agree.

'I hope she is going far away.'

We sing to God, asking him to save the Queen, the same one I have to wear my Sunday best for. Then we file into class and sit at our desks, but there is no Duncan.

One of the boys leans over to me and says, 'Duncan's back in the correction centre. He went there on the weekend. Must have been your good influence.'

* * *

It has been a whole week without Duncan and I have survived. It is Friday afternoon, with only quarter of an hour left until home time. We have baby chickens in our classroom, soft and yellow. We watched them hatch out of their eggs and now for the first time Mr Bleeser is going to let each of six lucky kids take one of them home in a shoebox and look after it for the weekend.

We have our hands up, all thirty-six of us, fingers pointing to the sky, our bums just off the chairs. We are all *sir, sir, sir*!

First up, he chooses me. He hands me a shoebox and, nearly tripping over myself, I go and choose a chicken. I choose the tiniest, most helpless-looking chicken, just as Jesus would. I place it so tenderly in the box, and can't bear to put the lid with fork holes over the top, but I know I have to get it home safely.

I walk home very slowly and when I get there I show Great-Grandma Lucy.

She touches the soft down and murmurs to herself. I think she likes the feel of the chicken.

'You'll have to get it some bread soaked in milk,' she says.

Then I show Grandma Lyne. 'Mmm,' she jokes, 'that'll be nice roasted up for dinner.'

'Graaan!' I say.

I am so proud that I was chosen to take home a chicken I can't wait to show my mother. She might even give me extra pocket money when she sees how good I am at school. She is in the kitchen making dinner, stirring tapioca pudding. Yuk.

'Look, look!' I say. 'I've got a chicken for the weekend. To look after,' I add, just to be sure she knows it's not for cooking and that it has to go back.

'How did you get that?' she snaps.

'Mr Bleeser gave it to me,' I explain, feeling nervous.

'What, he gave you a chicken — just like that?'

'Yes.'

'You didn't ask for it?'

I am silent.

'Well, I'm asking you a question. Teachers don't just give things to children without first getting their parents' permission. You must have asked for it!'

'Well, I put my hand up. We all did.' I am starting to cry.

'You can go straight to your bed, young lady, and stay there for the weekend! There'll be no dinner for you tonight! AND you can leave that bird right there on the table, thank you!'

I go to my bed, sobbing. I can't even take the little chicken with me.

Next thing I hear my father's footsteps stomping up the stairs. My mother is with him.

'How dare you!' he yells. 'How dare you bring home an animal without your parents' permission? And you call yourself a Christian! You are disobedient! Aren't Christian children supposed to be obedient to their parents? Isn't that right, Rowena?'

'Your father is right!' my mother yells. 'The Bible teaches us to honour our father and mother, and you have not obeyed us. How dare you bring home an animal without our permission? Did you ask us first? NO!' she answers. 'And now we are supposed to look after it all weekend.'

'If this is what Christian daughters are like,' yells my father, 'give me a non-Christian any day!' He picks *Prince Caspian* up off my bed, wallops me across the backside with it and throws it on the floor. He stomps off but my mother has not finished with me.

'You are a liar!' she says. 'How dare you tell Mr Bleeser that you could bring home a chicken without finding out from us? You will stay in your room all weekend and when Monday morning comes I will take you to school and you will tell Mr Bleeser that you lied about being allowed to take a chicken home and you will ask for forgiveness.'

So I pick *Prince Caspian* up off the floor, I smooth out the crumpled pages and I stay in my room all weekend. And I don't get to see the little chicken even once.

Monday morning arrives and I feel ill in my stomach. My mother drives me to school, a little late, and we arrive just as everyone is seated at their desks. She is carrying the little chicken in the shoebox. She marches me up to the teacher's desk. The class is straining to hear every word that passes.

Mr Bleeser stands up to greet her. I can see he knows it is something important that my mother has come to school first thing in the morning for.

'Go on,' she prompts me.

'I am sorry, Mr Bleeser, that I lied and said I could take a chicken home when I hadn't asked my parents for permission,' I say, looking at the ground and holding back the tears.

'You can sit down,' he says to me. I can't hear what he says to my mother because I am fighting too hard to stop crying in front of the whole class. Now that Mr Bleeser knows I am a liar, I know he will hate me. What will I do?

He smiles and nods at my mother. She smiles back and then leaves. I am sure that Mr Bleeser will make me stand up in front of the whole class, but he doesn't. He just says, 'Good morning, class.'

'Good morning, Mr Bleeser,' they all drone. I don't. I am still trying not to cry. Any minute I will be up the front while he tells them all what a liar I am. But he doesn't. We go straight into reciting our times tables instead. I keep on expecting Mr Bleeser to hate me, but he is even nicer to me than he already has been.

I love Mr Bleeser.

6

When I am not living at Mato and Granddad's I am living with my family at Grandma Lyne and Great-Grandma Lucy's house. We all live with them: my brothers, my sister, my parents and me. My sister and I sleep in the attic with Grandma Lyne, and that's great because we get to listen to her wireless, which she leaves on nearly all night. Every night she listens to Alex Kenworthy. She loves him. He is a godly man who gives solid Christian advice to lonely women whose husbands are not providing them with the leadership they need.

I am near the window that faces the street and in the morning I hear the *clop, clop, clop* of the milk cart being drawn by the horse and the *clink, clink, clink* of the bottles rattling against one another. I jump out of bed to watch. It is still dark when it goes by but you can see the milkman clearly in the glow from the street lights and I call to my Gran, 'Gran, quick. It's the milk cart!'

She jumps up, throws on her dressing gown and races downstairs and out into the street with a spade to get the horse manure for the garden, before any of the neighbours do.

Then she stays up and lights the fire.

My brother sleeps in the cupboard under the stairs and my youngest brother sleeps in a cot in the corner of my parents' room.

My two grans have their own kitchen and lounge room and my mum and dad have their own kitchen and lounge room too. I don't know who was silly enough to build a house with two kitchens and all these lounge rooms. There is also the front lounge room but that is where the piano is. My Great-Gran Lucy only ever sees two of these rooms: her bedroom and her lounge room.

She is in her nineties and has only one leg. My mother says if she just hangs on she'll get her letter from the Queen. She is the only one to have her own bedroom, because she moans all night. I can hear her cries. My mother says it is due to the pain in the leg she hasn't got. She can still feel it, although it isn't there.

Great-Gran Lucy sits on her couch all day brushing her long hair that has never been cut. Then she divides it into strips and twirls each one until it twists into a tight knot up on her head. Then in goes the hairpin to hold it. I sit on the floor to watch her do this whenever I can. I want to have long, long hair like hers, so no one will ever think I am a boy again.

My great-gran sits there with a crochet rug over her one leg and her knitting and her stick. She knits socks. She started during the war and the war has stopped, but her knitting hasn't. I don't know where the socks go when she has finished them. She won't go anywhere, because she says she has never been in a car and she isn't going in one till her funeral. 'Cars are unsafe! But for my funeral I won't get any say anyhow and by then it won't matter.' She says this every Sunday afternoon when my father suggests a drive.

He knows she'll say no.

She says there's nowhere she needs to go in a car and 'Homicide' on Channel Seven shows her all of Melbourne that she needs to see.

Great-Gran tells me stories about when she was a girl and travelled to school with her sisters on their horses. I sit on the floor at her foot and while she brushes her long white hair, I listen to her stories. She tells me that she was the first free child born on Kangaroo Island. I don't know what a free child is, but she seems glad that she was one, so I feel happy for her.

'The Abos used to come around,' she tells me, 'with balls of damper in their hands.'

'What's damper?' I ask.

'That's like a big ball of dough, like your mother uses to make scones. The Abos would come around with the damper, patting it from hand to hand, and ask for a bit of flour to add to their ball. Some of the meaner folks used to give them flour that had arsenic in it and then the poor Aboriginal mothers would take that damper home and feed it to their little children.'

'What happened to them then?'

'Well, they died, of course. What'd you think? Arsenic is poison. It kills yer. No one in my family,' she says heavily, 'ever did such a wicked thing. Pure wickedness,' she mutters.

Then she tells me the most amazing thing of all. 'My mother's stove,' she says, 'was outside, in the paddock. She did all the cookin out there: Sunday roasts, the lot.'

My father's family aren't worried about cooking on Sundays, so I'm not sure how saved they are.

Fancy having your kitchen outside! I am absolutely stunned as I try to imagine my great-great-grandmother in her long skirts cooking roast chicken outside in the pouring rain or the scorching heat. A kitchen outside. It's beyond thinking about.

I have to be careful when I walk past Great-Gran Lucy and lean over as far as I can to the side she is sitting on, to make my dress look longer on that side. She raps me on the legs with her cane if I don't get past her quickly enough.

'That dress is disgraceful!' she barks. 'Indecent! Pure indecent to be showing your knees like that! The world can nearly see your bottom!'

'But, Gran,' I plead, 'this is how everyone wears their dresses now. Minis are in.'

I have my tunic hitched up as high as I can. It is all bunched up around my waist because my mother will only shorten it to two inches above my knee, when anything less than four inches is positively embarrassing. I've gone to so much trouble in the mirror making sure the bunches around my waist look as inconspicuous as possible. There is no way I can pull it all out now, just to get past Gran and out the front door. So I lean over as far as I can.

'Rowena! Rowena!' she yells.

In comes my mother with a *what now?* look on her face.

'Rowena! How could you let this child out like this! Look! Look! It's shocking disgraceful! Young girls shouldn't be showing their ankles, let alone their knees and bottoms. Let it down at once!' So my mother kneels on the floor, pulls down my dress and out fall all my carefully manoeuvred bundles of gabardine.

'That's nowhere near enough!' snaps Grandma Lucy. Her stick gets the side of my legs and I yelp.

'But that's how they wear them,' my mother says on my behalf.

'No, it's not!' I protest. 'No one wears dresses this long!'

My mother scowls at me. 'I don't care what other girls do,' she says sternly. 'You are my daughter and you are a Christian. You must dress in a way that is pleasing to the Lord.'

'Decent? *Hmmph*! There's nothing decent about that length,' puts in my great-grandmother, so I dash to the door before I'm wearing a bustle.

Grandma Lyne is nearly seventy. She drives around Sandringham in her little red Triumph and the shopkeepers all complain to my mum because she won't use her indicators or stop at corners. My mother says she needs driving lessons and my father says her licence should be taken away from her and that she got it in a packet of Kellogg's in the first place. But Gran says, 'There's naught wrong with the way I drive. If I'm turning into a new street I always beep the horn to let them know that I'm coming.' My mother won't let any of us go in the car with her.

Grandma Lyne looks after us if my mother and father go to work on Saturday or Sunday or during school holidays. They have started their own business and are going to make a fortune because my father is such a clever man. He hasn't had a job since we left Lantana Street and he would just sit in his chair, his Mozart blaring, and yell at us whenever we upset him.

My mother gives my sister and me ten cents to go and buy a packet of chips in the afternoon, because we are always starving when Grandma Lyne looks after us. She always lets the boys eat first and Karyn and I have to wait until they are finished. And they are such greedy pigs that they never leave anything much for us.

'Why do the boys get to eat first? It's not fair!' I protest loudly.

'Because,' says my grandmother, 'they have to grow up to be big strong men and look after their families.'

'Well, I'm growing up to be a big strong woman! Besides, Dad doesn't look after our family, Mum does!' It is my mother who feeds us and who takes our temperature to see if we are really sick or just trying to wag school. It is my mother who cries when there isn't enough food and she's the one who cooks the food we do have. It is my mother who spends Saturdays with Grandma Lyne stirring clothes in the old copper, and I have to help hang the clothes out when I really want to play! And it is my mother who takes my brother to the hospital and sometimes comes home very late. My father sits in a chair or works on his boat or his car — and that is about it really.

'Women don't need as much food as men,' says my grandmother, ignoring my comment about my father. 'Yer've had your bowl of cornflakes for breakfast and that should do yer fer the day, you know.'

So My sister and I pretend to accept her answer, but really we rush off to our bedroom and put on the wigs that we love — hers have long pink plaits and mine has bright blue plaits — and off we trot, swishing our fluorescent long hair from side to side, around the corner to the milk bar to buy our packet of chips and twenty cents of boiled lollies that Grandma Lucy asks us to get for her when she hears we are going out. We prance along just like two adult women off to do their shopping. It's kind of good that Grandma Lyne won't give us enough food to eat, because this is the only time my mother ever gives us money for chips.

Grandma Lyne is chopping wood for the fire. She is really good at it. She heaves the axe over her head and brings it down on a piece of wood with a mighty thump and pieces of bark fly everywhere. My mother says it's disgraceful that she has to do it and that our lazy good-for-nothing father — *Please, Lord, convict him in his spirit and show him the way to You* — should do it. Fancy a man letting his elderly mother chop his wood!

Gran lights the fire too. Every morning before the rest of us are up she has it lit and roaring. We can boast that we've had the fire brigade to our house three times this winter alone, because our chimney keeps catching fire.

I climb up in the loquat tree and eat loquats while I watch Gran chopping the wood. I'm not really allowed to do it, because I am allergic to the caterpillars here and I come out in horrible red spots and have to take Condy's Crystals baths and then I'm red all over. I have a caterpillar in a shoebox with cling wrap over the top and fork holes so it can breathe. It is an emperor gum and when it turns into a beautiful butterfly I will let it go and it will be free.

Up the axe goes over Grandma Lyne's head and crashes down on the wood. *Whack!*

Suddenly my mother calls us all, 'Come quickly! Come quickly! Daddy has a surprise. Quick — come! Come!'

I scamper down from the tree and out to the front yard. My brothers are still shooting their cap guns at each other and we can't see a surprise anywhere.

'Look! Look!' says my mother. 'Here comes your daddy with a new car.' The biggest car I have ever seen is coming slowly down the road and I hate it immediately. It is a giant. It is ugly, the colour of my school uniform. It is grey!

'It's a Pontiac,' my father announces proudly to us all as he steps out of it. 'Only rich people have Pontiacs and now we have one.'

But we are not rich, I think. Sometimes we don't even have enough to eat and my mother says she doesn't know what she will do because our good-for-nothing father spends all the money he earns on himself and that stupid boat of his and gives her none to feed us with and she cries in church and then we get boxes of groceries delivered mysteriously to our front door and my mother cries again and thanks the Lord for his kindness.

'This car is great,' he says and he opens the back door. 'See? All you kids can fit across the back seat, it's so big. Davie won't have to sit on Mummy's knee anymore. This is a great car,' he goes on. 'It was a real bargain — only one little thing wrong with it. That's why it was so cheap.'

At this my parents have a quick conversation to themselves the way parents do all the time, like you're not even there. We all stand and watch them and then my mother says, 'Daddy got a real bargain. Isn't he clever? Only one little thing wrong with it — that's why it was such a bargain — the garage man couldn't work out what it was. He couldn't fix it, but that's because he's not clever like Daddy. Daddy'll have it fixed in no time. Won't you, Daddy?'

'Come on, hop in, we'll go for a spin,' he says. So we all scramble into the back seat and drive down the beach road.

We are having a family drive, just like a real family. My mother has put one of her wigs on for the occasion. I stare at the back of it and touch it every now and then because it feels nothing like real hair. It feels like dried-up bits of White Knight nougat bar when you have sucked on it and made it long and stringy. We only get as far as Black Rock because my mother has said something that my father doesn't like and now he is yelling at her. We are at the Black Rock clock and he has to stop because it is a roundabout, so he just gets out of the car, slams the door and yells at my mother, 'Serves you bloody well right!' And off he goes.

My mother gets in the driver's seat and drives us home. 'It's not your daddy's fault,' she tells us as she drives. 'He can't help the way he behaves. His father beat him and he was so ill when he was a little boy.'

And even though it is only four o'clock in the afternoon, we all have to go to bed.

It's not very long before I'm glad that I'm in my bed because my father has arrived home in a taxi and I can hear him yelling and breaking furniture and my mother screaming at him, 'Stop it, Vic! Stop it, Vic!' And I am scared and hiding under the blankets. There is so much banging and thumping and yelling and screaming that I wonder if there will be anything left of our house. I wonder if my grandmothers are okay and if it will ever stop. I am crying and so is my sister and my brothers in their beds are probably crying too. I wish I was at Mato's. I try to say Psalm 23 over and over because it worked for Daniel in the lion's den.

'The Lord is my Shepherd, I shall not want. He maketh me to lie down in green pastures.
'He leadeth me beside still waters.
'The Lord is my shepherd I shall not want,
'he maketh me to lie down in green pastures,
'he leadeth me beside still waters.'

I keep repeating the first two verses over and over, even though I know the whole psalm, because I am so scared.

I dread hearing his footsteps coming up the stairs, but they don't and I must eventually fall asleep because the next thing is I'm awake and it is morning.

A new day. I creep down the stairs and the lounge chairs are in pieces. The legs are off the dining-room table. The coffee table is in bits. There are torn-up books everywhere. The phone is ripped out of the wall. There is smashed china. It's a mess. The television is broken too. There are shards of glass and wires and valves all over the floor. Now I won't get to watch 'The Monkees'. I love the Monkees; they are so funny. They make me laugh so hard that I nearly wet myself. My father says they drive him up the wall and I laugh harder because that is what they are supposed to do to adults and what is really amazing is that he lets us watch it and doesn't hit us. In fact he watches it too. The drummer is so gorgeous. The big question at school is: who is better — the Monkees or the Beatles?

Everyone else is still asleep except Grandma Lyne, who has the fire roaring. I am as quiet as a mouse, so as not to wake my father. I peer around the lounge-room door where Gran is sitting by the fire sipping tea.

'Come on and sit by the fire,' she says, 'while I make yer a nice warm cuppa.'

I am holding onto the door so that I can lean round it and into the room to see her. I have to hang onto the door because there is a huge branch sticking out through the doorway and I can't get past it.

To get in and sit by the fire, I have to climb over this huge branch. One end of it is in the fireplace, with its leaves crackling and smoking; the other end is the one that's in my way. I clamber over and look at Gran with a *what's this?* look.

'It was too big to chop,' she explains, 'so I just keep pushing it further into the fire as it burns.' Then she reaches for the dented teapot sitting on the table in its knitted cosy and pours me a cup.

Pretty soon the fire brigade is back at our house.

'Beats me how she got the massive bloody thing in the house in the first place,' I hear my father saying to the fireman. 'She reckons she dragged it in.'

'Her and whose army, I'd like to know,' says the fireman.

That weekend the Pontiac is in pieces all over our driveway and stays that way until my father can sell it. He spends every Saturday out in the driveway, listening to the football and trying to fix it or working on his boat and swearing at us every time his team, the Saints, lose a goal or a point. He also yells at us every time the other team gets a free kick. We hate football.

We have to play quietly in the backyard, because if we make any noise he yells, 'You bloody kids shut up!'

Then if we forget and do make a noise, he gets out from under the car or from inside his boat, stomps over to us and yells, 'I won't have you bleedin kids fighting! Do you hear me? No fighting!' And then he wallops Davie and me and wallops Wayne for at least twice as long as he walloped us. Sometimes he doesn't stop till my mother comes running out saying, 'That's enough, Vic! Stop now, Vic!'

Sometimes my brother Wayne tries to help fix the car. He lies down beside our father and hands him screwdrivers and things, but I can't work out why because, sure as Jesus died for our sins, Wayne hands him the wrong thing and gets walloped. But the very next weekend he'll be out there trying to help again, when anyone can see that all he's going to get for his trouble is a thumping.

My father never can find the one little thing that's wrong with that car.

7

Wayne? Well, he is my mother's favourite, the oldest son.

He switched all the mail in our street's letterboxes.

My father bruises him on a regular basis.

My mother hit him so hard with a wooden spoon that half the spoon broke off and flew across the kitchen. He'd got up early and eaten Grandma Lucy's jar of boiled lollies.

Wayne learnt very quickly to pad his backside with clothing and books and then, bent over ready for his punishment, he grins up at us while we watch our mother try to smack him with the thick copper stick now that her wooden spoon is broken.

He is her favourite.

Wayne is in the Alfred Hospital again. He's there a lot. I get up in the morning and I put on my Saturday clothes. I bump down the stairs on my bottom, *thump, thump, thump* and when I get into the hallway I can see Grandma Lyne in her little kitchen getting three bowls of cornflakes ready and cups of tea. She is wearing her brown woollen skirt, her green twin set and her gumboots, ready for chopping wood.

'Where's Mum?' I ask. I never want to know where Dad is.

'Gone to get yer brother,' she says. 'They'll be back directly.'

'Is he coming home then?'

'He is. And you be sure to look after him.'

'What have they done to him?'

'They've patched the hole with Teflon and fixed his arteries,' says Gran, munching on her toast.

'What's Teflon?'

'Yer mother says it's the stuff they put on those electric frypans, to stop things sticking, just like the one yer mother's got.'

Thinking about my brother's heart having a Teflon patch on it is too hard, though I do wonder what kind of stitching they use when they are patching hearts. Gran patches our clothes on her treadle sewing machine and she always uses zigzag to make it tough. I hope they use zigzag on my brother's heart so it doesn't fray.

'Can I go and get the bread from Mum's kitchen?' I ask. Sometimes on Saturday we are allowed to have toast for breakfast. Gran only has brown bread.

'That white stuff'll block yer bowels,' she says. I get the white bread anyway. My dad says that brown bread is only white bread that has been dropped on the floor of the factory.

Karyn and Davie dawdle in.

'Yer mum's gone to get yer brother from the hospital,' Gran tells them. 'You all eat yer cornflakes and then you can hop on outside to play. They'll be back soon enough.'

We are outside hanging upside down on the monkey bars, bored. Gran is weeding her vegie garden. After what seems like forever Mum and Wayne turn up.

'I'm going in for a cuppa,' says Mum. 'It's been a long morning. You look after your brother,' she says to me. 'Remember, he's only just got out of hospital.' And she disappears inside the back door with Gran following.

Wayne grins, his face close to mine. Karyn, Davie and I clamber off the monkey bars.

'Look at this!' says Wayne and he pulls up his Miller shirt with its shiny buttons that I adore. Our mouths drop open. He has a scar that is half an inch wide and goes from his throat to his undies and four other smaller scars as well: one on each side at the top and one on each side at the bottom.

'Do they hurt?' I ask.

'Nah, you wanna touch them?'

'Nah.'

'What they did to me in hospital was they made me so I can fly,' he boasts. 'I've got super powers.'

'Oh, yeah? Prove it!' I say. Being the oldest, it is my responsibility to curb any sinful vanity. So he does. I watch as he climbs up to the top of the monkey bars. By the time he gets up there he's puffing and red but he keeps going. He stands up, balancing on the top; he spreads his arms wide and yells, 'Up in the sky, is it a bird? Is it a plane? No! It's Super Wayne!' Then he throws himself off the top of the monkey bars and hurtles to the ground.

'Muuuumm!' we all yell. Wayne is yelling too.

My mother bursts through the back door, stopping for only a split second to take in the situation.

'Go to your rooms!' she yells at us. She picks Wayne up and puts him in the back of the car and takes off. He gets to go everywhere.

I get to go to my room.

After ages I hear them come back and Gran calls us down for lunch.

Mum is muttering, 'Not even a day out of hospital. Not even a day, I tell you!' She glares at me from the stool she is sitting on in the kitchen. 'The white bread, Mum,' she says to Gran who is making her a sandwich.

Wayne has a big smile on his face. 'The doctor gave me a Wagon Wheel for being good.'

Since when are you good? I think. Then I see his arm. It's in plaster.

'Broken in three places,' says my mother crossly.

'Isn't it ace? I can get everyone to write on it,' Wayne gloats, so pleased with his morning's adventure.

'I asked you to look after him,' snaps my mother. 'You're the oldest and I expect you to be responsible.'

My brother is grinning from ear to ear and I am sulking. I didn't force him to show off.

My mother sighs. I can see she is tired from driving back and forth to doctors.

'If I take Wayne and that one,' and she nods at me, 'd'you think you could keep the littlies, Mum?' she asks Gran.

Gran sips her tea. 'I'll be right with the lot.'

'I want to keep my eye on Wayne, I can't afford any more incidents, and I'm not leaving the trouble-maker with you.'

'Where are we going?' I ask.

'To work. I was supposed to be helping your father hours ago,' my mother says pointedly.

My father designs and makes burglar alarms. He has just been on the news because he designed an alarm for schools that will go off if a fire is lit as well as if there is an intruder. There have been a lot of fires in schools lately, so he is getting lots of orders from the Department of Education. And now Wayne and I have been dragged along to work with them. They have an office in Melrose Street down in the Sandringham shops. They have several rooms there; an osteopath from England is in one of them. His name is Adrian, his wife has long blonde hair and they have a little boy named Jolly, which we think is pretty strange. Their last name is Good, so if you ask him his name he answers, 'I'm Jolly Good, thank you,' in his proper English accent.

Wayne and I are bored stiff at the office. We have coloured in and played with the tin of Matchbox cars. We want to fight, but we don't dare or we'll get beaten by my father.

Then suddenly I hear Wayne say, 'Hey, Mum, can we go and play downstairs?'

‘If you think you can behave yourselves and don’t get your plaster wet,’ she says absently, working frantically on her typewriter.

He tears off down the stairs and I am after him. We don’t even have to pack up the cars and textas. I know my brother. He has something on his mind, so I make sure to keep up with him. We get out into the street and I follow him around the corner until we get to the driveway of the hotel. We have never been in a hotel and I don’t even know what one is. I do know that they are bad, disreputable places. My Mato and mother say so and this was proved to me just last week when I saw two of my teachers kissing in the hotel car park the day my dad parked his car there. They’re not even married to each other, in fact they are married to other people, and my father said it would be best if I did not mention what I had seen at school.

‘Wait here,’ says Wayne and I crouch down behind the pink brick wall round the car park. I am nervous because this is closer to the hotel than I am allowed to be, but Wayne isn’t the slightest bit worried. He is definitely on the wide road to hell, but I watch to see what he is going to do. My heart is thumping madly because it’s sure to be something bad. I pull nervously on the end of my pigtails. My hair has grown quite long now. My mother seems to have forgotten to cut it and I love it long. I can nearly sit on it and I am so proud of my beautiful long almost black hair.

With his good hand Wayne musses up his hair, pulls his shirt half out of his shorts and sidles up to a man and woman coming down the street with brown paper shopping bags in their arms.

‘Hello,’ he says, all bright and chirpy. ‘My mother and father are too poor to feed us and I am hungry. Can you give me some money?’

I am in shock, these people will surely call the police and they’ll call our parents. Then my father will beat us and it will be mostly my fault because I am the oldest and I didn't stop him. I watch and tremble.

But the man laughs, puts his shopping bags on the ground against his legs so they don't fall over, shoves his hand into his pocket and hands something to Wayne.

He comes hurrying back and drops a two-cent coin into my hand. Then off he goes again. In no time we have ten cents. Enough for five cents' worth of chips, two potato cakes and one cent left over towards the next lot. We scurry down the road to the fish and chip shop with our hoard, get our chips and potato cakes, and, when we've finished, Wayne starts again and soon we have had three lots of fish and chips and can't eat one bit more. With our stomachs stuffed full we saunter back to Dad's office.

'Hello, what have you been up to?' asks my mother, standing at the top of the stairs.

'Nothing,' we answer together, wiping the grease off our faces with our sleeves. 'Just wandering around,' I add.

'Well, I've made you both a nice hot cup of coffee.'

'But I hate coffee,' I say.

My mother's face grows dark and she sighs. 'You have to learn to eat things you don't like. It is most ungrateful of you to turn your nose up at something that has been offered to you, young lady! How can I take you out in public if you haven't learnt that? Do you think Jesus would ever have said no to something that was put in front of him? You get in that kitchen, young lady, and drink that coffee now!'

I knew this was coming because last summer holidays we had a picnic in San Remo on our way to Phillip Island and my mother said I had to eat the tinned pineapple pieces she had opened. I hate pineapple, so she laid me down on the picnic bench and stuffed my mouth full of pineapple. Then she held my nose so I had to eat the pineapple to breathe again. Everyone in the park turned to watch and see the mother with her disobedient child.

I wish I'd had the strength to go blue and die.

The other things I have to eat are my mother's lumpy custard and her burnt porridge. She burns it every morning because she puts it on to cook, then goes to have a shower and when she comes out it is burnt. I wish she would teach me to make it and I wouldn't burn it. When I grow up these are the things I will never eat again: porridge, lumpy custard, pineapple, pears and coffee. And warm milk like we have to have at school every day although it always tastes sour. I wrote a note to the teacher once in red crayon, excusing me from having milk, but she made me have it anyway. She gave the note to my mum and she showed it to Mato, who laughed. The note said:

Dear miss knight,
please don't give Robbi any milk
love mum.

I am in tears. I really hate coffee. I really, *really* hate milk. And this is milky coffee. My mother stands in the doorway and watches to make sure I drink every last drop. As soon as she has gone back to the office I run to the toilet and spew the coffee up. Luckily I manage to keep my fish and chips. I hope my mother hasn't heard me doing it, because if she has she will make me drink another cup and I will be in trouble for spewing the first lot up.

Every time I vomit with carsickness going down Warrigal Road I get belted by my father.

I call out, 'Please stop the car! I'm going to be sick!'

He says to my mother, 'Do something with her, Rowena!' Then I am sick.

He stops the car to belt me, but he can't stop to let me vomit on the side of the road.

Wayne and I are in the office kitchen drying the cups. Mum comes in and says, 'Come with me, you two. We've got something to do.'

‘What?’ I ask.

‘Nothing. Just some business. Come on.’

We follow her out to the street, excited because maybe we are going shopping. We follow her into a hairdresser’s salon, which smells awful. There are women sitting in chairs with towels draped around their shoulders. They are reading magazines and have huge grey machines over their heads that are making a noise like a vacuum cleaner.

‘Look at the lovely locks on that girl!’ yells one of them over the din.

‘A raven beauty,’ the other woman yells back. I smile, proud of my long, long hair that reminds them of a bird.

‘How much will I get for it?’ I hear my mother ask a lady who is wearing a pink plastic smock.

‘Well, if we do it carefully and take as much as we can, I’d say — ooh — twenty-five dollars?’

‘That much?’ says my mother. Then she tells me to go and sit in a chair by one of the mirrors. I’m starting to get that sick feeling, as if lots of bees inside my stomach are stinging me, but after the coffee I don’t dare cause a ruckus.

Next thing I know the pink smock lady with fluffy hair has said, ‘Hello, dear. Want a change, do we?’

‘No,’ I say and she gives my mother a puzzled look.

‘Oh,’ says my mother firmly, ‘it’s just too much trouble to look after. I can’t stand all the tears over getting the knots out.’

I try to say something, but no voice will come out and before I know it, the pink smock lady has cut right through my hair, close up near my ears and she is saying, ‘Now, dear, we’ll just neaten it up a bit.’

I am trying my hardest not to give my mother the satisfaction of seeing me cry, but I am failing. I look just like a boy again.

After my really short hair is neatened up, the lady gives my mother the money and says to me, ‘Those tresses will make a lovely wig. What are you going to spend all that money on, dear?'

I shrug. Tears forcing their way out of my eyes.

'You can cut my hair for a wig,' offers my brother. 'I want a crew cut, but Mum will only let me have short back and sides.'

On our way back to the office, my mother snaps, 'Oh for goodness sake, stop sulking! Vanity is a sin, you know. You're overreacting as usual. It will grow back and I've got no time to cope with looking after long hair! I need that money to pay bills because your father spends money on himself and that boat that should be used to look after you children. So stop being so selfish!'

My brother and I are in trouble because with our bellies still full of fish and chips, we cannot eat our dinner.

'Why not?' my mother wants to know.

We say nothing, but sit there trying to force in the food. Two hours later, when we have still not been able to eat, my father wallops us both. I hit the wall on the other side of the room. He belts Wayne until my mother says, 'That's enough, Vic.'

'What's wrong with you?' he yells at me. 'You're supposed to be a Christian and you don't appreciate your own mother's cooking. Bloody ungrateful things you are! You can just both go straight to bed! Now!'

We're happy to go. I am crying, but I'm glad that we had the fish and chips. It was fun and I bet Wayne's glad too. He isn't crying. He gets hit so much he acts as if he doesn't care anymore.

On Saturdays we have to do our chores. They take hours and when I am big I will never make my children do any. Our chores change, but I always get the most to do because I am the oldest and a girl.

'You have to learn to run a house,' explains my mother. 'When you grow up you will get married, whereas the boys will have to go to work.'

Sometimes I do the ironing and, believe me, there is always a huge basket of hankies and tea towels and shirts. Sometimes I have to clean the bathroom. Whatever I do I get paid twenty-five cents pocket money. Every week Wayne asks to borrow mine and promises to pay it back. And every week I lend it to him, because the Bible says we should give to those who ask and are needy and I know that Wayne is needy. He has a bad heart and no one likes him at school because of it.

Not once has he paid me my money back, so he must owe me millions by now and I have to buy him a present for his birthday.

We never have parties and even if Wayne did have a party, no one would come. I know this really poor family, who have just moved into the area. Their kids go to the same school as us and sometimes we walk home with them. Their house is between the school and ours. It is really dingy and dark and they don't have a dad, which seems kind of lucky really because their mum is very nice. On the way home I think about Wayne's birthday and the poor family and how Jesus said to bring the poor into your homes and feed them and it seems like the perfect opportunity to do two good things at once. So when we all get to their place, I tell their mother that they are invited to our place that afternoon for Wayne's birthday.

'Yes, right now, for afternoon tea,' I tell her.

'Okay, then,' she says slowly, as if she is not sure. 'We'll be right over.'

Wayne and I get home, throw our bags in our bedrooms, change our clothes and there is a knock on the front door. My mother answers and it is the poor lady with her three sons.

They even have a present for my brother. He is thrilled.

No one but family has ever given him a present before. He unwraps it and inside is a Matchbox car. We all love Matchbox cars. We make cities and roads in the garden and play with them for hours.

My mother makes afternoon tea and brings out everything she has hiding in her cupboard — chocolate biscuits and all the cake in the cake tins. She quickly makes little squares of cheese and I notice that the poor family eat heaps. They must be really hungry so I can see it is lucky I invited them over and I am sure the Lord Jesus is pleased with me. Finally the poor family get up to leave and my mother shows them to the door. She looks really happy as if she has had a really good time doing the Lord's work too.

Then, when she has closed the door, she looks at me. 'How dare you?' she yells. 'How could you put me in such an embarrassing situation? I wasn't at all prepared for visitors I didn't even know were coming. I had to feed them all our food! Where do you think food grows — on trees? It takes money to feed people! I have enough trouble just feeding you lot with that lazy father of yours who won't support his family like a proper man! Go to your room and there'll be no dinner for you tonight while you think about how disgraceful you are!'

I go to my room and cry and sob because I didn't mean to be so bad. Soon my father is home and I feel sick as I hear him stomping up the stairs to yell at me too. I am frightened because I don't want him to hit me.

He yells at me, 'Some sort of Christian you are! You're a disgrace to us! That's what you are! A bloody disgrace! And you call yourself a Christian! How dare you bring people home and embarrass your mother like that!'

I don't understand why my parents hate me so much. I cry myself to sleep.

In the morning my mother says, 'I've decided that Wayne can have a birthday party after all.

'Wayne,' she says, 'you can choose eight people to have to your party. That's about the most we can afford.'

So they write out eight invitations for Wayne to hand out at school. Each one has a space at the bottom so people can say whether they are coming or not.

He invites the poor kids again. We are really excited as the week goes on. My mother has made a big pass-the-parcel with newspaper and lots of cakes. There will be potato chips and my favourite, Lollygobble Bliss Bombs. I wonder if anyone will come.

Two o'clock on Saturday finally comes and the doorbell starts ringing. In half an hour eight kids have arrived with parents and brothers and sisters in tow, and within another half an hour eight more kids have arrived with mothers and brothers and sisters in tow. The house is packed. My mother calls my brother aside; I can see she is a bit frantic. I sidle over to where she is talking to him so I can find out what is happening, but I can't hear over the din.

I find out after the party from Grandma Lyne that Wayne had given out all the invitations and then, when kids gave them back with a 'yes, I can come' on them, he tore the bottom bit off and gave all the invitations out again.

And he doesn't even get into trouble for it. My mother thinks it is cute.

8

Wayne has run away from home again. One time he packed a suitcase and dragged it round the block. Another time he headed off to Mato and Granddad's, but he only made it halfway. He was too ill to go any further and my mother brought him back. This time he's up the tree house in the backyard. Trouble is, it's Christmas Day tomorrow and Mum says if he doesn't come down he won't get any presents. She says this is okay by her. She'll just keep his present for his birthday and it will save her money that the Lord knows she sorely needs. I really want him to come down. I am worried that my parents will decide to save money on all of us.

I got to be Father Christmas in this year's callisthenics concert. My mother was really excited until after the concert when the teacher came up to me and snapped, 'Well, you were the worst Father Christmas I have ever seen! Never seen a Father Christmas look more miserable. Talk about depressing!'

'Couldn't you at least have smiled?' said my mother, joining in. 'Father Christmas is supposed to look happy, you know.'

'All you had to do,' says the teacher, 'was walk across the stage once, looking happy and saying, "Ho! Ho! Ho!" Couldn't you have managed even one smile at the audience?'

The thing is I hate callisthenics. I'm no good at it and my mother only makes me do it because my father's sister did it and now my beautiful blonde cousin Sharene does it. She is really good and wins heaps of medals. Grandma Lyne goes and watches her in the Royal South Street Competitions. I am lousy at it. I'm never in time with the other girls and I never win any medals. The teacher keeps me up the back where no one can see me and she tells me that she only made me Father Christmas so I wouldn't have to do anything but walk on stage with a sack of toys, wave at the audience, give out a few toys and walk straight off the other side.

So there I was, stuffed into a red suit with a pillow, a white beard hiding most of my face. Trouble was I was concentrating so hard on not stuffing up Father Christmas that I stuffed it up just like I stuff up everything else. Now my mother is really disappointed in me.

It's Christmas morning and we wake up early for our present before breakfast and church. We are supposed to care more about celebrating the birth of our Lord and Saviour with the fellowship of believers than about our presents. But when you're only ten it's a real struggle trying to look forward to church more than a present. I desperately want a soft baby doll that cries so I can love and care for it and pretend it's real.

I have one baby doll already. Her name is Joanne and I've had her since I was two. I play with her all the time and she sleeps in my bed, but I really want another one — one that cries. I just love babies so much and I can pretend they love me. I can't wait to be a real mother.

Whatever we get will be something our rich cousins no longer use or want. My stomach is in a tight knot as we sit on the lounge-room floor and my mother starts to give the presents out. I want that baby doll so badly. My youngest brother gets his present first and then my sister because it goes from youngest to oldest so I have to wait until last. At least with Wayne up in the tree house the wait isn't so long and I am just relieved that we, at least, are still getting our presents.

My sister unwraps hers. It is a beautiful baby doll in white crochet clothing. It even has a bonnet and when she turns the baby over there is a string on its back. She pulls it and the baby cries, just like a real one. It is so delicate and tiny. I am beside myself. Maybe, I think, there will be one for me too.

I get my present and open it slowly, carefully, because I know that no matter what it is I have to appear grateful. It is not only Christian, but polite. This has been drummed into me from as early as I can remember. Finally the wrapping reveals a hard, totally unhuggable big doll with brown hair. I smile and try to look happy, but I think she is the ugliest doll I have ever seen.

'See,' says my mother, 'she looks just like you.'

We go to church to celebrate the birth of the king of kings; my father stays at home and plays with the barometer my mother has given him for his boat. Afterwards, we have lunch with my father's family at our house along with our two grans and Grandma Lyne's brother and sister. Grandma Lyne has cooked roast chicken and she made the plum pudding with money hidden in it months ago. It is sweltering and my gingham dress itches like nothing on earth, but at least it's getting so small for me now that it looks almost like a mini.

Before lunch we open presents. Gran's sister, Auntie Elsie, always gives me a petticoat with a special place in it for two huge breasts, and although I don't have any breasts I smile and say thank you. My sister gets a singlet that has breast places too.

Mother has taken us shopping in Coles to buy Christmas presents and we have pooled our money and bought all the men California Poppy hair oil. We've even bought some for Uncle Ron who is bald, but he smiles and says thank you.

When someone gives a present to Grandma Lyne, she opens the package just enough to see what's inside and then she says, 'Why, thank you. This will make a lovely gift for Auntie Margaret next year.'

Once all the gift giving is done, Grandma Lyne takes us children upstairs and unlocks her big white wardrobe. Inside it is filled with gifts she has received in other years and she tells us to pick out what we would like. All the gifts still have their wrapping paper on them, but with the paper peeled back, you can see what is inside. I choose bouquet talc; it still has the rose-pattern wrapping paper on it and the little gift card with the Christmas bell. It says, 'To Lyne, Happy Christmas, Love Elsie'

I don't know what Davie will choose; he has a sort of blank look on his face. My sister chooses 4711 eau de cologne. When we have all chosen, Gran puts her gifts from this year into the cupboard and locks it until a birthday comes along or next Christmas.

Clutching our presents, we go downstairs for lunch. The grown-ups sit at the dining table and we sit at a card table with a cloth over it.

I hate plum pudding, but I want to get some money in my slice.

After lunch with Dad's family it's off to my mother's family at Mato's house. It's lucky that they are only several blocks away because my parents fight the whole time. It usually starts when my father says, 'Well, we're off to those bloody wowser in-laws of mine. I spose I gotta call her Tomato too, do I?'

'It's not "tomato"; it's Mato,' I protest, but not too strongly, because I don't want to make him angrier. Still, I can see that he thinks calling my grandmother 'tomato' is funny.

When we get there we all have to sit in a big circle while a grown-up plays Father Christmas and gives out the presents. The children always get one first. It's done slowly so that everyone can see what you've got and so you can thank the person who gave it to you. I love present-giving time at my mother's family because Mato and Granddad and Aunt Tonia always give me something I really love.

Mato always gets the best presents though, and the most, because we all love her so much. We watch as she opens her present from my rich Uncle Will. Carefully she peels off the sticky tape and pulls the paper open and inside is one of those new fibre optic lamps that twirl and change colour at the same time. I have never seen anything more stunning. Mato plugs it in and we children sit spellbound in front of it for ages.

After presents we eat salads and dessert is always something exotic that my Aunt Tonia has made — like passionfruit flummery. Then after dinner we have a concert and everyone takes turns at singing praise to our Lord on his birthday. Ours is a very musical family. Everyone can play an instrument or two and sing. When Mato was young she was renowned for her beautiful voice and she used to sing for the Lord at Belgrave Christian Conventions. My Aunt Tonia and Uncle Will sing 'Jerusalem, Jerusalem' together and I nearly cry because their singing makes me feel like the room is full of angels. I am the only one who doesn't sing. I tried to once. I love singing, but when I did sing they all laughed and my mother said, 'Just stick to drawing, Robbi.'

Now she doesn't even let me try and if I am singing along with everyone else I just mouth the words, because as soon as a bit of singing slips out — which it sometimes does — someone hears and gives me a strange look and I just want to die.

* * *

This is a special Christmas because Aunt Wilma and Uncle Daniel are over from India where they are missionaries. They came on a boat and it took them six weeks. They have brought us presents from India. Mine is an embroidered leather bag. I don't really like it, but I know I must treasure it because it has come such a long way. It must be valuable.

After our concert we all sit in the front room, the prayer room, where the slide projector has been set up. We watch slides and listen to stories of India and hear about all the heathen who desperately need saving and all about the Lord's work that is being done over there.

'This is our cook,' explains Uncle Dan, showing us a slide of a dark, chubby woman in a white apron. 'She chased a tiger out of our house with a straw broom. This is our house.'

And we see a slide of a charming little cottage surrounded by flowers. It looks just like the pictures of cottages in Enid Blyton's books. This isn't at all how I imagined India to be. When I grow up I will be a missionary and go and save the heathen from hell. I think I will go to Tasmania because I have heard that China, India and Africa are very hot. They are places all the missionaries go to, so someone needs to go to Tasmania.

After Christmas my mother and father go home with my brother and sister, but I stay with Mato and Granddad. Aunt Wilma and Uncle Dan are staying too, with their three children. Uncle George from Sydney is staying as well, with his son Chris, who is the same age as me.

Chris and I are told to go to bed. Our camp beds are made up in the vestibule.

'But why don't our cousins from India have to go to bed? They're younger than us,' we grumble.

'Your cousins are Uncle Dan's responsibility,' says my grandmother. 'You are mine and so is Chris, because his mother is not here.' I have never met Chris's mother. Her name is Mavis, but that is all I know. No one talks about her.

My three cousins from India can do whatever they want and their parents are really nice to them. I wish I was my cousin and had Auntie Wilma for my mother.

'Why can they do whatever they want?' I ask Mato.

'Because,' she says, 'they hardly ever see their parents. They are away at boarding school on the other side of India all year, while their parents do the Lord's work. Imagine how you would feel if you hardly ever saw your parents!'

I wonder what life would be like without my parents, but it is too hard to imagine.

Defeated, Chris and I go off to our beds. I get into my pyjamas in the bathroom and he uses the laundry.

Not long after that, we are getting on so well that we are both lying in my bed talking, talking, talking. We talk about the worst teachers we have ever had, about our favourite food. I say how great it must be for him to have no brothers or sisters, but he says it would be so great to have them.

'Have you ever kissed a boy?' he suddenly asks me.

'No,' I say and a strange thrill runs up my spine.

'Want to try it?'

'Well, we are cousins.'

'Yeah, it's okay to kiss your relatives,' he says.

'Okay,' I say.

'Okay,' he says.

'We *are* related.'

'First cousins.'

He leans over and we kiss quickly, so quickly that it has flown by before it happened.

'What on earth is going on in here?' demands my grandmother. She is furious. I have never seen her so cross. We don't speak.

'Boys and girls do not share the same bed.' She is not yelling. But if she did yell that is what she would be doing.

'Really, Robbi,' she says, 'I thought you were a good girl. I thought I could trust you and here you are letting me down. Chris doesn't know any better. His mother is unsaved, but you I expect better of. I am very disappointed in your behaviour. Back in your own bed, Chris. Now!'

We spend the rest of the night in our own beds without speaking.

On Boxing Day I go back to my parents and my brother comes out of the tree, where he has been hiding. He doesn't seem too hungry, so I think my mother or Grandma Lyne must have slipped food and blankets up to him. But now he has to wait until April for his presents. He only went up the tree in the first place because my father hit him.

9

I am sick in bed. And after I got sick everyone else in the family did too. Then they all got better, but I stayed sick. My poo is black and runny. Old Dr Sullivan says there is nothing wrong with me but a virus, but my mother says after what happened with Grandma Lyne she has good reason not to trust that Dr Sullivan. I am even too sick to go to Mato's, so my parents put me in the back of the car and take me to the children's hospital and I am vomiting the whole way, but my father doesn't even yell at me for it.

At the hospital they take blood and prick my fingers and I cry. Then they put me in boy's pyjamas in a room with other children and every night I vomit.

'If you are going to vomit,' says the nurse, 'then do it into your pillowcase.' I am scared of her so I don't tell her that the vomit just comes and I don't know it is going to. Then my mother comes to visit. She is crying and can't talk to me, so she sits by the bed looking at me, shaking her head and crying some more. I am too ill to talk to her so I just lie on the bed wishing she wouldn't cry. I know it's my fault that she is so unhappy.

She leaves, still dabbing her eyes with her hankie. That night one of the children in my room dies. No one tells us other children about it; it just happens and we know. It is the boy in the see-through tent who had just lain there and coughed all the time.

My Mato and Granddad visit me nearly every day and bring me ice-creams — the ones my mother says are too expensive — and pencils and colouring-in books, my favourite ones that you wet with water and the picture magically appears. They put the books on the bedside cabinet and I try to eat as much of the ice-cream as I can to show I am grateful.

Then the doctors in their white coats jab my fingers again and say, 'Just a little prick now.' But it hurts.

I wake in the morning and there are lots of doctors standing around my bed and their faces have changed from looking gloomy. They smile at me and say, 'We're moving you to a room of your own, young lady. You are contagious.'

Then I start to get better. When Mato and Granddad come to see me they are happy because I am sitting up in bed, painting with water. My father is not pleased though. Apparently anyone who has come into contact with me has to have a needle and he hates needles. The one time he comes to visit me the nurse pops her head through the door to tell him.

'Righto,' he says. Then he looks at me. 'Got to be going now, ducky. You get better.' And he is out the door and down the corridor faster than the Road Runner.

The nurse sees him making a run for it and chases after him. 'Sir, sir! You need to have your injection,' she yells. She must have caught him because the next thing I can hear is him swearing.

My mother says I have had hepatitis and I caught it off a girl at school. She says I have been in hospital for two months and it will be another month before I am out. Then I have to take six months off school and — the best news — no milk for two years. Yippee!

* * *

It is my brother Davie's birthday and my mother is on the phone to someone. She is crying. Her eyes are red and swollen. It seems so strange to be crying on his birthday. I stand by her and wait to find out why. At times like this, I have to guess how far away I should stand. Too close and she becomes aware and shoos me away; too far and I miss what's going on. Eventually she hangs up and says, 'Your granddad has gone to be with the Lord.'

'You mean he's died?' I say as tears fill up my eyes.

'Only his body has died. He is standing by the Lord's right side singing praises with all the angels,' she says, quickly pulling herself together.

After the funeral, where I get into trouble for crying, I move straight in to live with my Mato. I sleep in her big bed with her, on the side my grandfather slept on. It still has his smell. Mato and I hold hands every night while we go to sleep.

'I don't know what I would do without you, my popsy,' she says.

I feel so special to be looking after her. I am so happy I could live with Mato forever.

We go shopping together and we only have to drive to the end of Thomas Street to be at the Hampton shops.

'One day,' I say to her, 'I'll be driving you around. I might even be taller than you.'

'I'm sure you will, my popsy. I'm sure you will,' she says and squeezes my hand.

I will never love anyone as much as I love her.

In Hampton there is the best cake shop ever and I am always allowed to have one of their poodle meringues from the window. They are shaped like a poodle in two halves, sandwiched together with whipped cream. They have chocolate socks on each foot and a chocolate nose. My mother would never let me have one.

Mato and I cook meals together and she only cooks things that she knows I like to eat. We watch telly together and she is my best friend.

But shopping is the best. I love it. My father never goes shopping, so I only ever go with Mato or my mother. Shopping makes my mother happy too. She even smiles and laughs and buys us treats like donuts. Once she bought me some witchetty britches that I really wanted. Mine are pink and black with cream-coloured lace.

'Make sure you take the price off before we get home,' she said. 'I don't want your father seeing how much they cost.'

I like being with her when we are shopping, because shopping makes all our problems disappear.

While I am living with Mato she takes me to visit her sisters who are in homes. They are so old that they sit all crunched up in chairs, talk about the boyfriends they had when they were young and ask my Mato about her engagement to Joe, my grandfather.

Mato says, 'Joe has gone to be with the Lord, Winifred.' But her sister doesn't hear her and keeps on talking as though they are young.

Mato takes me to visit Aunt Tonia too. She lives in Greensborough, out in the country. It takes forever to get there and as always I am carsick going down Warrigal Road, but Mato doesn't hit me for being sick. She just gives me a plastic bag.

My aunt lives in Gladstone Street, which is just a dirt road, and her husband has a shop in the local shopping centre. I don't know what to think of her. She seems exotic and clever. She can make duchess potatoes and the best desserts with names like heavenly mash.

'You'll be an artist just like your aunt,' my mother is always saying to me.

'That sister of mine,' she snaps while she is cooking packet-mix cakes and I am helping. 'You're just like her: two peas in a pod.' I cringe; obviously it is not good that I am just like my aunt.

'You know she wanted you, don't you?' says my mother.

'What do you mean?'

'When you were born, she said I should give you to her, because I could have more babies and she couldn't have any.'

'You wouldn't have given me away, would you?'

'Sometimes I wonder that you're not hers anyway, you're so alike,' she says bitterly.

I don't mention this conversation to my aunt, even though I'm dying to ask whether she really did want me when I was a baby. My aunt is an artist. She teaches art and when I was younger I had to spend an entire day sitting on a chair while her class painted my picture. I want to be just like her. And she has had a baby anyway — a little boy named after Uncle William. So I guess she doesn't need me now.

She is changing his nappy when Mato and I arrive, and we follow her into the bedroom where the baby is up on the change table with a bare bottom, kicking his fat chubby legs in the air. My aunt quickly sends me out of the room because I'm not allowed to see what boys look like. I hang around the doorway so I am still sort of with them.

'I think it's okay,' says Mato. 'Ena lets her see her brothers.'

'Well, you can go and paint,' says my aunt, leaning through the doorway to block any view I might have of my baby cousin. 'I've put everything out for you on the kitchen table.'

I go because I know they really want to do grown-up talk about my uncle, who is strange and just as unsaved and good-for-nothing as my father.

On the kitchen table is the best assortment of paints and paper I've ever seen and I am in heaven. I paint and paint and forget the time completely. I must have twenty paintings done. My aunt is probably still feeding the baby. Aunt

Barbara, Uncle William's wife, has a baby too and she always goes into the bedroom and shuts the door to feed her. Breastfeeding babies must be dirty and shameful. Aunt Barbara's baby is named after Aunt Tonia and Aunt Tonia's baby is named after Uncle William and my mum is really jealous because no one has named a baby after her. I caught a glimpse once of Aunt Barbara feeding her baby. It was when my Uncle William was coming out of the room and I peeked and got into trouble for looking.

'Look at all those beautiful paintings!' says my aunt as she and my grandmother, who is holding the baby, come back. They have finished their talk. 'Spread them out on the floor so I can see them all.'

I do and I am really excited that she wants to see them.

'How much will you charge me for these?'

'What?' I say.

'Don't say "what"; say "beg your pardon",' says my grandmother.

'Beg your pardon.'

'All great artists sell their work. I'll give you twenty cents for each one,' says my aunt.

I am rich. I'm going to be an artist. Just imagine, getting money for something you like to do. I have four dollars. I have never had as much as that before. My aunt is nearly as wonderful as my grandmother. I wonder if I could be like her when I grow up.

'Well,' she says as we prepare lunch and Mato cuddles the baby, 'I noticed your mother was wearing nail polish the other day. Has she backslid from the Lord?'

Just wait till they notice that she has her ears pierced too, I think.

I consider before I answer.

'No. She says she has to wear it for work,' I mutter.

'She always surprises me, your mother,' says my aunt.

My grandmother and I drive home after the visit and I am

going to be rich when I grow up because I am going to be an artist.

These are some of the things my mother cooks besides lumpy custard and burnt porridge. Every night for dinner it is the same thing: we have potatoes and carrots that have been boiled for two hours. I know how long it is because she always puts them on to boil at four o'clock, when we get home from school. Then she takes them off the boil at six for dinner when my father comes home. We also have either beans or peas from the freezer and some sort of meat. I love it when we have sausages, but usually it is something that has been in the pressure cooker for the same amount of time as the vegetables have been cooking. For dessert it's always ice-cream and tinned fruit, either pears (yuk!) or peaches or apricots. On weekends we eat mince on toast, which my mother boils up and thickens with flour. The flour forms little white lumps in the mince. If visitors come she gets out the Royal Doulton, which I am going to inherit, and cooks roast chicken and for dessert she buys a pavlova from Safeway and puts cream and a crunched-up peppermint crisp on top.

Tonight, we are not even having visitors, but my mother has made a special meal. She and my father are really excited. They are being nice to each other and to all of us.

We are looking at each other as we eat, wondering when we are going to find out what is going on. Finally, as she slices the pavlova, my mother says, 'Daddy has sold the business and we are going to buy our own house.'

'Won't we live with Grandma Lyne and Grandma Lucy anymore?' I ask.

'No. Isn't that great?' she says. 'We will have our own house.'

'Will we get our own room?' I ask.

'You girls will share a room and so will the boys. Isn't that great?' says my mother. 'I won't have to do what those two old biddies tell me anymore.' I am shocked. I didn't know she felt this way about my grandmothers. Living with Grandma Lyne and Grandma Lucy is hard with Grandma Lucy always complaining about my clothes and Grandma Lyne spoiling the boys. And the worst thing is that we're not allowed to have friends over because my mother says Grandma Lucy is too old to cope with having children around.

'Will we be able to have friends over now?' I ask.

'We'll see,' she says, which means no. She and my father smile at each other. They are so pleased with themselves.

We are packing for the big move. My mother and father are very excited and they're not fighting anymore. Maybe they will like the new house so much that they will never fight again. It is a triple-fronted brick veneer in between Parkdale and Mentone, so Mum and Dad call it Parktone. They are so thrilled to be buying a brick home. The house we have been living in is two-storey. Yuk! It belongs to Grandma Lucy and it must be as old as her. We are really embarrassed by it. It is so ancient it is made of timber and has millions of redback spiders under the veranda.

Not only are we getting a new house, but there is also enough money left over for new furniture and a swimming pool. Mum and Dad have gone through Myers as if they will never have to worry about money again. You would think it really does grow on trees. New vinyl couch and matching Jason recliners that we are not allowed to sit in.

'They are Daddy and visitor only chairs,' my mother says.

New carpet. New bed and dressing table, with matching side tables for them. New kitchen table and chairs. Everything is in teak.

My mother is really praising the Lord now. My father is already digging the hole in the backyard for the pool. That's so we can pretend it is an in-ground one. I won't be able to stay with Mato every week when we move, but I will still be able to stay with her sometimes.

10

We have moved into the new house. The triple-fronted cream brick veneer with the cream brick fence that my parents have always dreamed of. There is a huge wattle tree in the front yard, which my mother says is going to stuff her sinuses no end.

The phone rings early one morning and when the phone rings strangely, with an eerie, shrill tone to it at a time when it wouldn't normally ring, you know that someone has died. And this time it is Great-Grandma Lucy.

The pastor talks about Grandma Lucy at her funeral. But the things he says make it sound as if he is talking about a stranger. He doesn't say a word about how she's never believed men landed on the moon a few years ago.

'It's all a hoax!' she growled at us. 'Impossible! Amazing how you young ones'll believe anything you see on that silly box.'

He doesn't mention that she never once in her life travelled in a car. He didn't say a word about how she rode her horse to school every day. I hate funerals and I don't like my grandparents dying. I cry.

'Don't cry,' says Grandma Lyne kindly. 'She had a good long life.'

Auntie Margaret is at the funeral in a huge bright aqua dress, laughing loudly and holding onto her new husband's arm and I hear the adults whispering about her remarrying, because it is sinful to marry twice.

Then they say, 'But he's a good man.'

I hate the funeral and I am never going to a funeral again.

My father gets tired of digging the hole for the new swimming pool, so it is half in the ground and half out. There are spades and picks everywhere, not to mention mounds of dirt and rocks all over the garden, which looks like an excavation site.

It is Saturday morning and he has gone out. It's peaceful when he is out. No yelling. No hitting. Our mother is happy and smiles and she potters around the kitchen. And if she feels really happy, she even makes us pancakes.

She still tells us that we have to go outside to play, once we have done all our chores and we are not allowed back in until four o'clock. She brings sandwiches out to us for lunch and we are allowed to drink as much cordial as we like, because it is so cheap.

We used to get out into the backyard and play doctors and nurses, but two things put a stop to that. They just happened to coincide. One: the lady next door heard us playing and dobbed us in and boy, did I get into trouble! My mother said that it was my fault and I should have known better, now that I was a Christian. I was sent to my room with no dinner. I didn't think about how it was evil and a sin that the Lord would not approve of. I should have guessed, though, that the tingle up my spine when we played wasn't coming from the Lord. Second: my brother Wayne started selling the boys in the street looks at us girls. Five cents a look and I wasn't happy about that. I wanted to swap looks and see the boys but they paid their five cents, looked and ran off and Wayne got all the money.

Anyway, we meander around the backyard bored and waiting for our father to come home, because he's bringing a surprise.

'He's here,' my mother calls from the back door. 'Quick! Go around the front and see.'

We all run to the front yard and there standing across the driveway is the biggest thing I've ever seen. It is on a trailer, but my father is standing in front of it and he is beaming. He's obviously going to be in a good mood for days, so whatever this is I'm glad he bought it and I say a quick prayer of thanks to the Lord.

'Look, Ena, look! Just a bit of paint, a bit of work and it'll be as good as new. I got it for a great price, a real bargain. Not much wrong with it at all. I'll just put it in the backyard to work on it. Should have it ready to go next weekend. How'd you like that, kiddlywinks? Next Saturday we'll all go out on the water.'

'Is it a boat?' I ask because it doesn't look like one.

'It's a trimaran,' he says. He's more proud of his boats than he's ever been of us, I think bitterly.

'What's a trimaran?' asks Wayne. He's hooked and he's in, always impressed by anything big.

'It's just like a catamaran,' explains my mother, 'only three instead of two. Three's better. It's better than a catamaran. Daddy is very clever. He always finds bargains.'

The trimaran is sky blue and I love sky blue, so maybe this thing will be okay. Maybe it will keep him in a good mood for months.

'I'll have to change the colour though,' he says. 'That's the first thing to do.'

'What's wrong with the colour?' I ask.

'Well, you can't have a blue boat,' he says. 'If it capsizes no one can see you to come and save you.' I hope he goes out sailing before he has a chance to change the colour. You never know what might happen.

'Daddy knows all about boat safety,' adds my mother. 'He's done a life rescue course.'

'Well, stand back now and I'll just put it in the backyard. I have to back it down, so stand well back,' he directs. My father gets in the car and pulls it out into the street so he can get the trailer on a good angle to back it down the drive. He starts revving and back it goes, straight into the letterbox, knocking one of their beautiful cream bricks off the top. It splats right onto the concrete driveway, breaking into dust and biscuit-size pieces.

'Fucking bloody blast! Why didn't you warn me, Ena? For God's sake!'

'Don't take the Lord's name in vain, Vic.'

Oh no, I think.

He stomps back to the car swearing the whole time. 'Shitting fucking bloody shit! Bloody useless woman! Jesus Christ!' He pulls back out into the street, takes a different angle and we back a bit further into the safety of the front yard.

Back he comes and hits the fence again, knocking a brick off that side of the driveway too.

'For God's sake, Ena! You get in and I'll direct! Christ Almighty!'

'Vic, please don't take the Lord's name in vain!'

'Fucking shit, Ena! I'll say what I bloody well please. You and your bloody wowser relatives! Get in the bloody car, Rowena!'

She gets in the car, pulls it out and tries again, while he yells, 'To your left a little bit, to the bloody left, Ena! Right! Right — shit, left, left!' And so it goes on and they actually get the monster down the driveway, where my father discovers that due to the new in-ground above-ground swimming pool, there is no way the trimaran is going to fit into our yard. He picks up the nearest spade, throws it at the trimaran and stomps into the house.

Tentatively we follow him.

The Mozart is on and he's in his chair.

'Robbi,' he yells. 'Make your father a bloody coffee!' I do and my mother makes him some jaffles with Kraft cheddar, his favourite.

We are all as quiet as mice. Hopefully he won't even notice we are there. I feel ill in my stomach because one wrong move from any of us and that will be it. He will lose it and start to throw us around like the spade.

We eat our jaffles in silence, sitting around the kitchen table. He is in the lounge room.

Then the Mozart stops. We stop eating and look apprehensively at each other.

He stomps in and throws his empty plate on the table so the crumbs bounce off the plate, and thumps on out to the yard and slams the door behind him. There is dead silence and then the chainsaw arcs up.

We listen for a bit, afraid to move.

'The swimming pool!' says Wayne finally and we tear into the backyard.

'It'll bleedin well fit now,' announces my father.

The pool looks fine, but he has chopped a third off the trimaran, right through each of the three ends. I didn't know boats were hollow down the middle. The three ends are lying where they've fallen, like amputated limbs.

He and my mother unhook the trailer from the car and push the boat into the yard. It stays there the whole weekend. The ends stay where they are too.

Months later, the boat is still where my mother and father put it. Now there are cans of yellow and orange paint around it and an assortment of tools and ropes, and every Saturday my father takes his radio out there, listens to the footy, swears a lot and works on his boat. The ends are still where they fell. When he is not looking we use them as cubby houses. It's a pity it wasn't a fourmaran because then we would have an end each.

Grandma Lyne is over, but staying out of my father's way because he yells at her all the time too. He's gone out now so she is sitting in the kitchen yakking to my mum. She is telling Mum how she has sold Grandma's Lucy's house for seventeen thousand and is using it to build a flat onto her daughter's house in Sunshine. Grandma Lyne turned up at seven this morning.

'How'd you bloody get here?' said my father, when he answered the door in his pyjamas.

'I walked,' she said. 'It's good fer yer health, yer know.'

'You're telling me you walked seven bloody miles. For God's sake, Mum, you're nearly eighty!' he snapped.

'Well, public transport is too slow,' she said and walked past him into the kitchen and waited for someone to pop the kettle on for her.

He just swore and disappeared.

My father always seems to bring home surprises on a Saturday and a few hours later we are called to view the latest as he pulls into the drive in a huge Ford Falcon.

'He got a real bargain,' says my mother proudly to us and, as if she knows what we are thinking, she adds quickly, 'And it hasn't got anything wrong with it.'

I believe her. The car is bright fluorescent lime. No one else could ever want it. You can probably see the reflection from the sunlight hitting it in Perth. I am never getting in this car. It is so embarrassing.

'Hop in,' says my father, 'we'll take it for a spin.'

We all pile into the back seat with Davie on Gran's knee.

11

My father has filled the pool with water and hooked up the old Hills slide so that we can whizz down into the water. The next-door neighbours' two tubby girls, Wendy and Debbie, are in the pool with us. Wendy is the same age as Davie and she is his best friend. Every morning she collects him before school and because he is always running late she grabs him by the ear, right in the middle of brushing his teeth, and hauls him out the door and off to school with toothpaste foam still on his face. But he doesn't mind, because Wendy is his best friend.

Last weekend we dressed the two of them up in Wendy and Debbie's parents' wedding clothes. Her parents are really short, but the clothes were still miles too long for Wendy and Davie because they are only seven. I married them and I did a really good job of it. I'm going to be a fantastic minister.

The pool is fantastic too and I practise baptising my brothers and sisters in it. I am going to be the best minister the Lord has ever had. Davie is next and I hold him just like a real minister does. I make him cross his arms over his chest and I place one hand on his crossed arms and the other hand on his back.

'Do you take the Lord Jesus Christ as your personal Lord and Saviour, believing in Him and only in Him for eternal salvation?' I ask him solemnly. 'Say yes,' I whisper to prompt him.

'Yes,' he mutters.

'I now baptise you in the name of the Father, the Son and the Holy Ghost,' I say and I push him backwards under the water just as I'd seen my grandfather do. Then I sing, 'Follow, follow, I will follow Jesus, anywhere, everywhere I will follow him.'

'Now it's Karyn's turn.'

'Can't I go forward?' she pleads. 'The water goes up my nose when I go backwards.'

'No, you have to go backwards or you're not rising from the death of your old life to a new birth in the Lord's life,' I say. 'You have to really bury your sins,' I add. 'No one gets buried face forward. Only wimpy Church of Christs baptise forward. We are Baptists and we do it properly.'

I know all this because my mother has told me. So I baptise Karyn backwards and she comes up spluttering but born again in the Lord.

Then my mother calls me. I clamber out of the pool and grab a towel that I throw around my waist to catch the drips. The others watch me getting out and wonder what I am in trouble for. I shrug at them, because I have no idea. I go into the kitchen and I'm careful not to slip on the tiles with my wet feet.

'What are you doing?' she snaps.

'Nothing,' I say.

'Out in the pool — what are you doing?'

I am silent, waiting for it.

'What you are doing is blasphemy! Baptism in the Lord is sacred and you are turning it into a game. I am ashamed of you. You should know better. I thought you loved the Lord and here you are making fun of Him!'

I do not tell her that I have been practising to be the best pastor the Lord has ever had, because I know that she will not approve. I am a girl. I feel so bad about shaming the Lord that I quickly pray that He will forgive me. I will ask for proper forgiveness later tonight when I say my prayers.

She sends me back out to play in the pool and I am relieved to have got off pretty lightly, with only my guilt. My brothers and sisters are relieved too because I don't baptise them backwards anymore with the water rushing up their noses.

At lunchtime Mum brings us out sandwiches and cordial and then we are back in the pool. We spend all day in the pool until four and we have the best time ever. Then she tells us to get out and take our bathers off on the back porch so we don't drip water through the house.

My father comes and sits in the camp chair on the back porch and watches us take them off. I hate the feeling that creeps over your skin when you try to take off your bathers. They cling to you and you have to peel them off. It always feels like the wet material is going to take the top layer of your wet chlorine-soaked skin along with it.

My mother comes rushing out the back door just as I am about to step out of my bathers. She throws a towel around me and steers me roughly into the laundry. She hurts my shoulders because she is doing it with such force. 'What do you think you're doing?' she asks. Whenever you're in trouble, she always starts by asking a question. I have learnt this.

'I was taking off my bathers.'

'You were flaunting your body in front of your father is what you were doing!'

I stand there. I don't really know what she is talking about, but I do know that I have sinned again. And I am sure she will not hesitate to explain further.

'You were exciting him with your body.'

'But the others are all outside getting undressed,' I protest. 'You told us to take off our bathers outside, so we don't drip all over the tiles.'

'Yes, but I didn't realise that your father was out there watching.'

'But you've never stopped him watching us before.'

'Yes, well, your father is interested in you now. Your body is changing and women's bodies do things to men,' she says. And I know I don't want to hear this. Inside, my head starts to scream. She goes on, 'Your father is a man and he can't help what his body does. Men can't help themselves. God made them that way. It is not their fault if they lose control of their bodies, but you are growing into a woman and it is your responsibility to make sure you don't lead any men on. If a man loses control of himself, it will be because you have led him on, past the point where he is able to stop himself. When things get to that point a man is no longer answerable for what happens. Do you hear me?'

'Yes,' I say, even though it seems so unfair. 'Why does it have to be my responsibility?' I say.

'Because you are a woman, or you will be soon, and women can control themselves. That is why. Men can't help what they do. You can! You are to save yourself for your husband. No good Christian man will want you for a wife if you are loose; your body belongs to your husband for his pleasure, whoever the man may be that God has picked out for you. Your father can't help it if he wants to look at you, but you will make sure you don't lead him on. Is that understood?'

'Yes,' I mutter, knowing that somehow my whole world has changed. I know that somehow I am even less safe with my father than I was before and knowing this sends a creepy-crawly feeling all over my skin, that creeps and crawls into my heart. I also know that my body is a bad thing. It leads holy men away from following the Lord and into backsliding. Why is it so horrible to be a girl?

I get changed in the laundry and feel totally alone. I can

hear my brothers and sister outside laughing together, but I am not with them because of my sinful body.

How am I going to manage this responsibility of not leading men astray, when it is obviously so easy for them to fall? After all, men have been falling easily ever since Eve showed Adam the apple. I have heard so many sermons about how evil she was for leading him astray, but now that I think about it, I realise that I have never heard sermons about Adam's sin of being weak and easily led. I wonder why men get to be the leaders of the church if they are so weak, so easily pushed beyond control as my mother puts it. If women can do this to them and women are the strong ones, then why don't we get to be the leaders? A bitter knot forms in my stomach, then I start to feel angry. Now I find out that women are pretending to be weak when really it's men who are the weak ones. I should have known. Just look at my mother and father.

The next Sunday the minister preaches about young girls dressing in a way that leads young men away from the Lord. Wearing off-the-shoulder peasant tops and such. I really wanted one of those tops that they sell in that new store, Target, for $4.95. I wonder if my mother has said something to the minister about me. I spend the whole sermon looking at my shoes, hoping that no one notices my red face, but I also feel angry because not once does he say that young men should not lead young women away from the Lord. It seems like the Lord doesn't care if women fall away. Now the minister is going on and on about hipster bell-bottom jeans that fit tightly around a young girl's bottom, which is a shame because I really wanted some of those jeans to match the top and I won't be getting any now.

It doesn't seem, with all these boys getting led astray, that there will be many good Christian ones left by the time I am twenty and ready to marry. I am a bit worried about this because I don't want to end up a spinster. I have to marry a Christian or I will be unequally yoked and in a marriage like the one my parents have. And I want to marry a man just like my grandfather, a man God tells me to marry so that I can have a blissful union like Mato and Granddad and never ever fight.

I glance quickly at my mother to see if she noticed the comments about off-the-shoulder tops and jeans and I can see that she is earnestly taking in every word. And there are tears streaming down her face.

The thing is, she cries every single Sunday morning during the sermon. Not just quiet, discreet little drops of tears; she has a waterfall cascading down her face.

It will be even worse this morning because we are having communion and I know that by the time communion is over her eyes will be red and puffy and lots of people will hover about her and ask her if she is all right and she will say, 'No, I'm not,' and she will sob a bit more. Then she will say, 'I just want that backsliding husband of mine to turn back to the Lord. Oh, when will the spirit convict him and bring him back to the Lord? During the week he beat Wayne and he —'

And she will give them all the details of my father's sinful ways and I quickly walk off because it is hard to listen to. Everyone knows that my father is a backslider, but I hate it that my mother is so terribly unhappy and is always on the point of tears.

'Did you listen to the sermon today?' she asks in the car on the way home from church. 'Or were you sleeping?'

'I don't see why it's such a big deal,' I mutter angrily from the back seat.

Then she pulls the car into the driveway and turns to me. 'Now you listen to me, young lady. I saw a man led away from the Lord once and it nearly ruined everything he had: his family and his work for the Lord. I once saw a father go white overnight because his daughter didn't stay pure. His family and work for the Lord were nearly ruined too. Would you like to be responsible for that?'

'No — what do you mean, she "didn't stay pure"?'

'She didn't wait for the man the Lord had chosen for her as a husband. She got impatient and didn't trust the Lord to provide for her.'

'How do you know?'

'She had a baby. You can't hide that sort of disgrace,' says my mother, looking out the car window. 'Now just remember that your sins will catch you out. I am your mother and if you do sinful things with boys, I will know about it.'

'How?'

'Because a little bird will tell me. Mothers always find these things out. You can't hide things from a mother. Mothers always know.'

I believe her. I don't like birds anymore, and I'm not even sure about the sparrows.

12

My mother has sent me on a Christian children's camp run by Mr White and Mr Coleman. They are two very old servants of the Lord. They have been running a ministry to children forever, though my mother says that before them it was Mr Roberts and Mr White, but that was back in her day and Mr White was younger then.

When I was eight Mr White and Mr Coleman came and did a mission at our church for a week. All of us ran to the church after school for mission every afternoon at four o'clock. If you were lucky and got enough of the answers right you won a chocolate frog. I knew I had a good chance of getting at least one of those frogs because I knew about God, Jesus and sin.

They showed us slides of 'The Pilgrims Progress' and had an altar call for kids to give their lives to the Lord. I really wished I could give my life to the Lord at every altar call because it is so moving. I would walk up the front, tears streaming down my face, my heart convicted by the Holy Spirit, ready to repent of my sins and hand my life over to the Lord while everyone sang:

Take my life and let it be
consecrated Lord to thee

or

All to Jesus I surrender,
All to him I freely give.

Now my mother says she has saved all of her hard-earned pennies just to send me on camp. I think she wants to get me away from my father, who hasn't worked since he sold his business. My mother is working as a secretary.

Every day on camp is the same. We have devotions after each meal and, of course, a church service on Sunday morning. Every afternoon we go for a long walk while Mr White and Mr Coleman rest, and in the evening we have more devotions and testimonies and an altar call. The camp leaders give testimonies about their sinful pasts and tell how the Lord has saved them and how their life is now perfect.

At lunchtime Mr White announces how many children have now been saved on camp and have given their lives to the Lord.

Then after a lunch of canned tomatoes on toast Mr Coleman turns on the projector so that we can sing songs. I notice while we are singing that Mr White and Mr Coleman are studying us and every now and then they lean over and whisper something about one of us campers. So then, I make sure I have a heavenly look on my face while I am singing. A look that shows that all that matters to me is the Lord, and soon after we finish Mr White calls me aside.

'We think you are ready to be a camp leader,' he says.

My mother will be so thrilled because that means I get to come to camp free from now on.

'Yes, yes,' I say. 'I'd love to be a camp leader.' Mr White walks away pleased.

But I have a hollow feeling inside. Being asked to be camp leader doesn't give me the sense of fulfillment I thought it would. I sit under a tree at the back of the girls' dormitory and think about it and I realise that only boy leaders are asked to take Sunday service and to speak about the Lord. The most you can do as a girl is give your testimony, and there is only so often you can do that, especially if you haven't had a very sinful life. I start to feel so angry with myself for being a stupid girl that I start to cry and Mr White walks around the corner and finds me. He fishes in his pocket and hands me a white handkerchief.

'What's the matter?' he asks. 'I didn't think being made leader was so important it would make you cry with joy.'

I blurt out, 'I want to be a boy! I hate being a girl. I am sure I was born in the wrong body! I want to be a leader in the church. I want to go out into the world as a missionary, maybe to Tasmania and preach the word of the Lord. I want to lead many souls to the Lord.'

So far the only souls I have led to the Lord are my little brother Davie and my sister and I'm sure my brother only gave his heart to the Lord because he wanted to go outside and play and I wouldn't let him until he had turned from his life of sin.

I tell Mr White, 'I don't want to be a girl and just take Sunday school or bring plates to meetings.'

He laughs and puts his hands on his big tummy and says, 'Goodness me! Being a woman is wonderful. Why, my mother was a woman and she was wonderful.'

That makes me cry more because I don't want to be just a mother and then my crying turns to laughter because I never imagined that someone as old as Mr White could possibly have a mother. 'Have you really got a mother?' I ask.

'Of course,' he says. 'Let's pray.' He prays, 'Dear Lord our God, please show Robbi the place that you have made for her in this world. Please show her the job that you have for her to do. Please help her to accept your will. Amen.' And he pats me on the head and walks off happy. But I am still angry.

* * *

I am at Mato's, sitting on the floor at her feet. I have upended her shoeboxes of old brown photos with ragged edges and strange-looking people who aren't smiling. I am rifling through them and I have photos spread all around me as I try to feel some sense of attachment to these people I have never met, who had lives so different from mine but are my relatives.

'Who's this?' I ask, pointing at a man in a soldier's uniform.

Mato leans over to see and I hold the photo up to her. 'Oh, that was my favourite brother, Claude.'

'What about this one?'

'That's your Great-Aunt Mabel when she was young. That's her beau who became her husband.'

Then I see a photo with people I recognise. 'Hey, this is Mum and Uncle William and Aunt Tonia.'

'Yes,' says Mato, 'and there is your Uncle Claude, who was named after my brother, and there's your Uncle George and Uncle Daniel.'

'Well, who is this other man?' I point to a tall, good-looking man with his hair swept back off his forehead in a wave. He is older than my uncles in the photograph and he looks uncomfortable, as if he doesn't belong.

'He isn't anyone important.'

'How did he come to be in the photograph?' I persist.

'Oh, he lived with us for a while,' mumbles Mato and she quickly starts scooping up all the photographs and puts them back in the shoebox. 'I think I could do with a lovely cup of tea, popsy. Why don't you put the kettle on for us?'

So I do, but I wonder who that man was and what he did that made Mato so upset she doesn't want to tell me about him. But we have a cup of tea and I tell her about the White and Coleman camp and she tells me that she and my grandfather went to Wycheproof and ran a two-week mission for their honeymoon.

I hear my mother's car pull into the driveway. She has finished shopping at Southland and has come to pick me up. I don't like Southland. My Grandma Lyne took my sister Karyn and me to Southland the weekend it was opened and in all that crowd of people we lost her. Karyn and I were frantic. We looked everywhere and asked in all the shops. We were starting to cry because Karyn was only five. Eventually we remembered that our mother said if we were ever out and had a problem we should look for someone in a uniform. So we found an official-looking lady and when we explained that we had lost our grandmother, she took us to the office and made an announcement asking our grandmother to come and get us. But she didn't need to because the next thing we heard was 'Hooo rooo!'

We popped our head around the door and there was Grandma Lyne in the next room, in the sick bay, having a nice cuppa and chatting to a lady who was offering her another Arnott's biscuit.

'I just felt a bit dizzy,' said Gran, 'so I thought twould be best if I got a cuppa. I could've had a turn, I daresay.'

My mother was really mad at Gran for that.

On the way home from Mato's I say to my mother, 'Did you have a man come and live with you?'

'Oh, my parents had lots of different people come. You have to keep your home open to the needy when you are doing the Lord's work. Why?'

'I saw a man in a photo.'

'What did Mato say?' she says, looking at me and not the road.

'Nothing,' I say quickly.

We head up Nepean Highway and my mother says, 'So did you meet any nice boys on camp?'

13

My brothers and sister walk home from their school together. My brothers will be stepping in every puddle they can find so that they can get new shoes. I ride from my school on my pushbike. It is a seven-mile ride. No one is ever home when we get there. Our mother is at work.

'I have to go to work,' she says. 'I would much rather stay home and look after all of you, but someone has to pay the bills and take responsibility for this family.' Our father never gets home until dinner is ready.

I hate going home to an empty house. The others dawdle and I ride as fast as I can, so we all get home about the same time. Because I am the eldest I get the key out from under the third pot plant from the door. I always stop to listen before I turn the key, to see if I can hear any noise inside the house, any creaks and groans that might be footsteps. When I can hear that the house is silent I turn the key and we go in, but I am still scared. There could be an evil man waiting in one of the closets until we are inside with the doors closed, then he will jump out with his knife and gun and do unmentionable things to us and kill us and my mother will come home and find our battered bodies.

I leave the front door open until I have checked in every closet and behind every door and under every bed.

Each night I prepare the vegetables and put them on. I have to have them on by four-thirty. Potatoes, carrots and frozen peas. At six my mother gets home, she turns off the vegetables, cooks the chops or sausages and gets ready to serve up. At six twenty-five my father gets home, kicks off his shoes, and his feet always stink. You can smell them from the other end of the house. At six-thirty we eat. My father never eats the vegetables, only the meat. He says he isn't hungry, but his car is always chockas with takeaway food wrappers a foot deep so you can't see the carpet.

Before my father gets home we have twenty-five minutes of peace with our mother. Twenty-five minutes of our mother being happy. She smiles and laughs and is kind to us. Sometimes, when she is in a really good mood, she brings home cream cakes to eat for afternoon tea before my father arrives, but tonight she walks in the back door and she hasn't brought us anything. I hang around her while she gets things ready for dinner. I know she doesn't like this, but I do it anyway.

Sometimes she says to me, 'Are you going to be forever tied to my apron strings?'

But tonight she hasn't said that. We don't talk but it is peaceful.

'Your father's . . .' she says to me out of the silence. 'Your father has decided that we will all be nudists.'

I catch my breath. 'What?' I gasp. I know what a nudist is because I watched the *Carry On* movie with Sid James on the telly on Saturday night.

'He has decided that we will all be nudists. Some nudists are very nice people,' she says.

'Well, I don't have to be a nudist,' I say.

'In the next school holidays, we are all going to a nudist camp. Your father has booked us in.'

'But I can go to Mato's,' I say.

'This is very important to your father, he needs our support,' she growls at me. 'We are going to a very respectable nudist camp and you will come, missy. It's a family camp and the whole family is going. We are also going to have nudist nights at home.'

'What?'

'Every Tuesday night is going to be nudist night. It will bring us closer together. It's important to your father.'

'But you don't have to agree to this!' I wail.

'I am his wife. The Lord requires of me that I submit as a good and obedient wife to my husband's wishes. Some day you will do the same with your husband. In the meantime you will obey your parents as the Lord directs in the Ten Commandments. Or would you prefer to disappoint the Lord?'

'But today is Tuesday!'

'That's why I am telling you now.'

I am shaking. I will never submit to a husband. I want to shout it, but my voice comes out low and quiet. 'I will never submit to a husband.'

'Then you will be answering to the Lord, young lady,' says my mother crossly.

'Do you mean I have to get naked tonight?'

'It will be good for you.'

'And I have to do it in front of strangers in the holidays?'

'They have trampolines there,' she says as if this is really going to seal it for me. I certainly won't be able to resist jumping naked on a trampoline.

'What? You think I want to trampoline with no clothes on?'

What if I have my period? I think. I will have to bleed everywhere, leaving a trail like Hansel and Gretel, or I will have the tampon string dangling between my legs like a loose thread and everyone will know I have it.

I imagine trampolining naked with my period, jumping up and down. My small breasts jiggling in front of everyone, my legs slightly apart so I can balance when I land on the mat.

There is blood going everywhere, spraying everyone in sight with a fine mist of red. My father is covered in my period blood. 'Come on,' he yells in his normal foul mood, 'we're leaving!' I am smiling because for once my period has been good; it has made us leave the nudist camp. I have had about six periods so far and I hate them.

'It's very healthy,' says my mother, bringing me swiftly back to reality. 'I know a teacher who is a nudist and it's quite respectable.'

I ignore her. I feel ill all the way through dinner. My brothers and sister don't know yet what is waiting for them. I hate my father. And I hate my mother. Why can't she say no to him? I will never make my children do something so horrible just because a man wants it.

I will be fourteen in the school holidays. I have never seen a grown man naked. I don't want to see anyone naked, man or woman, and I don't want to be naked full stop!

After dinner my father gets up and closes all the curtains. It is the only housework I have ever seen him do. He puts on one of his favourite records. It has songs on it like 'You Great Big Beautiful Doll' and 'Deep in the Heart of Texas'. He has a satisfied look on his face — no, more than satisfied: happy, expectant.

'Rightio,' he says, 'tonight we are going to be a real family. Come on, get your gear off.'

Davie is only eight. He thinks it is fun and strips off. Wayne doesn't care about anything so he strips off too. Karyn is only ten so I guess she doesn't care. She might as well be getting ready for the bath, so she is starting to take her clothes off too, and my mother and father are already naked. YUK!

My father is sitting in his chair but I try not to look at him. My mother is putting on coffee, going about business as usual except she is not wearing any clothes. I hope she doesn't burn herself.

'What's wrong with you?' my father barks at me. 'Some kind of prude, are you? Just like those bloody in-laws of mine!'

I know that if I don't take my clothes off he is really going to get worked up and we'll all cop it and it will be my fault, so I slowly peel them off. I do it sitting on the couch so I can keep as hidden as possible and when all my clothes are in a puddle on the floor I stay there on the couch, legs crossed, arms wrapped over my new, embarrassing little breasts.

My father is still scrutinising me. I imagine I am glued permanently to the couch and cannot move. I study my feet. Next I study the gold-flocked wallpaper that my parents love.

'Come over here,' he says, 'and sit on my knee.' And he pats his hairy leg.

I don't remember once, in my entire almost fourteen years, when he has wanted to give me even a fatherly hug and now when I'm naked and he's naked he wants me to sit on his knee. What if I can feel his thing?

'I'm okay,' I stammer.

'What, you can't even give your own father a hug?' he snaps at me. 'Karyn, come over here and give your father one.'

She runs over to him and clambers onto his knee. He hugs her and kisses her like a real father and then he puts her off again.

'See, it's not so hard to give your own father a hug. Your turn,' he says to me, except it's more of a command than a request and I know I am beaten, so I go over feeling so awful, so ashamed, because I am naked and I sit on his knee.

I wish Tuesdays didn't exist. I wish my parents didn't exist. I sit on his knee. I try to imagine a piece of cardboard is between us, separating our bodies. I can't look at him. Finally my mother comes in. 'Here's your coffee, Vic.'

I jump off his knee faster than you can blink as he reaches out for the hot cup. 'I'm so tired,' I say to my mother. 'Can't I go to bed?'

'It's only eight o'clock. I've never seen you want to go to bed this bloody early before,' says my father. 'I don't know what's wrong with these kids, Rowena. They don't want to be a family, bloody prudes, and it's that bloody Mato's influence, bloody Baptist wowsers!'

But my mother bundles us all off to bed and I guess they keep on being nudists for the rest of the night.

I lie there in bed trying to imagine what a respectable nudist camp is like. I don't imagine that they will have daily devotions or an hour of songs and praises. I wonder if there will be enough bushes for me to hide behind and if there will be lots of creepy old men like Sid James or that doctor from 'Lost in Space'. I hate 'Lost in Space'. It's so scary and anyone can see that horrible Dr Smith wants to do unmentionable things to that little boy. Maybe there will be creepy old men like that guy from 'Steptoe and Son', Alf Garnett, or the Bunker guy from 'All in the Family'. The world is full of scary men.

I go to see Alan Marr. He is our new minister. He has just arrived and he is a spunk. I tell him I need help to learn to forgive my father because at the moment I hate him. I don't tell Alan about the nudist nights. How could I tell anyone? It makes me feel sick just thinking about it. Alan prays with me and we look at Bible verses about forgiveness together, but still I hate my father. I really like being with Alan Marr, though, just the two of us together with the Lord's word. So I don't tell him it's not working and every week I get an hour with him while we pray about my problem with forgiveness. Alan has asked me if I want to lead the church service one Sunday. I will get to do everything but the sermon. I am so excited I can hardly contain myself.

I don't tell my friends that we are going to a nudist camp. I don't have many friends at school so it isn't really a problem;

the friends I do have are from the church youth group. David Danaher is my best friend and he asked me to go round with him. But he is shorter than me, so how can he protect me and look after me? David has that orangey blond sort of hair that flops in his face and he has even more freckles than me. We are the same age and I can say anything to him and he still smiles sweetly at me. His mother says she would like a daughter just like me; David is the oldest of four boys. He invites me on a date to the Royal Melbourne Show but we have to go on a train and his mum will pick us up from the station and that makes it seem like it's not a real grown-up date anymore.

What I really want is a boyfriend with a car whose mother won't have to pick us up.

Someone who is older and experienced who will just force himself on me so that I'm powerless to resist.

David asks if he can kiss me, but I have to save myself for my husband and the Lord. Older boys don't bother to ask, they just do it, which makes it so much easier, and more thrilling. It's so much better if you can't say no — even when you should. I know this because after youth group one night, Brian Lloyd just pulled me to him and kissed me. The big problem at the moment, though, is conscription. How can I get an older boyfriend when he might get conscripted to go to Vietnam?

Even more than a boyfriend who can drive, I want a boyfriend with long hair, and there is no way that David's parents would let him grow his hair.

When I was in the car with my parents and we were driving down the Calder Highway, we saw all these long-haired boys hitchhiking to Sunbury. Dad said, 'Bloody hippies!' but I thought they looked ace. I would have liked to pick one up and take him home, but he would have hated my dad's records. I wanted to jump out of the car and go to Sunbury too. Their long hair made my spine feel sparkly and

I sank into the back seat and imagined Clark Gable with long hair taking my face in his hands and kissing me before I could even say 'No — sorry. I'm saving myself.'

The man that I am really saving myself for, though, is Alan Marr. He makes the whole congregation laugh during his sermons. No one has ever made the congregation laugh in church before. I am going to marry him when I am older, and when I pray at night I ask the Lord to speak to Alan in his heart and tell him that he is to wait for me. He will just have to. Ten years isn't such a big gap; there was a sixteen-year gap between my grandparents and they were happy.

Alan will also have to grow his hair long. But at the moment I have to settle for Brian Lloyd, from youth group, who likes me. He has long hair, a motorbike and he is nineteen. He asked me to go round with him when he kissed me, so when I get back from the show I will say yes.

It is Sunday today and I get to be junior minister. I have chosen the hymns and I have written a talk for the little kids. I get to do everything but the sermon, which Alan will do. We all arrive at church — not my father, of course. I asked him to come but he said no and started screaming and yelling at us all. He screams and yells at the slightest thing, like the way my brother chews his food. You would think that my brother Wayne would learn not to sit next to my father. I always sit as far away from him as I can. But every meal my brother gets walloped for something and at the next meal he still sits down next to my father and smiles his big silly grin at him and gets walloped.

I jump out of the car as soon as my mum pulls into the church car park and rush off to the vestry.

'You all ready?' asks Alan. I nod. I am too nervous to speak. What if I can't make my voice speak when I get to the pulpit? I will open my mouth, nothing will come out, and 150 people will be staring at me, waiting for the word of the Lord.

'Let us pray,' says Alan. He prays, 'Dear Lord, please bless all who have come to hear your word, please speak through your servant Robbi today. Amen.'

He called me a servant of the Lord! Me? A young girl! I follow him into the church and everyone stands. I feel so important and special as I sit with Alan behind the pulpit while the congregation sings:

Worship the Lord in the beauty of holiness.
Bow down before him, his glory proclaim.

I say the call to worship slowly and clearly and announce the first hymn. The service seems to fly by and before I know it I am standing at the door with Alan and shaking people's hands on their way out. I know that this is what I am called to by the Lord — even if I *am* a girl.

14

'How much did we take today?' asks my aunt, trying to make it sound unimportant.

I am sitting with her in her car. We are close together because she has a VW Beetle and I can smell her lovely perfume. It fills the car. I am doing work experience in my uncle's jewellery shop. Not many customers come in and when they do my uncle hides and makes me go out to serve them. He is a scrawny man who looks like he could drop dead any minute and I can never understand a thing he says because he can't talk properly. My aunt has to tell people what he is saying because most of the time he just grunts.

'I've come for my watch! I left it here to be repaired six months ago! This is the fourth time I've come in for it!' the stocky man with the crew cut yells at me. He looks like a bull on two legs.

'Just a minute, I'll ask.' I say. I go out the back and look at my uncle who has heard everything. 'I Am Woman' by Helen Reddy is playing on the radio. He shakes his head at me, crouching there behind a filing cabinet. I have never seen a man look afraid before. I go back out to the lion and I am like Daniel. I say a quick prayer for protection.

'I'm sorry, it isn't ready yet,' I say.

'Fucking hell! What kind of outfit are you running here?

Bloody swindler! Just give me the bloody watch and I'll go somewhere else!'

When I go in the back room my uncle is already holding the watch at arm's length. He drops it into my palm and I give it to the customer. Then through the glass partition the man catches a glimpse of my uncle hiding. Off he goes, just like my father. 'You fucking useless sod! Getting a little girl to do your work for yer! What kind of man are yer? Bloody yellow coward! Get a real job! Shit, I'm outta here!' He storms out.

And he isn't the first. All the customers that come to my uncle's shop are angry and want their jewellery back. I hate doing work experience with my uncle. I really wanted to do work experience with Alan. Visiting the sick and needy would be fun, and the sick and needy would be grateful, unlike my uncle's customers. Besides, I still want to be a minister or a missionary even though I am a girl. And if I am going to marry Alan Marr we need to spend a bit of time together, getting to know each other, then he can see how much better it is to do the Lord's work with your helpmeet. Mato says that is what a woman is. She is there to *help* the Lord *meet* a man's needs.

But my parents say that I have a choice.

I can be a nurse so I can look after my children when they are sick.

I can be a secretary, because then I can help my husband run his business.

Or I can be a primary school teacher, and learn how to be a better mother.

I don't want to be a nurse because I don't want some male doctor telling me what to do all the time. I don't want to be a secretary because we have to learn typing at school and it is *soooo* boring, and I don't want to be a primary school teacher because my brother Davie's friend always has a snotty green nose. It is totally disgusting and

I couldn't stand a room full of sniffling, runny-nosed primary school children all day.

Because I come top of everything at school the teachers say I should become a doctor, but my parents say there is no way they are paying for any girl to go to university.

'Total waste of money,' says my father. 'We spend all that money sending you to university and you'll just go and have babies. Absolutely not!'

Now my aunt wants to know how much my uncle has taken in his shop today. He took twenty dollars from a repair he's actually done, but he told me to say two hundred when she asks.

I take a deep breath. 'Well,' I drawl, 'he said to tell you two hundred.'

My aunt sighs and shakes her head. 'I'm not stupid,' she says. 'I didn't come down in the last shower. What was it really?' She sounds sad, not angry.

'It was really twenty,' I confess immediately. I'm not suffering for my uncle. He's weird.

'He shouldn't make you lie to me,' she says. 'It isn't right. There are some things I must tell you about men.' She is almost whispering and shakes her head slowly from side to side. 'I can't imagine your mother will bother to tell you.' She frowns.

'What about men?'

'Men,' says Aunt Tonia, 'are untrustworthy. That is, of course, unless they truly follow the Lord. The only man I have ever known to truly do so was your grandfather, but most men don't and are only after one thing.'

'Money?'

'Your body! When I was your age,' says my aunt solemnly, 'a man did something very bad to me. You have to be careful and your mother should have warned you by now.'

'Who did something bad to you?'

'It was the local grocer and he exposed himself to me. Mato sent me to get some vegies and when I went into his shop he locked the door behind me and pulled down the blind with the closed sign. Then he opened his jacket and there it was. It was shocking. I didn't know what to do, or who to tell. I have never been the same since and I certainly could never go to the grocer's again. It's just lucky he stopped there because men will do anything. Your mother knows. You have to be careful to keep yourself set aside for the Lord, for the man he has chosen for you.' She looks at me seriously and her eyes are dark and questioning.

Maybe she can tell that I used to kiss Brian Lloyd, but that I dropped him and started going with Rodney Burlington. So recently I have been kissing Rodney Burlington from the youth group — and not just kissing either! He started by kissing me, but his tongue slid in my mouth and felt its way around my teeth and while I was considering whether this was enough to classify me as impure and was wondering if my mother could tell what I was doing, he moved his hands that were under my shirt around to the front. Each of his hands cupped one of my breasts and his fingers gently twirled around my nipples making them go hard and tingly and then one of his hands slid down my belly and into my jeans. Somehow he managed to get the button and zip undone and his fingers were inside my panties and almost inside me and every last bit of me tingled like a sherbet bomb exploding in my mouth. I couldn't say no. At twenty-four, he is nine years older than me, he has a Ford Fairmont with an inbuilt eight-track player, and he didn't ask.

'If you are to find a good Christian man,' my aunt says, 'you must remain pure for him. The Lord will have someone special for you. So you must not disappoint him. No man wants a used car when he can get a new one.'

I am never going to let Rodney Burlington near me again. There'll be no kissing! Nothing! I'll break it off as soon as I get home. It will be a relief because every time he drops me home in his Falcon, my mother says, 'Did he kiss you? How did he kiss you? How many times? Did he use his tongue?'

I just say no to everything and hope she can't tell what I've been doing, but I can always hear her saying, 'A little bird will tell me,' in the back of my head.

Then she says, 'Well, if a boy takes you to dinner or a movie, the least you can do is give him a nice kiss goodnight.'

And so I am totally confused. On the one hand I have to stay pure for my future husband, but on the other I am cheating the boys if I don't give them a thank you kiss for taking me out.

'I am surprised that your mother hasn't spoken to you about this,' my aunt is saying now. 'She's the one — well, anyway, she should. I never had a boyfriend until I married your uncle and boy did I get a few surprises on the wedding night!' I imagine my aunt bouncing back against the wall in surprise when my uncle shows himself on her wedding night.

'He had debts. Ten thousand dollars in debts and he never told me,' she says. 'No one else told me. And he didn't tell me he had muscular dystrophy either. I just thought he was tired all the time. Do you have a boyfriend?' she asks.

Luckily, her little boy in the back seat starts to cry so she doesn't ask me any more questions. I hope my face isn't too red because I feel hot and flushed, but she doesn't notice and I don't have to confess about what Rodney Burlington does. I will confess to the Lord later tonight and when He has forgiven me I will make sure it never happens again.

But Rodney Burlington has wandering hands. A lot of men have truly lovely hands and now that is the first thing I check out on a boy. My uncle's hands are awful: scrawny and weak. My father's hands are fat, chubby and grabbing. Alan Marr's hands are long and slender, with a gentle strength and knowledge in them. Rodney Burlington's hands aren't too bad, in fact they're pretty good, but I'll never let them wander again. I don't want a man like my father or uncle for a husband; only the husband the Lord has chosen for me — Alan Marr. He is ace!

We are going to Rosebud for the Christmas holidays so I will be away from the boys from youth group for at least four weeks. All that time with no boys! We are camping on the foreshore and I can't wait. The last holiday we had was at the nudist camp in Echuca. When we got there, my parents pulled up outside the office and an oldish man came out and poked his head through the window. I said a quick prayer of thanks to the Lord that he had his clothes on.

He told my mother and father where everything was — the toilet blocks, the tennis courts, all that stuff. Then he glanced in the back, saw all us kids and, looking right at me like he knew, said, 'Kids don't have to go nudist if they don't want to. We don't force 'em. They come back to it when they're adults.'

So I put on as many clothes as I could. Even though it was hot I wore my jumper, just to make sure. I hid behind a bush too. I stayed there all day and read *Gone With the Wind*. Rhett Butler doesn't give women the chance to say no. Nor does James Bond. They are real men.

Every time I saw my father, like at meal times, he would yell, 'I didn't bring us all the way here just so you could be a bloody prude like those bleedin wowser relatives of yours!' So I tried to sneak away as much as possible, to places where he couldn't find me. It was horrible and I couldn't wait to go home.

It's disgusting to watch your parents frolic around naked all day. It's even worse when they play tennis and their bits jiggle everywhere. Each day my mother said to me, 'Come on, Robbi, join us. Don't be a prude! Enjoy yourself and stop being a misery guts.'

'It's all right, Ena!' snapped my father. 'She just doesn't appreciate the things we do for her! She doesn't appreciate the nature *God* has created!'

I even showered with my bathers on. I had to: the showers were for men and women and only the actual toilets were separated.

'Of course the showers are for everyone.' My mother was exasperated. 'Everyone's naked anyway, silly! What would be the point of separate showers?'

If I wasn't reading behind the bushes, I was trying to straighten my hair. I have this horrible mop of shoulder-length curly hair. Full-on ringlets: how daggy can you get? And they're not even blonde. No one wants to have brown hair, but curly, unmanageable brown hair is truly embarrassing.

All the boys like blondes. Who is the favourite Angel? The one all the boys have posters of, Farrah Fawcett. Who is more popular: Agnetha or Frida? Agnetha with her long blonde hair. No one wants a poster of Frida, they just put up with her and the boys in ABBA to get Agnetha.

So I tried to bleach my hair with two bottles of peroxide and it went orange. Next I tried to straighten it with the iron and it frizzled and burnt. It smelt disgusting, like burnt custard. So all I could do was brush and brush with hot water and then try to hold the ends down while it dried. This took some work and had me tied up for hours in front of the mirror in the toilets, so I had no time for going nude.

My father seemed disappointed with the nudist camp, so now we don't have to have nudist nights anymore and for our next holiday we are going to Rosebud foreshore. That will be in the school holidays.

I don't go to the same school as the other kids in the youth group. Most of them go to Parkdale High but I have to ride my bike up and down hills for seven miles to go to Sandringham Technical School. My mother chose it because my grandfather once taught there, so she figured it had to be a good school. At school I am not very popular but the kids here accept me more than the kids in primary school did. There is a girl, Leanne, who is really unpopular because her clothes are always dirty, she has huge bushes of underarm hair that poke out of her summer uniform and she smells. The other kids are mean to her, so I am always nice because that is how the Lord Jesus would treat her.

The one thing that made me more popular was when I found out I could swim. We all had to compete in the school swimming carnival. I had learnt to swim when Grandma Lyne took me to lessons at the Brighton baths, but I wasn't very good because I am hopeless at sport. The only other swimming I had done was each year when my mother made us lie on a stool and practise as if we were in the water. We flailed our arms and legs about in the air, whining all the time, while she said, 'This is how they teach the champions to swim.'

I jumped into the pool for my heat, swam to the end and got out. No one else was around and I figured that was because I was so slow they had already finished, so I grabbed my towel and walked off.

'Hey! Where do you think you're going?' yelled the form six kid with the stopwatch.

'I've finished so I'm going to get changed.'

'Where do you think everyone else is?' he asked.

It was a strange question, but I knew you didn't mess with form six kids. 'Umm, they've already gone to get changed. I'm always last,' I said.

'You dag!' He laughed. 'The others are still only halfway down the pool.'

And that was how I found out I could swim: not only freestyle, but backstroke too. I could win the fast races and the long races. No one could beat me and — what was even better — because I could swim I was instantly popular. Once I found out I had to turn up to squad training at seven-thirty in the morning and that the pool didn't have one drop of heated water in it, I was less keen on swimming. But I was still glad that the other kids liked me.

At Sandringham Technical School they have a school disco, but I am not allowed to go. When I was unpopular I didn't mind, but now everything has changed and I want to go.

I am standing at the clothesline handing my mother wet clothes and I plead with her, 'Please, can I go? Please, please, please? Everyone is going!'

'We are not everyone!' she replies smartly.

'Please?'

'Absolutely not! We do not approve of dances. Dances encourage young people to sin.'

'But I won't sin, I promise.'

'You won't be able to help it. Once it goes past ten o'clock things start to happen.'

'Can't they happen before ten o'clock?'

'Don't get smart with me, young lady! Dances lead to other things,' she says as she shakes out one of my father's shirts.

'You can pick me up by ten,' I offer. 'Before anything happens.'

'Boys use dances to rub their bodies against the girls. They pull you indecently close to them, hold you tight in their arms.'

'Please can I go?' Dances are sounding better all the time.

'Baptists do not dance!'

'But the Bible says that King David danced in front of the Lord,' I protest.

'Fine,' snaps my mother. 'You can praise the Lord on Sunday morning, but no Christian daughter of mine is going to disgrace the Lord by going to a dance that encourages young people into the grasp of Satan.'

So I don't get to go to the dance because I'm Baptist and my mother doesn't believe in them.

All Friday night I mope, thinking of the other kids at the

dance, and on Saturday morning my father comes home with a surprise.

My mother calls us all to the front of the house to come and see. I throw down my book and saunter outside. My father has brought home a trail bike.

'He got it for an absolute bargain,' she says.

My father puts his car at the end of the driveway and we are all to take turns on the bike. First Wayne goes up the drive, swings in front of the car and comes back down. Then Davie. Then it is my turn.

'I don't want to,' I say.

'Come on. Don't be a sook,' says my father.

So I get on the bike and off I go but halfway down the drive I realise I don't know how to slow the thing down or stop. It is going too fast, so I pull on the handles, grip them tight, and the bike goes faster still. I am yelling, my Dad's car is in front of me. The next thing I know I have bounced off the bonnet of my father's car and am lying on my back on the pavement. I open my eyes and my mother's face is the only thing I can see.

'Just keep still,' says my mother. 'I'll go and ring an ambulance.'

I hold my thumb up in front of my face. It is a funny shape, bending all the wrong way, and it hurts. Soon my mother is back, leaning over me and saying, 'The ambulance will be here any moment.'

'Where's Dad?' I ask.

'Oh, he's inside sitting on his chair. He can't cope when anything happens to his children, he doesn't know what to do. He is no help at all when I need him most.'

Soon I am lying in the back of the ambulance, fascinated by my wonky thumb.

Next I am in the Alfred Hospital where I find out I have dislocated it and sometime on the way in the ambulance it has just popped back into place.

‘And a lucky thing for you, young lady,’ says the doctor. ‘It isn’t a pleasant thing when we have to put it back into place for you.’

I have also cracked several ribs, but that’s okay because now I am back in my bed listening to the Beatles special on 3XY. There is a whole weekend of their songs because the Beatles have broken up. It’s pretty groovy when you are too sick to do anything, but not too sick to enjoy being in bed.

I keep the radio down low so that my mother can’t hear me listening to non-Christian songs. On Sunday morning she comes into the bedroom and says, ‘Would you like me to tune the radio to Sunday service so you can still worship the Lord on his day?’

‘Ohh, I don’t feel well enough to listen to the radio,’ I moan. Then as soon as she has gone to church I get out my earphones and listen to more of the Beatles.

When I am well enough to get up the trail bike is gone.

15

At Rosebud we have a huge orange tent and two little blue tents, one for the girls and one for the boys. The big orange tent is for my parents and it has the kitchen in it. We are camping on the Rosebud foreshore. Every morning we run off to CSSM, which stands for Children's Special Service Mission, but everyone says it stands for 'Come Single Soon Marry' because all the young Christian adults in their early twenties run it and they soon pair off and get engaged. Alan Marr will be here on the last night to give a special sermon and there will be an altar call. Peter Grey is coming too. He is a clown and acrobat and so fantastic that people are sure to turn to the Lord when they see how amazing he is.

I have decided that I should witness to the Lord whenever I can, so I have painted the words JESUS IN ME LOVES YOU down the back of my red Exacto windcheater and on the front I have painted JESUS WAS HUNG UP FOR OUR HANG UPS. I wear it everywhere. My father sniggered when he saw it.

When I wear it boys yell out at me, 'Hey Jesus in you, can give me a little lovin!' but I know the Holy Spirit will convict them in their hearts so I keep wearing it. I wear it all over Rosebud, even when it's hot. Unfortunately I had to get my mother to cut my hair off because it turned orange and there was the fried bit where I ironed it, so I have short hair again.

But the boys still yell out at me for a little loving in my Exacto, so I don't think I look like a boy anymore.

I thought I would have to spend four weeks without boys but there are two boys I like camping near us. It's lucky that I've dropped Rodney Burlington. One is an Italian boy named Alex, who is nineteen and an art student at Prahran. He is quiet and gentle and we sit together on the sand dunes in the evenings and watch the waves. Sometimes he draws. It feels so pleasant and safe just sitting with him. The only trouble is that he is a Catholic.

'Oh oh oh,' says my gran, who has come down for the day. 'Yer can't marry him! T'would be a mixed marriage. Oh dearie me, you'd have to bring the children up Catholic, yer know. They make you, or they won't marry you.'

'Gran, I'm not going to marry him. He's only asked me on a date and we're not even going until we get back from the holidays,' I say.

The other boy I like is Geoffrey. He lives in Kew and goes to a private school. Like me he is sixteen and we talk and talk and talk. He is a Methodist, but he seems really nice and goes to a church youth group too. He lies in his sleeping bag on the ground outside my tent and we talk and talk through the doorway. He has asked me to go to the Sorrento cinema with him to see *Sunshine*. I know the girl dies, because I read about it in Gran's *New Idea*.

'Well,' says my mother, cutting sandwiches for lunch. 'You know why he's taking you to see that film, don't you?'

'Because he thinks I'll like it.'

'Oh, Robbi, you are daft sometimes,' she says. 'Because, silly, he knows you will cry and then he can comfort you and put his arm around your shoulder. Then,' she says, 'his hands will start to wander. And before you know it, he won't be able to stop. Boys plan these things, you know.'

Gee, I think: all that from some comforting! I will have to be careful.

So Geoffrey and I go to see *Sunshine* and I steel myself. All the way there I say to myself over and over: no matter what, I'm not going to cry. So I try not to care all the way through the movie when she is dying. I try not to care when John Denver is singing 'Sunshine on my Shoulders'. I try not to cry when we are walking back to Rosebud. Every time Geoffrey asks me something I just go 'Mmm-hmm'. Because I know sure as the Lord died to save us that if I open my mouth to speak I will cry instead.

'Did you like the movie?' he asks.

'Mmm-hmm.'

'Would you like me to buy you an ice-cream on the way home?'

'Mmmm-hmm.'

'Would you like to walk along the beach or the road?'

'Mmmm-hmm.'

'Well, umm, is it all right if I kiss you goodnight?'

'Uhh-uh!'

Geoffrey goes off to his campsite with a disappointed slump to his shoulders and I crawl into bed and sleep. I am so proud of myself that I didn't cry and Geoffrey didn't have to comfort me and I have lived up to my promise to the Lord and remained pure, a vessel of the Lord.

In the morning I wake up and bawl my eyes out. See this is the thing: my parents are only happy with me when I have a boyfriend. They don't want me to study, which is what I like to do best, because they think it is a waste of time. They want my brothers to do apprenticeships but they want my sister and me to marry and have babies. Otherwise I'd be just as happy to concentrate on my study.

So I go out with a boy from our youth group, who is older, has a car and seems a bit wild. My mother says some of the boys aren't really there because they love the Lord, but because they want to meet girls. So I go out with one of them. More than cars, money and motorbikes, these boys have long hair. And I have trouble controlling what they do because they're not polite. They don't ask and, to be honest, after going out with them a few times I think they're boring, so there isn't much else to do but a lot of kissing and petting.

I never actually do the petting so that must be a fraction less sinful. I have never looked at or touched a boy anywhere I shouldn't. It's where they touch me that is the problem.

I know that the Lord's word says anything below the neckline is sinful, but it just doesn't feel that bad when it is happening. It's afterwards that I feel bad and then I feel worse when I realise that I don't even like the boy who did it.

Eventually I break it off with him and he goes to see my mother, who makes him coffee and says, 'Why did you break it off with Steve? He has a good job as a salesman.'

And my father says, 'You know Robbi thinks there is no one out there good enough for her. Any normal girl is happy to have a boyfriend, but not Robbi. With her it's God, God, God!'

So I go out with Steve again to make my mother and father happy and the petting starts again. I feel so guilty that I am asking the Lord for forgiveness constantly. Then I break it off a second time — but this time for good.

Then I am relieved because I didn't really like him anyway and now I am no longer sinning and can concentrate on following the Lord on the path that is narrow and rocky and on my school work which I am really good at.

So I don't even look for a boyfriend, and I meet a boy who is really nice. A boy I really like; a boy like David Danaher or Geoffrey Upton.

We become friends and eventually I go out with him.

I go out with him, but I don't let him touch me, kiss me, or even hold my hand. That way I can be sure I won't slip into sin. I will keep myself for the Lord. I am happy. I have a nice boyfriend and I have the Lord and I don't have to ask for forgiveness every time I see him. But the boy looks more and more dissatisfied with things until he looks positively unhappy and he becomes distant. Then he breaks it off with me and says he really likes me but he can't stand this not-even-kissing stuff.

And I say, 'Well, if you care about me you will respect my wishes and wait for me.'

And he says, 'I do respect you, more than any other girl I've ever met, but my mother says I should break it off with you.'

Why do boys always have to talk to their mothers?

I feel hurt and my parents are unhappy because I don't have a boyfriend, so I go out with the next boy who comes along and in no time he is boring, we are petting and I am asking for forgiveness.

I am playing canasta with my father at a card table outside the tent.

My mother is on the beach with my brothers and sister and other campers are lounging around outside their tents too. I love playing canasta. The other campers taught my parents to play and they taught me, so sometimes when the adults need an extra player I get to stay up really late playing and eating chocolates while my brothers and sister have to go to bed.

My father smiles as he deals and I smile back.

It is just the two of us playing canasta, which is great because he is being really nice. If only he could always be like this! Maybe if he sees how nice it is to be kind, he will keep on being kind forever.

I pick up my cards and sort them out. I have a fantastic hand, but I pick up and discard and so does my father. He puts out a few melds and he is thinking he has a really good hand. I pick up from the deck. It is just the card I need and I lay all my cards on the table. I have gone out concealed.

My father's face goes red. He slams the rest of his cards on the table, stands up and with both hands tips the card table up into the air and sends all the cards flying.

'Go to bed!' he yells.

I look around me. The other campers, including Geoff, Alex and their parents are staring at us. Can't my father see that I am too old to be sent to bed? His face is growing angrier, he is a volcano bubbling, ready to erupt. I can't win and I crawl into my tent.

I am crying. All this has happened just because I beat him at a silly game.

Once he took me fishing at Inverlock. It was a family holiday with my grandparents, my aunt and her strange husband. My father took me out fishing on the lake, because neither of my brothers wanted to go. This one time they must have had more sense than me or maybe they didn't want to keep trying to please him. Maybe they realised that pleasing my father was impossible. Anyway, out in the little boat, fishing like a disciple of the Lord, I caught a rainbow trout. My father didn't catch anything and when we got back to shore he was huffing and heaving all over the place.

'Rowena!' he yelled. 'Ena! Last time I take a bloody girl fishing! She didn't shut up the whole time we were out in the frickin boat! How can you catch a bloody fish with a bloody girl yap yapping the whole bleeding time?'

All this because I'd caught a fish and he hadn't.

He was so busy stomping around that he left me in the boat. I couldn't get out and my grandfather bent down to lift me out. His tall lean body stretched over the water to get me, then he fell — *smack* — into the water, crashing his head against the boat on the way down.

He was very ill after that and died.

* * *

So my father has tipped up the card table, knocked the cards flying and sent me to bed because I beat him. It was my own stupid fault. My aunt and mother both told me that you should never beat a boy at anything.

'They have fragile egos,' said my aunt as she dunked her arrowroot biscuit into her tea.

'If you beat a boy at anything,' said my mother, 'he won't find you attractive.'

'They don't cope with losing,' said my aunt.

'If you ever play tennis with a boy, you make sure you are gracious and lose,' said my mother.

'I'm never going to play tennis,' I said. 'It's boring and, besides, I'm no good at sport.'

'She's just too clever and vain for her own good,' my mother said to my aunt as if I was no longer there. 'God has made us as a helpmeet for men, young lady,' she says to me, putting her mug of tea firmly on the table. 'Not to upstage them.'

I have no words in my mouth willing to come out in my defence, but I know in my heart that they are wrong. Either they are mistaken or I am sinful, vain, proud and absolutely hopeless at being a submissive woman, so I will make a dreadful wife. I get that bitter knot in my stomach again.

I know it is all there in the Bible. Men are created in God's image. Men are leaders in the church and women are to keep silent. A woman must always submit to her husband, because he is her spiritual head.

The males in our family always get fed first, they get the biggest portions, the best part of the chicken, they always get asked if they want a second helping and always get to walk away and leave the dishes. My brother is never told that he can't do this and can't do that. Even though my parents want him to be an apprentice, they always say, 'Wayne, you can be whatever you want.' He never has to be in by ten at night and when they found him with a girl in his bedroom once they laughed and said he was sowing his wild oats.

I hate being a girl. I am sure I was made in the wrong body. When I have children I hope I don't have any girls because I would give anything to be a boy.

But now I am angry. I know that I mustn't question the ways of the Lord as only God knows what is best for the human condition, but surely if God wanted me to be so submissive he could have made it so that I would like it.

16

My mother and father are screaming at each other again and the swear words are flying out of my father's mouth. 'Fucking shit, Rowena! What I have to put up with! Bleedin, frickin hell, Rowena! Christsakes, Ena!'

It is six o'clock at night. My brothers, my sister and I are sitting around a card table outside the tent, in our bathers with beach towels wrapped around our waists, our hair stringy from the seawater, playing 500.

We don't know what to do, we don't know where to go, so we just stay there in the middle of the camp ground feeling stupid while our parents scream and screech.

'Fuckin bloody shit!' yells my father.

'Vic! Vic!' cries my mother. We have no idea what they are fighting about.

Suddenly my father takes to the big tent with the tomahawk used to hammer the pegs into the ground. He smashes the poles and we wince with every chop.

Now he is ripping the canvas, hacking at the tent and swearing at the top of his lungs, and all of us kids except Wayne start to cry.

My father is a hurricane. 'Fucking shit and hell!' he yells.

'Stop it, Vic, stop it!' my mother yells back.

Pieces of canvas are being ripped from the tent and there are plastic camping plates and cups flying everywhere. We are as still and quiet as mice, hoping he won't notice us because we don't want to end up like the tent. All the other campers have disappeared. Then he gets in his fluorescent lime green car and slams the door so hard that the car rocks on its wheels. My mother and he are still screaming at each other and she runs to the car door. Don't stop him from going, I think.

'Let him go. Let him go,' my brother Wayne whispers to himself.

'Don't think you're leaving me here with all the children!' yells my mother.

There is dead silence. My father looks at her and then at us, standing in a line.

He gets out of the car, slams the door again and storms over.

'I'll take Robbi and Davie,' he says, pointing at the two of us. He thunders back to his car, gets in and turns the radio on loud. It is the Bee Gees singing 'Massa-a-a-tu-sis'. One of his favourites. He drives off, making the wheels screech and dust fly everywhere.

My mother, with her swollen red eyes, turns to the four of us, still standing there in a line. 'Daddy can't help the way he behaves,' she says. 'His father used to beat him up and he was very sick as a child. He can't help it.'

Yeah, I think to myself. Well, I've been beaten as a child and I will never do it to my children!

'Well,' she says to Davie and me, 'you'll be going to live with your father. We're splitting up.'

'We don't want to go,' I say. I think I could spew up at any second.

'But you can't leave him on his own,' she says.

'I don't care if he is on his own. He leaves *us* on our own. I don't want to go and live with him.'

'Really, you are so unChristian sometimes, Robbi,' she says.

'I want to stay with you, and so does Davie,' I say on his behalf. He nods in agreement. Davie never says anything much except to his best friend, Wendy.

This is not the first time my father has left us. Last year he went to Sydney. My grandmother took me there to visit him and I had a good time going everywhere on the double-decker buses with her. My father was living in a one-bedroom flat so she slept on the couch in the lounge room and I had to sleep in his bed. I was so scared that I slept on top of the blankets. He asked me why and I said Sydney was hot. Then he laughed, but he didn't make me get under the blankets. He yelled all the time at my poor old gran, but he was nice to me.

But when he came back to Melbourne I knew his good mood wouldn't last.

My mother has collapsed into a camp chair in tears and we are all sobbing. The other campers have come out now and Alex's mother puts her arm around my mother's shoulders and his father pours something into a glass.

'It's whisky,' he says, handing it to her. I wonder if I should tell them that she has never touched alcohol before. I wonder if she will use this as a chance to witness to them and explain that we don't need to drink because we have the Lord looking after us. Besides, as Mato says, alcohol is evil because men grow to love it more than their families. She says she's seen many a child go hungry while the father is drinking in the hotel.

But my mother just thanks Alex's father for the whisky, downs it in one big gulp and holds her glass out for another. Then she starts to tell Alex's parents all the grimy details of everything my father has ever done to her.

'He doesn't wash properly, you know, and I get terrible infections and the way that he hits Wayne over and over again — he has such a vile temper. Oh, I know it's not his fault, he can't help the way that he is. His father used to beat him, you know, and he had polio as a child — couldn't walk for six months. He had a terrible childhood. He's never really had a father so he doesn't know how to behave and he doesn't love the Lord. He did once but now Satan has a good grip on him so he takes it out on us. The other day he —'

Alex can see the look of horror on my face. As if what my father did wasn't enough, now we have to talk about it! He gives me a tap on the shoulder and nods towards the beach. So he and Geoff and I go off and watch the waves.

In the morning we pack up what is left of our tent because we are going back to Melbourne. It is all on top of Mum's red Hillman. She sends us to the toilet, one last time before we leave, and complains about her stress headache as she massages her temples with her fingers. I can see that she is in no mood to be argued with so I go, even though I am too old to be told to go to the toilet and camping block toilets are always wet and smelly.

Alex waits outside for me. He is squatting down behind a bush in his tight Levis. He is so dark and handsome, and has the blackest eyes. I don't care at all that he is a wog. He looks nervous, as if he is hiding.

I am a bit embarrassed that he is waiting for me outside the women's and I quickly wipe my hands on the back of my cut-off denims to dry them.

'Hi,' I say.

'Hi.'

'What's the matter?'

'What are you doing?' he says, standing up and plunging his hands into his back pockets.

'Oh, we're going back to Melbourne today. I think we're

going to my grandmother's, but I don't know. My mum is too upset to talk. She just cries all the time.'

He is shuffling from one foot to the other.

'I can give you my grandmother's phone number if you like,' I offer.

'No, it's okay,' he says. 'Umm, look, this isn't my decision, but, umm, my parents won't let me go out with you. I'm not even supposed to see you.'

'What? You're not meant to be talking to me, you mean?'

He nods.

'Why?' I ask, only just holding back the tears.

'It's not you,' he says. 'It's your parents.'

'But your parents gave my mum alcohol last night.'

'They were only being kind. She needed help.'

'But I'm not my parents,' I protest.

'Yeah, I know that, but my parents are Italian. We're wogs, right? Family is everything. They're already upset because my older brother married an Australian girl and she won't breastfeed her baby. She says it's disgusting, so they're worried about Australians generally. They don't understand how a mother can't want the best for her baby and ... well ... they just don't want me involved with someone like your father.'

He looks up towards the campsite to make sure no one can see him talking to me.

'If it got serious with you,' he says, 'my parents would have to get to know your parents because they take family seriously. They were happy for me to go out with you even if you are Australian because they liked you, but not after last night. They think children turn out like their parents, and I have to do what they say. They are my parents and they will buy me a house when I marry.'

'It's my father?'

'My parents were shocked last night. It's not you. I really do like you a lot. An awful lot,' he says. He kisses me softly on the cheek, then walks away.

My eyes fill with tears and they spill down my cheeks. I feel so alone and he was really nice. Sometimes it just isn't worth it hanging out for the nice boys and I will never be like my father. I hate him.

When I get to the car my mother thinks I am crying because my father has left. But I think his leaving was the best thing that has happened to me in the past twenty-four hours.

17

We go straight from the beach to Mato's house in Thomas Street, Hampton.

My Aunt Tonia lives there too now because she has left her floppy husband. Once she painted a picture on the garage wall of Granddad, Mato and me hopping into an old jalopy. It's still there, but it has faded.

Aunt Tonia had a large extension put on the back of the house for Mato and everything in it is new. Mato has four beige Jason recliner chairs, a television, a beige laminate kitchen table and chairs, a bathroom, beige carpet, beige curtains and a bedroom with a beige bedspread. It's all brand new! I think Aunt Tonia chose everything because she loves brown colours, whereas Mato always chooses blue.

Mato has great big windows so she can see the whole backyard and she has a new oven and refrigerator, but she never uses them because she always eats with Aunt Tonia. Because of the extension there is plenty of room for all of us. I get to sleep in Mato's room on a stretcher beside her new single bed. At night she says to me, 'I love you, my popsy.'

My mum cries all the time, but I don't know why. I would have thought she'd be happy to be away from my father, because she complains about him every chance she gets.

'Your father won't eat vegetables. I don't know why I bother to cook for him.'

'Your father is so lazy I don't know how he can live with himself. I am so exhausted I don't know what kind of man lets a woman do all his work for him.'

'Your father wants his husbandly rights every night and I'm always getting infections.'

I can't imagine what sort of infections she gets, or where, and I look at her shocked when she says this. But I know it isn't true about the husbandly rights bit, because my sister and I are in the bedroom right next door and at night we can hear my mother saying, 'Come on, Vic. Come on.'

And he says, 'Not now, Ena. No, Ena. Don't do that, Ena. Go away, Ena.' And my sister and I giggle. Then sometimes we hear the bed squeaking and we put our heads under the blankets and try not to listen.

But my mother gets my father back. She always says, 'Go and give your father a kiss goodnight.' Or, 'Go and thank your father for the present.'

She gets in quickly before we have even had a chance to go, and I feel sorry for my father because it must seem to him that we are only ever being nice to him because our mother has made us.

Mato and Aunt Tonia have lots of adult discussions with my mother and she is always in tears, her eyes red and swollen. I try to listen but I can't get close enough without them noticing. I want to know what is going to happen to us. But I only manage to hear one thing.

'What did the doctor say?' says Mato.

'She's having a nervous breakdown. He's given her something,' says Aunt Tonia. 'Sshh! We've got big ears listening!'

* * *

It is easy for me to go to school from Mato's. I just take my bike, ride to Cheltenham and catch the train to Frankston where I go to school. I found out about an art course at a school where you don't have to wear uniforms, you call the teachers by their Christian names and there are no rules. Kids even smoke in class, which I would never do, but it is nice to know I could if I did want to.

I am really glad to leave my old school because they had a special stream of kids who were to specialise in maths and science. Just heaps and heaps of maths and science every day and that was the stream I was put in. Worse still, there were only two girls in the class — Kathy and I — and the boys teased us continually. The science teacher muttered, 'I don't know why they put girls in science,' and he ignored us.

We got As anyway. Then the teachers wanted me to study hard so I could get into medicine at Melbourne University. My parents wouldn't let me study until I had done my chores, which didn't leave me enough time. I hated science anyway because science is evil. It was designed by Satan to lead the unbelievers and weak astray. So when the teacher talked about evolution, I recited psalms in my head and I tried not to listen. When he talked about dinosaurs I knew it was the devil trying to lead me down the path that is wide. So I put my hand up.

'Yes,' he groaned, 'what is it?'

'Sir,' I said, 'the Lord created the world in seven days and gave man dominion over the earth and told him to be fruitful and multiply.

'Sir, dinosaurs and evolution are inventions of the devil designed to lead the weak-minded astray from the truth.'

'Are you finished?' he said and then not even waiting for my answer, in case I went on witnessing, he put down his chalk and said, 'Tomorrow we will study biology.' And he looked at me as if to say, *Got a problem with biology?*

I asked the principal to take me out of the specialist stream and put me in art, but he said art was for kids who couldn't do anything else.

So I prayed to the Lord about this problem of having the devil's words thrown at me in science every day and I got an idea. The next exam we had, I drew pictures all over the paper and didn't answer a single question. But instead of putting me in art, they made me go to the school chaplain once a week for counselling. He was a Uniting Church minister. 'The devil disguised in lamb's clothing,' said my mother.

Then I found out about Frankston and I was saved from the wickedness of science.

I especially love it at Frankston because, apart from English, all my subjects are art subjects. After I took my mother to meet the principal and sign the forms, she came home and said to my father, 'We always knew Robbi was an artist like her aunt.'

'Won't pay the bloody bills!' he said.

'That's okay,' I told him. 'I'll just marry someone rich.'

He looked up and smiled at me. 'Knowing you, that's exactly what you'll bloody well do!'

And for once I had said something that made him happy.

These are the subjects I take: pottery, drawing, painting (which is my favourite), graphic art and photography.

I hate photography because the teacher always shuts himself in the dark room with me, then waits and as soon as there are not many of us in the dark room he says, 'I'm going to start developing now. Will you all wait outside? Ahh, Robbi, I'm going to need an assistant.'

When the door is shut and the room is black he says in a low, croaky voice, 'Can you just scratch my neck for me? I am itchy just here.' Then he says, 'Lower. Scratch a little lower and I need you to rub just here — lower, lower.' I feel sick in my stomach, as if I have worms crawling around nibbling my insides away, and I think I am going to throw up. But because I have always been taught to obey my elders and those in authority I scratch his neck for him and his skin is rubbery and goose pimply.

The next time he shuts the dark room door he wants me to scratch his chest or his back and it's always lower, a bit lower. Now I am starting to get scared and I wonder what he is going to want scratched next. So I have made a decision. I have never once wagged, but I am going to wag photography even though he gave me an A+.

And I deserved that A+. We had to take a photograph of speed. Everyone else took a photograph of a car, a motorbike or a train in motion, but I took a photograph of a girl, her mouth poised open over the top of the drinking fountain, the water spouting out of the bubbler and over her face and open mouth. The boys laughed at my photograph of the speed of water, though I couldn't see what was funny about it. The teacher grinned and stroked it lovingly and took it home so I had to print off another copy. But I will never go to photography again.

I go home on the train happy because I am on my way to Mato's house and I never want to live with both my parents again.

This time I get home from school and my mother is sitting beside the kitchen table with a cup of tea and she is crying again.

She hasn't touched the tea and it has gone cold. So I head for the lounge room to watch David Cassidy, who is so handsome and has that long tousled hair.

'Come back,' calls my mother. 'I have to talk to you all. Get your brothers and sister.' We all sit on the floor at her feet waiting to hear her news. I have a heavy feeling in my stomach because I am sure she is going to say that we are going back to live with my father.

'I have arranged,' she says, 'for Wayne and Karyn to go to a Christian boarding school.'

'But how can we afford that?' I ask.

'I have spoken to the principal today on the phone. He is a lovely Christian man and we only have to pay what we can.'

'So when are they going?'

'We're driving them up there this weekend. I have prayed about it and I think this is what the Lord wants. Wayne needs to be away from your father, somewhere your father can't get to him.'

'What about me?' I say. I need to be away from him too.

'You're older and you can handle your father. Besides, you're his favourite. If anyone is ever to lead him to the Lord it will be you. You're the only one who will be able to do it,' she says.

'I am not his favourite,' I plead, hurt to the core. None of us is; only his boat. My mother is simply saying this to hurt me and to justify sending Wayne and Karyn away.

Once she said to me, 'I have to spoil Wayne and ignore you because you are your father's favourite. I have to balance things out.' And I thought then, How can she call me his favourite just because he doesn't hit me as hard as he hits Wayne? What about Karyn? I thought. He doesn't hit her at all, so why isn't she his favourite? I could tell my mother was only saying this to cover the fact that Wayne is really her favourite.

I don't want the responsibility of leading my father to the Lord. It is too heavy a burden, and I don't want him in heaven with us, so I'm not sure I even want him to get saved.

'What about Davie?' I ask. 'Is he his favourite too?'

'Davie is too little to be away from home.' I know she is getting back at Davie and me for being the ones he chose. But he only chose us because we are the least trouble and I am old enough to cook for him.

So the next weekend we are driving to a little town just out of Wangaratta called Thoona and a school called Canaan

Christian College. The countryside is just beautiful, with rolling hills and imposing gum trees under which sheep like fairy floss graze without a care in the world.

We deliver Wayne and Karyn and, after looking over the school and settling them in, we are on our way back to Melbourne. Back to the grey, overcast city. I would give anything to stay in the sweet, vibrant countryside.

When only one person is away from your family it is weird that it is so much quieter and their absence so visible. Now we have two people away and, of course, not having my father around is like missing a whole army battalion. My mother is constantly in tears but she really cried the other day when she ran the sewing machine needle through her finger. She dunked it quickly in a sink full of cold water and the water turned bright red. I wish I could get a glorious red like that when I try to paint. I stood there mesmerised until Aunt Tonia gave me a disapproving look and let the water out. Then she bundled Mum into the car and took her to the doctor's to get the needle out. It was stuck right through her finger. She has a thick bandage on it now, which makes it hard for her to drive.

We are going to our house in Parkdale to pick up a few things. As my mother pulls into the driveway you can feel the emptiness and silence of the house, but as we get to the front door the Mozart is booming out at us and it is not silent and empty after all. My father is in his chair in the lounge room and I thank the Lord that he has his clothes on. He doesn't say anything to us; just peers at us as he rocks back and forth in his chair with one leg thrown over the side.

My mother sits down in a chair near him and motions for me to sit on the pouffe between them. I sit because I can tell that this is not a time to do anything but try to be as invisible as I can. I feel sick in my stomach and look around for a bowl in case I need it. They don't talk and the silence is painful.

Finally my father speaks. 'Well, tell your mother,' he says in a deep, menacing voice that I have never heard before, 'tell your mother that perhaps she can let me know why she has left her husband. It's not what one would expect of a good Christian wife. Is it, Rowena?' he snipes.

I have never seen him like this. He is not yelling or screaming or throwing anything around and the sickness has reached my throat now.

'Tell your father,' says my mother, 'that I haven't left him. He has left me.'

'I'm not the one who doesn't live in the marital home, Rowena!' he shrieks.

He has cracked already. I try to edge off the pouffe, but my mother glares at me, so I sink down into it.

'What do you want, Vic?' she whispers.

'Well, Ena, I want what any man wants. I want my family, don't I? A man is supposed to be the king of his castle, Ena. What sort of a castle is an empty house, I ask you!'

If a man is the king of his castle, I think, then surely his family are his slaves.

'Tell your father that you don't want to live with him because he hits you,' my mother says to me.

I look at him.

'Have I ever hit you? You tell your bloody mother that I never laid a hand on any of my kids,' he says as he slams his hand down hard on the coffee table and makes me and the mouldy old coffee cups jump. Now I am surely going to be sick and I clamp my hand over my mouth. I don't know what to do. I look at my mother. If I say that he hits me, I will get hit for sure. And if I say that he doesn't, then I won't get hit, but my mother will be furious with me for betraying her.

So I say nothing, and they wait.

'You're a fucking liar, Rowena!' he bellows and they are off, yelling and shouting at each other, so I sneak out to the car, curl up against the tyre and then I start to weep and shake. I feel so tiny and weak. I want to be home with Mato, snuggled against her in bed. Safe.

Eventually my mother comes out and she is crying. 'Hop in the car and stop blubbering,' she says to me. 'He didn't do anything to you, did he? No!' she says. 'So stop snivelling and get in. You're not showing much trust in the Lord when you cry every time something happens that you don't like,' she says as she backs out the driveway. 'Don't you trust that the Lord has your life in his hands? Everything that happens to you, you know is in God's control, so why shed tears every time your father loses his temper? Really, Robbi, you're too old for such antics.'

I say nothing. I can't help it if I am scared of my father and if I don't have enough faith in the Lord. I will try to be better. I will ask the Lord to forgive me and to help me be stronger for Him, but I hate it when my parents shout at each other. I just want to die.

'What do you think?' she says, snapping me out of my thoughts that I know are selfish and not pleasing to the Lord.

'What do I think about what?' I snivel, drying my eyes.

'Do you think I should go back to him or leave him?'

I don't know, I think. I am only sixteen and he's not my husband.

'We-ell?' she persists. 'You must have some kind of opinion!'

This is dangerous ground, but eventually my desire to be rid of him and my mother's insistence that I answer her takes over and I say, 'I think you should leave him.'

'That is not what the scriptures would tell me to do,' she says. 'Mato won't approve.'

I say nothing. I can't win.

'Well,' she says, 'I'll have to go and see Daddy again and you'll have to come. It's better if you're there.'

We get back to Mato's and Mato can see I have been crying. 'Are you all right, popsy?' she asks, looking from me to my mother and back again.

My mother stares at me.

'I'm fine,' I say.

When we are in bed Mato holds my hand and tells me a story. 'The Lord was going to take me to heaven to be with him so I would have seen my Joe again. My life has been a long wait since Joe went. I have been waiting till the Lord sees fit to take me to join him and Joe. I was going down a tunnel, with a white light at the end of it, and when I got to the end of the tunnel the Lord Jesus was waiting for me. I looked back down the tunnel and I could see you, my popsy, lying asleep on the camp bed beside me and I said to the Lord, "I can't come with you. I want to so much and I miss my Joe, but I cannot bear the thought of my granddaughter waking and finding my dead body." And the Lord said to me, "You are my faithful servant. The choice is yours." So I came back, my popsy, because I love you so much.'

'Did this really happen?' I ask.

'Yes. It happened just last night, but I couldn't leave you. No matter how much I miss my Joe and no matter how much I want to join the Lord, I couldn't leave you.'

And we squeeze each other's hand, tightly.

All I can think about now is my parents screaming at each other with me stuck in the middle and that it's going to happen again and again. At school and during lunch, it is all I can think about. Going home on the train I can't think of anything else. My friend is telling me that she likes a group called Led Zeppelin, but I've never heard of them because they're not a Christian band and, apart from the Beatles and the Monkees, I only know about Christian bands, but all I can think of is my parents at war and me in the middle.

I watch the stations go by: Kannanook Creek, Carrum Downs, Chelsea, Edithvale, Aspendale. Suddenly the train is at Parkdale and although I am supposed to go to Cheltenham and then ride to Mato's in Hampton, I'm going to jump off.

'What are you doing?' says Leanne. 'You don't get off here.'

'I'm running away from home,' I tell her. 'Well, I haven't *got* a home but if I did have one that's what I would be doing.'

'Do you want me to come with you?'

'Nah, I'll be right,' I say. 'I don't think I'm going far.' And I jump off the train with my heavy school bag slung over my shoulder. Suddenly Parkdale railway station seems a vast and vacant place and I realise that I have no one to run to. Normally I would go to Mato's, but I can't because my mother is there and it is my parents that I want to get away from. I can't go to Grandma Lyne's because now that Great-Grandma Lucy has died, Grandma Lyne has sold her house and gone to live in Sunshine with her daughter. Anyway, she is my father's mother, so she probably thinks that whatever he does is okay.

The only place I can go to is our minister's house. I am part of his flock and I need advice from the Lord. I need to talk to someone wise who will look to God to help me. He is our new minister, because Alan Marr took a job at Blackburn, the biggest Baptist Church in Victoria. They have a congregation of over a thousand and they are all wealthy. Or so my mother says. 'Everyone in the eastern suburbs is wealthy, so they will be able to pay Alan a lot more money and he needs that, now that he has a wife and a baby on the way,' she says.

Our new minister is John Parker and he has two daughters, one a year younger than me and one a year older. They are really pretty with long straight hair. All the boys really like them and I am rather jealous of them if I am going to be honest. They also have really loving Christian parents and their names are girl's names: Cheryl and Jennifer.

So I hitch up my heavy school bag and start the march to the minister's house in Mordialloc. I have no idea what I am going to say to him when I arrive or what he is going to say to me and I worry all the way there, trying out different sentences to see how they sound.

'I've run away from home.' Sounds immature and I am sixteen now.

'I hate my parents.' Sounds too teenage and easy to dismiss.

'Are Cheryl and Jenny home?' Won't get me what I want. What do I want? I ask myself and realise that what I really want is never to have to live at home with my parents again. I might be only sixteen, but it is time I left home.

'I need to talk to someone.'

'Come in,' says Mr Parker. 'I was just going to sit down to afternoon tea. You can join me.'

I walk through their front door and aromas from their kitchen swirl around me. Their house always smells of hot lamb casserole and freshly baked biscuits. I follow Mr Parker into his study and Mrs Parker brings me a mug of tea and puts down a plate of biscuits. She is short, with a round friendly face, shoulder-length hair, and she is comfortingly plump. My mother is five foot eleven with broad shoulders. She is an imposing woman.

'How are you, Robbi?' says Mrs Parker, smiling at me.

I look mournful. I want them to know just how bad I feel. 'I'm okay,' I mumble.

She gives Mr Parker a meaningful look and departs, shutting the door softly behind her. I can hear the television on and she is in the kitchen laughing with her daughters.

'So, Robbi, tell me what's been happening for you,' says Mr Parker. Ministers never have to beat around the bush; everyone is just waiting to pour out their souls to them. So out it comes. I tell him that I am running away, but I am not sure where I'm going so I came here. I tell him how much I hate living at home. I tell him about the meetings with my parents and me stuck in the middle. I tell him that my mother is blaming me because they have split up. I tell him that my mother says if it wasn't for me they'd be back together by now; that she is only separated from her husband to please me, because when she asked me if she should leave or stay I said leave.

'Dear me,' he says at last. 'Do you mind if I go and have a little chat with your parents?'

'No,' I say. 'Provided you don't mention that I have come to see you today. I don't want them knowing anything I've said and I want to leave home.'

'I think we can arrange alternative accommodation for you, at least for a while. To give you a break, so to speak. But you'll have to go back to your mother until something can be worked out. I'll talk to them.'

So I head back to Mato's house, where my mother is still crying and drinking tea. She looks at me distrustfully as I walk in late. And it doesn't take her long to tell me what has been 'worked out'.

'Pack your things,' says my mother after school a few days later.

'Why?' I ask. Maybe the pastor has arranged somewhere for me to live.

'Because we are moving back with your father.'

'Why?' Why would she want to do such a stupid thing?

'Because your father and I had a long talk with the pastor and it is obvious that you are not coping with us living apart. You were going to run away. So we are getting back together for you.'

'But I want to move out of home. I don't want to live with you and Dad and the continuous fighting. I can live here with Mato,' I say desperately.

'Daddy is going to change,' she says. 'He promised the pastor and we have to be fair and give him a chance. Besides, there is no room now that Aunt Tonia lives here. Anyway, you are *my* daughter, not Mato's. I am your mother and she is your grandmother — though you seem to forget that!'

'Well, I can live somewhere else. I can board.'

'Listen to me, young lady. First of all, we can't possibly afford to pay for you to board somewhere when you have a perfectly good home to live in. Secondly, it is already stretching our finances having to pay for Karyn and Wayne to be at Canaan College. Thirdly, you are too young to be living away from home. You can leave home at a suitable time and that will be when you get married like any good Christian girl who is obedient to the wishes and God-given authority of her parents. Now pack!'

So I am back at Parkdale and every time my parents fight, which is often, my mother says to me, 'I wouldn't be here if it wasn't for you. I made the break. I only came back because of you.'

My father is worse than ever. He hits us, sends us flying across the room, and yells all the time at Davie and me and, of course, Wayne, when he is home on the weekends or for holidays. Sometimes my brother Davie and I crouch down in a corner together and cry while he continues screaming at my mother and wallops Wayne, who doesn't seem to have the sense to get away. Then I get a lecture from my mother about not trusting in the Lord.

I notice that she is often up till midnight doing the housework. The other night she was hanging clothes on the line at eleven-thirty while my father lay sprawled across the lounge-room carpet watching television. He never helps and just yells if she gets in the way of the TV.

Other times he isn't so bad and it's just:

'Robbi, make your father a bloody coffee and some lunch!'

'Robbi, leave that stupid homework and do the dishes, school is a bleeding waste of time on a girl. You're just going to have babies anyway!'

'Robbi, finish the bloody food your mother cooked for you and be grateful. Don't give me any of that bleedin I-feel-sick crap!'

'Robbi, for God's sake go and put some lipstick on before you go out. You look bloody dreadful. A woman is undressed if she isn't wearing make-up!'

'Robbi, for God's sake go and put on a dress and some high heels. You look like a bloody tradesman!'

I'm not a woman; I am sixteen. I look to my mother who says, 'Your father just wants you to look attractive.'

Then when I have done what he says and put on a dress, high heels and make-up and I feel like an absolute idiot, he comes up and puts his hands on my breasts and squeezes them. 'Growing two little beauties you are,' he says. 'She's gonna be all right, Ena. She's got two little beauties here,' he yells to her in the kitchen.

But that isn't as bad as what he did to her the other day. The couple from across the road came over for coffee and my father came up behind my mother and plunged both his hands down her dress. He grabbed her breasts, jiggled them about and out of her dress, then he said to Mr Collins, 'How'd yer like a bit of these, hey?'

I wanted to kill him. There and then I could have got my mother's Wiltshire, plunged it through his hard heart and sent him straight to hell even though he'd had no chance of being saved.

My mother went bright red and said, 'Stop that now, Vic!' in a joking kind of way.

I hate it when he touches my breasts.

When Wayne comes home for the holidays, my father won't stop hitting him. My mother says to me while we are doing the dishes, 'Your father better watch out, because one day soon Wayne is going to hit him back and *then* he'll be sorry.'

I'm not sure whether she means Wayne or my father.

18

'By the way,' my mother says to me, 'I've decided that you are old enough and mature enough to be baptised. Make sure you invite your father; you never know when the Lord will speak to him, when the Holy Spirit might convict him in his heart and bring him back into God's family.'

I can't believe it! This is going to be the most exciting time of my entire life. I will give a testimony for the Lord. And I will go down into the water and wash off all my past sins, and as I come up out of the water to my new life in the Lord everyone will sing:

Follow follow I will follow Jesus,
anywhere, everywhere I will follow him.

A baptism is the most rousing, truly moving event you could ever hope to see. My mother is going to buy me a new dress for the occasion. Mato will come and my aunt, Tonia and everyone in the church will be there.

Because we are Baptists you can only be baptised when you are considered adult enough to have made an adult decision to follow the Lord. I have been wanting to get baptised since I was nine and at last my mother has said yes.

I ask my father to come. 'We'll see,' he mutters, annoyed because I am getting baptised and because I interrupted him watching a rerun of 'McHale's Navy'. Lucky it wasn't 'The Flintstones', because that is his favourite.

During the ad break he comes into the kitchen and screams at my mother and me. 'I don't know why you had to turn all our kids into bloody wowser Christians just like that bloody family of yours! Why couldn't they be normal kids, Ena? What sort of mother are you? What sort of bloody daughter have I got that wants to get drowned like a bleedin ruddy rat?'

I guess that means he's decided no, he's not coming. So I don't mention it again in front of him.

I have to go to six weeks of baptism classes, which will be easy because I have known all the answers since I was eight. And I get a new dress. It is long and green and the material clings to my body. My mother buys me a pair of cork heels to go with the dress. We get all this in the new shop called Venture. With my corks on I am six feet tall and so slim. I weigh fifty kilos and my dress sweeps along the floor as I walk. I can't wait to wear it at my baptism.

The best thing in the world has happened: my father is sick. Our house is so happy and quiet. He can't get out of bed because he is far too ill and he has been like that for five weeks now.

He is so sick he doesn't even ruin my baptism. The night of my baptism I arrive at church early and hang up my green dress on a hook in the vestry. I put on the white, starchy gown. Mrs Parker, the minister's wife, is there to help and look after me.

Then, as the service is to begin, I and the others being baptised walk into the church and sit in the front pew. It is cold and I am so nervous I don't know which of the two is making me shake and I don't hear a thing the pastor is saying. Finally he calls me up and I walk to the pulpit. I stand in my bare feet and white gown behind the pulpit and grip its sides hard to keep myself steady. I have practised my testimony over and over on our reel-to-reel tape recorder. I still don't have a life of sin to confess, except for petting with the boys and I'm certainly not going to confess that in front of the whole church and Mato. But I hope the Lord and Mato will be proud of me anyway.

I talk about how I was brought to the Lord by my mother when I was eight and how having a personal relationship with God through Jesus His son has been the most wonderful thing ever to happen to me. When I have finished my testimony they all sing a hymn while I walk to the baptismal where the pastor is already waiting for me. I wonder whether the water is cold. I step into the baptistry and Pastor Brian Parker puts his hands on my shoulders and says to me in a loud voice so everyone can hear, 'Do you, Robbi, take the Lord Jesus Christ as your personal Lord and Saviour, promising to serve Him and only Him for all your life, passing into everlasting life with Him?'

I say, 'I do,' and he plunges me forward into the water. He doesn't do it backwards like my grandfather did. I mentioned to my mother I was getting baptised forward and she said, 'Well, no one follows the Lord like your grandfather did.'

When I come up I briefly lose my breath and realise that my father was right: I do feel like a drowned rat. But now I belong absolutely and totally to the Lord. Now I can become an official church member and vote in the members' meetings. Apart from that I thought I would feel different, closer to God, but I don't. I feel just the same as before I was baptised — only wetter.

Afterwards I change into my new clothes, and at the end of the service there is a special supper where everyone congratulates me on being baptised and I walk around six feet tall in my beautiful green dress, fully aware that the boys can't take their eyes off me and David Danaher and Rodney Burlington just kind of follow me around like hovering shadows. If only my father could see me now, he might be proud of me.

So my dad is in hospital. My mother says he has diabetes and he has been sick for years. She says this is why he has always been so bad tempered, and he has been in a permanent hypo. We will all see how different he is when he gets out of hospital. He nearly died because of not being diagnosed and he has probably been diabetic all his life, she says.

I know she wishes he would make a deathbed conversion, but no such luck. I am not a doctor, but I think he is diabetic because he eats McDonald's every night on the way home from work and that is also why he never eats his vegetables. He has a Mars Bar every day for lunch too and after dinner he and Mum sit in front of 'Mission Impossible' with a bag of chocolate that she buys from the seconds shop in Mordialloc.

My father will be in hospital until he is stabilised and we kids are hoping that won't happen too quickly. We went to visit him and, even though he isn't supposed to eat any lollies, we could see for ourselves that he had Cherry Ripe and Violet Crumble wrappers stuffed under his mattress. He likes being in hospital and he calls the nurses 'ducky' and reaches out to pinch their bottoms.

But you wouldn't believe it. My father comes out of hospital and my mother goes in. And with my mother not around, my father isn't so bad. For three weeks my father doesn't yell once or hit us or anything. He still doesn't do any housework, but he does come home one evening and announce that he has a new job, selling heaters. He lets me put records I like on his stereo and I dance around the lounge room playing them full blast. He just smiles and says there is no accounting for the bad taste of the young and when I put on the radio he says jokingly, 'These bands you are listening to have a very limited vocabulary. All this Diamond bloke can say is "Cherry Cherry".'

But he lets me listen.

He comes home with chocolate eclairs and vanilla slices and still eats more than the rest of us. Then he says, 'Look, I've got this terrific machine. It just pricks my finger like this, doesn't hurt a bit, then it measures my blood to tell me how much sugar is in it. If I've eaten too many cakes and my sugar level is up, I just inject a bit more insulin.'

'Can we see what our blood sugar is?' we all ask.

'Sure,' he says. 'Doesn't hurt a bit,' he assures us as he pricks our fingers.

Our sugar is all okay.

No one will say what is wrong with my mother. Mato and Aunt Tonia keep having those secret talks in the corner of her hospital room and looking at us kids in a funny way and when I ask them what is wrong with her they answer, 'Nothing you need to know about.'

But I do need to know what is wrong with my mother and I decide that when I have kids I will tell them what is going on.

For three weeks I do the ironing and the cooking and the washing and finally my mother arrives home one afternoon to us and the new colour TV that my father has bought with his new salary. He flicks it on and we are absolutely spellbound by the coloured Bugs Bunny on the screen. He's not grey after all, we laugh. It is only a little TV because that was all he could afford in colour. Our old black and white one was big but my father is very proud of his colour TV and he is happy that we are pleased with it.

With my mother home everything returns to normal. She has to stay off work for six weeks to rest and something is different about her. It is as if I hear everything she says differently, through new ears.

* * *

I am sitting in the lounge room cuddling and patting my Persian rabbit. His name is Shadrach after one of the three followers of God who were thrown into a pit of fire, but the fire didn't burn them because they were faithful to the Lord. Shadrach is house-trained and he wakes me up at seven every morning when he nuzzles into my face. He loves to drink Milo and will steal anybody's if they leave their mug lying around. Shadrach won't eat his food unless the rest of the family is sitting down to eat and if we forget to feed him he stomps his feet — *thud, thud, thud* — until we do. I nagged my parents silly to get Shadrach for me and I love him. I have his brush and I am sitting on the couch, teasing the knots out of his long soft hair, when I hear my mother on the phone telling a friend, 'Yes, I've just got out of hospital. No, I had a hysterectomy.' Then she says, 'Well, I've had seven children.'

Seven? I do a quick count; nope, there are definitely four of us.

'I had a miscarriage between Robbi and Wayne, and between Wayne and Karyn,' she goes on.

Okay, so that makes six, I think. Four of us, plus two miscarriages.

Soon she says goodbye and rings someone else. 'I've just got out of hospital,' I hear her saying to the new listener. 'Oh no, nothing serious. I just had a miscarriage, that's all. Yes, it happens. It's my third actually.'

Then she is on the phone to someone else. 'Yes, yes,' she is telling them, 'yes, I had my ovaries removed, cysts. Yes, that's right.' Every person she rings gets a different story.

Later that night she is doing the washing and she starts to yell at us. We rush to the laundry to see what is wrong. 'I told you all to put your washing out.'

'But we did,' we plead.

'No, you didn't! I know washing when I see it!'

'But, Mum, I did the washing,' I tell her.

'Don't you answer me back, young lady,' she growls. I am worried about her because she seems so confused.

The next night I bring a friend home from school, a boy who likes me. Michael is a real dag, but he is fun to talk to. I am nervous about bringing him home in case my father is there, but luckily he isn't. Only my mum is.

'Sit down,' she says to him. 'I'll just make you some Milo. Go and change out of your school uniform, Robbi.'

So I go and change into my week clothes and as I come back to the kitchen I can hear my mother saying to him, 'Yes, well, the problem with Robbi is she is very lazy. Have you noticed that, Michael? Oh well, you'll find out for yourself. She just won't push herself to do anything. Never do today what you can put off until tomorrow — that's Robbi. She can also be extremely bad tempered. You should see what we have to live with in the mornings: not only the temper, but she isn't a very good-looking girl first thing in the morning. In fact she's downright ugly. Mind you, I think sometimes she just isn't very fortunate in the looks department. Now her *sister* is a sweet-looking girl, but Robbi won't do anything to improve what God has given her. I pity the poor man that decides to marry her and has to wake up looking at her in the mornings.'

I am mortified. I look around frantically for a hole I can jump into and bury myself in. The hallway where I am standing closes in around me and I drop against the wall. Suffocation doesn't seem a bad way to die, compared with having to walk into the kitchen after what my mother has just said. Michael will never want to see me again. I stand there; my palms are all sweaty and I feel so ill that I clutch my stomach. Finally my mother interrupts the description of me that she is giving Michael to call out, 'Robbi, what's keeping you? It doesn't take that long to change your clothes! Don't you remember you've got a guest here in the kitchen?'

With that command I know I cannot hide any longer. Keeping my eyes to the ground I go into the kitchen and Michael mutters something about having to get going or his mother will wonder where he is and I walk him out to the front gate, where he climbs on his bike and off he goes.

The next night I get home from school and I don't bring a friend. I promise myself that I will never bring a friend again.

My brother is already playing in the backyard with Wendy, his best friend from next door. Wendy and he go everywhere together. The evidence of his after-school snack is on the kitchen bench. The cake tin is out with the lid left off and the dregs of lemon cordial sit thickening in the bottom of the glass. I will have to clean that up later, I think.

The lounge room is in darkness. The curtains are drawn and that is really strange because my mother always has the curtains open during the day. Only the white netting stays drawn to make sure no one can see through the windows. My mother is sitting in the lounge room and she looks dreadful. She sways from side to side in her chair.

'What's wrong?' I ask her.

'Sit down here on the pouffe,' she says, and she draws it up to her feet. 'There is something I have to tell you. Now I have never told this to anybody,' she says solemnly, 'but I am going to tell you. You are just like me and I worry about you.'

'Why? I'm okay. You don't need to worry,' I assure her. I'm not like her, I assure myself.

'Oh yes, I do need to worry because I was once a girl like you. In fact I was younger than you and if you don't watch it you are going to end up just like me. Your father and I are both concerned.'

'What am I doing wrong?' I ask, really worried now about just how much trouble I am in.

'It isn't what you are doing; it is what you are *going* to do.' What on earth am I going to do that I don't even know about? But I don't say anything, because I don't want her to stop talking. But she does.

'How can you tell what I am going to do?' I ask finally.

'Mothers can tell these things about their children. You must always remember that I know you better than you know yourself. I was thirteen,' she says, and I lean forward to catch every word because suddenly I can tell that this is going to be better than 'Days of Our Lives'.

'I was thirteen years old and I was disgraced by a boy. He was twenty-eight. He was a minister, too. He lived in my parents' house and was a migrant from another country. They took him under their roof. I disgraced them as well because I was a minister's daughter and I was supposed to set an example. Your granddad had to move to another town, we went to Ballarat and I had a year off school.'

'You had a baby?' It has taken me a while to realise what she means by 'disgraced'.

'Because I had disgraced my family and the man, I couldn't marry the boy that I truly loved. Your grandparents made me write to him and explain that we could not marry because I had been defiled in the eyes of the Lord. He deserved a wife who would only ever be his. It wouldn't be fair on him to expect him to take on a girl in my circumstances. I thought the other man loved me. He was much older than me and he told me he loved me. But your father was the best I could get for a husband after what I had done.'

'But that was years before you were married,' I say. Even though it is all coming out a bit jumbled I get the gist of what she is saying. 'Surely if someone loved you he wouldn't care what you did before he met you.'

'Life isn't like that, Robbi!' she answers crossly.

'So where is the baby?'

'Your grandparents took care of all that. And what happened turned your grandfather white overnight and nearly ruined his career, his work for the Lord. Now listen here, young lady. It is important that you don't end up like me. You're just like me and I don't want you to be a disgrace to your family. Wouldn't it be terrible if you were responsible for taking a man away from his work for the Lord?'

I think of Mato and how horrified she would be if I ever got pregnant before I was married and I determine to be more vigilant in my resistance to the temptation to pet. I will make sure I never forget to read my Bible and I am going with Rodney Burlington again but in future I will stop him from getting me to lie down naked with him. He never gets naked and I wouldn't want him to. I have never seen a man naked because I was so careful not to look that time at the nudist camp or when my father was naked. And I have never touched Rodney Burlington or any other boy anywhere I shouldn't. 'I won't do anything,' he always says. 'I promise I just want you to take your clothes off so I can feel you close.' And he keeps his word. We don't do anything that we haven't already done — which is me lying there feeling shocked that I am doing this and praying for forgiveness, but unable to stop him because it feels so good with his fingers delving into places that my own have never been.

I am still a virgin and I can't get pregnant, though sometimes I'm not sure just how far those little sperm can travel and my girlfriends at school don't know either. Perhaps they can crawl out of a boy's jeans and into a girl's naked body. Sue Johnson thought she was pregnant because she got in the bath with her boyfriend, and they say in health classes at school that it only takes a microscopic drop and *wham* — you could be pregnant!

I certainly can't ask my mother how far sperm travels because then she'll know for sure what I've been doing with Rodney Burlington. And there is no reason for her to know because I am not going to do it anymore. Besides, it's only Rodney who does anything; I just lie there. Even though I have never touched his penis or even looked at it I feel guilty because the pastor says anything that goes below the neckline is fornicating and a sin, and Rodney goes below my neckline every chance he gets.

'So,' my mother is saying, 'you must make sure that you obey the Lord and stay chaste.'

I think of the Bible verse: Faith, hope and chastity and the greatest of these is chastity. Or is it charity?

I suddenly feel sorry for my mother, who looks so distraught about what she did when she was thirteen.

19

My mother, father, brother and I have driven to Canaan College to pick up Karyn and Wayne for the holidays. It's a beautiful sunny day, the sort that makes the countryside seem exquisite and I am jealous that Wayne and Karyn get to live away from home. I so desperately want to stay here where you can hear the silence for miles. Our house is never ever silent.

Wayne and Karyn come running up to the car and drag us off to see their dormitories, which are just rows and rows of bunks. There are families everywhere and teachers answering parents' questions. My mother has to go and see the bursar about fees. Wayne is playing with Davie and Karyn has gone off with her friends, so that leaves the choice of staying with my father or following my mother. I am never good in crowds of people that I don't know, so I tag along behind her.

'Come in, come in,' says the bursar, a woman with greyish hair and glasses that have thick rims. She is wearing a grey woollen suit so that she looked very grey, but kind.

She smiles at me standing just behind my mother and I try to smile back. My gaze is drawn to her window and the beautiful view of the countryside calling to me, calling me away from the stress of living with my parents, of being afraid of my father, of disappointing my mother. I start to daydream about living in the country, in a little cottage surrounded by gentle animals that keep me company, when suddenly something the bursar has said captures my attention.

'Mrs Dusty,' she is sitting behind her desk and telling my mother about the school. 'I imagine you've had a good look around when you've brought Wayne and Karyn up here, but let me tell you about our teachers. You know our principal, Mr Barry Johnson, of course, who is our English teacher, and his wife, Julie, does all the cooking for the school. Then we have Glen Hedges, the maths teacher. His wife, Sarah, is the secretary. An art teacher comes in once a week. Then I'm the bursar, my husband, Frank, is the gardener and handyman, and we did have Joanne, a young girl who was the art teacher's assistant, but she has left us.'

I don't wait to hear any more. I am out the door, across the hall and knocking on the principal's door. I am so fast I don't even give myself time to think about what I am doing, so I can't get nervous.

'Yes,' answers a deep voice in response to my knock.

I go into his office, I can't help noticing the beautiful view from his window, but I drag my eyes away and look at him.

'I was wondering if you need a new teacher's assistant. I am really good at art,' I say.

'Hmm, yes, we do need a new assistant. Maybe the Lord has sent you along for us,' he says.

A good start.

'How old are you?' he asks. 'Our last assistant was seventeen.'

'I'm seventeen in the holidays,' I say hopefully.

'What year are you in at school?'

'I'm in form five and I really want a break before I think about form six,' I say, thinking that what I really want a break from is my home.

'When were you born again?' he asks me.

'I gave my heart to the Lord and have known him as my personal Lord and Saviour since I was eight,' I answer confidently; I am on familiar ground now.

'Hmm,' he says. 'I find the best way to make decisions about these things is to ask the Lord and see what he has to say. Will you pray with me, Robbi?

'Dear Lord,' he prays as we both bow our heads, 'young Robbi here has come to us with a wish to serve you in this school. We ask for your wisdom and guidance in this matter as we seek to do your will. Grant us your grace, understanding and direction as we ponder this issue. Your will be done and all glory be to your name, Our Lord and Saviour. Amen.'

I do not know if I am meant to add something so I just say 'Amen' too.

'I will wait for the Lord to speak to me and I will let you know,' says the principal.

I wander out to look for my parents and I am so excited my heart is up in the sky somewhere. They are putting bags into the boot of the car and my father's face has clouded over.

'Where did you get to, missy?' asks my mother with the distrustful look on her face that she often has.

'Just wandering around.' I cannot bring myself to tell them about the principal. There is no point getting them all riled up about something that probably won't happen.

'Well, we're just about ready to go,' says my father. He is desperate to get away from this Christian place.

'Umm, I just have to go to the toilet,' I say frantically and off I shoot back to the principal's office. I knock on his door and this time I am so nervous, I am trembling. He'll say no he'll say no, I tell myself over and over so that I won't be too disappointed.

'Yeeeess,' he drawls and I poke my head around the corner. 'Ahh, you'll be living by faith, you know,' he says.

'That's okay. My grandparents spent their whole life living by faith,' I tell him.

'We can only pay you fifty dollars a week. Any more than that and you will have to trust the Lord to provide. When can you start?'

'Next term when school goes back.'

'All the staff live in the caravans you will have seen dotted around. We've got an old one you can have. Your predecessor was happy enough with it.'

'That's great,' I say. 'Thank you. Thank you so much.'

'All right, then. See you in two weeks. Oh,' he adds, 'you can have every third weekend off.'

I am so excited that I can hardly contain myself as I go back to the car. We all pile in the back and my father starts the engine and heads down the long dusty driveway. As soon as he is out the school gates, my news bursts out of me.

'I am going to be a teacher's assistant at Canaan.'

'What?' says my mother.

'I'm going to be a teacher's assistant at Canaan College. I just got the job.'

'What job?'

'A job as the teacher's assistant at Canaan. The last girl has left and I've got the job.'

'What about school?' says my father. 'You're giving up school just like that, are you?'

'Only for a year.'

'Once you leave school you'll never go back,' says my mother. 'We always wanted more for you than form five. Leaving Certificate won't get you very far in the world, young lady.'

'So you're leaving home — just like that?' continues my father. 'After all we've done for you, this is the way you thank us, is it? We don't get a say in it. Just up and off, are you?' he yells over his shoulder at me.

'I'll be able to look after Karyn and Wayne,' I say, but I

notice that Davie is looking sad and I shrug my shoulders at him.

'You're a very ungrateful young lady, you know that?' says my mother and on and on and on they go — for the whole four hours it takes to get home.

When we get there, they have exhausted themselves, so they stop talking to me altogether.

'Can I have a drink, Mum?'

Silence.

'Can I watch TV?'

Silence.

'Can I help with dinner?'

Silence.

'Is it okay if I go to the movies with the youth group on Saturday night? We're going to see *Jonathan Livingstone Seagull*. It's a Christian movie.'

Silence.

So I arrange to go anyway. The silence goes on unbearably and I swear I will remember it and never give my children the silent treatment.

Suddenly we hear my father screaming at Wayne, who is sitting at the table drawing, and I immediately feel ill although I am not the one he is yelling at.

'You ruddy frickin idiot! You're a bloody useless sod!'

'Vic.' My mother holds her soapy hands over the sink and my father screams at her.

'Don't bloody undermine me in front of my kids, Ena!'

He stands over Wayne ready to throttle him, but Wayne stands up and he is the same height as my father and he swears and yells back at him. Their faces are inches from each other. But my father is unstoppable now and he whacks Wayne.

Wayne scrunches his fist and wallops him back and as my father falls into a chair in shock, Wayne is out the back door and gone.

I don't know what to think about this. I feel a foreboding that seeps through me like black ooze. Will this mean that we have two male tyrants ranting, screaming and hitting, or will my father change now that he can't get away with walloping Wayne?

But when Wayne comes back they both act as though nothing has happened, except my father is kinder to Wayne. It is a subtle change and you would miss it if you didn't know, but he smiles at Wayne now and speaks to him normally.

Trouble is, he is worse to Davie.

Finally we arrive back at Canaan. Karyn's friends run up to join her and we take Wayne to his dormitory.

The principal has spotted us and comes over. 'Mr and Mrs Dusty, how are you? We've got nearly the whole family here now, haven't we? The Lord be praised.'

My father winces and my mother smiles warmly. 'Yes,' she says, kindly and still smiling, 'it seems so. We hope Robbi will do a good job for you. This is just what she needs. A break from school and this will be such a lovely Christian environment for her.' She puts her arm lovingly around my shoulder.

I smile weakly at the principal.

'I see you've got a swimming pool there,' says my father, all blokey and on comfortable ground.

'Yes,' says the principal, 'but we only use it for baptising the students who have accepted Jesus as their Lord and Saviour.'

At this my father has to physically hold himself back from whopping the principal. He would happily feed all of us Christians to the lions.

Life at Canaan College is hard, but good. I love helping in art classes, but unfortunately I don't love my other jobs. Every night I have to soak a huge pot of rolled oats and in the morning I have to be up and in the kitchen by six-thirty to have the oats ready for breakfast at seven-thirty. There are about fifty students at Canaan College and porridge for fifty is a lot to stir and stop from burning. I also have to supervise the students as they wash their clothes in laundry class. The clothes get washed in two old twin tubs under a veranda and the water is icy cold on the children's hands, so they cry and I feel like a right royal heel. I also have to help with cleaning and cooking, especially on Sundays when the principal's wife makes a roast dinner for the whole school and boils raisins to make the non-alcoholic grape juice for celebrating the Lord's Supper. She never digs out the eyes on the potatoes for the roast, though. She just hacks off a whole piece of potato if it has an eye in it. I tell my mother about this and she says the principal's wife will always be poor if she is going to waste food like that.

The principal always takes the church service as he is the spiritual leader of the school, but his church services go for two hours! A Baptist service never goes a second over one and a quarter. In the services at Canaan we don't sing hymns, we sing choruses that I have never heard before, and while we are singing the bursar raises her arms to the heavens, closes her eyes and starts to sing in tongues, waving her arms about as though she is unable to control them.

I have a lovely old caravan to live in with floral curtains, a tapestry-covered couch at one end and a double bed at the other. I put my poster of Clark Gable on the ceiling and lie in bed and dream of one day having a dark and glorious husband like him. I have a frypan to cook in when it is my weekend off and I notice my skin is getting a bit oily, but at least I don't have pimples yet. I have a record player and I play my Christian rock records as loudly as I can and fill the little van with the thump of music. Rodney Burlington, who I've been back with for a while now, comes up nearly every weekend to visit me and I lie naked beside him, with him fully clothed in his jeans and shirt, in the little caravan, absolutely terrified that someone will knock on the door and discover me. And now he wants us to get engaged.

'But I'm only seventeen,' I say.

'My mother was seventeen when she got engaged to my father and they got married when she was nineteen.' His family is English. He says his father was a chief engineer on the Westgate Bridge and now that the bridge has collapsed they have fled back to England. But Rodney has stayed behind because he has a good job in the bank.

'I don't know,' I say slowly. I'm not sure I want to get engaged. The truth is I don't really like Rodney that much. It's just that every time I try to break it off with him he gets angry and then gives me presents.

'We're nearly having sex, so you're nearly my wife anyway!' he says, getting angry. 'For goodness sake, we've been going together for two years now. You *have* to get engaged to me!' And he kicks the cupboard.

I know we are not nearly having sex because my mother made me read the lifetime books when I got my periods, and I've seen Rodney angry so many times. He drives his Ford Falcon really fast, and if another car does something he doesn't like he pulls in front of them and keeps putting his brakes on so the other car nearly runs into him. I am scared when I am in the car with him. I am scared right now because he is angry. I don't know what to do about his anger so I hop in his car and we drive to Wangaratta, where he buys me an engagement ring. I don't like it but it is the cheapest one in the shop and it's his choice.

I turn my engagement ring over and over on my finger. It makes my finger sore and I pull it off and put it in my pocket. It doesn't seem to fit my finger very well and, besides, it is ugly. I have tried to like it because you should appreciate anything someone gives to you, but it really is unattractive and imposing. It has a loud angular diamond in the middle and two small blue stones either side that look like little blue pimples on the face of the ring. It is sterile and modern.

I am sitting on a chair in the principal's office.

'It seems to me, Robbi,' the principal says thoughtfully, 'that you don't really want that ring on your finger or the man who gave it to you.'

'I don't know,' I say. 'We've been going out for a long time.'

'Let us pray about the matter.

'Dear Lord Jesus our Saviour,' he prays, 'you have taught us that marriage is a holy sacrament, a bond that no man can break asunder; you have taught us that marriage is a holy institution that one must only enter with the utmost seriousness and consideration. You teach that a woman must surrender to her husband in all things and that he is her spiritual head and her lord. Please, Lord, we pray that you will give Robbi guidance as she considers whether this is the man you have chosen to be her spiritual head, the man she should be bound to until death does part them. Give Robbi your wisdom, we pray. Amen.'

I say 'Amen' and wipe away the tears rolling down my cheeks. The very thought of having to be with Rodney Burlington until death makes me feel that my life is over. And the thought of having to be subservient to him makes me feel that I will never see light again.

'We've been going out for two years,' I say. It is hopeless. After all, I am engaged. It's a done deal.

'Marriage is a holy union,' says the principal. 'A husband is the head of the wife as Christ is the head of the church and the wife must submit to him in all things. Are you ready for that, Robbi?'

The next weekend Rodney drives me down to Parkdale in his V8 to see my parents for the first time, now that we are engaged. We walk in the back door. He is tall and proud, glad that we are engaged, sure that my father will treat him as an equal now that he is going to be his son-in-law.

My father gets up from his chair when he sees us and turns down the stereo; my mother is standing nearby.

'Robbi, give me the ring,' says my father. I hand it over to him, amazed that he is interested in my engagement ring. Maybe he wants to check that I have been bought a good one.

'Rod,' he says, looking him straight in the face, 'Robbi doesn't want to get married to you. She's too young. She's only seventeen, for God's sake! This is ridiculous.'

'I'll wait for her,' says Rodney defiantly.

'Rod, Robbi doesn't want to ever marry you — not now, not when she is older, not *ever*! Now, it's been nice knowing you, Rod, but it's time to take your ring and never see her again.'

Rodney looks at me, but I say nothing, I am stunned, though I am brimming with love for my father. This is the most wonderful thing he has ever done for me.

Rodney leaves and I am crying with relief.

'How did you know?' I ask.

'We are your parents,' my mother says matter-of-factly. 'We know when you're unhappy. Now go and put some coffee on for your father. I think he deserves it.'

And that is that. I was engaged for two weeks.

I am getting very tired at Canaan College. I have to work such long hours and not once have I been paid fifty dollars. My clothes are really worn out and my skin is so greasy. I have burns on my face because I hate plucking my thick dark eyebrows so I tried to thin them with Nair cream. It burnt my skin so I am bathing my eyebrows with milk every day and hope they are better by Sunday. The gorgeous maths teacher Glen Hedges and his wife are taking me over to

Shepparton Baptist Church on Sunday night for a special youth service.

I didn't realise that Canaan College is Pentecostal. A few years ago all good Baptists knew that Pentecostalism was not of the Lord, but inspired by the devil and a practice to keep well away from. Our pastor preached many sermons about its dangers — especially speaking in tongues. But here at Canaan they say that if you don't speak in tongues you are not fully baptised in the Holy Spirit and God's power cannot flow freely through you. I have been praying to the Lord to make me speak in tongues if it is His will, but it hasn't happened. The principal has prayed for it to happen and laid his hands on me, but it hasn't yet and I feel like I am only half a Christian.

During the special youth service I pray that the Lord will make it happen, but it doesn't and we sing, 'I'm on the Top of the World', but the words are changed so that we are singing about Jesus.

Then we are going to the hall to have supper and, after that, back to Canaan. I turn to get my bag and as I straighten to leave the pew I find that I am face to face with Clark Gable. He is standing there, flesh and blood and just as beautiful as I've imagined. Dark curling hair and eyes that twinkle and glitter impertinently at me.

'Hi, I am Graeme,' says Clark Gable. 'I've been watching you all through the service. Couldn't take my eyes off you, in fact. So what brings a gorgeous-looking girl like you into church on a cold Sunday night — and before you answer, may I escort you to supper?'

I am totally, completely besotted and instantly in love. I don't take my eyes off him for an instant. His friends wink and nudge each other but introduce themselves to me and are very polite. It is painful to have to take my eyes off him and be polite to them, but I do it because it is important to make a good impression on his friends. They are all students at

Dookey Agricultural College. But none of them is as good-looking as him. He is tall with broad shoulders, hair twisting and curling just below them, and he has lovely deep brown eyes with black lashes that would put mascara companies out of business. His voice is deep and runs over me like the sauce on my gran's chocolate pudding, warm and sweet. When he laughs he sounds just like my Auntie Margaret and his friends look embarrassed, but I don't care. How often does a person laugh anyway?

Graeme, it happens, laughs a lot.

All the way home the Canaan teachers tease me. 'Robbi's in love,' they sing. 'Robbi's found true love.'

For the first time ever, I love my boyfriend. The five-page letters start to arrive instantly and the roses and the visits. He rides over on his pushbike, all the way from Dookey to Thoona. He makes me laugh. He is kind. He introduces me to non-Christian music and now my record collection includes Alice Cooper and Queen. I don't let him kiss me because after Rodney Burlington I have learnt my lesson.

Then one night he says, 'Robbi, I really don't understand this no-kissing business and it's driving me crazy. Surely God meant us to enjoy kissing? It's only normal. You are so beautiful I really have to kiss you.' And he does, without asking.

He lifts my chin up to his face and he kisses me softly but firmly, our bodies press together and I can feel his body hard against mine. Rodney Burlington might have put his hands all over me, but I never got close to him — I never felt his body. But I want to feel Graeme's body and I can. His body is handsome and smells divine.

I can do it! I can speak in tongues. It's just happened. I was praying to the Lord and it started to come out. I can sing in tongues too. I am now baptised in the Holy Spirit as well as water. I am a complete Christian. The words just pour out of my mouth in praise to God without my even thinking about it. It is as if someone else is speaking through me. Praise be to Jesus our Lord and Saviour.

I tell the principal I can speak in tongues and he says, 'Praise the Lord for his goodness!'

I tell the bursar I have been baptised in the Holy Spirit and she says, 'Hallelujah, thank you Jesus!' Then she looks at me strangely for a few moments before she says, 'You're a strange girl, Robbi. Your little sister, now *she's* a lovely young girl. I think it would be a good idea if you left Canaan. It isn't good for your sister to have you around. You ruin her chances to make friends. She's a sweet girl, your sister. You're like opposites. The real problem with you, Robbi, is that you try too hard.'

I feel like I have been hit with a cricket bat. What does my sister have that I don't?

Why am I bad for her? What makes me strange? Why is it that everyone likes her, but not me? What is it about me that is so horrible and unlovable? How can you try too hard? I've always thought trying was good. I want all of these questions answered but I am too frightened of the answers to actually ask the bursar what she means. One thing is obvious: she doesn't like me and probably no one else here does either. I run to my caravan, throw myself on the bed and cry.

Why does no one love me, Lord? I must be truly awful if no one can love me except my grandmother. I realise that I have to leave Canaan as soon as possible. They don't really want someone like me here, even if I am now filled with the Holy Spirit.

20

I am back home and I am sick. I got a mosquito bite and my whole leg has swollen up from my ankle to my groin and I am on antibiotics. My mother says it is because I wasn't looked after at Canaan College. She says she can't believe that I was never paid a single cent the whole time I was there, when I was working twelve-hour days. She says that it's time Wayne and Karyn came home too. She hopes I have learnt that home is the place the Lord means me to be. So I lie in bed and listen to Skyhooks and Status Quo on the radio until I am better.

Graeme is coming over tonight for my eighteenth birthday. I am wearing my pink satin top and a pair of chocolate brown satin pants that I got at the opportunity shop. He arrives in his Mini Minor. He is taking me out for dinner.

'Hello, beautiful,' he says when I open the door and he hands me a corsage in a box, a lovely white orchid. He leans over and kisses me as he pins it to my chest. My parents really like Graeme. Me, I love Graeme and I imagine being his wife, having his babies and growing old with him.

'Come on, let's go,' he says.

'Have a good time, you two lovebirds,' my mother says and winks at him.

‘What was that all about?’ I ask him as we get in his car.

‘Nothing, nothing.’

‘Where are we going?’

‘Aha — surprise!’ he says.

We drive towards the Nepean Highway and he says, ‘Oh no! I’ve left my wallet back at your house. I must have taken it out of my pocket when I was pinning the corsage on you. Better go back for it.’

We get back to the house and as soon as we get in the lounge room everyone yells, ‘Surprise!’ All Graeme’s Dookey friends are here and my old youth group friends and his two sisters, his mum and dad, Grandma Lyne, Mato and Aunt Tonia, who rarely come to our house because of Dad.

Graeme and his friends give me a card they have all signed, a Royal Doulton egg cup and a beautiful dress. Aunt Tonia gives me a Bible that has all four versions, The King James, The Revised, The New English and The Living Bible in it. It is huge and very impressive. Mato gives me money to buy something I really want and my parents give me a dolly lamp that is fuchsia pink and covered in lace. I pretend to like it — and I might have liked it when I was six.

I am overwhelmed. I say hello to everyone and go into the kitchen to help my mother.

‘About time someone gave me some help!’ she snaps.

‘Thank you for the surprise party, Mum. It’s great,’ I say and go to hug her, but she pulls away and keeps cutting up cubes of cheese.

‘Don’t thank me! Graeme organised it. Guess he doesn’t have to do all the work, does he?’ she says nastily. ‘Your father and I are stuck with the entertaining — not to mention the expense! By the way, now that you’re eighteen we expect you to have your driver’s licence by Christmas, because after that we won’t be driving you anywhere. If you haven’t got your licence, you can walk.’ And she storms off, leaving the cheese.

Graeme is standing in the doorway, and he has heard everything. Before I can speak he says, 'Your parents are awful to you. My parents would never treat me the way yours treat you.'

'But I've always assumed that most parents are like mine,' I say. 'It's the nice ones who are the exception. Besides, my mother is okay; it's just because she has to cope with my father.'

'No, Robbi,' he says firmly. 'Other people are not like your parents. My parents think yours are weird.'

I swallow my pain. 'Let's go and party,' I try to say bravely.

After the party I don't see Graeme. He cancels a date because he has to work on his mother's car, or he can't come over because he has to go away with his family for the weekend, so I fret and mope and miss him. Then finally the phone rings and he says he is coming over. He takes me to the beach at Ricketts Point and we sit in his car and instead of not being able to keep his hands off me he is distant and preoccupied and stares out at the deserted beach.

I want to be anywhere but here. I know what is coming and I also know that there is no way I can stop it.

'It's not me,' he says at last. 'It's my mother. She doesn't think you are good for me. She thinks that we're too young to feel this seriously about each other and, um ...'

I wait for it.

'Well, I don't think she likes the thought of me having too much to do with your parents.'

Don't leave me! Whatever the problem is I'll change it, I want to plead, but I don't. I try to turn my heart to stone so that I don't cry in front of him.

But I am broken-hearted. I listen to Stevie Wright sing 'Evie' and to Joe Cocker singing 'You Are So Beautiful' on the radio and I cry in my bed. I pray that God will bring

Graeme back to me but he doesn't, and I am having a hard time believing that God has anyone better than Graeme planned for me.

But I drag myself out of bed and decide that I have to do something. Two weeks of moping about is enough. I have to get a job or go back to school so I organise to do both and I will decide later. I go to an interview in Cheltenham for a job in a milk bar.

'Are you good with maths? Can you count out change?' says the owner, sifting through papers and not looking at me.

'I was top of the year.'

'We need someone honest,' he says, but he still hasn't bothered to look up.

'I'm honest.'

'They all say that.'

He seems a bit grumpy. I think he needs the Lord.

'Okay, give me your phone number and I'll call you,' he says, still sifting through the papers on top of the lolly counter.

'Umm . . . if you give me the job,' I say, 'I won't be able to work Sundays.'

This will be the end of the job.

He sighs. 'Why not?'

'Because Sunday is the Lord's day and I need to go and worship him.'

Finally he looks up and he stares at me, his eyes wide open. 'When can you start?' he says.

So I work in the milk bar and I am terrible at it. I get flustered and give the wrong change. Then one day the owner says, 'We are letting you go.'

I go and sit a test for the Commonwealth Bank and two weeks later I am called for an interview.

'You came second in our test,' says the man in a pin-striped suit as he shakes my hand and ushers me into a small cubicle. 'And it was a good group. We've never had such high scores before. You got ninety-eight per cent and the boy who beat you got ninety-nine per cent. So you want to work in the bank. It's a fine career choice. We'll start you as a junior teller and see where you go from there. Of course, only males can become managers — we can't have women managers — not fair on men to expect them to take orders from a woman.'

'How much will I get paid?'

'Ahh, good question,' he says and looks in his manual. 'Sixty-seven a week,' he says, looking up at me. 'Of course, if you were a boy you'd get ninety-nine dollars fifty.'

'What? You mean I get thirty dollars a week less, just because I am a girl — even though I got such a high score in your test?'

'That's it,' he says. 'Nothing I can do about it. You girls go off and get married, have babies — you don't need the money. You don't have to support a family one day. When do you want to start?' I sit, offended, then I stand, shake his hand and say 'I'm sorry, but I don't,' and walk out, disgusted with myself for being born a girl. I arrange to go back to school.

It is Christmas and everyone has had a present except me and my parents are giving each other strange looks. 'What do you think?' my mother says to my father. 'Shall we give it to her?'

'Give me what?'

'Your present is outside,' says my father.

I race out and there — wrapped in toilet paper, going both ways around it and over the top with a toilet paper bow — is a beautiful black car.

'Oh, I love it! I love it! What sort is it?'

'A Hillman, 1959, made the same year as you. Daddy got it from his sister Clare. She bought it for Sharene, but they couldn't get it going properly. Daddy will have it going for you in no time. Do you like it?'

I love it!

'Actually, Ena, I think it's a 1956,' says my father.

'You need to give us two hundred dollars to cover the cost,' says my mother.

The car is so lovely. It has running boards and is shiny black, smooth and round. You start the ignition with a button and it is the coolest, grooviest car I have ever seen.

My father doesn't get around to fixing it and the engine cuts out every time you slow down, so I have to make sure that my timing is right at intersections so I can fly through the lights, because once it stops that is *it*. You have to call the RACV.

I drive it every day to school in Frankston, careful not to have to stop at any lights, juggling the clutch and the accelerator. But my car is the most wonderful thing I have ever owned and I will never part with it. I give it the name Hezekiah.

Being back at the Frankston school is good and the other students accept me as part of the group. They stop talking about sex when I am around, but they are kind about it. They are trying to protect my innocence. This time I get invited to the parties. One girl is even living with her boyfriend and she invites me to her house.

'Would you like some cider?' she asks as I sit at her table.

'Sure.'

She pours me a cider and teaches me to play Euchre. Her boyfriend comes in and sees that my glass is empty. 'Would you like another glass?' he asks.

'Sure,' I say as I make my bid on hearts. I love apple cider and I drink many more glasses and Fran and her boyfriend start to give each other odd looks. After a couple of hours I look at my watch and I am shocked that it is so late. 'I have to go,' I say. 'I'm going to my aunt and grandmother's tonight. My aunt is taking me bowling.' Fran and her boyfriend are giggling, but I don't get the joke.

‘Are you sure you’ll be okay on the train?’ says Fran’s boyfriend.

‘Of course. Why not?’ I say and they look at each other, shrug and grin.

When we get to the bowling alley everything seems a bit blurred and I cannot for the life of me get the bowling ball down my lane. I toss it down and it jumps the gutter and goes straight over into the lane of the men playing next to us. I smile stupidly at them and say sorry. They smile back, nudge each other and nod agreeably at me. I toss the ball again and it flies backwards. It goes anywhere but where it’s supposed to and I can’t wait to get into bed.

When I wake in the morning I have the most shocking headache. I can hardly lift my head off the pillow and I am too sick for school.

‘What did you drink last night?’ asks my aunt, handing me a mug of hot tea.

‘Just cider.’

‘What sort of just cider?’

‘Apple.’

‘No, I mean was it alcoholic?’ Alcoholic cider — I have never heard of such a thing, but it was pretty yummy. My aunt tells me I’ll feel better if I get out of bed and go to school. So I do, but it’s a struggle.

I get through school with my headache and when I get home I dump my heavy bag and folio by the back door. I am desperate to lie down and head through the kitchen to my bedroom. My father is sitting at the table. He is out of work again.

‘What do you think you’re going to do next year?’ he says, between mouthfuls of cheese jaffle.

‘I’m going to art school,’ I say, hoping this won’t take long and I can go to bed.

‘We’re not paying for it. You know that, don’t you?’

‘I really want to go.’

'We're not paying for a girl to go and do some bloody art course!' he says angrily.

'What's wrong with a teaching contract?' asks my mother as she slices cheese for more jaffles.

'It's a good secure job,' says my father. 'They pay you while you study.'

'Nothing's wrong with it, but I don't want to be a teacher. I don't want to *teach* art, I want to do it myself. I want to paint.'

'You could be a nurse, you know,' says my father. 'Nursing is a good job for a girl.'

'I don't want a whole bunch of stuck-up doctors bossing me around,' I say, sitting at the other end of the table.

'You could end up marrying one, you know,' says my mother, as if this is a huge selling point.

'But I don't *want* to marry someone who does something. I want to do something myself.'

'If you end up in an art course,' she waves her finger at me, 'you better not start dressing like one of those artists. We didn't bring you up in the gutter and we don't want you to look like that's where you've come from. I don't know what's wrong with nursing.'

'If you do art,' adds my father, 'don't expect a cent from us.'

'You'd make a lovely nurse,' says my mother.

'Don't bother, Ena,' my father says scathingly. 'A doctor's not good enough for Robbi.' He slams back his chair and goes for another jaffle. I am amazed he actually stands up to get it himself.

So I go to the Victorian College of the Arts. I just rock up and say to the first person I can find, 'I want to come to this school next year. I want it more than anything in the world. I've brought some of my paintings for you to have a look at so you can tell me if I need to do something different to get in here.'

'Come with me,' the man says and takes me into a huge studio. 'Wait here and I'll see who I can find.' I wait and wait and the whole time I wait I pray, *Please, Lord, let me get in. Please, Lord, if it is your will for me to come here, make them like me.*

About twenty minutes must have passed and finally a stocky man with a bold smile comes in and scans the full length of my body, smiling mischievously all the time. He gets so close to me, face to face, that his confidence is almost arrogant.

'So you want to be a student here,' he says. 'Let's have a look.' I am not sure whether he means me or the paintings. Then he says, 'By the way, I am Gareth Sansom, head of the painting department.' I'm actually talking to the head of the painting department! I try to catch my breath.

'Now you know the competition is really stiff for places,' he says. 'You know, don't you, that you have basically no chance of getting in? We can pick and choose our students, and we only take the cream. We have applicants from all over Australasia — about five hundred for the painting school alone — and we take fifteen. So my advice is don't get your hopes up. Now let's see what you've got.'

I show him my three paintings. He sits and stares at them and says nothing, nothing, nothing for what seems like forever. I desperately need to go to the toilet. I cross and uncross my legs and cross them again.

'Why do you want to paint?' he says finally.

'It's what I've always wanted to do, nothing else. I love painting.' I decide not to tell him that I really want to become a candidate for ministry in the Baptist church, except they won't take you if you are too young and have no life experience or if you are female. I don't tell him that I am coming to art school to get life experience, because I really do love painting and it is the other thing that I want to do — but it is my second choice.

'Well,' he says, 'you're going to need a lot more work for the interview. Make sure you have lots of drawings and try to free up a bit. See you back here in December.' And he goes.

I take all the work I have to the interview, plus photos of the chess set I made in pottery and won an award for. There are three people interviewing me: two art teachers and a third-year student. They look at my work, then call in Gareth Sansom, who smiles and says hello and walks straight out with one of the interviewers. There is an uncomfortable silence until the man who went out with Gareth Sansom comes back in and says, 'Come with me, please.' He takes me into an office and says, 'This is the Dean, William Kelly.'

'Sit down,' says the Dean. I sit, my knees are shaking so I put my hands on them to clamp them down. 'I don't know why, it has never happened before, but Gareth Sansom wants you in the school. He is head of painting, so I can only assume that he knows what he is doing,' the Dean says.

I drive home in Hezekiah and I don't see the lights turning red. I am going to the Victorian College of the Arts! As I run in the back door I scream at my parents, 'I got in! I got in — just like that — I got in!'

'You'll start dressing like one of those artists and make me ashamed of you,' says my mother.

My father just keeps reading the *Herald*.

21

Now that I can speak in tongues I don't feel like I fit in at Mordialloc Baptist Church anymore. The folk there don't believe in baptism of the Holy Spirit and some of them think speaking in tongues is downright evil. I know, because that's what I used to think. So they don't pray in tongues and don't sing choruses of praise with their hands held high to God. I need to go to a church that is filled with the Holy Spirit, so I am going to one in Mentone called The Church of the Open Door. It is Fundamental, Evangelical, Ecumenical, Charismatic, Pentecostal. Well, that's what the sign at the front says. It is a breakaway of a breakaway of the Assemblies of God Church.

Now that I am filled with the spirit, I am leading people to the Lord all over the place.

I have brought my sister Karyn to the Open Door and her boyfriend, Sam. I have also brought my new boyfriend, Simon Reynolds. He was a leader at the camp my mother sent me on and I had a crush on him. He has shoulder-length hair and a huge motorbike. I started writing to him, then I went in Hezekiah to visit him and he asked me out. After Graeme I have given up on the staying pure bit, so Simon and I wash each other's hair and play pool in his bedroom on his pool table. Then we lie in his bed and listen to his favourite band, Yes, with his bedroom door locked. Then he kisses me, my top comes off and we get hot and sweaty with him kissing and touching me. But at least he is now filled with the spirit too.

I have also brought my new boss to church. She is a rich lady named Mavis Wright and her husband is an electrician. She advertised for a nanny to work in the holidays looking after her five primary-school-aged children and I applied. But I only work for her in the school holidays, when her children are home from boarding school.

'I can't work on Sundays,' I said as she showed me over her two-storey brick house in Beaumaris.

We sat in the sun by her heated saltwater pool. 'Why not?' she asked.

'Because I serve the Lord Jesus Christ and on Sundays I go to worship him. Do you know Him as your personal Lord and Saviour?'

'Well, I do go to church at Easter and Christmas,' she says. 'We're Anglican.'

'Ah yes, many people go to church and they think that makes them a Christian, but they're not Christians,' I tell her. 'To become a Christian you must be born again. You must have a life-changing experience of God. You must have a personal relationship with Him that can only be attained through His son, Jesus Christ. Without God my life would be miserable, but knowing Jesus has meant that I can face anything and feel secure that my life is in God's hands. God has a wonderful plan for my life.' I bring my Bible out of my handbag and we walk back inside to the family room while I flick through the pages.

I am on a roll.

'See? Here is Revelation 3:20, this is Jesus talking to you,' I say. '"Behold I stand at the door and knock" — that's the door to your heart — "and if any person hears my voice and opens the door I will come into him and sup with him and he shall know life everlasting."' I look at Mrs Wright and tears are rolling down her cheeks.

'Maybe that is what is missing in my life,' she says. 'My husband spends so much time at work and I am so depressed I can hardly get out of bed each day. I can't face the thought of the children arriving home from boarding at Grammar and having to look after them. My life is a mess.'

I know this is true because she showed me the tray of pills and vitamins she swallows each day and it must take her half the day just to get them all down.

'Jesus will give you a reason for living,' I say. 'He is the answer to all of life's questions and the only road to eternal life is through Him.'

'How do I make it happen? How do I have a relationship with God like you have?' she asks. So I tell her to kneel on the floor, right there in the middle of her family room, and I kneel with her. 'Now pray after me,' I say. 'Dear Lord Jesus, you are the light and the way, I confess to you all my sins and ask that you would forgive me and give me everlasting life. Please come into my heart and make me a child of God. Amen.'

Mrs Wright looks at me through her tears. 'You've got the job,' she says.

And now her whole family comes to church: all five kids and her husband.

All because of me.

Pastor Greenslade at The Church of the Open Door is about eighty-five years old, all hunched over and he coughs and splutters all the time because he has emphysema. Nevertheless, he shouts from the pulpit, holding his King James version high in the air, 'God said it, I believe it, so that settles it!'

And we all call out, 'Amen! Praise you, Jesus! Thank you, Jesus!'

He says that if the King James version was good enough

for the apostle Paul then it is good enough for him. I don't think he has read the bit at the very front of the Bible, where it says:

> Translated by His Majesty's most special command, appointed to be read in churches by the most high and mighty Prince James. King of Great Britain, France and Ireland, defender of the faith in 1611 AD.

When we talk to each other at the Open Door Church, we make sure to include the Lord in everything we say. So instead of saying, 'I am going to do such and such tomorrow', we always say, 'I am going to do such and such, Lord willing', to show that we know we are at the Lord's mercy and that we submit to God's will in all things, no matter how small. Lord, should I buy chocolate or flowers as a gift for Mrs Wright? Lord, should I buy chips or Twisties for a snack?

We call each other 'brother' and 'sister' to show we are part of the true family of God.

We give each other holy hugs.

Every morning I put on the Lord's Holy Armour with which we fight the evil spirits of Satan. In Ephesians 6:13–17 it says, 'For we wrestle not against flesh and blood, but against principalities, against powers, against the rulers of darkness of this world, against spiritual wickedness in high places. Wherefore take unto you the whole Armour of God, that ye may be able to withstand in the evil day and having done all to stand. Stand therefore, having your loins girt about with truth.'

And here I pretend to put on the loincloth of truth. I mime tying a knot in the invisible cloth that girds our loins. 'And having on the breastplate of righteousness.' So I pretend to put on a breastplate like knights wear in medieval films. 'And your feet shod with the preparation of the gospel of peace.'

And I pretend to put on shoes that are the holy word of the Lord. 'Above all the shield of faith whereupon you will be able to quench all the fiery darts of the wicked.' And now I pretend I am carrying a shield, which is our shield of faith. 'And take the helmet of salvation.' Of course I pretend to put on a hat. And finally, 'The sword of the spirit', and I pretend to swish a mighty sword through the air and cut the devil's minions to pieces.

Now that I am filled with the Holy Spirit, I try to witness to at least three people a day. So I just walk up to people on the street or in a train and say, 'Do you know that God has a wonderful plan for your life?' Or I say, 'Do you know Jesus?' Sometimes, especially if they are young men, they will talk and argue with me for ages, but I am always praying that underneath the Lord is speaking to them and even if they don't convert then and there, who I am to judge whether the Holy Spirit is convicting them in their heart?

Pastor Greenslade says that I have a spirit of rejecting food upon me because I feel so ill all the time and I can't eat what my mother puts in front of me.

He says that if Simon Reynolds and I are petting, he'd better marry me quickly and keep me pure in the Lord's eyes. But I don't answer because although I like Simon a lot, I don't want to marry him.

Pastor Greenslade says we must all write letters of protest to the government about the evil film, *Life of Brian*. We have never seen the film because it is evil and would taint our souls, but we still write the letters. He says that all non-Christian music is of the devil and so I throw out my Alice Cooper, Queen, Meatloaf and Rod Stewart records. I wince as I toss them into the garbage bin, they crash against the metal sides and — *snap!* — the bonds of Satan are broken.

Pastor Greenslade says that if you have enough faith you

can live forever and that people only die of disease when they lack faith in God's power to heal them.

He says that Jesus is coming back really soon — before 1984 — and that is only five and a half years away. He says that if we young people want to get married and have children, we'd better do it mighty soon or we'll miss out. I am beginning to realise that if I am ever going to have sex I will have to marry someone. I don't want to still be a virgin when the Lord comes back.

Every Sunday night Pastor Greenslade slays people in the Holy Spirit. He puts his hand on their forehead and prays loudly in tongues, and the whole congregation sings louder and louder, 'From the rising of the sun, to the going down of the same, the Lord's name is to be praised.' And we all raise our hands in the air to the Lord in heaven. Then the person falls down in raptures with the Lord. You can feel the spirit. The air is thick with the Lord's presence. Sometimes the person who has been slain lies there for half an hour. I really want to get slain in the Lord.

Now that I have brought Mrs Wright to the Lord she no longer needs me to work for her. She looks after her children herself now, and I work for Sandringham Council, in the home help department. I go to old people's homes and clean them. The old ladies really love me because I am so respectful and because I even move their chairs and vacuum underneath. They give me little presents like embroidered lace handkerchiefs or tea strainers. I do the home help for three hours from eight in the morning till eleven, and then I drive on my little motorbike to school. To make up the hours I have lost in the morning I stay at school until seven at night. This is the only way I can support myself. I pay my parents twenty dollars a week board.

I get up every morning at five and spend a couple of hours meditating and praying to the Lord and reading my Bible. It was really hard when I first started doing this. I got down on my knees and prayed and prayed and finally, sure that at least an hour and a half had passed, I looked at the clock to find I had only been praying for five minutes. I never admitted this to anyone and I can hardly admit it to myself, but praying is really boring. Now, however, through practice and perseverance, I am spending at least two hours from five-thirty to seven-thirty in quiet time with the Lord. It means I am exhausted all day, but spiritual.

It is Friday and I have to fast from when I wake up in the morning all the way through art school, which is really hard because the other students around me smoke dope and eat chips all day. Even by the time I get to school, my stomach is rumbling and instead of thinking about the Lord I am thinking about hot chips and Mars Bars. I go to my cubicle where I have an easel and paints, turpentine and oils and I try to concentrate on painting. Blondie is playing on the radio and other students are sitting around their studio areas chatting. To stave off the hunger I decide to get a cup of tea, which is allowed. I grab my mug, but someone has emptied their bong into it. Yuk!

I get my handbag and walk to the cafeteria where I buy a Violet Crumble and I eat it so fast that I don't enjoy it and then I feel guilty because I cannot go without food even for one day for the Lord, when children in Ethiopia go without food for years.

Fridays pass dreadfully slowly. It's like waiting for Christmas when you are little. But finally it is time to leave school and I ride straight to The Church of the Open Door, where we continue to pray and fast. We stay up the entire night at church until the sun comes up, praying and singing to the Lord in tongues.

When we have finished, I stand and stretch the pins and needles out of my legs and a girl named Karen says to me, 'I really like your boyfriend Simon' and I say flippantly, 'You can have him if you want.' And a few weeks later they are engaged, so I guess they'll be right when the Lord comes.

The groovy thing about the College of the Arts is that there are basically no classes apart from life drawing on Thursdays. We haven't had a male model yet and I am a bit nervous about that. Each of us has a studio space and we are supposed to spend our days painting and learning to be self-motivated. The lecturers occasionally come out of their cubby holes where they play chess to comment on our paintings. Once a month we take our work into the common room where Gareth Sansom tells us what is wrong with it.

I am sure that art school is filled with evil spirits; someone has stuck up pictures of naked men in the girls' toilets so I have to close my eyes when I go to the loo and ask the Holy Spirit to protect me from evil while I am having a wee. Also someone has written 'Women's Liberation — Let him sleep on the wet spot' on the toilet door. I have no idea what that means but it is sure to be bad.

So I walk around at art school praying in tongues so that the Holy Spirit can cleanse the school and the other art students put down their bongs and stare at me in disbelief. Maybe the Holy Spirit is convicting them in their hearts.

22

There are two new boys in the church and they are sharing a house that is on the beachfront in Mentone. We all go over for a youth group night and I notice they are only renting half the house. The other half is empty. The house is old and rambling with a massive patch of parsley growing under the back tap and I love it. I also like one of the boys, who has the most amazing eyes you've ever seen. They are so large, so deep and so blue a girl could get lost in those eyes forever. He is really good-looking, in fact drop-dead gorgeous. And I desperately need to leave home. It is unbearable with my parents. Now my father doesn't get stuck into Wayne anymore — not since Wayne hit him back. He gets stuck into Davie.

I go to the real estate agent and say, 'I want to rent the other half of Number Two Napier Street.' The house is an old double-fronted cottage with a big wide front veranda. It is the sort of house that you imagine pottering around in on lazy sunny days and I really want to live there with Mark and Rick.

'You know that house is going to be demolished, don't you?' says the middle-aged agent with the beer belly just back from lunch. He smells of meat pie.

'Yeah, I know the two guys renting the other half,' I say.

‘So you’d only be able to stay there for six months, you know. The plans have been approved and everything.’

‘How much is it?’

‘Forty dollars a fortnight,’ he says.

‘I can afford twenty.’

‘Have you got a job?’

‘Yes, I work for Sandringham Council. I do home help. I go to school after I’ve finished work and I support myself.’

‘We’ll let you know,’ he says.

The following week I am moving in and my mother isn’t talking to me again. When I go home to pick up a few things she is talking to Wendy’s mother. Wendy is still best friends with Davie. ‘Sorry, we can’t keep discussing this. There is a stranger in the house,’ she says, not looking at me or saying hello.

I don’t care, because living with Mark and Rick-of-the-beautiful-eyes is the best thing that’s ever happened to me. I paint pictures of them both. I paint Rick with his arms outstretched praising the Lord. I paint Mark reading a book and I paint our house. Mark paints every wall in the lounge room a different vibrant colour. One wall is orange, another blue, another green and another purple. He says they all symbolise the passing of time during the day.

With the two of them I learn about food I have never tasted before, like muesli and yogurt, and we eat bucketloads of baked beans that we mix with vegetables and turn into a casserole. We make heaps of vegetable soup with lots of parsley in it.

Mrs Wright gives us household items and we thank the Lord for her goodness. Rick and I spend hours and hours praying together, and on Sundays after church at the Open Door we walk the streets and witness to people. I have never felt so spiritual before. I have no temptation to kiss boys at all.

* * *

Three people in our congregation have just died. One of them was a young mother with three little children, so Pastor Greenslade is preaching harder than ever before that with faith you can live forever. He yells it from the pulpit, angry that any in his congregation should lack faith. The harder he preaches the more he coughs and splutters and his wife runs up to the pulpit to support him as he wobbles on his feet. The congregation mutters about the lack of faith of the three who have died and I look over to the husband of the woman who died. They had three little girls. He is sitting in the pew with his head in his hands, tugging at his hair. He rocks back and forth while his little girls hang onto him looking deserted and lost. He is pallid and his pain forms an arrow that shoots across the church and into my heart. I turn back to Pastor Greenslade.

'I want to hear of no one in my flock lacking faith!' he yells. 'We will conquer the devil! We will conquer death and live victorious with the Lord!'

Everyone yells, 'Amen, Jesus! Praise be to God most high! Hallelujah! Thank you, Lord!'

'There are saints who walked this earth with our Lord Jesus Christ and are still walking this earth today. I will never die, but live eternally in faith.' The pastor doubles over, coughing and spluttering with the exertion.

I look back at the man who has just lost his young wife and he is not listening. He is still rocking gently back and forth, back and forth, and I can see that he is crying and a dark, uncomfortable weight settles in my heart and I do not join the others shouting praises to the Lord. I stand, stony and silent, and I know this is wrong. How can lack of faith be the cause of death? What about when innocent little children die? How can you say a young child lacked faith? What about when Mato came to one of Pastor Greenslade's healing services to get her arthritis healed? The pastor said the Lord wasn't healing arthritis that night, he was doing leglengthening. So Mato still has arthritis and I know how strong her faith is. I suddenly realise that if it is lack of faith that stops people getting healed, then the fault can never be with God or more importantly with Pastor Greenslade's healing.

I stare at Pastor Greenslade as he keeps shouting at his flock. He spots me and my rebellion is not missed. He sees me and he takes note. He glares at me from the pulpit; his eyes have turned to ice. After his sermon he announces that a girl is pregnant so she has been banned from the church for eight weeks and when she comes back she has to marry the boy who got her pregnant. He is Pastor Greenslade's stepson. Pastor Greenslade says he hopes they are married before the Lord returns.

'Robbi, phone!' yells one of the students, so I put down my paint brushes and answer the telephone, which is covered in paint, in the student common room.

It is a man from the church, who is about forty years old and has a big sloppy belly that hangs over his jeans. When we have to give each other hugs in the Lord at church, he calls me 'sister' and hugs me, pushing his body into mine until I break away and say, 'Peace be with you, brother.'

'How did you get this number?' I ask him.

'I rang the school and they put me through to you. Pastor Greenslade told me where you are so I'm ringing with his blessing.'

I wait for what he has to say.

'I am ringing to ask if you will marry me.'

'You're asking me over the phone?'

'Well, I didn't want to waste any time.'

'Aren't you in love with June?' I say. Everyone knows he is.

'Yes, but she won't marry me.'

'So you're asking me instead?'

'Well, you're good-looking, you know. I've always thought so.'

'I'll have to think about this,' I say, not wanting to hurt him. 'I will have to ask the Lord.' But I already know the Lord is not going to tell me to marry this man. I mean, I have hardly spoken more than two words to him and he thinks it's okay for us to get married. I know there is a bit of urgency about the matter with Jesus coming back so soon, but not so urgent that I feel I have to marry someone twice my age with a big belly. When I see him at church on Sunday I will say that I spoke to the Lord about it and I feel that it is not God's will for us to marry.

Rick-of-the-beautiful-eyes and I pray together and I start to have difficult thoughts of him kissing me, but we stay pure and only pray. We stay pure as we cook vegetable soup together and as we go shopping in Mentone together. I take my pet rabbit in a basket and he sits there with his furry little head peeping over the top of the wicker and the vegetable shop lady gives him a carrot every week. Rick and I stay pure as we talk and pray till four in the morning. We stay pure as we ride the night train to Sydney for a special Bible study week.

At the Bible study week I am told that I have to wear a scarf over my head because a woman should never be seen in public with her head uncovered. I feel that tight angry knot again. Why should I have to cover my head as though I am shameful and if my hair is my crowning glory why not let someone see it? The Bible study leader says it is obvious that the Lord wants Rick and me to be together and that before we marry we must confess any past sex to each other so that when we marry we are pure for each other.

So Rick and I ask the Lord if we are meant to marry and we feel that God says yes.

We have known each other for three months.

So we confess our past sexual sin to each other. I haven't

actually had sex so I don't confess anything and I hope that Rick has a lot of experience — dark and mysterious. It would be nice to be thrown into the hands of an accomplished man, but it turns out that while he has a bit more experience than I do, it certainly isn't enough to fill a manual.

On the way back to Melbourne in the train Rick says to me, 'Well, we better get married soon.'

'I s'pose,' I say, as an amazing thrill runs up and down my spine.

It is going to happen — really. Getting married means that I won't ever have to go back and live at my parents' house again. I'll be eligible for a government student allowance and I will be able to stop doing the hours of housework I do every day before I go to school. And I won't have to stay at school until seven at night to make up the hours. Getting married means I will be able to have sex before the Lord returns and I won't have to ask the Lord for forgiveness. Being married will mean that someone will love me and it will be his job to look after me.

'I better ask you properly,' says Rick. 'Robbi, will you marry me?'

'Yes,' I say and try not to sound too needy or desperate.

The first fight comes after pre-marriage classes with Pastor Greenslade.

'You have to submit to Rick in all things,' he says as his wife nods at his side.

I look at him, a shrivelled-up old man, and I look at his wife, a woman full of vitality and spunk, and I say, 'I just don't get it. I've been told this all my life and it seems so unfair. Why can't I make my own decisions? I am an adult just like Rick is!'

'Women are weaker,' says the pastor. 'Women were the first to fall to the temptation of the devil in the Garden of Eden. That is why you must suffer pain in childbirth.'

Well, forget that for a joke! I'm never having babies, I think.

'God knows that you need the protection of your husband,' he says. 'Without your husband's spiritual protection you are vulnerable and defenceless against the powers of Satan. A woman must never answer the front door. It is the husband's job to be the public representative of the family. In your wedding service I will ask if you will honour and *obey* your husband. Unless you promise to do so, I will not marry you. The word of God says, "Wives, submit yourselves unto your husbands, as unto the Lord. For the husband is the head of the wife."'

'But my grandmother loved the Lord and she didn't promise to obey her husband. She refused,' I tell him.

'In my church,' says the pastor, 'women will obey men or all the upheaval of the devil himself will be set upon us. God has designed this order for a reason and you will not question his ways, young lady. I have felt for some time —' His wife starts to nod again. She knows what is coming and so do I. 'The Lord has spoken to me about you,' he continues 'and you have many evil spirits upon you that need to be cast out. You have a spirit of rebelliousness and a spirit of faithlessness. But you also have a spirit of seductiveness, which must be dealt with. Now we will pray for your spirit of seduction to be cast from you.'

Through all of this Rick says not a word and I hate him for not sticking up for me. I thought he was my friend.

The next fight comes when I say that I am keeping my own name.

'Don't be ridiculous, Robbi. A family must have the same name.'

'Then you change your name to mine.'

'No! I've had my name all my life, I'm used to it, it's a part of me, and I couldn't possibly be called something else.'

'Exactly!' I say.

We fight again when I say that I want to be married in Hampton Baptist Church. 'This is our family church,' I say. 'Nearly every relative I have has been married there and most of them by my grandfather.'

So we go to see the minister.

I explain why I want to get married in his church — but not by him, by Pastor Greenslade — and he is most accommodating.

'Tell me, how long have you two known each other?' he asks.

'Three months,' we answer and I see his jaw drop.

'Ahh, so when exactly are you getting married?'

'Well, we've been engaged for two weeks so the wedding is in six weeks: December the first.'

'It is usual if someone is getting married in my church that I give them a bit of pre-marriage counselling. Are you happy with that?'

We both nod. The pastor is the head of the church and not to be argued with and Pastor Greenslade always says that if we disagree with him over anything, he will speak to the Lord and the Lord will tell him what is correct.

'Now this is a difficult area, but how are things sexually?'

'Oh — we've never kissed each other,' I say. 'We're waiting until we are married.'

He coughs and says, 'What — nothing?'

I nod.

'No sexual relations at all?'

I nod.

'It seems to me,' he says, 'that you'd better get started if you're going to be married in only six weeks!'

So that night Rick says, 'Well, the pastor said we'd better get started.' And he leans over and kisses me and it feels like I am kissing my brother. It feels wrong. It must be because we are not married yet and I am sure that when we marry it will be right.

Pastor Greenslade won't let us get married at Hampton Baptist Church. He says a man's church is his own and he won't be going into another man's domain. He is angry because I won't wear a veil over my face and I won't walk to the bridal march. He is also angry because I want to pick my own hymns and he says this is the worst wedding he has ever had to do, that I have a shocking problem with authority and it will all come to no good!

I am beginning to think that I will not be able to get away from Pastor Greenslade soon enough.

I take Rick to meet Mato. She is so excited that I am getting married. Rick, Mato and I pray together and she is glad that I am marrying a good Christian man.

Rick takes me to meet his parents. He drives up to his house in Mont Albert Road and it is huge, monstrous. You could sleep a whole country of starving kids in his parents' house. He tells me on the way that he has never been eligible for government support and his father pays him an allowance of sixty dollars a week, which is more than I ever earned. Rick is studying to be a vet, but he has taken a year off. He was a boarder at Scotch College and says it was awful. I don't know what Scotch College is, but it sounds okay. Rick says he has had a hard life because he had to go to boarding schools and when he wasn't boarding the chauffeur sometimes drove him to school, which was really embarrassing, and he had to get the chauffeur to drop him off around the corner.

When we get to the house, dinner is all prepared and set out in a huge dining room. There are more knives and forks than I have ever seen, just like in a movie. Rick takes me upstairs and shows me his bedroom, which has its own bathroom and a balcony. I gaze at it all in utter amazement. His bedroom is larger than half my parents' house.

Back downstairs he introduces me to his family, and there is his father, coming towards us in his suit, with a drink in his hand. He walks stiffly as though he has a beam of wood bolted to his back.

'Well, Dad,' says Rick, 'I've got some good news. I'm going back to university.'

His dad smiles and mutters, 'At last.'

Then Rick adds, 'But I'm getting married in six weeks.' And his dad tries not to choke on his drink.

His mother shakes my hand awkwardly and says, 'Oh, this is all so sudden, isn't it! You're both so young.'

'I'm nineteen,' I say.

'I was twenty-eight when Bill and I married,' she replies.

Rick is only five foot six and his brothers are taller than him. They both smile and have open, warm faces.

'And this is my sister,' Rick says.

His sister smiles awkwardly and his mother says, 'You will make Cassie a bridesmaid, won't you?'

I don't want bridesmaids, but I say, 'Yes, of course,' because I really want them to like me.

We sit down to dinner which starts with an entrée and Rick's dad pours wine for everyone but Rick and me.

'So what school did you go to?' his mother and father ask me almost at the same time.

'The Victorian College of the Arts,' I say, but they mean secondary school. Did I go to Lauriston or Presbyterian Girls or perhaps Fernbank?

'No,' I say. 'I went to Sandy Tech.' They look shocked and there is a silence before his dad speaks.

'You mean you didn't even go to a high school? You haven't even matriculated?'

'What do you need a high school for if you are doing art?' I say. 'I got into the Victorian College of the Arts without it.'

‘Are you going to get married at St John’s in Kew?’ his mother says, tactfully changing the subject.

‘The Church of the Open Door,’ we tell her.

‘Except I really wanted to be married at Hampton Baptist Church,’ I add. ‘But Pastor Greenslade won’t let us.’

‘Baptist,’ repeats Rick’s father. ‘Baptists are a sect!’

I cannot begin to describe the shock I feel. Here is an Anglican, a pretend Christian who doesn’t even begin to understand the need to repent of his sins and be born again. He not only drinks whisky before dinner, but a different wine with every course. He has never been baptised according to the institution of Christ and the practice of the apostles; he has never taken the word of the Lord to the unsaved and *he* dismisses Baptists as a sect! Baptists are the only truly faithful; we spring from the loins of those who were persecuted for remaining true. Even in the face of death at the hands of Luther and his followers, who threw pregnant Anabaptist women into rivers to drown, the Baptists remained true to God’s word.

‘Bill is an elder at St Andrew’s,’ says Rick’s mother proudly.

An elder! That’s the same as a deacon in the Baptist Church, but a deacon is someone who has proved his ability to help in the spiritual leadership of the church. To be elected a deacon is to be recognised for your gifts and qualities. It means you are respected, but most of all it means you are committed to the work of the Lord.

Rick’s father only goes to church at Easter and Christmas. How can he possibly be elected an elder? It only goes to show how far the Church of England has fallen!

His parents ask if we can’t be engaged longer. We say that we don’t see the point; they shake their heads and say they will arrange to meet my parents. We can’t explain to them that God has told us to get married and that we are following his will. Their heads continue to shake, but no words will come out of their open mouths.

23

She is still not talking to me and I thought they would be happy I was getting married.

They know that we are vegetarian so they give us a set of steak knives for an engagement present.

My mother is on the phone to Rick's mother. 'Oh, yes,' she is saying, in a la-de-dah voice I have never heard before. 'Oh, yes, we will get our personal tailor to sew Karyn's bridesmaid dress. Oh, no. They want to have the reception here. No, she wanted a picnic, but I told them that that wasn't suitable for a wedding. Oh, yes, I will have the house staff organise everything. Yes, yes. Morning tea it will be. Well, that would be lovely if you'd like to bring some sandwiches. No, the caterer is making the wedding cake. Yes, I'll talk to you soon. Lovely to speak to you and, yes, we look forward to Sunday. Bye now.'

'Mum! We don't have a personal tailor or house cleaners and *you're* making the wedding cake!' I say as she hangs up.

'Yes, we do. Rose is going to make Karyn's dress.'

'Mum, she's a family friend — not a servant!'

'Rick's mother is having Cassie's dress made professionally. Rose could be a professional seamstress if she wanted,' says my mother sharply.

'Well, Rick's mum can afford it.'

We head over to Rose's house to fit my mother's wedding dress on me. I don't want to wear it because it seems like bad luck. After all, the dress hasn't done her marriage much good. But my mother got so upset when I told her, I had to relent. The dress has hoops in it, a high cut and an unattractive neck. It looks stiff, uncomfortable and *so* fifties.

'Will Rose be able to cut out the bits I don't like?' I ask on the way over in Mum's Hillman. It is night and the stars seem so far away.

'Of course! She's a wiz when it comes to sewing,' my mother says. 'She's a very lucky woman, Rose; she has the most wonderful husband. What I wouldn't give for a husband like Skipper. He's a lovely, lovely man.'

'Mum, have you got a crush on this man?'

'Don't be silly! Grown women don't get crushes. But you know I only married your father because I thought I couldn't get anyone better — not after what I'd done when I was thirteen. No one else would have wanted me, but your father said he didn't mind. Your grandparents were so upset when I said I was going to marry him. They could see what he was like. They could see his vile temper and they warned me, but I wouldn't listen. You always pay when you don't obey the Lord and by not respecting my parents' authority I was disobeying the Lord. Your sins always find you out.'

I don't say anything because I don't know what to say, but I feel sorry for my mother and her life of punishment.

Rose cuts up the dress, gets rid of the hoops and when I put it on it makes me feel like a Disney princess. If I could sing I would sing, 'Someday My Prince Will Come'.

Rick told me that my Uncle William called him up and said, 'Look, Rick, I know I don't know you very well, but I was praying to the Lord and I just felt I should say something.

Your father is probably the sort of man to mention this, but you and Robbi need to organise some contraception before you are married.'

So here we are, sitting in a cold corridor at the Moorabbin community centre. It is all so sterile and I am nervous. When a lady finally calls our names, we walk into her equally wintry, sanitised office. Her smile is supposed to put us at ease but I am holding back the tears.

'Now, what can I do for you?' she asks nonchalantly.

'We are getting married in two weeks,' says Rick.

She waits. Silence. We look at her, she looks at us. The look goes back and forth until finally she says, 'And what sort of contraception are you using?'

'We're not getting married for two weeks,' I say.

'Yes, I heard that. But I assume that you've come to a family planning clinic because you want to change your contraception.'

'No, we're not using any,' I say.

'That's very dangerous. What have you used in the past?'

'None — we haven't used any,' I say, finding this all very difficult and embarrassing.

'Oh — you think you might be pregnant?'

'No, I'm not pregnant. We're not getting married for two weeks,' I say yet again.

She sighs and turns to look at something on her desk. 'What are you here for then?'

'Because my uncle thinks we should talk to someone about contraception before we get married.'

Finally it has clicked and she tries with all her social worker training not to show how shocked she is. 'Your uncle suggested you come here?'

'Yes, but I told him that we are going to trust the Lord for our contraception,' says Rick.

'We'll just accept whatever the Lord sends along,' I add and I smile at her.

She clears her throat, gives herself a shake, thinks for a moment and says, 'Are you at school? Working? What do you both do?'

'We're both at school,' says Rick. 'I'm starting my fourth year of veterinary studies at Melbourne University and Robbi is starting her second year of painting at the Victorian College of the Arts.'

'So you both study full time?'

'Yes.'

'And you both want to finish your studies?'

'Yes.'

'Well, it seems to me that if you don't use some kind of contraception the Lord is certainly going to send along some little bundles that will make it very difficult for you to do so.' She gives us two fistfuls of condoms and a prescription for the pill.

Mato is thrilled I am getting married, but she is worried that Rick doesn't wash his hair often enough and that he might not let me come to visit her. When I tell her that it is up to me who I visit, she is shocked.

'Does Rick approve of that attitude?' she asks. 'After all, he is your spiritual head now.'

She is also horrified that I haven't got a trousseau. 'Well, you must have a glory box, popsy!' she says as she hands me my bolognaise sauce on toast.

I shake my head and sip my tea. My grandmothers have got so much stuff from saving the Lipton's labels. One year Grandma Lyne had enough to get me a school bag, and that was great because I was embarrassed about my old leather satchel and the one that Lipton's sent was navy vinyl. Now, of course, I would give anything to have the old leather one. It would match fantastically with the old thirties dresses that I scour op shops for and my flat school sandals that I wear over bright red or green tights.

'I knew you'd start dressing like one of those artists!' my mother says. 'I'm so disappointed in you, Robbi.'

But Mato never comments on what I am wearing. She only ever smiles, wraps me in her arms and says how lovely it is to see me.

'So, no glory box,' says Mato. 'Your mother hasn't prepared you very well for marriage.'

'She hasn't really talked to me since I moved out of home,' I tell her.

'What do you mean she hasn't talked to you? She has to say *something*.'

'No, she just ignores me. If I say, "Hi, Mum", she is silent. "Can I have a drink?" Silent. "Can I choose my wedding cake?" And then she barks, "You'll have whatever cake I can get made in such a short time young lady!" Then it's back to not talking again.'

'All right then,' says Mato. 'After we've had lunch, we're off to get you a trousseau, popsy.'

'What *is* a trousseau anyway?'

'A trousseau, my dear, is the things you need for your wedding night. A new bride must have new pyjamas and underwear and a new dress to go away in. You certainly won't get them after you're married! A woman knows that once she is married her family comes first and she has to go without. You'll need every spare cent to provide food and clothing for your husband and family, so you must at least have new things to start married life with. Besides, wouldn't you be embarrassed on the wedding night if you didn't have new pyjamas?'

'But I don't wear any.'

Mato coughs. 'You don't wear pyjamas?'

'Nah, don't like em. They get all twisted up.'

'Well, you'll need some nice lacy ones for your wedding night. You can't prance around naked in front of your husband.' She looks at me strangely. 'Your mother has spoken to you about the wedding night, hasn't she?'

I shake my head and go on enjoying my lunch.

'Well, what are you going to do?' she asks.

'About what?'

'About your wedding night, popsy.'

'What do you mean?' I've suddenly twigged where she is going.

'I mean, what are you going to do about what men like — what they expect on the wedding night?' She is trying so hard not to look embarrassed.

I stare at Mato blankly. I want to hear what she will say next and I am enjoying her discomfort.

'What are you going to do about performing your wifely duty?' She leans over the table towards me. 'What are you going to do to avoid it?'

'Nothing,' I say slowly. 'I expect to enjoy it.'

'Ooohh!' says Mato. 'That certainly wasn't done in my day.'

'What do you mean?'

'Your grandfather never saw me naked,' she says. 'Not once in our entire married life.'

'But he was your husband.'

'I would have been too embarrassed.'

'How did you manage it? How did you handle sharing a bedroom and not letting him see you naked?'

'I made sure I changed when he was out of the bedroom, or I changed in the dark. And he never saw me with make-up on. I was born without it and I never once wore it. If a man is to marry you he should know how the good Lord made you. Make-up is an insult to the Lord's handiwork. You are telling the Lord you don't think his creation is good enough.'

'But you had three children,' I say. 'So he must have seen you naked sometimes!'

Mato sighs. 'I'm sure that the good Lord had only one intention and that was procreation. Your grandfather and I only procreated. That was the only time I had to perform my duty. Three times. Three children.'

'Oh,' I say, 'I think Rick is going to expect a little more than that.'

'God has made sex for the purpose of procreation only,' says Mato firmly. 'A good Christian man will understand that.'

We clean up the dishes and hit Myer where Mato lets me choose a dress, a bra, some panties and a nightie. She also wants me to buy a girdle and is shocked when I tell her that I don't wear one.

'But how do you hold all your bits in?' she says.

Altogether our purchases come to over a hundred dollars. We go to a coffee shop for Devonshire tea. I leave the bag containing my trousseau on the floor and it gets stolen. I am distraught and feel guilty that I've been so careless.

'It's only money,' says Mato. 'Don't fret. The Lord always provides for our needs. We will pray for the person who stole these things because they obviously need the Lord in their heart and we'll buy them again. What's done is done.'

So we go back to Myer and Mato buys them all again.

'I understand now,' says Rick's mother running up to the car. We are leaving Mont Albert Road after the do where the two families met. 'A friend of mine has a son who is a born again Christian and she explained it to me,' she says excitedly. 'You have to get married young so you can have sex.'

I've been nervous about what Rick's family would think of mine, but even if they didn't like them, his family would be too polite to let on. I did hear my brother Wayne boasting that he is an assistant stationmaster now. Rick's uncle nodded politely and pretended to be impressed, but he has his own insurance company. It's huge.

On the morning of the wedding my mother wakes me up.

'Mum, it's only six in the morning and the wedding isn't till ten!' I groan and roll over.

She grabs my big toe and twists it. She has always used this technique. 'Say good morning, Jesus,' she says.

'It's six o'clock, Mum.'

'Yes, and you have a lot to do before ten, young lady. Make-up, hair. Now say good morning, Jesus.'

'I'm not wearing make-up. It's fake,' I grumble. 'And brushing my hair will take two seconds.'

'Robbi, you have to wear make-up on your wedding day. What will Rick think he has married? What will his family think of you?' she sighs.

She tries again, 'Say good morning, Jesus.'

I mumble, 'Good morning, Jesus', full of resentment at being made to say such a stupid thing but she won't let up till I do.

'What do you want for breakfast?' she asks.

'Sausages.' I love them and there probably isn't any real meat in them, so they could be considered vegetarian.

I have never once in my life been asked what I want for breakfast by anyone except Mato. This feels a bit like the Last Supper. I know that on the one hand my parents are proud of me for marrying Rick and they have been talking to me again since they saw the house Rick's parents live in. On the other hand, they resent me because they feel I am making a good marriage and will have something they have never achieved.

Rick's family have given us a refrigerator and a bed, mattress and some linen for our wedding.

My mother and father have given us a deep freeze to put the meat in that we are going to cut with the steak knives.

'But we're vegetarian,' said Rick.

Holy cow! Obviously his parents haven't taught him to accept every gift as a great treasure, even if you hate it. There's trouble coming. It's rolling towards me at a hundred miles an hour and I don't know how to stop it.

'If you don't feed your children meat, they will be malnourished and die!' my mother said. 'And then you will go to jail for manslaughter. Do you want to be responsible for killing your own children?'

'Mum, first of all we're not having children,' I said just to shock her. 'And second, they will hardly put us in jail for feeding our children nice healthy vegetables. Lots of people are vegetarian and their children don't die,' I said. 'We can fill the freezer with vegetables.'

'Can't you take the deep freeze back? We won't use it,' said Rick.

And the trouble hit.

'It's all right, Ena!' growled my father. 'If they don't want our gift; if they're too bloody good to accept our gifts; if they don't realise that we're only trying to help! Last bloody frickin gift we'll give them! Ungrateful little sods!' he yelled. He slammed his coffee cup down on the table and stomped around the lounge room.

The freezer went back and nothing was bought to replace it.

I finally crawl out of bed, throw on a shirt and some jeans. I have woken up on the day of my wedding feeling miserable — and not just because of the huge pimple that has shown up on the middle of my chin. I sneak out the front door, leave the enticing smell of sausages behind and go for a walk. When I reach the park, I hide in the concrete play tunnel and pray.

'Dear Lord Jesus, I feel like I am losing my life and my closeness to you. After today I will be under the authority of my husband and I will no longer be free to be myself and make my own decisions. My husband will stand between me and you, Lord.

'I have loved you, Lord Jesus, and I have loved being your disciple, but I so wish I had been born a boy.' And I cry.

I go back home and throw on my wedding dress and brush my hair.

‘I’ve bought you some pantyhose and high heels,’ says my mother tentatively holding a pair of white shoes towards me.

‘I’ve got jiffies and I don’t wear pantyhose unless they’re coloured tights,’ I say showing her my bare, unshaven legs.

‘You will put on a little make-up won’t you?’ she pleads. I look out the window and see that my father’s car is missing from the driveway.

‘Where’s Dad? I’m going to be late you realise,’ I say changing the subject away from my appearance.

‘Oh he just had to run your Grandma Lyne to the church. He’ll be back by ten,’ she says.

But my father doesn’t come back until half-past ten so by the time I get to the church I am nearly an hour late. I take his arm and walk up the aisle to one of my favourite hymns.

Now thank we all our God,
With hearts and hands and voices,
Who wondrous things hath done,
In whom His world rejoices,
Who, from our mother’s arms,
Hath blessed us on our way,
With countless gifts of love,
And still is ours today.
Oh praise him! Oh praise him! Alleluia, alleluia,
alleluia!

I reach the end of the aisle where Rick is waiting for me and Pastor Greenslade mutters, ‘You’re late!’ Then he glares at me and I know that we hate each other.

I hate him for making me promise to obey and for saying I am full of evil spirits.

I wonder if Rick knows he is marrying a vessel that Pastor Greenslade says is just about controlled by the devil. Pastor Greenslade has hated me since the day I did not shout that death can be overcome. He hates me because I am a rebellious woman.

He uses our wedding to preach that it is a woman's duty to obey her husband and then he talks about how sinful divorce is. He says that anyone who is married for a second time must return to their first husband or wife, because otherwise they are living in adultery with a man or woman who is not their true spouse in God's eyes. We have a lot of wedding guests who are married for the second time.

Then Pastor Greenslade asks me if I will obey Rick. I cannot bring myself to do it, but I don't want to have an argument with him in the middle of my wedding. So I cross my fingers behind my back as I repeat his words on 1 December 1979.

Part Two

Faith

24

I step through the church door out into the warm and pure morning sunshine and the smiling faces of family and friends, with their cameras clicking wildly like uncontrollable twitches. I am now married and tonight I will have sex for the first time. I will no longer be a virgin. I will be a mature woman. And I will never set foot in The Church of the Open Door again!

All the guests squash into my parents' backyard with the cut-off trimaran and eat sandwiches and cake. Then Rick and I hop into Hezekiah and head off to start our married life. As we head for Rosebud, people beep at us all the way because 'Just married' has been scrawled across the bonnet of the car and there is a constant rattle coming from the back.

'I'll just stop and check,' says Rick. This is probably the fourth time he has tried to find the rattle, but hasn't been able to. He walks right around the car but he can't find a thing. There are no tin cans tied to the bumper, so we keep going. People in other cars point and laugh at us and we rattle all the way.

We arrive at the little timber cottage that has been lent to us by Mum's friends Rose and Skipper, and I get the luggage out of the boot. Rick scurries off to one of the rooms and shuts the door behind him; he is praying.

The old man weeding his garden next door looks up at me and says, 'Someone 'elpful's put stones in yer 'ubcaps.'

'Thanks,' I call back.

Rick has been praying constantly and I have busied myself unpacking our food, clothes and blankets while I wait for him, but I can still hear the murmur of his prayers through the wall. This is not how I imagined my honeymoon. I imagined being swept off my feet, then the two of us would sit on a veranda together, sip tea and declare our undying love. I imagined we might chat for hours about the children and grandchildren we would share. We would spend hours in passionate lovemaking. I feel so alone and I throw myself on the double bed that has waited patiently for us and I cry. I want to go back to Mato, but marriage is forever, until death do us part. If I go home to Mato and my mother, they will only say that even if I haven't lain in it yet, it is my bed and I'd better make it!

I am married. In the eyes of the Lord.

Finally, Rick stands in the doorway, walks over to the bed and kisses me. I have just turned twenty, I have never had sex and I am desperate to try it. We pray that the Lord will bless our union and then we both start taking our clothes off but we are both inexperienced and before I have time to think of the Lord, as a good Christian woman does when she has sex, it is over and it hurt.

All night I wait for morning and at first light I sneak out of bed to wash my face and brush my hair. I remember my mother's words and I don't want Rick to see the repulsive woman he has married. I crawl back in beside him and lie still, so as not to muck up my hair, and I wait for him to wake up.

I make him pancakes for breakfast, using the recipe my mother taught me, and Rick says, 'I like my mother's pancakes better. Hers are thick and fluffy.' Mine are thin and funny shaped. I don't admit to him that I was aiming for a heart. I have failed at breakfast, I decide to shower away my disappointment and I strip off and pull the shower curtain aside.

Then I scream. In the shower is a huntsman spider the size of Tasmania.

Rick comes running from the lounge room where he is again praying. 'What's wrong? What's wrong?'

'There is a spider,' I blubber. 'It's huge and evil.'

'Is that all? It's only an insect, Robbi. It can't be evil.'

'It's not only evil, it's wearing dark glasses and has friends! It's a member of the spider mafia!' I say as I back my naked wet body down the hallway away from it.

'I think I should leave the spider there,' he says, 'so you can learn to deal with your phobias.'

'I'm quite at home with my phobias. You've got to get rid of it!' I screech from the safety of the hallway.

'It's at home in the bathroom.'

'I am not having another shower until it's gone! It's me or it!'

'Well, you move it,' he says.

'You're the man. You do it!'

And I win. But it is just the start of our battle.

We drive from Rosebud to Woodend to finish our holiday, because my mother arranged the cottage for us with Rose and Skipper who own it.

'How long do you want your honeymoon to be?' she asked.

'Three weeks.'

'Three weeks? You don't want a three-week honeymoon!' she exclaimed.

'Yes, we do,' I said.

'Heavens, no! You'll be sick to death of each other after three weeks,' she said. 'That's no way to start a marriage, young lady!'

'Mum, we're spending the rest of our lives together! Can you book it for three weeks?'

She went back to her sewing and didn't say another word until we were leaving for the honeymoon. 'Now, I booked you in for two weeks. That's what you wanted, isn't it?'

So now we are on our way to Woodend for the third week, making sure we don't stop at any lights because the car might stall. My head is pounding and by the time we arrive it feels like it is going to explode. It is the pill so I stop taking it and even though someone says to us that people who use the rhythm method are called parents, that's what we use — along with condoms. Somehow condoms seem seedy when you are respectably married.

It is Christmas, we have finished our honeymoon and my parents give us an electric knife to cut the roast from the freezer that we haven't got and which we are going to eat with the steak knives. Rick just shook his head.

Mato gave him some shampoo.

We are with his parents in Barwon Heads where they book the tennis court and play for two weeks every year. I can't even get the ball over the net, but from Rick's parents I do learn what Stilton cheese is and pâté and smoked trout. I also learn about olives and avocados and I drink wine for the first time. I make sure to have only one glass, because more than that and I feel a bit silly. I notice how kind Rick's mum is to her children and I want to be like that when I am a mother.

The dishes have been cleared from the table, two at a time because stacking, I find out quickly, is frowned upon. Rick's father is cutting himself a slice of Stilton cheese and suddenly loses his temper. It comes from nowhere, but I guess it must have been brewing to explode like that. 'What is she doing here? This is meant to be a family holiday! Why is she here? She's not family!' he says.

I look at the other people round the table. Rick, his mother, his two brothers and his sister.

His father can only mean me. I am feeling uncomfortable and scan everyone's faces to see what they will do. I look to Rick, expecting him to get angry and remind his father that I am his wife. But he just sits there as if he has no connection to me at all. Everyone sits there dumbfounded and finally Rick's mother says in a small, croaky voice, 'Bill!'

I am going to cry and I don't want them to see me so I run off to a corner of our bedroom. His sister Cassie comes in and puts her arm around my shoulder, but I say to her, 'Only non family in here,' so she goes away hurt and doesn't talk to me again.

Rick doesn't say anything to me or to his father and I feel betrayed. I really wanted his family to like me. I want to leave and not be where I am not welcome, but I don't know what will happen if I do. Perhaps they will hate me even more than they do now.

The day finally comes for Rick and me to leave Barwon Heads. I no longer have to play bad tennis or be careful what I say or balance peas on my fork. Leaving makes me feel like I am really beginning my married life. We head to Werribee to live. We have sold Hezekiah for fifty dollars, which breaks my heart, and I tell myself that one day I will have another old car, and we buy a VW Beetle with money from Rick's parents. On the way to Werribee, we stop at the Lort Smith Animal Hospital to pick up our dog, which we are rescuing from the lost dogs' home. Dishevelled and scruffy, he looks exactly like a lost dog should. We go to Melbourne Uni so Rick can enrol and I sit outside on the grass in the early summer morning to wait for him with our new dog.

I have called the dog Caleb, which is Arabic for 'dog', and I hold him close and hope he will love me. With the sun shining, it is warm but not hot — one of those moments when you imagine that nothing could ever go wrong in your life again. I look around the courtyard at the arches that seem ancient and I see these advertising people — sunglasses everywhere, power suits, models in gallons of make-up, lights, cameras and loads of self-importance — filming on the grass. I feel relieved because, close up, the models have in fact very bad skin and don't look superior at all. One model has walked the same patch of grass over and over. She just can't get it right, whatever 'it' is. A man comes up to me, lowers his sunnies down over his nose and says, 'Can we use your amazing dog in our commercial?'

'Are you sure?' I stammer.

And off goes my beautiful but disgustingly dirty new dog. Only one hour out of dog prison and already he is a star. This has to be a good start to our marriage.

We have moved to Werribee so Rick can be close to his school and I travel to Melbourne for art school. At art school I stop praying in tongues. I have had enough of Pentecostalism to last me a lifetime, but I tell my lecturers, Libby Gower and Janine Burke, that I am married now and that I have to be submissive to my husband in all things. They say that I have a promising career in art and they are worried that I might get pregnant.

'It's okay,' I assure them. 'We trust the Lord with our contraception. If I get pregnant it will be God's will.' They give each other strange looks and next morning call me into their office.

'We're worried about you,' says Libby.

'Read this,' Janine says. I feel intimidated by her, because she is so forthright. She thrusts a book into my hands — it is about the oppression of women through the English language.

'Tell us what you think when you have read it,' says Libby.

I read it on the train to and from school and I have never read anything like this in my life. I didn't even know people thought these things, let alone wrote them in books. Women have been written out of history and pretty much out of the Bible and the knot of anger inside me grows bigger and almost overwhelms me. I think, yes! Why is it that we don't know the name of Noah's wife? After all, she was on the ark too. She probably did all the cooking, cleaning and washing and she doesn't even get a name. And why was the father in the Old Testament praised for being willing to throw out his virgin daughters to be pack-raped so that he could protect his two male guests?

I try to tell Rick about the book, but he is not interested.

We are going to Werribee Baptist. Rick wants to go to an Anglican church and looks at me darkly when I say that I have to go to a church that is Christian, not one that has caved in to the demands of society and state.

At church the pastor preaches about a virtuous woman in the book of Proverbs.

'A virtuous wife,' it says, 'has a price far above rubies' and she does all these things:

She is trustworthy and maintains her husband's good character.

She does her husband good all the days of her life.

She finds wool and flax and works with her hands.

She buys food from afar.

She gets up while it is still night, while everyone else is sleeping.

She buys land and plants an orchard and a vineyard.

She has good strong arms and loins.

She sells merchandise.

She weaves.

She gives to the poor and the needy.

She is not afraid of the cold because she has made warm clothes for everyone.

She makes tapestries and curtains.

She makes fine linen and sells it and delivers it to merchants.

She only speaks words of wisdom and kindness.

After reading my book, I think she sounds like a slave. Then the pastor jumps to the New Testament and talks about Mary and Martha. Martha does all the things Proverbs says you should do. She cooks and cleans and yet Jesus rebukes her and says she should be like Mary: willing to just sit at his feet, listen and pray.

That's all very well, I think, but I bet Jesus enjoyed that meal Martha made for him, and I bet none of the apostles offered to cook for her so she could take a break and listen to him. I start to feel quite angry because as I listen to the pastor it becomes obvious that he expects women to do all the stuff in Proverbs and pray and worship the Lord as well.

I am being suffocated. I don't like being married after all and the experience hasn't made me like being a girl any better. I wonder if I can ever find a way to be a good Christian woman and have the things that I want. I want to feel equal to men. I want to believe that I am created in God's image too and I still want to be a minister of the Lord, to spread God's word to the needy.

I hold that little book close to my heart on the train to Melbourne and I feel its questioning, its demands and its angry words about the treatment of women through the ages and it gives me hope. But it is a hope that is at cross purposes to my faith and I don't think I can find a way to have both. So when Libby and Janine say 'Well?' with such hope in their eyes, I say only, 'Yes, it was interesting.' And I leave their office quickly and go back to my studio space. They don't know, however, that they have planted a seed.

25

Grandma Lyne visits me at art school and I know when she arrives because I recognise her clomping up the stairwell. She arrives in her floral frock with a brown vinyl handbag and she wanders around and looks at all the paintings. She is fearless. She walks up to Steig Pierson, who is painting a massive canvas, all in shades of black. It is so big he has to stand on a ladder to reach the top.

'It's very nice,' says Grandma Lyne, 'but don't you realise it won't fit in anyone's lounge? In fact, now I really look at it, I don't think you're going to find a lounge suite that will match that painting.' She fishes in her handbag and brings out a handful of cuttings, 'Here,' she says, 'I bought these fer Robbi. I thought she might like to copy some of them instead of those paintings she does, but now I can see that you could use a few too.'

And she hands Steig pictures of lakes and gardens and mountains with perfectly formed clouds hanging above them that she has cut out of *New Idea*.

'Come on, Gran,' I say, taking her arm.

Steig smiles at me and I smile back.

Gran and I head off to Coles cafeteria, which has been my favourite place to eat with my grandmothers since I was little. I always choose exactly the same things: fish and chips with a little white plastic cup of vinegar and pikelets with jam and cream. We queue up to choose our food, carry our trays and plonk ourselves down in the springy leather chairs that they've had there since I was little.

'So you're married,' Gran says as if she is trying to let it sink in.

'Yes, Gran. Yes, I am.'

'Ahhh, yes. Well, I remember when your mother and father got married, of course. Wasn't too long before you came along.'

I pour my little white plastic cup of vinegar over my fish and chips.

Gran goes on, 'Yer mother left you with me when you were little while they went on a holiday. Then when she came back to get yer, yer wouldn't go to her, of course. Yer hadn't seen her fer two weeks. Yer were only little and yer mother said, "Well, if she wants yer, yer might as well keep her." And I would have. Do you know that yer father only has one testicle?'

'Yes, I did know that. He lost one in a bicycle accident, didn't he?'

'Yeees,' she drawls, thinking things over. 'Only one. I always thought he must have the testicle fer girl children because you came along first. But then yer brother came along and, well now, I've never known what ter think about that — or yer mother, fer that matter.'

'I don't think they get a boy testicle and a girl testicle, Gran. I think the sex is in the sperm.'

'Well,' she says dismissively, 'I daresay you know more about these things than me. I organised fer yer mother and father to have single beds after that. I rang up Myers and traded in their double bed fer two singles. I thought it might be best after yer brother came along, but yer mother didn't appreciate it one little bit. Do yer know yer grandfather left me after the war? Came back from the war to another woman. I always told people I was a widder, but I wasn't really. I was deserted. Did yer know that?'

'Yes, I did, Gran. But it doesn't really matter now, does it?'

She always talks like this, rolling from one subject to another, and all I have to do is say, 'Yes, Gran' occasionally. I don't think many people listen to her, so she tries to get in as much as she can as quickly as possible.

'I had to go out an earn a livin then,' she continues. 'I looked after two spoilt brats fer a rich lady. Had to leave my own two at home with my mother, yer Grandma Lucy, and then I took in sewin on my treadle. I know yer father used to take yer to see yer grandfather and that woman once in a while. They had two girls, didn't they? I think I saw em once. Nice-looking girls. Looked like yer Aunt Claire.'

'We only saw them once or twice,' I say, although it was a bit more often than that. 'He just sat in a chair, yelled at us kids, and only got up to wallop his daughters.'

'After he left,' Gran says, happy to hear how awful her ex-husband was, 'I thought about changing back to my maiden name but, well, it wasn't done in my day. Still, I think it's all right that you kept yours. And at least yer not in a mixed marriage,' she says, changing tack. 'Yer don't want to be in a mixed marriage. You'd have ter bring yer children up Catholic.'

'You better eat up, Gran,' I say. 'I've got to get back to the school.'

After we've had lunch I walk Gran back to Flinders Street Station. I put my arm through hers to steady her, just as I do with Mato. We make our way along the narrow lanes and she says, 'Yer know I was never friends with yer t'other grandmother. She was a bit hoity-toity, and everyone else liked her and wanted ter be her friend. I remember she had the Baptist women's meeting at her house. Well, it was the manse, of course, and everyone came and bought plates. So I offered to have the next meeting at my house. I cooked cakes and biscuits and date loaf and not a soul turned up — 'cepting her, but she *had* to come, being the minister's wife an all. Maybe it was because I didn't have a husband. I don't know, really.'

I suddenly realise that I have never thought of my Grandma Lyne as much more than my father's mother. I really don't know her that well. I have never known about her pain and suddenly I see her differently. My heart breaks for her because it is so awful to be rejected by people you want as friends. Sometimes I think we never leave the schoolyard. How can I tell her that she is different, eccentric, wonderful? She walks seven miles in her seventies to visit her son, tells promising young male artists that their works of art are beyond the average person's lounge room. How could she have possibly been accepted by conservative housewives in the thirties who abhorred a woman alone? She went out to work to support her family. She was a single mother when they didn't have single parent pensions.

'You were ahead of your time, Gran,' I say, squeezing her arm.

'Oh, I don't think so. Trains can leave early, you know,' she says. 'I daresay I better git a move on if I'm to catch that train directly.' She gets the train for Sunshine and I go back to school.

The pastor comes up to Rick and me after church on Sunday morning.

He shakes Rick's hand and nods at him in that how-yer-doin-mate way that men do.

'We have a Bible study on Saturday mornings, at seven. You might like to come,' he says, leaning over us because he is very tall and Rick is rather short.

It is probably just Rick who is being invited, but because he doesn't make it clear, I assume he means me too.

'Now, Robbi,' he goes on, 'we thought you might like to help in the Sunday school.'

'But I don't know anything about children,' I say.

He chuckles. 'Well, you better get used to them sooner or later. Oh, and if you could bring a plate on Sunday nights towards supper, I am sure the other ladies would appreciate it.'

When I turn up to Bible study with Rick, the pastor says, 'Well, this is unusual. Not many men bring their wives to Bible study.'

And I say, 'He didn't bring me. I brought him.' All the men chuckle as if what I have said is cute.

Then there is an uncomfortable silence until the pastor shuffles in his chair and says, 'Mmmmm, well, we'd better get on with it.' As if he has only just realised that I am not going to get up and make them all cups of tea.

Rick and I fight all the way home from Bible study. We hate being married and we hate being married to each other, but we both know that it is forever. Every time we fight, I go and find a dark corner, I crawl into a small ball and shake and cry, just as I did when my father yelled. Poor Rick wonders what he has married.

We are really poor because we are living on a government allowance, which we are now eligible for because we are married students. It is seventy-five dollars a week for a married couple. We eat vegetables out of our garden and buy powdered milk. We only buy milk in a carton if we are having visitors, because they all screw up their faces when we say we only have powdered milk. We don't have a television or a stereo. No television is great, but I miss the music. We buy flour and make our own bread, which you have to eat the day you make it or it is pretty hard going.

I don't mind being poor because I am used to it and I know it is only temporary. It's what you expect if you're a student or newly married, and gives you something to tell your children about in later years. But my Aunt Tonia gives us money and boxes of groceries when the Lord tells her to.

'You don't need to,' I tell her.

'Of course I do,' she says. 'That is what families do for each other. Besides, your grandparents gave me boxes of food and money when I was first married, so now I am doing it for you.'

She's terrific my aunt. I wish she was my mother.

Now Rick and I fight about housework.

'It's not fair that I have to go to school, do all the travelling and do housework on top of it!' I yell at him.

'Do you have hours and hours of homework to do?' he asks. 'No! Well, I do! I have to study, study, study if I'm going to get honours. Besides, you're only doing an art course. I'm doing vet science. It's my work that will pay the bills, Robbi. I don't really see what your problem is anyway. My mother always got the housework done and she managed to play tennis. I would go to school in the morning and when I came home in the afternoon my room would have been tidied and my bed made.'

'Rick, your mother has people come in to do everything,' I say, totally frustrated with him, regardless of whether my feelings are fair or not. 'She has an ironing lady, a gardener, a cleaner, someone to maintain the pool.'

He stares at me.

I know I have lost, so I stomp off. But at least I have had the last word. He goes back to his books that are the size and weight of encyclopaedias and surround him in geometrical mountains. I take the dog as an ally, do the housework and finally crawl into bed with a book.

He studies until midnight and at midnight he comes to the bedroom door and says, 'Are we going to have sex?'

I just look at him. I don't know what to say. I don't want

to have sex like this. I imagined it would always be romantic, spiritual even — never perfunctory.

'It's just that if we're not going to have sex, I'll keep studying,' he says.

'It will get better,' says an older Christian friend. 'When my husband and I first married we fought non-stop for the first three months. Then everything settled down.'

So I organise a celebration to mark our three-month anniversary and the end of our fighting. We are going to Tasmania in the term break. It is really cheap because we are students. We will hitchhike our way around and camp.

My Calvinist uncle picks us up at Launceston airport and we throw our bags in the boot of his station wagon. My cousin Carey is in the front seat and his younger brother Riley is in the back with us. They are all in their farm clobber: flannelette shirts, Yakka pants and gumboots. We clamber in beside Riley.

'Hi, Riley,' I say. 'What have you been doing today?'

'Studying the five states of human deprivation,' he says. 'State one, the total depravity of man. We are born into sin; for by the disobedience of Adam who was tempted by Eve are we all made sinners. State two: the wickedness of Eve —'

'So how are you, Carey?' I say quickly.

Our bags are dumped in the guest room and my aunt has made us hot steaming cups of tea.

'So what are you planning to do when you've finished studying?' asks my uncle as we sit around the table in their large farmhouse kitchen.

'I'm very interested in large animal practice,' says Rick. 'Breeding, disease control.'

My uncle, being a dairy farmer, is impressed and asks Rick more questions. I am starting to feel ignored. Whenever we are with Rick's family they are only interested in Rick and when we are with my family they are only interested in Rick too. So eventually I pipe up.

'I'm at art school at the moment, but I want to go to theological school and become a minister.'

My aunt stops mixing a cake and a shadow falls over my uncle's face.

There is silence.

Finally my uncle says, 'You are a female. In our church, women are not permitted to speak to any man until they are spoken to. They submit to the authority of men at all times. The scripture says that a woman's voice must not be heard in church and if she has a question about spiritual matters, she can ask her husband when she gets home. 1 Corinthians 14:34–35 says, "Let your women keep silence in the churches, for it is not permitted unto them to speak; but they are commanded to be under obedience, as also saith the law. And if they will learn anything, let them ask their husbands at home: for it is shameful for a woman to speak in church."'

I look at my aunt and she is nodding.

I am confused. How can she feel this way? She is a woman. How can she not want equality?

'Your desire to become a minister is not of the Lord,' says my uncle and he dismisses me and continues his conversation with Rick. Rick says nothing and the gap between us grows wider.

Rick and my uncle get on really well and I am mighty pleased when my uncle drives us to Queenstown and we continue our journey.

Kind people pick us up as we hitchhike, though some of them think we are runaway teenagers because we look so young and clean-cut. It takes some doing to convince them we are married and over eighteen.

We land in St Helens at nine o'clock at night. We are hungry and tired but the pub has finished serving dinner. We hire a caravan and head off to find some food somewhere else. We walk into the only place open, a restaurant with crimson carpet, white tablecloths, low lights, gentle music and loads of ambience.

The owner comes over.

'We have ten dollars,' says Rick. 'Do you have an entrée under ten dollars that we can share?'

The owner sighs; he shows us to some seats and says grumpily, 'I'll bring you some soup.'

Rick and I take in our lovely surroundings and soon the owner places the soup in front of us. We bow our heads and say grace while the owner stands there gaping.

'What are you doing?' he asks, as if he doesn't know.

'We were giving thanks to God for the food,' explains Rick.

'Look, I'll give you both a three-course meal,' he says. 'On the house. Choose whatever you want.'

I scan the menu, looking for something that is not too expensive, and settle on Chicken Provençal. Rick chooses rabbit in beer. It is the best food I have had yet and as it nourishes our bodies I feel it feeding my soul too. Maybe this is a sign that things are going to improve for us.

We get up to leave and to thank the owner, but he says, 'No, no, no. Sit down. I'll bring you some coffee.'

'Umm, can I have tea? I can't drink coffee,' I say apologetically.

And we are brought dessert and coffee and tea, with after-dinner mints.

Rick and I look at each other and smile. We could never afford a meal like this in a restaurant and here we are getting all this for only ten dollars. All because we said grace. We thank the Lord for his graciousness and the restaurant owner for his generosity. But we still fight the whole way round Tasmania.

When we arrive home we collapse into bed, exhausted from our trip and all the arguments. I am enjoying that morning sleep and the snug warmth of the doona tucked around me when my dozing is interrupted sharply by tap, tap, tap on our garden path. And then *rap*, *rap*, *rap* on our bedroom window.

'Who on earth is that?' Rick says, rolling over. 'It's only six-thirty! Who on earth could be coming here this early?'

As soon as he says that, I know who it is. It's my gran! I leap out of bed, throw on my silk dressing gown and open the door to Grandma Lyne. I notice she plans to stay awhile. She has an overnight bag and I am thrilled. Even though she isn't my favourite grandmother I still love her very much.

'Gran, Gran,' I say. 'It's so early! How did you get here?'

'Well, I took public transport as far as I could, and then I walked, didn't I. Walking's good fer yer. It keeps yer fit. So are yer going to make me a cuppa, or are yer going to keep me standin here?'

'No, no! Come in, Gran. Sit in the kitchen and I'll get Rick to light the wood stove. I'll make us a cup of Earl of Lipton's.'

'Just plain old Lipton's is plenty good enough fer me.'

'It is Lipton's, Gran; we just mix it with Twinings to make the Twinings go further. Rick, can you light the fire in the kitchen?' I call out on my way past our bedroom.

I settle Gran in a chair by the table and put the kettle on. She is folding up her white stick to put it in her handbag.

'I'm legally blind now, you know,' she says to me proudly.

'No, Gran, I didn't know that.'

'Oh, I am. You have to be legally blind to get the white stick and a blind pension. I had a dickens of a job getting it, but in the end I kept pestering and they had ter give it to me. My white stick is very useful, did you know that?'

'No, Gran.'

'Oh, yes. If I want to cross the road it's so easy, now that I've got my white stick. I just put it out and off I go across the road and everyone stops for me because I'm blind. I don't even have to stop and look and see if any traffic's coming anymore. Very useful, my white stick.' And she tucks it in her brown vinyl handbag.

I pour her a cup of tea.

'Only half full,' she says. 'Any more than that and I'll spill it because I can't see it — being blind, you know. More sugar than that, thank you. I like two good teaspoonfuls.'

Rick walks in looking very sleepy and I make him a cup of tea the way he likes it with lots of milk. The exact opposite to the way I like mine. He takes a gulp and starts to scrunch up paper for the fire.

'You need to put Epsom salts around those lettuces,' says Gran, looking out the kitchen window at our vegie garden. 'It will make them heart. You need to plant marigolds too; I can see you've got thrip.'

Rick and I look at each other; I can see he is thinking, 'I thought she was blind.' I just shrug and smile.

Rick starts muttering because he's got a splinter from the wood.

'Beg yer pardon,' says Gran. 'I didn't quite catch that. I can't hear too well these days. I'm quite deaf, yer know. I went to the doctor, yer know,' she says, turning to me and forgetting whatever Rick has been saying. 'I complained about my sight and my hearing and he said there's nothing they can do about it! Nothing at all! All that medical knowledge and they can't do anything about my ailing health! He said I've got Uldedge. "Mrs Dusty," he said, "you've just got to live with this. It's Uldedge. There is nothing we can do fer yer."'

'What did he say that you have?' I ask.

'Uldegde.'

'Rick, do you know anything about Uldedge? Do animals get it?'

He looks up from poking at the fire. 'Never heard of it,' he says and goes back to it.

I start making some Vegemite toast for Gran and me. I dab the Vegemite on in little pats just like Mato used to do for me when I was little and finally it dawns on me.

'Gran, he said you have old age!'

'Nope,' she says. 'He never said a word about my old age.'

Rick looks in the bread bin. 'Is this all the bread we've got?'

'Yeah, we need some more, don't we.'

'I'll just nick down the shop and get some, special treat.' He goes to find his wallet and I follow him up the hall to the bedroom and say quietly, 'You might want to get some chocolate for Gran while you're at the milk bar. She loves it.'

'Oooohh, oooo,' Gran calls out from the kitchen. 'If you're getting chocolate Rum 'n' Raisin is my favourite.'

26

I am so ill, I can't stop vomiting. I can't even keep icy poles down and it's February and so stifling hot! I just want to crawl into a dark space and hide. I've been to the doctor and he says I can't possibly be pregnant because my period was only a week ago.

But he's really excited because he thinks I might have caught brucellosis.

We have moved to a beautiful new house. It was the first convent in Werribee and it has a rambling veranda covered in banksia roses and big French doors. There's also a massive lounge room with wood panelling. I love this house and it only costs us forty-five dollars a week. We have sheep in the back half of the garden to keep down the grass and a massive vegie garden full of corn, zucchini and tomatoes.

My parents have moved to the country and Davie didn't want to go, so he has moved in with us. But I don't think he likes living with us very much. For a start, he misses his best friend, Wendy.

Rick has been working over the Christmas holidays at Werribee Park as a stockman with the cattle and I have driven over to pick him up in our Veedub, in my cut-off denim shorts. The other stockmen all whistle at me and it now looks like I have brucellosis which I would have caught from the cattle.

Six weeks on and I am still vomiting. I am sitting in the doctor's waiting room, staring at the brick walls and wondering whether I will ever be well again. Finally, the nurse arrives and I stand up. She shakes my hand.

'Congratulations! You're pregnant. Let's make an antenatal appointment for you.'

I am stunned. I feel numb.

'What day suits you best?' she asks and when I don't respond she adds, 'You're going to have a baby.'

'No, thanks,' I blurt out as I rush from the room. I can feel her staring after me; she thinks I am heading straight for an abortion clinic, but I'm going back to school. I am not pregnant. I can't be.

Trouble is, I keep vomiting all the time, I only want to eat donuts and in the end I have to admit that I am.

'Why don't you have an abortion?' says Virginia, a girl at art school, as she passes me on the steps. I stop dead in my tracks and I can't express my horror adequately. If I don't believe in divorce, then I certainly see abortion as nothing less than the cruel murder of a defenceless, innocent victim. But I don't say anything, because Virginia is already on her way down the stairs. I say a prayer for her that the Holy Spirit will convict her in her heart and the Lord will lead her to him and save her from her downward spiral into sin.

I realise, however, that I can't stay at school. It's useless. I am just spending all my time in the toilet throwing up anyway. So I go home and prepare for the baby.

I stand in the kitchen, gazing out the window, watering my herbs and imagine myself cuddling this perfect baby. I was told in Sunday school that our Lord Jesus never cried when he was a baby and I am sure mine won't either.

Suddenly Rick's mother's face is in the window. 'Cooeee!' She taps on the glass and startles me.

'Guess what? I'm pregnant,' I blurt out, startling her back. 'You're going to be a grandmother.'

'Where is Rick?' She looks alarmed.

'Studying,' I say.

She drops her bags on the kitchen table and as she rushes down the hall she calls out, 'Oh, Rick! Oh, Rick, darling!'

She gives us forty dollars a week when she finds out that, although I'm pregnant, we live on pumpkin from the garden and big bags of skim milk. With that I buy a few luxuries like dried apricots and real milk. The only other luxury we have is when Rick offers to neuter a friend's cat in exchange for dinner. One friend works at Werribee farm and he not only gives us dinner, but a piglet from the farm all ready for roasting. We are ethical vegetarians. That is, we don't eat meat because we believe if we stopped grazing animals and used the land for farming, there would be enough food for the world. But if someone gives us meat, if it is just a delicacy or used for celebration or if we are out to dinner and are served meat, we eat it. It is more important not to insult other people than it is to stick to your principles. We invite friends over to share the roast pork and have a party, but I can hardly eat any of it, I feel so ill.

I manage to get on the train with an ice-cream container in case I'm sick and rattle all the way to Melbourne so I can defer my studies. The teachers shake their heads as if I am a lost cause. But now I am home again the vomiting is bad.

'Do you want me to ring the doctor?' asks Rick.

'I don't know,' I moan. I am too sick to make decisions.

Rick rings the doctor. 'My wife is vomiting every half hour. She can't even keep water down.'

'It's normal. Don't worry about it!' barks the doctor. Even I can hear him while I lean against the wall clutching my ice-cream container like a safety blanket.

I lose heaps of weight until finally I am saved when the doctor gives me a prescription for Debendox. I down at least four a day and at last I can crawl out of bed, and I do that to bring back our sheep. They have followed my brother Davie to school.

I crawl out of bed to pick vegetables, but I cannot eat them, and I get out of bed to go to church, where at morning tea the women balance their tea cups on their laps and tell me horror stories of ghastly births, horrific childbirth pain that lasts for weeks, of women being practically sliced in two and appalling mistakes made by doctors that leave both baby and mother maimed for life. They tell me that women's bodies are destroyed and sometimes they need thousands of stitches to put them back together again and I am filled with terror. Then — worst of all — they tell me that they shave all your pubic hair off!

My mother never told me about these aspects of having a baby. She always made it sound so romantic. 'One day you will grow up and have a baby boy and I will be a grandmother. A little baby of your own.'

It doesn't seem so little, now that I think about one growing in me and about how it is going to get out!

Rick drives us home from church and I tell him, 'We are not having our baby in a hospital! No one is shaving me! And there is no way some scrawny disgusting baby is ever putting his lips on my breasts!'

After lunch I put my head in his study and say, 'We are going to the new birth centre at Queen Victoria Hospital. You have to come to classes.'

'As long as it doesn't interfere with my studies,' he says, momentarily lifting his head out of his books.

'This is important! You have to come or they won't let us have the baby there!'

But Rick is angry. Angry that I am pregnant. He is angry that my pregnancy is interfering with his studies, and that he has to stop studying to come to birthing classes. We are late to every class and then after we have fought all the way to Melbourne, he gets out of the car and stomps off to the class and I am so angry that these classes are not important to him that I run up and wallop him hard in the middle of his back.

He turns and looks at me. He is stunned. I don't think we will be late to the classes again.

Davie cannot take the fighting and my being sick, but most of all he wants some meat and is sick to death of vegies, so he moves to live with Mum and Dad in the country. The next thing I hear is that he and Dad are nearly killing each other. But I don't worry because I am pregnant and when you are pregnant it fills your every waking thought. I wonder what thoughts filled my brain before.

I am two weeks overdue. If the baby doesn't come this weekend I have to go to hospital and be induced. I try every housewives' tale I have heard.

I mix a large glass of orange juice with half a cup of castor oil and two tablespoons of bicarbonate of soda, pour it down my throat and instantly I want to spew. I rush to the bathroom but I don't vomit and the baby doesn't come. I do get terrible diarrhoea though.

I run a hot bath and sit in it for an hour, but all I get is wrinkly skin so I go for a ride on a friend's motorbike over bumpy back streets and dirt roads and I go for a long walk. I am so tired I fall soundly asleep until I wake up at midnight; I have a terrible urge to go to the toilet and suddenly a pain sweeps across my lower back and then another and another on top of it.

I call out to Rick, 'I think something is happening!'

'I'll just ring the birth centre and check,' he says. He talks to someone there and calls out to me, 'How long between contractions?'

'Nothing!' I yell back.

He comes into the bathroom where I am bent over the toilet vomiting.

'They say there must be time between contractions, probably about twenty minutes. They say that if you can't tell any time between the contractions, then they mustn't be very strong yet.'

At that comment I curse, 'Oh God, why wasn't I born a male?'

'But they think we should go in so they can check,' he says calmly.

We grab the bags I packed weeks ago and I hobble out to the car, clutching my belly with one hand and an ice-cream container with the other, but we always have to push-start the car to get it going. We can't call the RACV because we called them out so often that the RACV guy just started coming by every morning to start our car and now head office won't let him come anymore. So Rick pushes the car and I try to steer, grasping my stomach with one hand because of the contractions and holding the ice-cream container and the steering wheel with the other.

I yell and screw up my face just as he gives a big push and we end up in a ditch.

So I have to get out of the car and, despite my contractions, lean against it with all my might and help get it out of the ditch. Then we push-start it all over again. This time I try to concentrate harder on the steering and I don't close my eyes when I feel a contraction.

Finally we're on our way to have a baby, rumbling down the highway. I have a contraction, then I vomit and I call out, 'I don't want this baby! I never wanted this baby! I want to finish art school!'

Another contraction and more vomiting and I call out, 'I don't want this baby! I don't want it!' My body is betraying me by giving me a baby against my will.

We fly through the Westgate toll bridge, the man takes one

look in the window at me with my ice-cream container, my huge belly and he lets us through without paying, and when we get to the birthing centre the midwife, Maria, says to Rick, 'She's pretty freaked out, she's not going to make it without drugs. She'll have to go to the hospital.'

I am walking around in circles. I am walking fast. I don't want anyone to come near me. I think I want to die. Everything is spinning.

Suddenly all this water gushes out of me as if I am a waterfall and the midwife says, 'Forget I said that! There's a baby coming!' And she says to me, 'Do you think you can lie down?'

And I do, though it is the last thing I feel like right now. But I am used to doing what I am told.

Then Maria says, 'I'm going to have to do an episiotomy.' I get an almighty contraction, she slits with the knife and out of my body slips Jacob Asher, a dark-haired little human and she passes him to me. I clasp him to my breast and I fall in love, truly deeply in love, for the first time in my life. He is the most exquisite, gorgeous creature I have ever laid eyes on and there is no way a plastic bottle is ever going to touch his pure delicate rosebud lips.

'He's so tiny,' I gasp.

'No, he's big,' says Maria. 'I reckon when we weigh him he's gonna be about nine pound. What are you going to call him?'

'Jacob Asher,' we say and the band goes on his little arm. Then they take me through to the hospital and stitch me up and it is so bad — 'about twenty stitches' they tell me, like it is a war wound I can be proud of. The stitching is much worse than the labour and I need lots of gas and look at Rick through the blur, with the gas mask held tightly over my nose and mouth. He is all soft-focus like in the movies and I think perhaps I do love him after all.

Rick goes off to the birth room next door to study. His final exams are in two weeks and even though they said he could sit for them in January rather than November because of the baby, he said he didn't want special treatment. He had worked hard and didn't want them put off.

'Oh, Rick, congratulations! Oh, Rick, Rick — oh, darling!' says his mother as she flounces in with Harry and Cassie, his brother and sister. She brings out a camera and takes photos of Rick with the baby, photos of Harry with the baby and Cassie with the baby, then hands the camera to Harry to take photos of her with the baby. But no one takes a photo of me. I want to put up a flag, wave it around and yell out, 'Excuse me, but I'm the one that just gave birth to the baby! I'm here! I do exist!'

But instead I sulk.

In the afternoon we take the baby home and Aunt Tonia and Mato come loaded with gifts for the baby and I glow with love and gratitude and the knowledge that I certainly exist for them. Grandma Lyne and my mother come too.

Rick puts the kettle on and the women all sit around on my bed, taking it in turns to cuddle the baby. He doesn't even whimper at being passed around like a box of chocolates.

My mother says, 'Here's a present for the baby,' and hands me an old tattered book.

'This is my old school bank book,' I say.

'Yes, I'm giving it to you for the baby,' she says.

'But it's mine. I saved my pocket money in it. Twenty-five cents a week and my birthday money.'

'Yes and I saved it all these years for you. I thought you might like to buy something for the baby with it.'

'He is so beautiful,' says Aunt Tonia, getting out her camera. 'Rick's parents must be so pleased that you have given them a grandson.'

'Yes,' I say, 'he's their first grandchild, so I think they're pretty thrilled.'

'But they must be delighted that he's a boy, not a girl.'

‘I don’t think they care as long as the baby’s healthy,’ I say.

She looks at me sceptically. ‘I’m sure they do care. They’re just too polite to say. Everyone wants a boy first.’

‘Shouldn’t you put him down?’ says Mato.

‘Why?’ I ask.

‘Because you’ll spoil him if you cuddle him. We were only ever allowed to pick our babies up for feeding and then it was straight down in the cot so we didn’t spoil them. And you must only feed him once every four hours. If you feed him more than that he won’t learn that he can’t have everything he wants in life.’

‘Oh no,’ I say, ‘I am going to feed him whenever he wants.’

Mato looks horrified. ‘But if you do that you’ll be in trouble with the maternity sister.’

‘What do you mean?’

‘If our babies put on more than four ounces a week we got in trouble for feeding them too much.’

‘I’m sure that doesn’t happen anymore,’ I say.

‘Can’t you call him something other than Jacob?’ says my mother.

‘Yes — aren’t you worried that he’ll get teased at school with a name like that?’ says Aunt Tonia.

‘You really should call him something ordinary like Michael or Matthew or Derek. Derek’s such a nice name,’ says Grandma Lyne.

‘Calling him Jacob is dangerous,’ adds my mother. ‘People will think he’s Jewish and you’ll get letter bombs from Arabs.’

Rick is standing in the doorway with the tray of cups and the teapot and we just smile at each other.

Jacob is four days old and he is yellow with jaundice. We take him down to Queen Victoria Hospital. They take blood from his little foot and he looks so betrayed when they hurt him that I burst into tears. They send us home and as we walk in the front door the phone is ringing. Rick answers it and I go with my mother to put the kettle on.

Just as I am putting the tea leaves into the pot, Rick is back in the kitchen.

'He has to go straight back,' he says.

'What do you mean?'

'Jacob, his bilirubin count is really high. That was the hospital. They said don't do anything, just put him in the car and go straight back. He has to be admitted and they'll admit you too.'

'Okay.' I try to ignore the sick feeling growing quickly in my stomach. 'Let's go,' I say and take Jacob from my mother's arms.

'I can't go,' says Rick. 'I have to study. I've already lost too much time. You'll have to go yourself.'

'I'll take you,' my mother says. She puts the baby and me in the car and off we go, back down the Geelong road. Is my baby going to be all right? Is he going to die? I am so worried that I am only just holding back the hysteria and tears.

'You know that he'll always be like this, don't you?' says my mother, as she drives.

'Who are we talking about, Mum?' I mumble.

'Rick. He's never going to be a husband to you,' she says. 'If he can't stand by you now when you need him, this early in your marriage, then he never will. What sort of man is happy to let his wife and new baby go off to hospital on their own? He will never put his family first. It will always be his work first and you a poor second. He is not much of a husband, if you ask me.'

She talks like this all the way to the hospital and by the time we get there I really am hysterical. The hospital staff think it's all about the baby, but I am also beside myself because of the things my mother has been saying about my husband.

They take Jacob from my arms and put him in a special ward under lights that will make his jaundice go away. I am scared. He is part of me. If something happens to him I will be lost.

'He'll have to go on a bottle,' says the doctor. 'The heat from the lights will make him really thirsty.'

'No, no, no, I'll feed him,' I say and I cry. The tears tumble down my face.

The doctor is young and thin with an unruly mop of black hair. He looks at me sympathetically and says, 'Okay, we'll give it a go. We'll weigh him before and after you feed him to see if he is getting enough fluid.'

I am put in the maternity ward where the nurses say to me in their most derisive voices, 'Oh yes, you're the birth centre mother, aren't you?' As if my baby wouldn't be sick if I'd had him in the hospital.

All the other mothers are surrounded by vases of flowers and cards with pictures of teddies and storks, and have their babies next to them. Visitors come to see them and bring even more chocolates and flowers. I am so lonely in hospital. My baby is away being treated in another ward and I can only give him a cuddle when I go to feed him. I ring Rick's mother because she lives near the hospital and I tell her we are here.

She says, 'Good luck then.' And I hang up the phone feeling depressed and alone.

I do not see Rick for the whole four days that we are in hospital; I guess that he is studying. Finally he comes to collect us and take us home and I am still having difficulty walking because of the stitches. After making fried eggs and tomatoes I clamber into bed and Rick comes too.

'Rick, I'm really sore,' I say.

'It's been a week, Robbi. You can't still be *that* sore.'

'They said at the birthing centre it could take up to six weeks.'

'Yeah, that's for women who have forceps. You just don't want to make love with me!'

I am crying but he doesn't notice and I think that Rick always gets what he wants and I start to hate him with a deep, menacing, unforgiving hate.

27

Rick finishes studying at Werribee and graduates with honours.

I hear that Alan Marr is pastor at the Baptist Church in Yarraville and has started the Westgate Christian Community, and we move there to join the community. Maybe this will be the church where I find a home.

We have our dog, our baby and our VW Beetle. We have to be careful because every time the dog sees a VW open he jumps in, whether it's ours or not. One time a lady had just finished putting her two kids and groceries in the back and the next minute there is Caleb sitting in the back, between the kids and on top of her groceries. Maybe these cars symbolise freedom for him, because we took him from the lost dogs' home in one. It's very handy having a VW because whenever we forget the keys and lock them in the car, we only have to wait for someone else with a VW to show up and we ask to borrow theirs. The keys all seem to be the same.

We rent a little one-bedroom house with an asphalt backyard. In the front yard is a rectangle of grass about two feet by three feet and completely surrounded by concrete. That little patch is the only green we have, so Rick and I let it grow free, as long as it wants. Our small green rebellion against all the inner-city concrete. It is so blistering hot in our little rented house that Rick and I are sitting on the front doorstep. I have put the baby, naked on his sheepskin, at my feet.

The screech and wailing of a fire engine gets closer and closer and ends up in our skinny little street. This brings out all the neighbours and Rick and I watch in amusement as people come out to look, but our amusement turns to horror when the fire engine pulls up right in front of us.

The fireman leans out the window and says, 'We've had a complaint about your front yard. Someone's rung up and said it's a fire hazard.' He checks it out. We look at it too. It is a very sad excuse for foliage of any kind. He looks back at us. 'Couldn't set a rag alight with that,' he says. 'Grow it as long as you like.' And off he goes.

The two old ladies who live either side of us are muttering to each other, nodding and looking pleased with themselves.

One of them said to me the other day, 'Oh, is that baby on breast milk?'

I said, 'Yes, he is.'

'Well,' she said, 'you should put that baby in a competition. If that's all breast milk, you should put him in a competition.'

The lady on the other side said to me, 'Did you know that the house two doors down is a brothel, and before that it was an opium den?'

I didn't think opium dens were around anymore but I just smiled and said, 'Really?'

We can hear everything that happens in the old ladies' houses, because we are all jammed in so tight.

I try to avoid these two after the fire engine business. Then I hear a knock on the front door, I wander down the hallway and open it to another old lady with an impressive bust. She isn't one of the neighbours. I've never seen her before, but my baby would sure like to get hold of those breasts.

'I'm Mrs Williams,' she says. 'I'm Doris's sister, Mrs Stewart's sister — you know — she lives next door. She asked me to check on the baby because she hasn't heard him cry. I used to be a maternal nurse.' And with that she is halfway down my hallway and I'm shutting the door and following her. 'He might be weak. He might not be getting enough food,' she says.

'I thought you only check on babies when they do cry,' I say, but she ignores me. She is in hot pursuit of my baby.

Jacob is lying on his sheepskin, goohing and gahhing.

She takes one look at him and says, 'Oh. Oh. Oh, there's no need to worry about him, is there?'

He is enormous. He is the fattest, most contented baby you ever saw. People think he is seven months old, when in fact he is only two months. He smiles and gurgles.

I stand there, silent, and wait for her to leave.

'Oh well, I'll just go and tell Doris there's nothing to worry about. She's a bit of a worrier, my young sister.' And she is back out my door as fast as she came in.

Rick has been given a job tutoring at Melbourne Uni, so he's driving back to Werribee every day. He gets paid twelve thousand a year. We have friends at Westgate who are in their first year of a teaching contract and they get twenty-four, but still Rick yells at me at the end of every month when there is no money left over. I'm stuck at home with a baby and no car. Rick's mother offers to take me out, but I wait and wait and she doesn't show up. So I put Jacob in the sling and walk down to the Yarraville shops where the Macedonian ladies pinch his fat cheeks and make them go red. Then they give him hard Greek biscuits to suck on.

Wednesday evening wc go to what is called Small Group. There are lots of groups at Westgate Community and the idea is that it is easier to support and be close to a small group of people than a hundred and fifty. In Small Group we meet in a different member's house each time and share a meal. After dinner we have a Bible study or a discussion about social justice and we take it in turns to lead. Even the women. We discuss our lives and share our resources. I want to buy a food processor so I can make really smooth pumpkin soup. The problem is that a food processor is an unnecessary material object, so I ask the Small Group if they think it would be okay for me to buy one. I will share it with all of them, of course.

We shop together at Victoria Market. Mostly Christopher, another Small Group member, and I do the shopping for all of us, because we are the ones at home. I don't mind, because Christopher and I get on really well and have become good friends.

Alan Marr is in our group too, but he does not realise how much I loved him when I was fourteen.

Since Rick and I married, George Bush has started a war with Saddam Hussein. Like everyone else I know that is about my age, I worry about it. In the middle of the night I wonder if Armageddon is approaching; the nuclear arms build-up seems to be a sign that it is.

I have been taught since I was little that the rapture is coming and all the faithful will be taken to heaven while the unfaithful will be left for the tribulation. Aunt Tonia is so convinced the tribulation is coming that she has spent heaps of money stocking up, because the Bible says that those who do not have the mark of the beast upon them will be unable to buy or sell anything. She has bought a stereo and television, telephones, food — all the things she might want but won't be able to buy because she will refuse to have her body stamped with the devil's mark, which we all realise now is not 666 but a barcode. At our Small Group dinner, while we are all sitting around a fire in Alan's backyard, I confess my fear to him while no one else is listening.

'I can't sleep at night sometimes because I am so worried that the tribulation might be coming and the Antichrist and the rapture,' I say quietly so no one else can hear.

'I don't believe in any of that stuff,' he says flippantly.

I am shocked, but I also feel a glimmer of hope, as if someone has lit a match in the dark corner of my soul. What if he is right and none of this is true? 'You don't believe it? But it's in the Bible, in Revelation,' I say, trying to sound as calm as possible, but really my heart is racing at his blasphemy.

'No, I don't,' he says. He probably has no idea how important this is to me. 'There have been Antichrists throughout history, people who have been so destructive to humanity and to peace that that's all you can call them. Look at Idi Amin, Hitler. And there have been many times when faithful followers have been convinced that their time on earth was at the end. I don't think in Revelation the writer is talking about one Antichrist in particular but any Antichrist who arises and threatens the beauty of God's creation. The writer of Revelation is writing to anyone who suffers oppression. It is a story of good triumphing over bad, a story of revolution. It is just like a cowboy movie: a few good guys against loads of bad guys and for most of the movie it looks like the good guys are cactus, but in the end they win. The book of Revelation is a cowboy movie for the first century.'

'But what about the tribulation?'

'Tribulation arises any time there is an Antichrist. And as for the rapture, well, there's no Biblical evidence for the rapture. It is a post-Biblical doctrine, only believed by a select few.'

I mull this over and realise that it makes more sense than anything I was brought up with. I realise that it is much easier to believe in a loving God if that loving God is not inflicting tribulation upon the world and only rescuing from this tribulation a select few who happen to be born again. But if I take this on, I think to myself, what other things have I been brought up to believe that can be challenged? Might there also be other ways of interpreting what the Bible says about the place of women?

On Sunday we go to morning and evening service. At Westgate Baptist Community the church services are creative and alive and I relish them. Alan Marr preaches sermons that are real and meaningful, not just full of platitudes, and he makes us laugh. I study his sermons carefully so that when I get to preach I can be just like him. Ross Langmead, the other minister, writes songs that are just for our community, so they make sense because they are about things that have happened. One couple adopted a baby from overseas and he wrote a beautiful song just for them. My favourite song is, 'Brother, let me be your servant, Let Me be as Christ to You'.

Of course in the second verse we sing 'Sister' instead of 'Brother', and that is what is so wonderful about Westgate.

There are about a hundred and fifty people at Westgate, so the children have a superb time playing together and a real effort is made to celebrate them as part of the community. Jacob is too little to play yet, so I put him on his sheepskin on the floor and he continues to gurgle and smile. After the service we have morning tea and the children tear around our legs laughing and screaming and eating too many Arnott's biscuits. Then we go and study the book *The Road Less Traveled*, together.

There is a lot of talk at Westgate about voluntary poverty, though it seems to me that most of the people who talk about how wonderful voluntary poverty is have never seen their mother crying because there is not enough food, and have their parents to fall back on if they should decide they have had enough of poverty. True poverty isn't pretending you are poor when you're not, or even making yourself poor. True poverty is when you have no way out.

But we try to live our lives simply and share our possessions, though this is fraught with danger because some people are more willing to share than others and some people are not very good lenders.

There is a preaching team that includes women and I am amazed and delighted and hope that one day I will be asked to join. There are even women on the deaconate. But what is really miraculous is that everyone just acts as if that is perfectly normal.

They all love Rick at Westgate and say to me, 'You are so lucky to be married to Rick. He is so spiritual.' And I try to smile, because I don't feel lucky at all, even though I know I should. I don't think anyone likes me much and why should they? Even my own parents don't. But I like being a part of such a vibrant church.

I paint huge banners for the church when we have special events, and I paint the church's ugly windows so that they look like stained glass. Christopher takes up a collection to pay me for it. 'We pay the pastors for their work,' he says. 'I don't know why people always think it's okay not to pay artists.' And he hands me a hundred dollars.

We start a house for homeless youth, a job creation program and a medical clinic that is a cooperative, where the patients employ the doctors and every one is bulk billed. I am so excited that we belong to a church where we are trying to live just as the church did in the New Testament: caring for the poor and sharing our resources. We are also committed to social justice, a term I have never heard before. But we write letters to Amnesty International and watch movies about the horror of nuclear arms. We also watch *Life of Brian* and laugh.

And I think, at last! We are living church the way Jesus meant us to.

I need to go back to art school and finish my degree. Rick says he will mind Jacob while I go back, but every time someone rings up and asks him to work he says yes.

'I have to keep my hand in,' he says. But I know he also feels embarrassed saying that he can't work because he is stuck at home with a baby. My friend Jill can see how frantic I am becoming about finishing my course and offers to mind Jacob for me.

I stand in my studio space; a large white canvas glares at me and dares me to transform it, but I can't paint anymore. The paintings I have attempted are piled against the wall. They are flat, boring and brown and my heart isn't in them. Once again the lecturers are shaking their heads at me. I don't know why I can't paint. Maybe it is because my mind is on my baby and I don't really want to be at school, but at home with him. He is thirteen months now, with springy ringlets and he is so cute. He makes me laugh and smile. Maybe I can't paint because I don't know what to paint about. I am trying to paint about social justice, but the result is just predictable and ugly.

Gareth Sansom calls me to his office. He gets straight to the point. 'You've forgotten how to paint,' he says. 'There is no point you being here. Go home to your baby. We are going to let you graduate anyway.'

I am pleased. I don't know any of the students, because the ones I started with have left, and I can't paint. But this doesn't mean I won't be able to paint in the future. I just have to find what it is I am supposed to be painting about.

Now that I am home again I have time to wander to Alan's office, pushing Jacob in the pram. I walk into his office and he swings around on his chair and smiles at me.

'What about the submission of women?' I say and I am so nervous wondering what his answer will be that I cannot stand still.

‘Sit, sit,’ he says and pulls up a chair. ‘I don’t believe that anyone should be oppressed in the name of religion. We have to look at the Bible in its proper historical and sociological context.

‘The Bible also says that men should always have beards, but we know that law is outdated. And we don’t stone our sons for disobedience or gluttony, but in Deuteronomy 21:19 it says that a son who is disobedient, a drunkard and a glutton shall be stoned.

‘The Bible not only gives guidelines for the submission of women, but also for the keeping of slaves. We are able to see that the keeping of slaves is immoral, even though the Bible does not condemn doing it. But we are unable to see that the submission of women is cultural too, and not theological. It is an outdated, immoral practice. The male-dominated church has been very good at keeping the rules that maintain the status quo, but not so good at acknowledging other rules as outdated. The Bible has to be brought alive to each new generation by reinterpretation. Here, let me lend you this book.’

He hands me a book called *All We’re Meant to Be*. ‘It is an exploration of the impact of liberation theology on the Biblical interpretation of the role of women,’ he says.

‘Liberation theology?’

‘Yep. I think you’ll enjoy this book.’

I want to tell him that I have loved him since I was fourteen and I imagine taking his face gently in my hands and kissing him fully, passionately and deeply on his lips.

‘Anyway, just bring it back when you’re ready,’ he says, shattering my daydream.

My feet are walking out of his office but my heart is skipping. I feel free, but disconnected from my family. Suddenly I am on a different road from them, one that no one in my family has travelled on before me. It is the road of questioning, the road of being rescued from fundamentalism.

It offers the freedom of not having to interpret literally passages of the Bible that are nearly two thousand years old. The freedom of being able to search for truth instead of fact.

My sister Karyn is still firmly entrenched at The Church of the Open Door and wants to find a nice Pentecostal husband. I know that Mato and Aunt Tonia would think Alan Marr has been corrupted by theological school. When I told Aunt Tonia I wanted to go to theological school she was horrified and said, 'But you'll lose your faith!' And I thought that if my faith is so easily cracked and shattered, why would I want to keep it?

'How can learning about the Bible make you lose your faith?' I said.

'All I know,' she answered, 'is that young men go off to theological college full of faith in the Lord and they come out with their faith destroyed. Theological college is the den of the devil.'

'I have had my faith since I was eight years old and I'm sure I can hang onto it,' I said. But now I want to go to theological school more than ever. I don't see how education can corrupt you. It seems the more I learn, the more freedom I have.

So I enrol for theology classes at Whitley College and Rick decides to enrol too.

I sit in Ancient Greek and learn that the Holy Spirit is female in Hebrew in the Old Testament and that in Greek she became neutral and in English male. So I find the woman in God.

In New Testament I learn that the gospels were written decades apart and that they do not really tell us very much about Jesus, but they tell us a lot about the early church: what the early church thought of Jesus and how the early church treated its women. Not how we should be treating women now! I learn this from a large, wonderful man named Athol Gill, who has started a Christian community called the

House of the Gentle Bunyip. I have the greatest admiration for the House of the Gentle Bunyip because they actually live in communal houses and have common meals.

In Philosophy I learn about Kierkegaard and Nietzsche and what these great thinkers thought about God. The windows in my world start to open and the air is fresh and life-giving.

But although I want to study, I get pregnant.

I am back on Debendox and I struggle through my theological classes while a lovely lady named Shirley looks after Jacob.

And before long I'm at the birthing centre, and Seth is born in three hours, just like Jacob. I have to go to the hospital soon for stitches, but not as many as I had with Jacob. I am so in love with my new baby that I am crying tears of joy. He is sweet and small and perfect. I sit, cuddling him and feeling pretty cocky. Having babies is not so hard; it's a bit of a breeze really. Three hours of reasonable pain, but pain you can handle and that you know will end.

Rick read *Brave New World* while I was in labour.

Maria the midwife comes in. 'The doctor is ready for the stitches now, so we will just wheel you into the theatre,' she says. I clutch my baby as she wheels me in and once we are there, I reluctantly hand him to Rick while I push the gas mask to my face. I take a few deep sucks and look over at Rick holding him. Rick has gone all blurry once again, just like in the movies, and I realise with sadness this time that he isn't blurry because I love him. It's because of the gas.

So I suck even harder.

After the stitches — only six this time and nothing to boast about — Maria calls all the nurses from the hospital to come and see the beautiful olive baby with the longest, most amazing eyelashes you ever saw.

We take him home to the house Rick's parents have helped us buy. It is in Anderson Street, Yarraville, and cost

$32 000. Aunt Tonia and Mato arrive with gifts for Seth and some for me because it is my twenty-fourth birthday in four days' time, on 29 August. My sister and my parents arrive to stay for a week. My father plonks in a chair and doesn't move.

I climb into bed to feed Seth and Mato and Aunt Tonia sit on the end of the bed and we talk about how beautiful my babies are. I am so lucky to have such wonderful women in my family. Soon Grandma Lyne arrives and my mother is making copious amounts of tea.

'So what is his middle name?' asks Mato.

'We haven't got one yet,' I say and pull Seth tighter to me, so he knows we love him even though he hasn't got his full name yet.

Karyn says, 'Call him Micah. It means "one who is like the Lord".' I like the sound of Micah, so we do.

Out of the blue, several days later, my father gets off his chair and says, 'I could renovate your bathroom for you while I'm here, if you like. I could make you some kitchen shelves too, if you tell me what you want.'

'Really?' I ask.

'Well, as long as you pay for the materials.'

So I flick through magazines and show him what I like. Next thing he is out the door and off to the hardware store.

'Will he finish it?' asks Rick, when he gets home and finds the bathroom in pieces.

But my father has it all done in a couple of days and he and my mother head off.

So now I am at home with two little children, babies really, and Rick is working for Ian Gawler at Yarra Junction. Ian has a veterinary practice there that Rick runs while Ian concentrates on establishing his centre for cancer patients. Rick leaves for work at six in the morning and doesn't get home until seven at night. It is a long day for both of us.

He is in bed reading and I am stripping out of my clothes, so exhausted from running around all day that I just leave them in puddles where they fall. Rick looks over the top of his book and says carelessly, 'I liked your body better before you had children.'

I am mortified. I am fat. He's right. I weigh fifty-six kilos now and I was fifty before I had babies. I quickly throw my pyjamas on to hide my ruined body.

Now while Rick goes to work I don't eat. Or if I do eat I go to the toilet and stick my fingers down my throat. Or sometimes I eat chocolate-flavoured laxatives, because I read in a women's magazine that they can make you thin. When Rick comes home and I put our dinner on the table, I don't eat and I just say, 'Oh, I'm not hungry. I ate earlier.'

For two days of the week I paint while Seth and Jacob go to Shirley's. She is a wonderful lady in her fifties, who was having a sad time because all her family had left home and she was lonely. I got pneumonia when Jacob was ten months old and the Westgate medical clinic arranged for her to come to our house and look after me. She has been minding Jacob ever since, and now Seth as well. Because she has two children to care for again she no longer feels bad and I love having two days to myself to paint.

And I have found what I want to paint about. I paint about my life at home with two babies. I don't try to create paintings that have deep social justice or religious meaning; I just paint about what I know. One of my paintings is called 'Sometimes I can't even go to the toilet by myself'. I paint in bright colours and I paint freely, because I don't feel any pressure to be a budding artist. I'm just a housewife, so who cares what my paintings are like?

When I have a collection of about sixteen paintings I trudge around the art galleries of Melbourne, showing them my work and hoping for an exhibition.

'Your work is good,' says the guy at Pinacotheca Gallery, 'but not aggressive enough.'

'Too sophisticated for us,' the woman at the naive gallery says, as she flips through my work.

'No, sorry, far too naive for us,' the guy at Niagara Gallery tells me.

'Your work is good,' says the guy at Rhumbarella Gallery and I sigh and get ready for another rejection. 'When would you like to have your exhibition?'

So now I am working towards my first solo exhibition. Alan Marr gives me a book called *Making All Things New* by a Catholic priest, Henri Nouwen, to celebrate my achievement. Inside he writes: 'A book by my favourite author for my favourite artist.'

'How much will holding this exhibition cost us?' Rick says. 'If you insist on working, Robbi, you should do something that brings money into the household. Your painting is just a drain on our resources. We pay for a studio space each week already, and now an exhibition as well.'

Then he does what he always does when he gets home from work. He goes for a run and studies theology.

I do my theology study in the afternoon while 'Playschool' is on. I watch the time anxiously and as soon as that clock is ticking close to three, I switch on the television.

'Boys,' I call, 'time for "Playschool".' But I have put the television on too early and the ABC is showing the last moments of a ballet. I think it must be *Swan Lake* but I only think that because it's the only ballet I know. I lean over to turn it off until later, but I can see that Jacob is spellbound. There are men, who I think look very gay and prissy, prancing around in their tight leotards and jockstraps, but Jacob is mesmerised.

He points and says to me, 'That's what I am going to do when I grow up.'

'Do you mean that?' I say. What am I saying? He is only three years old. Next week he will want to be a fireman. 'Perhaps you would like to be a vet?' I add. 'Like your father.'

'No,' he says, still watching the TV. 'I am going to do that — that dancing on a stage.'

'Well, you can do anything you want,' I say, 'as long as you enjoy it.' I say this because I know it is the right thing to say to your child, and while I know that I cannot stop him from becoming anything he wants, I can certainly encourage him to choose things I approve of. For example, if he wanted to join the army I would feel compelled to encourage him to have pacifist beliefs, to see the army as legalised killing and the epitome of male aggression. But he wants to be a ballet dancer and I don't have a problem with my children being interested in the arts.

I try to do my essays while the children are watching 'Playschool'; it is very hard to concentrate on what I am writing when in the background I can hear 'The wheels of the bus go round and round'.

If Philip Quast is on I get up and watch with them though, because he is pretty cute.

I am trying to write an essay about a book called *Shantung Compound* and I don't think I am going too well. I can hear the boys laughing hysterically so I leave my papers all over the kitchen table and go to see what the ruckus is about.

They are sitting on the edge of their bean bags, pointing at the television, so I turn to look and John Hamblin is singing, 'One, two, three, four, five, Once I caught a fish alive'.

And when he gets to 'this little finger on the right' he holds up his rude finger to the camera, Jacob, Seth and I crack up. It has instantly become our favourite song.

When I walk down the street with the boys, the old ladies look at Jacob and say, 'Oooh, his hair is so pretty. It's wasted on a boy.'

Seth has olive skin and fine blond hair that flops down to his big brown eyes. A lady stops me in the street and says, 'What nationality is his father?'

'White Anglo-Saxon Aussie,' I say.

'No, really, I don't mind, you can tell me,' she insists. 'Is his father Italian or Greek?'

'No, he's not anything,' I say. 'Just plain old white Aussie.'

'Really, dear, you shouldn't be married to an ethnic man if you are so embarrassed about it,' she says. 'The poor little dear is obviously from a Greek or Italian background and you shouldn't make him grow up ashamed of it.'

One of my ancestors must have been a Spanish milkman.

I have written a paper about the humanity of God, which sounds pretty rambling to me. I have written that where God is seen as most human, in Jesus suffering and vulnerable on the cross, near to death and unable to save himself, we find God at his most miraculous and omnipotent.

The lecturer, Graeme Garret, raves about my paper and shows it to the other lecturers. Rick is not happy and finds it hard to talk to me for a few days.

To make matters worse, Jacob informs me that not only does he want to be a ballet dancer when he grows up, but his favourite colour is pink. And he asks please could I buy him only pink clothes from now on? He says his name is Sandy now and he is a girl.

Rick, Jacob and I are sitting outside a counsellor's office for an appointment Rick has arranged because Jacob wants to wear a see-through negligée to kinder and tells everyone he is a girl named Sandy, despite the fact that I have bought him pink jocks and socks so he can wear pink in private.

I figure this is happening because his best friend is a girl and he'll sort it out, but Rick is worried.

Finally a short, plump, conservative-looking woman with

thick glasses, short permed hair and what my grandmother would call 'a lovely frock' opens her door and peers out. We stand up and I see she immediately notes that I am a couple of inches taller than Rick, who she has spoken to on the phone. I know I am in for it, that she sees this as an issue. She opens the door wide enough to shake our hands and I protectively take Jacob's hand in mine. As we step into her office I notice a poster on her wall: 'Christians aren't perfect, just forgiven.'

I moan inwardly. I am toast!

'Now,' she says, sitting us down, 'tell me why you have come to see me.'

'I'm worried about my son,' says Rick, looking over at Jacob who is happily playing with dolls he has dug out of a toy box, having discarded the trucks, transformers and Voltrons. 'He only wants to wear pink and he says his name is Sandy. He is wearing see-though negligées. I think he is having problems with role modelling and is exhibiting inappropriate behaviour. Perhaps he feels disassociated from his maleness.'

'Where did he get the negligées?' asks the counsellor, looking only at Rick.

'I got them for him from the op shop for dress-ups,' I say meekly.

'Oh,' she says. 'I thought they might have been yours.' But she still doesn't look at me.

'So you see,' says Rick, 'he even does it when he goes out in public. He is having problems differentiating between life and make-believe, reality and fairy tale.'

'How old is he?'

'Three and a half,' he says.

'Now, this can be quite normal for a three year old, but not with this amount of determination.' She looks us both up and down. 'It is obvious,' she says, and finally looks at me, 'that you are too dominating in this relationship. Jacob is modelling himself on you.'

‘But I don’t wear frilly negligées,’ I say, trying to joke.

She ignores me and goes on. ‘Rick, you need to take the leadership role in the family. You are its head. Robbi, you need to step back and allow Rick his rightful role as head of the house.’

We get outside and back in the car — not soon enough for me — and I tease Rick and say, ‘Ooooh, I’m just one big head!’ And I roll my head around on my shoulders until I see that he is angry.

‘You have to stop dominating me!’ he hisses.

But when friends come over, he laughs about what the counsellor said and rolls his head around on his shoulders saying, ‘Ooooh, I’m just one big head.’

I don’t eat lunch. I am getting really thin again and a friend who is a vet has given me diet pills that she orders for fat corgis.

My exhibition opens. Rick’s mum kindly pays for the framing and I sell over half my paintings. That’s really good for a first solo exhibition. So I am happy on the outside.

28

I read in the paper that you can have young people come to live with you, young teenagers who have offended and been institutionalised. You get paid quite well, but that is not what attracts me. I have always wanted lots of children and I love having them around. I enjoy Seth and Jacob so much and we have a spare room and of course the support of our community, so this will be social justice in our own home.

Rick is all for it and we will get paid $110 a week.

We have done the training and our first young boy is coming. His name is Geoff. He hasn't been to a normal school in a long time because he has been at a correctional institution called Taurana.

We organise for him to go to Footscray High School but he doesn't turn up. He likes to arrive home at four every afternoon. That gives him enough time to get a snack so he can be in his room by four-thirty. That is the time you get locked up at Pentridge. Then he gets out his smokes, lies on his bed and listens to Slim Dusty, which is what his big brother listens to in Pentridge. He is practising for when he gets there.

On Saturday we take Geoff to visit his mother in St Albans. She is angry and hostile towards us and eventually she says, 'If the bloody government wants to pay me an extra $110 a week I'll do a good job of looking after him myself!'

I feel guilty when she says this because it does seem unfair. She needs the money a lot more than we do and Geoff really wants to be with his family.

After six months he leaves and goes to a residential house. The next we hear of him he is in custody again.

We get a boy who has alopecia and refuses to wash. He smells so bad that the whole house starts to reek. One day Jacob tells me that this boy tries to make him put his penis inside Seth's bum and that he frightens him. I call the social workers and ask them to move him out fast.

We get a girl, Tracy, who is fourteen and an incest victim. She swears at the teachers at Footscray Girls High and they call us in tears. She hoards food in her room — half-eaten cans of baked beans, packets of biscuits, cheese that is mouldering — and the mice come in and have a banquet. She starts to take my jewellery and my underwear and chops up baby Joanne, my doll. Even though it is only a doll, I have had it and loved it since I was tiny. She gets her period and leaves used pads and tampons around the house. You open the cutlery drawer and there it is waiting for you. Or you find a used pad hiding in among the towels in the linen press. She tells me, while I am hanging out the washing, that she would like it if Jacob and Seth died and she could be my daughter. I am at my wits' end with her. I am exhausted and I am in tears constantly, because I cannot cope with her. I know she is a damaged child, but I want her to be damaged somewhere else.

Rick is supposed to go away to Goulburn on the weekend for a meeting of representatives from Christian communities around Australia, but I don't want to be left with Tracy, so he lets me go instead. I am taking Jacob with me, but because Rick and I fight we miss the interstate train and have to go up in a car with some people from a community in Dallas. By the time Jacob and I get to Goulburn I am so worn out and on edge that I cannot handle it. I snap at Jacob when he makes up silly five-year-old jokes. I complain that my community is unsupportive, when really I mean my husband. I want to tell the other delegates that I shouldn't be here. That this is not me. That I cannot deal with this girl in my home and I cannot manage my life. I am sure the other delegates think I am weird — and they're right.

The other problem is that I am finding community life quite hard. I feel alienated from it. Most of the people in our community come from nice families in the eastern suburbs. They know how to be nice, how to talk about inconsequential things as if they are important, and I simply can't relate to them nor can they to me. And there is bad feeling in the community. People have expectations of what community means and should be, and when those expectations aren't met there is bitterness. Some of the bitterness is mine. I know I need to grow up, but I don't quite know how to do it.

As soon as I get home I ask for Tracy to be moved.

Next we are getting a boy who is sixteen. He set the last residence he was living in on fire and took to a social worker with a knife. Another time he pointed a loaded gun at his mother, so now she won't have him back home. I am really worried about this one. The phone rings and it's our social worker, Noreen.

'His name is Mark and he should be there any moment,' she says. 'Now lock all your windows and doors.'

I ask why.

'Because his girlfriend's father has a gun and is trying to kill him. Mark is really worried about it.'

'What did he do to his girlfriend?'

'Oh no, it wasn't his girlfriend,' she says. 'He slept with his girlfriend's mother.'

So I run around, lock everything up and there is a knock on the door.

On the veranda is a social worker I know and a short, freckled kid with a wild mop of red curls and a smile that beams pure innocence.

He fits right in with our family: plays with Jacob and Seth and comes on family outings. He decides to cook us spaghetti bolognaise for dinner one night and he buys pet mince. But we eat it anyway. He is sweet, polite and cheerful and when he leaves six months later I am sad to see him go.

I need a rest and at Westgate we have discovered Catholic Contemplation.

I go to Laverna, a Franciscan monastery, to spend a week in retreat. And I really need it. I live in a little room that is bare, apart from an old rickety bed and a bedside table, but I love it.

What I enjoy most is the evenings, because the priests drink red wine with dinner.

'Why do you wear those long robes?' I ask the priests over dinner. Baptists don't wear ceremonial garb.

'To identify with the poor,' one priest answers.

'It was the ordinary clothing of the working class in the time of St Francis,' says another.

'So how much do they cost now?'

'About $600 each.'

'If you want simple clothing why not a flanelette shirt and a pair of jeans?' I ask, but they have no answer. Then they ask me to dance with them. So three of them and I go to their huge, ornate lounge room.

Even though I don't dance, I think with a priest it must be all right. So we put on a record and dance wildly around their lounge room. I throw my arms about in a pitiful attempt at dancing and the priests' robes flap in the air as they fling their legs about and jig around the room. I dance until I am exhausted and it is such fun that I do not want to stop.

I meditate in my room all day, every day, and in my meditations I try to empty my mind. As I do, I feel my body floating to another world. I drift into the sky and I look down and see my body sitting cross-legged on the floor in my room. I float off to an island where I find Jesus and he wraps me in his arms and kisses me passionately and we talk and talk as I lie in his arms.

I write down in my journal all that happens to me in my meditations and after my retreat I give them to Alan Marr to read, because he is my spiritual director. At the end of my week away I don't want to go home — not because I want to stay in the monastery forever, but because I realise how unhappy I am at home. But I have to go, because I don't know a way out of the unhappiness. And Rick needs to have his turn at having a retreat. He goes to a monastery where no women are allowed — and certainly no wine or dancing.

29

I am pregnant again and Debendox has been banned. What am I to do? Nine and a half months of vomiting in front of me. I cannot stand the stifling heat so I am at Highpoint West, where there is air conditioning and I am vomiting in the ladies' toilets. Poor Jacob and Seth stand outside the cubicle and explain to people that their mummy is having a baby and they have to wait until she stops vomiting.

Eventually I stop for a little bit and I take them into Target to look at toys. On the way I am distracted by the pretty pink baby girls' clothing and sift through the racks until I suddenly realise that I cannot see Jacob anywhere. I look in every direction. I check the toy section and the panic sets in, sinking further into my stomach like a barbed anchor with every moment. I imagine the worst possible scenarios. Thinking for even a minute that your child is gone and you may never see him again leaves you shattered for the rest of the day.

'There he is!' says Seth, pointing.

'Where?' I turn to look and I see Jacob, high up on a huge pot plant. He is weeing on it. The plant is artificial. I walk away and pretend he isn't mine.

We hang out in the air-conditioned cool until it is time to go home.

'I don't want any more young people living with us,' I tell Rick after dinner while the children are in the bath. 'I don't want to get another one. I want to stay like this. Just us.'

I have had enough of strangers in our home. I use being pregnant again as a reason, but Rick says he can't understand how I feel. He hasn't had to live with them; he only sees them at night when he gets home. And as he makes sure he plays tennis all day Saturday, he doesn't have to see them on the weekend either.

So now while Rick is playing tennis or at work I can take the children with me to visit Mato and I'm not always worrying about another undomesticated teenager. The children run down Mato's driveway and I follow. The painting of Granddad, Mato and me is still on the garage wall, faded and tired. It points to a childhood gone, but it still fills me with a warm, safe feeling.

'My aunt painted that,' I tell the boys, but they are not interested.

I love visiting my grandmother. We sit and drink tea from her Royal Winston cups. She puts little curls of butter on the table in a dish and cuts large fresh chunks of soft white bread to go with it. Sometimes you can almost pretend you are enjoying tea in an English home. But she has started to say silly things.

She puts her head on my shoulder and says in a little girl voice, 'Are you going to look after me?' It is disconcerting when someone who has watched over you all your life suddenly becomes a child.

But I say, 'Of course I am.'

Then she looks up into my face. 'You know, Mabel got asked to a dance last week. Fancy, a dance! Joe would never take me to a dance. Joe is taking me to the Belgrave Convention and I am going to sing on the stage. Joe is leading the prayer meetings.'

I remember this happening when I was young, this returning to youth of those close to death. I saw it when she took me to see her elderly sisters and I am scared. How can I live without Mato?

I make her a pot of tea and bolognaise sauce on toast and because it is a weekday we put on 'Days of Our Lives'.

'Oooh! Look! Look! That man, he isn't really a doctor at all. I saw him in "The Young and the Restless". He's a world-renowned chef. Oh, she's going to die if she lets him operate on her. Did you know that Rose isn't pregnant at all?' Mato says.

'Rose who, Mato?' I ask.

'Rose that is pregnant to Storm. She's lying.'

'Oh, you mean someone from "Days of Our Lives",' I say.

'Do I?' she says. 'Why is the Lord waiting so long to take me? I so miss my Joe. Sixteen years is a long time to have to wait to see him again. It's just never been the same without Joe. I've just been waiting, that's all — waiting. You know the Lord nearly took me once?'

Then she turns and looks into my eyes and says, 'I've never had any real friend except you, my popsy.'

'Why, Mato?' I ask.

'Because you can't have friends when you are the minister's wife or people in the congregation accuse you of favouritism. It is better not to have friends at all. And then of course you are always on the move. Every four years off to a new church, but when the Lord calls you, you accept these things. I've always had you though, my popsy.'

She is eighty-six years old and I love everything about her: her smile, her voice and her fragrant hot Anzac biscuit scent that makes me feel safe. Mato never complains about my untidy hair or that my sons call me Robbi. She listens to my questions but still treats my faith with respect even though it has shifted away from her own beliefs. She knows that Rick and I now drink alcohol and go to a left-wing church and still she always welcomes me with a smile that reaches into my heart and wraps its arms around me.

'I am so pleased you are pregnant again,' she says as I put the boys into their car seats. 'I am asking the Lord to give you a little girl this time.'

Rick is doing night shift at a vet clinic in the eastern suburbs. I am scared on my own in the house so I put the boys in the car and take them to my parents. They live only one suburb away, in Seddon on top of the old State Bank. Wayne is married and living in New South Wales; Davie has gone to live with him. Karyn is in a flat with her friends.

Jacob and Seth run up the stairs to the flat and I follow with overnight bags. 'Mum!' I call out. 'Where are you?' And I take two steps at a time.

'I'm in here, in the bathroom.' Mum is at the sink washing something.

'Whatcha doing?' I ask her.

'I found this little kitten and it's full of fleas so I'm giving it a flea wash,' she says.

I pick up the bottle. 'Mum, this is flea wash for grown dogs! I don't think you can use it on an abandoned, sick kitten.'

'It's all I've got and it will do the job.' She dries off the bony little wretch and hands him to Seth to cuddle. He adores cats.

My father sits watching the telly and as it is tea time I suggest fish and chips. Rick and I never eat it because he doesn't eat junk food. Sometimes I buy the boys fish and chips for lunch when Rick's at work and they think it's a real treat.

As I sit on the floor with my parents, our dinner scattered on the paper in the middle, I breathe in the aroma of the hot chips and think how much luckier I am than Rick. I don't think he has once in his entire life spontaneously shared fish and chips on the floor with his parents. Meals with Rick's parents are glorious three-course affairs.

Fish and chips are special though, and blaze a trail of delicious warmth all the way through you.

After dinner I bath the boys and put them to bed in the spare room. As I am reading Dr Seuss, I can hear in the background that my parents have already settled in front of a video. I kiss the boys goodnight and head to the lounge room to relax with them, hoping the video is one I want to see. Through the doorway I can see the television screen and a woman on it is doing things with her fanny that you could only do if you were born with a deformity. 'This is porn!' I blurt out.

My father swings around on his chair and grins at me. 'Yeah, why don't you watch it with us? You might learn something.'

'There's nothing wrong with it,' my mother says defensively. 'Daddy wouldn't watch it if there was.'

'It's only the God-given human body,' he says. 'Don't say you're going to go all prudish on us, are you?'

So I sit and I watch and I am shocked, both by the images and the fact that I am watching them with my parents. By the time the movie is over I feel like I never want to have sex again. It's all so clinical. How boring to spend twenty minutes watching penises ejaculate from every possible angle! I feel offended that my father would put it on in front of me, his daughter.

He goes to bed and, as we clear up the kitchen, I say to my mother, 'He used to touch me up.'

'That's absolutely ridiculous,' she says. 'I don't know why you make these lies up. Your father always did his best by you.'

So I crawl onto the fold-out couch, beside my two sleeping babies, feeling miserable.

Mato is really sick, but I'm sure she will be all right. I ring Aunt Tonia to arrange to visit her.

'I've had to put Mato into a nursing home,' she says. 'I really need a break. It's only for a week to start with, just to see if she likes it or not. If she isn't happy I'll bring her back home.'

'Well, when can I go and visit her? Can you give me the address?' I ask.

'No, I think it's a lot better if you don't see her,' she says.

'Why not? She would want to see me,' I say. I am feeling very distressed by the thought that I can't see Mato. What if she needs me? She would want to see me even if it made her tired.

'No, it's better if you don't see her,' my aunt says firmly. 'You'll only get her excited and that won't be good for her health.'

Mato doesn't even make the week. She dies in the nursing home away from her family and I don't even get to see her and tell her how much I love her. But I hope she knows.

My uncles fly in and a funeral is arranged at Hampton Baptist Church. They talk about how pleased we all are that Mato has gone to join the Lord and what a blessed occasion this is.

Another uncle starts an altar call. 'If there are any of you here today,' he says, 'who do not know Jesus Christ as your personal Lord and Saviour and may be afraid of death, you may wish to put your hope in Jesus Christ our Lord. If you are wondering why it is that we are not sad today at our mother's passing, I will tell you. It is because we are rejoicing that she has gone to be with her Lord and Saviour. She is by his right side and we know that this is what is awaiting us. For in God's mansion there are many rooms for all who wish to give their hearts to the Lord and put their trust in him. If you would like to know how you can be like us and stand firm in the face of death, then speak to one of us after the funeral.'

I am in the third pew. I have tears streaming down my face. I look over at the choir stalls. My granddad made them. I remember clearly running around the church, pretending I was mother Mary with my doll Joanne as baby Jesus, while my grandfather sawed and nailed, like a carpenter, just like our Lord. I have sat in this church and played with Mato's fur-lined kid gloves. I was a flower girl in this church when my granddad married my Aunt Tonia to her weird husband.

My mother leans over as we are about to stand and sing 'Blessed Assurance Jesus is Mine, Oh What a Foretaste of Glory Divine'.

'Stop those tears,' says my mother. 'Do you think Mato would want to see you like that?'

We sing, and as we sit down my mother says, 'Goodness, Robbi, there are many unbelievers here today and we must witness to them and show them that we believe in life ever after, that our faith is in the Lord our God.'

Inside the house, where Mato made me Vegemite toast and had her tin of Arnott's cream-filled biscuits, we are drinking tea and eating cakes after the funeral, and I am still crying.

My mother says, 'Mato wasn't unhappy about dying; she was looking forward to joining her Lord. Stop letting her down with those self-centred tears. You are thinking only of your own sorrow!'

I feel totally desolate without Mato in my life and there is no one I can tell. No one to whom I can say, *She was my mother*.

After having young people live with us Rick has decided he doesn't want to be a vet after all and has found a job as a social worker. Being a vet will only lead us out of the community, he says. After all, there isn't much need for community development in pet care. But his job as a social worker will lead us into the community and will enable him to be more involved in community programs. Rick is doing night shifts at the residential house for children in Sunshine and I never sleep well when he is away at night because I am afraid. So after I have tucked the boys safely into their beds and watched as much television as I can stand, I get into bed but leave the radio on all night to stifle the night creaks and bumps and listen to poor lonely people trying to sell themselves as attractive potential mates.

'I am thirty-five, a little overweight.'

'How overweight are you, Gerald?' asks the radio presenter.

'Oh, I'm 112 kilos and I like to drink and hang out with the boys, and I'm on the dole at the moment. But that's going to change. I'm looking for a slim attractive female around twenty-two who works. I'd like her to be — oh, I'm not fussy — but I'd like her to be 36–22--36.'

'Are you single, divorced?'

'Yes, I'm separated.'

'How long have you been separated, Gerald?' The presenter sounds as if he has better things to do.

'She left yesterday morning.'

We've had our house broken into three times, but I think it was the kids who stayed with us, because they only ever took the stereo that Rick's parents bought us when they were overseas.

The phone rings shrilly, like it does when there is trouble, and interrupts the next caller, Martin, who is fifty-five and wants a female in her early twenties. I look at my watch. Half-past midnight. I jump out of bed, pick up the receiver in the hallway and a strange deep voice says, 'This is Senior Constable Fitzpatrick. Your mother-in-law has asked me to call. Your husband's sister Cassie has been killed in a drowning accident. Can you come over? Your mother-in-law is alone.'

I ring Rick at work and tell him. Then I ring a friend to come and stay with the children and I drive over to pick Rick up. When I see the withdrawn look on his face and the sheet of pain that separates him from the rest of the world, my heart aches for him. By the time we get to his mother's, most of his family is there.

They become really close to each other and a beautiful funeral is held at Woodend in the front garden. Everyone talks about how Cassie touched their lives. There are no altar calls.

30

Rick has a new job and no longer has to do night shift, which I am very pleased about.

But, even better, I've got a job too, just ten hours a week. We have started a Transitional Accommodation Program at Westgate in conjunction with Melbourne City Mission. It is a housing program that gives long-term homeless men a house to live in and teaches them skills to help them stay off the streets and in permanent housing. I have been involved from the beginning. Rick still complains that my painting only takes money out of the house but now I will be working in the transitional house and getting paid.

First I have to help interview men and find four who seem suitable. We already have three, so there is one place left. Melbourne City Mission has suggested a candidate and Rick, Alan and I are interviewing him this afternoon. He has a strange name: Jurgen. I imagine he will be a balding, overweight alcoholic with an addled brain who has spent a lot of nights in the Fitzroy Gardens or at men's shelters.

Four o'clock and Rick, Alan and I have drunk too much tea and coffee in Alan's office and there's no sign of Mr Jurgen Friedman.

'I have to go and pick up the children,' I say. 'Shirley said she could mind them until four.'

'Okay,' says Rick. 'We'll give it another half-hour and if he doesn't show, we'll figure he isn't coming.'

I get home with the children and I have just finished making face sandwiches with them when Rick bursts in the front door.

'You wouldn't believe it!' he says, as I put the plates down in front of the boys on their little table.

'Well, go on tell me,' I say and I put the kettle on.

'Alan and I had given up on this Jurgen character ever showing so we left, and as I was driving home I see this guy with long blond hair down to his elbows, a coat that fair dinkum must be a relic from the sixties — you know, American Indian tasselled look — faded flared jeans with floral patches sewn on them and get this, feathers and beads braided everywhere into his hair! And suddenly I have a hunch this must be him! So I stop and ask him if he's looking for the Transitional Accommodation Program and sure enough, it is him. Anyway, I take him up to see Alan and he's in. He was pretty stoned, I think. He's on a methadone program, but I think he was on something besides the meth. You're going to hate him.'

'I don't have to live with him,' I say. 'I just have to work with him.'

Besides working for the transitional house, I am also on the pastoral care team at Westgate. It is run by a young man who Alan brought back from one of his conferences and gave a job as pastor. It's easy to become a pastor if you are a man. This guy is so lazy that everyone talks about it. Then the deacons decide that every pastor will be accountable and that the church will run feedback groups on each pastor's performance. Russell is first and when the feedback starts to come in, it is negative. So it is quickly decided that feedback forums aren't much good. Russell never prepares anything for the pastoral team, but I am also on the preaching team. I try to make my sermons just like Alan's: personal and real. My first sermon is a hit. I'm so nervous I have to hold onto the pulpit for support, and I end up with bruises on my knees where they bang together from anxiety. But I keep my voice steady and calm and, most importantly, I remember to step back from the microphone in case a bit of singing slips out. After church people come up to me and say, 'Robbi that was a good sermon. I really enjoyed it.' I am pleased and look to Rick standing by me but his face is dark and angry, his lips are pressed tight and I know he will be angry with me for days.

He would be happier if people hated my sermons.

Rick and I are also leading Lent services on Wednesday nights. Normally Baptists don't use a church calendar, but Alan thinks it might be good if all the Small Groups go to a mid-week service leading up to Easter and asks Rick and me to run them. We take it in turns and I absolutely love doing this.

After church we all have morning tea and then Bible study. The children go off to Sunday school and have a good time with all their Westgate friends. Rick and I always invite people home to have lunch with us and so our Sundays are spent with Rick socialising and me making lunch for everyone.

At the transitional house the men call me sweetie, darling, gorgeous — anything but my name. Well, except Troy, that is, who won't call me anything at all. Every week I say to them, 'My name is Robbi, guys.'

'Okay, then — sweet Robbi,' says Ron, an alcoholic who is forty-five but looks sixty-five. He seems a damaged but kind man.

'So how is it going here?' I ask them and sip the tea that Jurgen has made for me.

'Good, good, love,' says Ron. 'Bloody young Troy is a waste of space, but Jurgen here makes a mean sausage dish.'

'Yeah,' says Jurgen, 'but you make great steak and chips. Just like in a pub.'

'Jurgen has been doing most of the washing and housework,' says Ron. 'He'd make some bloke a bloody beaut wife.'

We discuss dividing up the bills and start to talk about what will happen when their six months in the house ends and they need to be ready to move on to their own accommodation. We talk about how their job applications are going and whether they are managing to stay off their drugs of choice. When the meeting is over we arrange a time for the next one, the following week, and because Jurgen believes in chivalry towards women he walks me to the car.

Rick is working until midnight at least three nights a week now. I assume it is because he wants to. He's always been a workaholic. My father snorts when I tell him.

'He's obviously having an affair!' he says.

'The only affair that Rick is having,' I say, 'is with his job.'

'I doubt it!' says my father. 'No man works until midnight unless he's getting something to keep him at work.'

I ignore him. I know Rick wouldn't have an affair without first discussing all the relevant issues and drawing up a 'purpose and mission' statement.

I am in Nagambie. My parents seem to move every two years. They have lived in Canberra, Queanbeyan, Seddon and now Nagambie. My brother Davie has moved back in with them. They open a coffee shop and my mother is making people cappuccinos. She puts red food colouring into the cappuccino froth and turns it bright pink. She serves this to customers. Coffee with bright pink mountain peaks.

'Mum, you can't serve that to people! They didn't ask for it!' I say.

'Of course I can. It will brighten up their day. Just get that can over there will you.'

'What for?'

'It's oil. Give those spuds in the bain marie a good spray, will you?' she says.

'Why?' I'm a bit doubtful.

'It keeps them looking like they've just been baked. I spray them every hour and then they last for days.'

The children think it's fantastic being able to have milkshakes for free.

A lady comes into the café and in a very proper voice asks for a curried egg sandwich. I can't find curried egg anywhere. 'Mum where's the curried egg? A lady wants a sandwich,' I tell her. She is in the kitchen making packet cakes to go on display with a homemade sign.

'I'll fix it,' she says. She wipes her hands, comes out into the shop and turns on the hamburger grill. She slaps an egg on it and the grease swims around it as it cooks. When the egg has been flipped, and is coated thickly with grease, she smacks the egg on a slice of white sandwich bread, sprinkles some Keens curry powder on top and slaps on another piece of bread. It all gets slapped again, this time onto a plate. I can see the slices of bread are already turning to mush with the oil. This creation is handed over the counter to the waiting customer who looks at her sandwich in disbelief. But luckily she is a woman so she does not argue and I try to shake my head at her as if to say, I'm sorry but your sandwich is out of my control.

Soon after, a man comes in with two little children and orders the soup for them. I notice they don't eat much and they certainly don't bother with the toast that my mother had to take out the back and scrape the burnt bits off.

I give Jacob and Seth some vegetable soup too, and get some for myself. It seems like the healthiest thing going.

'Just wait for it to cool a bit,' I warn the children. I take a spoonful and spit it out. It sprays everywhere and the children burst into spontaneous giggles. I grab their bowls and head out to the kitchen.

'Mum, how did you make this soup?'

'It's just vegetable,' she says matter-of-factly.

'Yes, I know. But what's in it?'

'Nothing. I just put all last week's leftovers in a big pot during the week and they become next week's soup.'

'Mum, it tastes like vinegar. You can't serve this to people.'

'It's not that bad,' she says. 'You always were a fussy girl.'

I can see my mother's cooking hasn't improved at all. I have also noticed that while she has been doing all these things, my father has been sitting in a chair all day reading the paper, gazing out the window and giving her instructions.

Finally, it is time to shut the coffee shop and my mother starts to clean. She wipes out the bain marie while my father sits. She sweeps and mops the floor while my father sits as she does it and she sips from a gin bottle. Davie comes in, looking miserable too. He grabs himself a pie, puts it in the microwave and ignores my father still sitting in the chair. I follow him out to the kitchen.

'What's going on, Davie? How long has Mum been at the gin?'

'Gin? Mum doesn't drink. You know that,' he says sarcastically. Then he adds, 'Ever since we moved here. It's pretty bad. Dad is so mad; he's such a bastard. He nearly killed me the other day. He reckons I'm stealing from the shop. Stupid bastard! What would I want to steal his money for when I've got a perfectly good paying apprenticeship? I won't talk to him! They're both mental. They've lost it. I'm going up north. I've only stayed to make sure he doesn't kill Mum.'

I feel sad because they all seem so unhappy. I hope Davie gets away soon and I feel guilty that I got away so early.

I take the children home. On the way, the boys fight in the back of the car.

Jacob says to Seth, 'God is a boy!'

'No!' says Seth. 'God is the Holy Syrup!'

'No, God is a boy!'

'No, God is the Holy Syrup, like Golden Syrup,' Seth explains.

'No, God is a boy!'

'No,' I tell them, 'God is a boy and a girl.'

'Oh,' says Jacob. 'Do you mean that God watches the cricket and does the dishes?'

Is that what Jacob thinks? That Rick watches the cricket and I do the dishes?

It is a long drive and I arrive home tired. I shove the kids into bed and climb into my pyjamas. Just as I am about to switch on the radio and hop into bed, the front door bell rings. I open it nervously because it is about ten-thirty and there is Jurgen, stretching right to the top of the doorway as he inclines against the door jamb, a bold, mischievous grin on his face.

I can't help but notice his six foot two inches of perfectly shaped male body, crowned with that long blond hair. I involuntarily suck in my breath. Composing myself I say firmly and curtly, 'Yes? It's very late, you know.'

'I love it when you play the strict schoolteacher,' he coos. 'You don't by any chance have a uniform hiding in your cupboard, do you? Perhaps a cane as well?'

The impertinence of this man infuriates me. He just cuts straight across any barriers that are supposed to exist between us.

'What do you want, Jurgen?' I say, trying to ignore his comments.

'Well,' he says, stepping into the hallway before I invite him — which I wasn't going to do. 'The thing is, you see, that I have this thing for pregnant women and you, my dear, just happen to be pregnant.' He looks down at my belly and adds appreciatively, 'Very pregnant.'

This man belongs in a midday soap, not roaming the streets of Melbourne and spending nights at St Vinnie's.

'Jurgen, I am a happily married woman and you and I have a professional relationship. I am your social worker and you are my client,' I say, trying to nail the fence back up as quickly as possible, and not succeeding.

'I just want a nice strong coffee.' He shrugs. 'We've only got instant at the house and I'm German. I like real coffee. Come on, teach, you'll make me a coffee, won't you? I'll give you some company that anyone can see that husband of yours doesn't bother to give you.'

I follow him into the kitchen and notice that, unlike most men who plonk into chairs, Jurgen effortlessly folds his lithe body into the kitchen chair with the simplicity and silent smoothness of a cat. I make him a coffee and, despite my efforts not to, I enjoy his company. He is intelligent, warm and he talks to me as if I matter. I am surprised by him, so when he asks if he can come again, I say yes. He comes over nearly every night that Rick isn't home.

'Actually, I was on four drugs when I applied for the house,' he tells me, not a bit ashamed about it. 'I was drinking a bottle of scotch a day, I was on the meth program, I was on valium (the doctor gave me that for my nerves) and of course I was still shooting up. I'm down to just two drugs now.'

'Which are?' I enquire, not at all impressed.

'The valium and the meth, of course. They're free aren't they? I've been taking heroin since I was fifteen when a bloke at work gave it to me.'

'You were at work at fifteen?'

'Yeah, well, I didn't know English when I went to school and they didn't have aides and stuff then, so it was pretty hard.' Then he looks right into me. 'Do you know,' he says, 'if you were my wife, there is no way I'd be leaving you alone at night to the mercy of rogues like me.'

'I can look after myself,' I say, feeling a bit like a character from a movie. This conversation has taken on an unreal quality.

'We'll see about that,' he says. 'I have every intention of seducing you away from that husband of yours.'

As soon as he says this, I know that if I want to save my marriage I should resign as worker for the house and never lay eyes on Jurgen again. He is so attractive physically with his blue eyes and Nordic looks. He could have walked straight off a commercial and, if you ignore the addictions, he is attractive as a person. There are so many rules to be broken here. But I have faith in myself. I have no intention of letting this man, this heroin addict, ruin my marriage.

'I am married,' I tell him. 'I am a Christian married woman.'

I don't believe in divorce, I think. Adultery is a grave sin.

Jurgen is a client; it would be unethical to be involved with him.

I have children.

Jurgen is a homeless drug addict.

Not a problem, I think. I can handle this.

'When this baby is born,' I say to Rick one night when he is home, 'I don't want you to go back to work for a week. I want you to stay home with us. You know that you can. I want you to bring me flowers and chocolate and champagne. That isn't too hard, is it? I want to be spoiled after the pain and nine months of pregnancy.'

I get a gripping, wrenching pain and look at my watch. It is about ten o clock and I ring Rick and ask him to come home from work. We put the sleeping boys in the car and head off to the birthing centre. When we arrive the midwife says, 'I don't do episiotomies. I've never done one and I'm not letting you break my record.'

I am most grateful when Indea Eliza arrives that the midwife doesn't believe in episiotomies, but after six hours of labour I am not so cocky.

I am in love again. I have a gorgeous, sweet, delightful daughter. She is perfect and I am determined that she will never feel unwanted because she is a girl. I will provide her with a happy, healthy role model of adult womanhood — and suddenly it hits me: I'm not happy. I never daydream about my bright future, or about growing old with Rick in the country, or about possible artistic accomplishments. Instead I am sad, at a deep inner level where no one can see and where I expect little for myself and, except in brief moments of clarity like this, I can't see. But giving birth to Indea has put me up in the clouds; for the time being, at least.

Rick's parents want us to call her Cassie, but I think it is too soon. So his father calls her Bangladesh or Pakistan, but not Indea.

Rick has bought bottles of pink champagne and when his friend Mick turns up they drink it in the living room. I am in the bedroom with the baby. Alone. Finally Mick goes home, but is back again by ten the next morning.

'Can't you get rid of him?' I complain.

'I can't be rude,' says Rick.

But you can be rude to me, I think. And I have given you three babies.

Rick goes back to work. Indea is two days old. Resigned, I go back to work too. Indea is two weeks old and the men's eyes pop out when I start to breastfeed her during our meeting, but they soon get used to it and calm down. Jacob is at school and when Seth is not at kinder or at a friend's house, he goes to Shirley's. But I am changed. Having a daughter has done it. I am determined that I will be a good strong role model for her. She will not grow up believing that women are second best. She will not grow up believing her needs are less important than a man's. She will not grow up with a weak bullied mother, and it dawns on me that if I am to give her this I will need to leave her father.

31

We arrive at Lakes Entrance: Joanne, a friend from our management committee, the children and I and three of the men, Jurgen, Ron and Steve. All piled into our Econovan. I try to get Rick to come, but he has to work. I barely have my foot out of the van before I ask Joanne to watch the kids while I find a phone box near the camp-ground office. I ring Rick and plead with him once more.

'Robbi, I have too much work. There's a funding proposal to finish.'

'Please, Rick,' I say. 'It's really important that you be here this weekend. One weekend away from work won't hurt, surely?'

'I just can't do it, Robbi. I'm sure you and the kids will have a good time.'

'But I really need you.' And as I say it, I give up. On the hope that he will put us before his work; on the hope that he will rescue me from being tempted by Jurgen. I give up on everything — most of all I give up on our marriage.

'Don't be silly. You've got Joanne, Jurgen, Steve and Ron there. You'll be right. I'll see you on Sunday night. I tell you what — I'll come up on Sunday afternoon if I can. Okay?'

His voice sounds distant and no longer a part of my life. I hear myself say 'okay' as I hang up, and when I get to our caravan the men have erected tents for themselves and Joanne has cooked kransky and it tastes so hot and nourishing that I can feel its warmth all the way to my soul. I feel as if I have never been really warm. Ron hands me a cup of tea and says, 'You all right, love?'

'Yep,' I say.

We have a great time swimming in the lake, wandering around the bush, and I am starting to relax and feel happy for the first time in years.

We have had dinner, the children are asleep and Jurgen says to me, 'Let's go skinny-dipping, just you and me. Come on.'

I have been skinny-dipping plenty of times with Rick and other friends, so there seems no harm in it. Except that Jurgen is my client.

If I act as a social worker, then I cannot possibly go with him. But we are trying to treat people as Jesus treated them, so we don't behave as social workers. So if I am to treat Jurgen equally and as a true friend, I must say yes. These are the silly thoughts going through my head, and then I tell him okay.

The moon is smiling down on us, the water is secret and dark, covering our naked bodies, there is silence around us except for the occasional call of an owl, and then Jurgen pulls my body up against his with nothing but the flimsy softness of the water between us. But I stiffen and pull away.

'I'm only going to kiss you,' he says and does, without asking, and his kiss is deep and hungry and speaks to that part of me that it seems no one else can.

I sink into indecision and immobility, and I am suddenly being swept away on a journey that I know I am allowing but that I seem unable to stop. A journey that will change everything I have known. I know I cannot return to my marriage.

* * *

I am home again, the children are tucked in bed and I say to Rick, 'I want to split up. I don't want to talk about it for hours. I don't want to go to any more counsellors. I think we should split up — at least for a while.'

'So,' he says, 'is there any hope that we could work things out?'

And I say, 'Yes,' because I really think there might be.

'Is there someone else?' he asks.

I am dreading this question. 'Not really,' I say. 'I mean, I don't want to split up because of anyone else. I don't think we have ever been happy. It's remarkable, really, when you look at how we got married, that we have lasted so long.' Then the need to be truthful takes over. 'I — I'm attracted to Jurgen.'

Rick looks at me, silent for the first time in his life. I can see that he is in pain but I'm not sure what the pain is about. I don't feel like it is pain over losing me, but the pain of all the things associated with losing me. How will it affect his image of himself? What will people think of him? I don't think he actually likes me very much, but somehow he feels I belong to him. I feel compelled to say something.

'I kissed Jurgen,' I say helplessly.

'You kissed him!' Then, 'Oh, Robbi!' he moans and puts his head in his hands.

I know I should be racked with guilt about the kiss, but instead I feel guilty because telling Rick about it makes me feel free and happy.

Rick buys me the presents I have wanted all our married life. Presents that symbolise love and devotion: flowers, wine, records, lingerie and jewellery — and they have all come too late.

We are still sharing the same bed because I guess it is difficult to break a habit of nine years. The days are heavy

299

and hard, the nights are thick with angst. I am reading in bed and Rick says, 'What do you think about me having an affair?'

'It's up to you,' I say and keep my head buried in my book.

'But I want to know what you think.'

'I think you should decide for yourself what you want to do.'

'This girl at work, Linda, wants to have an affair with me. She is fun and attractive, she makes me laugh. I feel light when I am with her,' he says.

'How long has she been wanting to have an affair with you?' I ask, thinking of my father's words.

'A while.'

When Rick arrives home I put the rest of the lentil pie on the dining table for him. The children are bathed, I've read to them and they're asleep in bed. Rick sits down to eat and says, 'I'm going to Woodend for the night. I am taking the children.' Then he adds, 'And Linda.'

'Okay,' I say. 'When?'

'Tomorrow. I'm taking a couple of days off work.'

'Okay,' I say.

I am waving goodbye to my husband and children, who are going on their first family excursion without me, but it's not family because Linda will be there. I watch as the car disappears at the end of the street and I run inside and I ring Jurgen. He is no longer in the house and has moved to a private rental with Ron, so I guess the program has worked. He is happy to have me over tonight.

All day I can think of nothing but spending the night with Jurgen. I buzz around the empty house. I put the kettle on and let it boil dry. I make myself lunch, but I don't eat it. I wander down the street and finally the clock hits five and Jurgen will be home from work.

I walk timidly into his house and head to his room to put my bag in there. His room is filled with candles and roses. And as soon as I see that I know what is going to happen. I have never had sex with anyone but my husband and I know that this isn't just sex at all.

If I have sex with Jurgen my marriage will end. If my marriage ends I can never become a Baptist minister. I can't become a Baptist minister without my husband's approval and support and I am never going to get that from Rick. But still, if I have sex with Jurgen and my marriage ends I will lose everything. I will be ostracised by the church community, by my family and certainly by Rick's family.

But it is inevitable unless I turn around right now and walk away. My legs are not taking me anywhere though. It is some other part of me on this journey and making love with Jurgen is the start of it. I know it will happen and it does. Slowly, tenderly, because I am scared. After tonight there will be no going back and I don't know any other way to go forward.

'First time I've made love to a virgin in a long, long time,' says Jurgen.

'You know I'm not a virgin,' I say. 'I have three kids, for God's sake.'

'You might as bloody well be,' he says.

I want to thank him for being so gentle, for taking so long, but I am in shock at what I have done and the words will not come out of my mouth.

Ron makes me bacon and eggs for breakfast. He is polite and says nothing about my spending the night in Jurgen's room. Then Jurgen goes to work and I head for home. I walk in the front door of my house feeling strange and different. I will never be the same person again. And this house seems foreign, as if it belongs to someone else.

Rick calls and he is still in Woodend. 'How was your night?' he asks.

'Great,' I say. 'I went to see Jurgen.'

'How was it?'

'It was great,' I say. 'Really great.' Not thinking at all about what I am saying but glad that Rick seems to want to stay friends with me. As soon as the words are out though, I realise how stupid I am. 'So how was your night?' I ask lamely, because I don't really want to know about it. But I do want to take the focus off me.

'Pretty awful,' he says and I can hear his anger. It is like a knife twisting in my heart and I know that we are destined only to hurt each other.

'What do you see in him?' asks Rick when he gets back, and there is an edge in his voice. I can see his distress, but I don't know how to help him and save myself at the same time.

'Jurgen is such a failure,' he adds bitterly.

'I thought we didn't believe people could be measured by how successful they are in the world. I thought we believed in the kingdom of Jesus, where those who are weak in the world's eyes are really the strong,' I say.

I cannot say that I am attracted to Jurgen because he is the opposite of Rick.

Rick is short, dark, wealthy, educated, privileged whereas Jurgen is tall, blond, poor, uneducated. He started life in Australia in an old army shed, the sort new migrants went to, born to displaced parents because his father was Jewish and spent the war in a concentration camp. Jurgen still says his sentences back to front as he would in German.

Alan doesn't know Rick and I are splitting up and he has offered me another job.

There is a famous female minister at Port Melbourne Baptist Church. She married a divorced man so the Baptist Church refused to ordain her because they considered her to be an adulterer even though she has never been married before. He is an ordained Baptist minister. The Baptist Union are quite happy for him to stay ordained, even though he is the one divorced, but they won't ordain her.

She has cancer and needs an associate pastor to assist her. I am thrilled to be asked and I go to see her.

Adele Davies is a vibrant, no-frills sort of woman, strong, daunting, and I instantly love her and wish she was my mother.

'I really want to do this,' I say, my knees jigging up and down. 'But I ought to tell you that I am having an affair with a man who was my client.'

As I listen to myself say this, I realise how far I have removed myself from the possibility of ever becoming a Baptist minister and how far away I have moved from my upbringing. I wait for Adele's anger, for surely I have insulted her and the church to assume that I have anything to offer them, considering what is happening in my life.

'We're a pretty open church here at Port Melbourne,' she says, leaning back in her chair and putting her hands behind her head. 'You obviously have gifts and talents we can use. So I hope we can support you in whatever you are going through personally.'

I am so shocked at her reply that I have to hold back the tears. I feel as if this is the first truly affirmative thing anyone has ever said to me since Mato died.

Finally I have achieved my childhood dream of being a minister. I applied for a job at Westgate once, when the community decided we needed a female pastor, and I told them I had been called by God to the ministry since childhood. But Russell, who was interviewing, said the job had effectively been given to a friend of Alan's who was coming back from New Guinea.

'Frankly,' he said, 'we wanted to give you the job, but everyone knows that Alan thinks the sun shines out her arse;

there wasn't much we could do.' I liked Russell a lot after he told me that.

When I didn't get that job, Alan arranged for a lovely woman named Anne to mentor me through the process of becoming an ordained minister. The first question she asked as she sat down at my kitchen table was, 'How does Rick feel about your wish to become a minister? Has he given his support?'

I didn't stop to think. 'I have been called to this since I was eight years old,' I said shortly, 'and I will do it with or without Rick's support!' I didn't admit that he would never support me.

She sat back on her chair in shock and we didn't meet again after that.

But even though I am now a separated woman, Port Melbourne Baptist Church wants me just as I am and inducts me as an assistant pastor.

I rarely see my sister, but she turns up as Rick is moving into a friend's bungalow and is lugging his boxes down the garden path.

'Robbi's having an affair with a heroin addict!' he says.

Karyn looks at me and cannot hide her dismay. She is still a Pentecostal.

I just shake my head at her.

'Is it true?' she says.

'Yes. Do you want a cuppa?' What else is there to say?

Staying in the home I shared with Rick is no good. He walks in all the time without warning and he is always angry with me. The arguments are nasty and loud.

I spend months trying to rent a house, but no one wants to rent to a single mother with three children. Then Port Melbourne Baptist decide they will rent a house for me.

So I move into a tiny single-fronted Victorian house in Port Melbourne with the children's beds, half their toys, the fridge and the telly. The children think moving is great because I give them a four-litre bucket of ice cream and three spoons to keep them busy while I help the moving men with the furniture. By lunch we are gone and in the afternoon Rick moves back into our old house.

Jurgen is on a holiday at Her Majesty's pleasure in Pentridge. He'll be away for six months. All through the court case I felt it couldn't be me sitting here. How could a good Christian girl end up watching her lover sentenced for petty crime and drug dependence? And I knew the answer. I have stopped being good and this is where I have ended up. The court case was such a farce, however, that I will never trust the judicial system again.

But the prison is worse. There are signs saying that the wardens have the right to body search you! My heart pounds wildly as I line up and the wardens check me out. It pounds the whole time I am at the prison. This is such an alien, vile world and I don't belong. I try to remember the Bible verses where Jesus tells his followers to visit those who are in prison. I put down in the visitors' book that I am a pastor and I wear a little cross badge but the wardens scan my body with leery smiles and I am put in a tiny room and kept waiting for three hours. Finally Jurgen appears.

Today I have to talk to him through a glass partition. Sometimes I can visit in a garden and touch him, sometimes in a common room, but there is no consistency or any way of predicting.

'What happened?' I ask after my three-hour wait.

'It's the screws playing games,' he says. 'They've been sending me back and forth for three hours with slips of paper. I get over here and it's "No, you've got the wrong colour slip". And I go back and they say, "We ain't giving you any other colour, mate". So I've been doing that for hours, till finally they go, "Piece of paper? You don't need a piece of paper. You've got a visitor waiting to see you".'

It's the system, but there are children visiting their fathers every week and it breaks my heart to see the poor children getting stuffed around like this. Surely they have a right to be treated with dignity and to see their fathers without unreasonable waiting.

I talk to Jurgen for the hour we're permitted and I am sad he is in jail. He seems to be in shock and scared about it too. He writes me pages and pages of love letters in beautiful script that dances exotically across the pages. His words tumble into my heart and I can see why women fall in love with prisoners, though sometimes it is hard to unite the intelligent, sensitive letters with the man behind bars. But in some ways I am glad he is not around, so I can concentrate on splitting up with Rick.

This is the most terrible thing that has ever happened to me.

Rick has told his parents all the sordid details of our marriage so I have lost his family. He needed their support, but I know now there is no way we can ever get back together. How could I ever face them again?

I have lost most of our friends and I have lost him; someone who has been part of my life for nine years, suddenly gone.

'I thought you were a lesbian,' says Rick's friend. 'I'm so surprised you're having an affair with a male.' I wonder what she is really saying when she says this.

I have lost my community because divorce just doesn't happen among its members.

I have lost my family. My mother rings up and screams over the phone, 'We are so ashamed of you! It's disgraceful, leaving your husband like that. Poor Rick. What must his family think of us? You really are turning your back on the Lord, aren't you?'

I can hear my father in the background yelling, 'And she calls herself a bloody Christian!'

My Aunt Tonia is convinced that I have backslidden into the vile clutches of Satan and won't talk to me. She fusses over my sister and acts as if I am invisible.

I am so depressed. The children are at Rick's this weekend and it is late at night. I cannot sleep, the hours tick by and sleep recedes even further from me. I find myself in the van, driving to Rick's, to the house that was my home. I sneak quietly in the back door, curl up on the couch in the lounge room and cry silent tears. As morning approaches, I sneak out before Rick wakes up. I just wanted to feel like part of a family again. If Rick had come out I would have done anything to get back together, but in the cold broad daylight I know the only way we can get back together is if I am sorry for what I have done and spend the rest of my life being totally indebted to Rick for taking me back.

'Can't you give Jurgen up?' he asks me. And I can't give him up. Rick's face is creased with pain and anger, his eyes are drawn and weary. I feel tenderness for him but cannot go to him because of the wall between us. I know he thinks I do not care, but really my heart is broken for both of us. For some naive, stupid reason I thought he would love me if he didn't have to be married to me.

Every time I have to see him to collect the children or work out some other detail he always has 'Somebody Did Somebody Wrong' by Paul Kelly playing on the stereo. He must have it cued in case I turn up.

I sit huddled in a corner and cry and cry and rock back and forth. No one has ever loved me except Mato. To be so unloved I must be worthless, of no value to anyone, I tell myself. I imagine Rick wanting me back despite Jurgen, and saying, 'I know I haven't been a good husband, I don't care what you have done, but I want you back.' That is the miracle I hope for, but it doesn't happen. He just yells and screams.

So my friend Joanne gives me some cookies to cheer me up.

They are wonderful cookies and I sing and dance around my house, then I get out my paints. I am in a world of my own, slapping paint around the canvas. I am sure that I am painting a masterpiece, then the front door bell rings. I pull the door open. It is Rick's friend, Mick.

'I've come to talk to you about how you're destroying your marriage. Adultery is a sin,' he says. I cut in and say, 'Fuck off', and before he can reply I shut the door.

In the morning I look at my paintings and I throw them in the bin.

I ring my mother, but no one answers. I ring my brother, my sister and finally Aunt Tonia who says, 'Your mother has gone to live in Queensland. She told me she had said goodbye to everyone. Didn't she tell you? She has left your father.'

My mother has left and hasn't even said goodbye to me.

32

I try to concentrate on my work. The church pays me two days' salary to do whatever I think will spread the Lord's word in Port Melbourne. I introduce myself to the local social workers, who are delighted to find a young female pastor because they themselves are young and female, and we set up some programs for women in the Ministry of Housing flats and workshops for women escaping domestic violence. We start positive parenting classes and write a report about women suffering mental illness when they leave abusive situations.

In the communion services Adele and I use real wine from grapes grown, harvested and bottled by Adele on her country property. Adele, Julie and I have girls' nights. We sit up late, tell each other our secrets and finish off the communion wine.

Port Melbourne Baptist Church also pays me to preach every second Sunday. I preach about the motherhood of God and the old ladies say, 'That was lovely, dear. I haven't heard anything like that in church before.'

When I preach that true spirituality isn't cutting yourself off from life in a monastery or spending hours in prayer, they smile and say, 'That was lovely, dear. I always feel so good after your sermons.'

These women have never been able to cut themselves off from life to become 'spiritual'. There have always been children to feed, houses to clean and a husband's clothes to wash.

I preach that we can find God in the smiles on our children's faces, in their exuberant hugs in the morning when they wake full of surprise that they are alive and ready to play for another day. And the women nod because the lives they have lived are being affirmed.

I tell them that we are all God's angels and that we minister to one another. And they say, 'Oh, isn't that a lovely thought!' and hug each other.

When I turn up for church in my mini-skirt and leather boots, they smile and say, 'If we can handle Adele in her trousers and jumpers, we can cope with you.'

And when I turn up one week with my long frizzy hair dyed bright orange, they say, 'Perhaps you should put a blue rinse through it, dear, to tone it down a bit.'

Jurgen gets out of prison and moves in with me. 'Just till you find a place of your own,' I tell him. 'And no drugs or you're out!' So he comes to church too. He is happy to be part of a family, thrilled at becoming respectable, and he almost skips along the road as we walk to church.

We drag the children along and they grumble, 'Why do we have to go to church? It's so borrrrring!'

'Because it's my job,' I say, 'and it would seem strange if I didn't bring you. Besides, I need someone to give the children's talk to.'

We all sit round in a circle, twelve or so elderly women with their handbags, perms, floral frocks and me. There's Julie too, the church secretary, with her two children, Jurgen and my three kids. Adele usually goes away for the weekend if it is my turn to take the service.

'Isn't it lovely to have a man around?' the old ladies coo.

Joyce makes Jurgen sponge cakes for morning tea. 'It's so nice to have a man at church again,' she giggles as she hands him a massive slice.

He plays up to them, helps them through doors and eats plenty of their cake at morning-tea time, oozing compliments between mouthfuls.

Lois, an old lady who waddles to church every week with her most precious possessions crammed into a torn vinyl shopping trolley that she drags along behind her, suddenly reaches down into her trolley and drags out a shovel.

'What's that for, Lois?' we all ask.

She motions to Jurgen, then smiles coyly at him. 'I thought Jurgen might dig up a plant I want.'

Jurgen takes the shovel and heads off with Lois, his hand under her arm to steady her as they go. Then, as we are washing the morning-tea dishes, he arrives back.

'Did you get the plant?' I ask him, but he nods towards the door. I walk out of the kitchen so no one can hear us.

'The plant she wanted me to dig up was right in the middle of someone's front yard,' he says.

I can't help laughing. I realise I have a lot to learn about real Christian community from this tiny group of elderly women and Adele, Julie and Jurgen. They offer each other and me more acceptance and love than I have experienced in any church before.

Lois lives in a ministry bedsit, a small room with a bed on one wall, the kitchen on another and a tiny bathroom. I am on my pastoral visiting round and I sit in one of Lois's two lounge chairs. She keeps a two-litre juice bottle beside her at all times and soon I realise the bottle contains wine. Even though it is only ten in the morning, she sips away.

She says to me in her raucous, friendly voice, 'Now listen to me, love. You've got rid of yer husband and that's good. But yer don't want any man livin with yer. They'll only make yer work fer them. Cookin and cleanin and such. Now you listen to me: yer jus let a man come around once durin the week on, say, a Wednesday and on the weekends. That's enough to keep any healthy girl goin and that's all yer need him fer.'

'Is that what you think, Lois?' I grin.

'You bet your sweet bikkies I do!' She takes another swig.

'I'm quite happy with Jurgen,' I say. 'He's a good man.'

'None of em are good, love!' she says. 'They only pretend.'

I don't tell her that I am happy to have sex with Jurgen anytime I can get it. I don't tell her that if he's *pretending* to be good, that only makes him more exciting.

During the day I visit the other women from the congregation too, and by the end of it I am full of biscuits and tea.

I open my eyes and look at the clock. It's six-thirty and the thumping on the front door has woken us both up. I scramble to the door in my pyjamas. The knocking becomes so ferocious that the children wake up too, become frightened and scurry to my side. I hardly turn the handle before the police barge through, four of them. Big, intimidating and aggressive. They throw Jurgen against the wall. I am in my pyjamas and the children are crying. I pull them safely under my arms.

'Your ex-husband told us where to find Jurgen,' says one of the policemen. 'You can thank him for this little visit.'

They ask us both where Jurgen was last Thursday night and I keep the children tucked under my arm. Jurgen is too afraid to speak so I tell them that he was at his year twelve English class and that he has to sign in and out so they can check that he was there. I tell them I picked him up from class. The police believe me and get up to leave.

On their way out the door, one of them says to me, 'What does a girl like you see in a bloke like him?'

His colleague pushes him out the door and says, 'Don't worry, love. We know Jurgen isn't like most of them.'

I am shaking, but for the children I act as though having the police barge through your door early in the morning is perfectly normal. I get them ready for school. I still drive them to school in Yarraville every day, which is quite a drive.

Jurgen is back at his job working for Vic Rail at the Newport workshops. The supervisor says to me, 'I know Jurgen was in jail, but he's a really nice bloke. I've been saving this job for him while he was in. I just put him on compassionate leave. I said that he was visiting his dying mother.'

We move into a house in Newport, which is only twenty minutes over the Westgate Bridge from Port Melbourne, and closer to the children's school. All the affordable houses in Port Melbourne are too small for us now that Jurgen has moved in. He clearly considers I have given him a home and he hasn't even been pretending to find a place of his own.

He gets excellent marks in English and encourages me to take up my theological studies again. So I go back to college.

I am packing up my books after a lecture on Biblical exegesis when one of the Jesuit priests sidles up to me. 'Would you like to come to lunch?' he asks. 'My shout.'

'Yeah, sure,' I say and off we go. Students have lunch together all the time.

We go to an Asian café and over lunch we are discussing nothing when he suddenly says, 'It's eight years since I have had a woman.'

I try not to choke and put down my chopsticks. Where did this come from? And, more importantly, where is it going?

'I don't want to go to a prostitute,' he goes on, 'and I was wondering if you would sleep with me?'

'You mean you're not even going to chat me up first?'

He looks at me blankly. He has no idea what I am talking about.

'You're not even going to tell me how attracted you are to me?'

'I just want to have sex and I don't want to pay for it,' he says.

'Why have you become a priest?' I say.

'In my country it is the only way a poor son can get a good education. I had to leave my girlfriend of eight years, but I did not want to end up a poor farmer. The Catholic Church offered education and financial security and I was clever.'

I leave him as he pleads with me not to tell his superior about his proposition and I head for my next class: Pastoral Care and Counselling.

'First thing today we are going to do a spiritual exercise,' Bruce the lecturer says as he walks into the classroom with the kind of aura that immediately silences all chattering. 'I think there will be something here for everyone. We have a prayer, a meditation to be done with a tree and a Bible reading to contemplate. So come and choose what you most identify with.'

I don't want to do any of them. For me, spirituality is no longer about spending time meditating or praying, but about how you live your life.

'Does anyone want to nick down to the pub for a quick drink?' I ask my friends. They giggle. There is nothing as spiritual as a nice glass of wine shared with friends.

I realise that Lois is very lonely in her little bedsit and that she hates meals on wheels so at church on Sunday I ask the women, 'How would you feel about cooking a meal? A large meal.'

'What do you have in mind, dear?' asks Lorna.

'Well, it seems to me that there are a lot of lonely people in Port Melbourne, stuck in bedsits, eating meals on wheels, which is a great service mind you, but not very appetising. I thought maybe we could put on a community lunch once a month. Cook a three-course meal, charge five dollars to cover costs so we can keep doing it if it works and get all these lonely people together over food.'

'I'll make the cakes,' says Joyce. 'My husband Herb and I had a bakery for twenty years.'

Soon I have offers of soup and roasts as well and we advertise our lunch. We have three weeks to get bookings. Probably no one will come.

'Any bookings?' I ask Julie, as I arrive at work the next week.

'We're booked out,' she says. 'We got to forty; we can't fit any more in the hall than that. I've started a waiting list for the next one.' And so the community lunches become a Port Melbourne institution.

I also start a monthly staff lunch at the local pub. Adele, Julie and I go off and get sozzled and laugh a lot. It is very healing.

I introduce mulled wine to the deacons' meetings. These old women have never had wine and after a lot of do-you-think-I-should-oh-all-right-just-a-little-nip-then, and lots of giggling, they decide they like it. Soon our church meetings don't finish until midnight.

'That was the best deacons' meeting I've ever been to,' Norma says as she wobbles out the door to go home.

Every month I also attend the local ministers' meetings. This meeting is called the 'ministers' fraternal', of course. There are two Catholic priests with red noses, three Uniting Church ministers who are real blokes, a couple of well-spoken Anglicans and me. Naturally, I am the only woman and they make jokes about having to change their language to include me — but of course they don't. Because I am young and female they pretty well ignore me. I want to make jokes about finding a good layman, but I don't.

* * *

Each week I do the motherly stuff and take Jacob to ballet and Seth to drama lessons. I take the children with me to visit Grandma Lyne in the Westhaven old people's home too.

It is hard for Jacob because all the old ladies at the home tug at his curls and say, 'Oh, how lovely. I wish I could get hair like that without having to pay for it.'

Jacob is good and smiles sweetly and Seth hides behind my leg. Indea is shy and clingy and stays firmly planted on my hip.

Gran did have a room of her own, but now she is in the hospital. Jacob and Seth don't like going to visit her because she smells funny and dribbles.

'She hasn't always been like this,' I say. 'She is very old.'

We pass the reception desk and smile at the staff who know us by sight and we find Gran sitting by her bed in a Jason recliner, looking at a *New Idea*.

'Is that you, Karyn?' she calls out.

She knows it is me because I am the only person who visits her. 'No, Gran, it's me and the children. You know it's me,' I say.

'Oh well, I just thought it might be your sister.'

'How are you, Gran?' The children plonk themselves on the floor and start playing with the toys I have brought for them.

'I'm all right. It's tripe today. It's always tripe on a Thursday. I like tripe days. They do it just lovely here. It's good fer yer, yer know. You should eat more tripe. We ate a lot of it during the war I daresay.'

'I daresay you did, but I can live without it. But, Gran, it's Wednesday today.'

'Of course it's Wednesday,' she says, annoyed with me. 'What do yer want to know if it's Wednesday fer? What do you do on a Wednesday?'

'Well, I visit you for a start and I take Jacob to ballet.'

'Has he still got those curls? I can't see. It would be such a pity if he lost them all. You used to have curls just like his, you know. I daresay he got them from you. Still, I suppose those curls are a waste on a boy. Freda would like to see him though. She loves curls, even if they are on a boy. Pity the other one doesn't have any.'

'Oh, I don't think he's too worried about it. Seth's hair is dead straight, just like his father's. I don't know yet what Indea's will be like. It isn't long enough.'

'So,' says Gran, 'how is Rick? You must be so proud to be married to a vet.'

'Gran,' I say firmly, 'he's not a vet anymore and he's not my husband anymore.'

'Oh yes, who's your friend?' she grumbles.

'Jurgen. You've met him several times now.'

'Well, I don't know. What was wrong with Rick?'

'Listen, Gran, are you going to come over for Christmas? We'll come and pick you up.'

'Nope, I'm not coming. Not if Rick isn't going to be there. Besides, I get car sick. Half a mile and I vomit everywhere.'

'We can give you a bucket.'

'No, I'm not coming! Does Rick mind what's-his-name?'

'Jurgen — and it's not really any of Rick's business, is it? I'm not married to him anymore.'

'More's the pity,' she mutters.

The tea lady has arrived. A round woman with a heavy accent and a friendly face. She is wearing a blue apron over her clothes and says to Gran, 'How yer doin, Slim? We all call her Slim on account of her last name being Dusty. You know, Slim Dusty,' she tells me.

'Look at this,' says Gran. 'Look at this in the *New Idea*. Ten children in this family and every last one of them blind.'

'You tell your gran to be good. No more shenanigans,' the tea lady says to me as she wanders off to the next bed.

'What's this, Gran?'

'I've been going fer walks early in the morning when I can't sleep and t'other day the doctor saw me and brought me back 'ere, an he says don't you go walking around in the early morning, it's not safe. But I ses to him, I've got my stick. I can whack anyone I need to with my stick. Jus get me some more sugar out of my drawer over there, will you? I pay them all this money to be ere and I can't even get a cuppa when I want it — or how I want it,' she grizzles.

'How early are these walks, Gran?'

'Well, I leave about five, but the doctor didn't find me till six. It was getting light then anyways.'

I open up her drawer and a faded sepia photograph of a child is lying inside.

'That's Derek,' Gran says. 'Where's my sugar?'

'Derek was your oldest, wasn't he?' I take the lid off the jar of sugar she has stored in her drawer and spoon some into her cup.

'Yes, yes, he was. He died of the polio. He was such a lovely young fellow.'

'How did it happen, Gran?' I know the story from my mother, but I ask knowing that Gran has probably never talked about this before and she seems to want to.

'First the war, then the polio,' she tells me. 'Every family had it, I guess. Some had one down with it, but I had all three. Derek was the worst, then your dad and then the little one Clare was least hit. She didn't get it too bad. Funny — you'd expect it t'other way round. You'd expect the youngest to be the weakest. I walked to the doctor's — old Doctor Sullivan down in Bay Road — when those kids was sick. I told him they were all down with the polio and he says, "How'd you know it's polio? You're not a doctor."

'He was always acid like that. Then he says, "Hmmpph! Everyone has someone sick with the polio. Yours can't be too bad or you wouldn't be here now, would you? You're just a panicky mother! I can't be in all places at once! I'm only human!"

'So I go home and by morning little Derek, such a lovely little boy with beautiful curls, is dead. Well, after that yer dad and Clare were in the hospital quick smart without a by-yer-leave! Derek was only a boy and such a head of curls. Yer should have named one of yours Derek. I would have liked that. Yer can take that tea away. It's stone-cold now.'

'Jurgen is really nice,' I say. 'Perhaps we'll have a baby and we could name him Derek.'

'I spose he's not a bad fella. I'll think about Christmas,' she says. 'That nice minister of yours, he comes every week, yer know, an takes devotions. I always tell him about how you're getting on.' She means Alan Marr.

'I'm not at Westgate anymore, Gran, remember.'

'Hmm,' she says. 'But those men at Westgate are such lovely fellows. What's his name?'

'Do you mean Russell or Alan?' I ask.

'The young fella.'

'You like Russell, do you?'

'Oh, yes. He lets us sing as many choruses as we like.'

'Well, I miss Westgate Community, Gran, but I'm at Port Melbourne now,' I say.

'Hmmm,' she says. 'I bet the singing isn't as nice as it is at Westgate.'

The singing at Port Melbourne leaves a lot to be desired, but I love my work and they support me. Each Baptist church is completely autonomous. This is the reason you can have Baptist churches that are alternative and committed to social justice and Baptist churches that are rigid and strict. Each church is allowed to appoint its own pastors and Baptists believe passionately in the priesthood of all believers. This is the belief that every man, woman and child has direct access to God and to God's word, the Bible. So the pastor of a church does not necessarily have to be someone who is trained and ordained. The pastor may be someone who has shown that he or she has gifts of leadership.

But I know that I am never going to be ordained by the Baptist Union. It is a conservative body and I most certainly don't fit the mould. The Uniting Church in Fitzroy has approached me and offered to see me through candidacy and ordination within the Uniting Church. 'The biggest difference between Baptist and Uniting Church,' they say to me, 'is infant baptism. How do you feel about infant baptism, because Baptists are very anti infant baptism and you have been Baptist all your life.'

'I don't have a problem with it,' I say. 'Once I would have, because I believed that you could only be a part of the family of God after you had experienced conversion. Now I believe that we are all part of each other, that our lives are intertwined and that we should welcome our children into our community with ceremony. So I believe in the baptism of infants now — though my poor grandmother will be turning in her grave to hear me say it. She and her family left the Methodist Church and became Baptists over that issue.'

The Uniting Church are happy with my answer and they offer me a job, basically doing what I am doing at Port Melbourne but with a different title. The job is to start next year so that I can warn Port Melbourne in plenty of time that I am leaving. Meanwhile, the Uniting Church asks if I can preach there once a month and I say yes.

So although I am a pastor at Port Melbourne Baptist I am also now a member of Fitzroy Uniting Church and I go over to preach.

Fitzroy Uniting is at least twice the size of Port Melbourne and has a congregation of about thirty-five. So it too is a small, struggling church. The congregation is committed to social justice. Probably the most left-wing congregation I have ever encountered, it is colourful and includes a transsexual and people who seem to live on the streets.

I enjoy being with them once a month, but I do find it alien because I don't quite understand the workings of the Uniting Church. They have a central body of government and a hierarchy that doesn't exist in the Baptist Church.

When the local Uniting Church minister who attends the ministers' fraternal meetings hears of me preaching at another Uniting Church, he asks me to preach at his church too. He asks me to preach on Mothers' Day because I'm a mother. So I go and preach about the motherhood of God and ask everyone to light a candle and to name out loud a woman who has been significant in their lives. I name my two grandmothers, Hilda Prestonia and Edith Lyne, and after the service I am flooded with people telling me how much they enjoyed my service.

Several men come up to me and say that they felt a bit strange when they first heard a woman would be leading the service, but actually it was lovely to see a woman in the pulpit. And I think maybe there is hope for change.

When I am at the next ministers' fraternal meeting, the men all speak to me and ask me to lead them in prayer. I guess now that I have preached in one of their churches, and it was a success, I have proved myself. But sometimes it is hard just to get the opportunity to do that.

33

My children really like Jurgen. He makes them fried rice and pancakes, plays his guitar and lulls them off to sleep, and he plays chasey with them. He minds them while I go to study Clinical Pastoral Education at night. In Clinical Pastoral Education we give a verbatim report of counselling sessions we have held during the week and then analyse them. But tonight I have to do a presentation of what spirituality means to me. The other students have given long talks with lots of Bible verses thrown in, but I cook everyone gado gado and give them red wine to drink.

I tell them that food is religious. Sharing it is the most significant ceremony we have with others. I say that true spirituality for me is enjoying the company of other beings and celebrating life together. And then I tell them to dig in.

We have a lovely night together, the two tutors, the seven other students and me. We eat, drink, we tell each other jokes. We celebrate the life God has given us.

I am getting home a bit early and as I walk up the front path I can tell the children are asleep in bed, because the house is so silent.

Jurgen comes to the door; he pokes only his face out into the dark of the night. His cheeks are flushed with embarrassment or something. He holds the door slightly ajar and doesn't want to let me in.

'Come on, open the door, Jurgen,' I say anxiously. Maybe he has another woman in there. But the door doesn't budge.

'What's going on?' I ask. I am worried about the children now. Jurgen hasn't used while he's been with me, but what if he has started again? He sighs and opens the door.

I look him over as I step inside and I can see why he didn't want to let me in.

'I wasn't expecting you yet,' he stammers.

'I can see that. Class finished early,' I say shortly, trying desperately to control my emotions.

'I couldn't help it,' he says. 'The kids were asleep and I couldn't resist the temptation.'

Jurgen is dressed in my clothes. He has my dress on, my make-up; his hair is in pigtails with ribbons. I can see from the bra strap showing that he has my underwear on too. I look at his legs and sure enough he has my tights on.

'How long have you been doing this?' I ask. My throat is dry and I can hardly speak.

'Since I was eight,' he says, like a child who has been caught out.

'Are you gay?'

'Sometimes.'

'Are you a transvestite?'

'Seems that way, doesn't it,' he says shamefully.

I am angry and I don't know why. I feel like my privacy has been violated. I don't mind the fact that he is bisexual, because I thought as much anyhow; there had been little hints along the way. But I do mind him raiding my drawers, wearing my clothes and pretending he is a woman. How does he know what being a woman is like? Has he grown-up as a girl? Has he been told 'no' all his life?

Well, as an immigrant growing up in Australia during the sixties he probably *was* often told no, but that doesn't make me feel any better. Then I realise how much Jurgen has changed me. For the first time in my life I like being female thanks to him. When I am with him I wouldn't want to be anything but, and now he is threatening this by trying to be female himself.

'I am the woman in this household!' I yell at him. 'If anyone is going to wear sexy underwear it will be me. You get to appreciate lace and silk *on me*! On *my body*! Not on yours!'

'Honey, honey,' he says soothingly, 'silk and lace I love on you. Your body I love. Women's bodies I have always loved. There is nothing more beautiful to me than your vagina. It's just that one of my own I've always wished I had.'

I know that this is what makes Jurgen such a good lover: he deeply, honestly adores women with every last cell of his being. He has not one misogynistic bone in his body.

So I soften. 'Please, don't do it while you're with me,' I say.

'Okay, fair enough,' he says, but I keep a close eye on my underwear.

Jurgen is kind to me and when I am ill he looks after me and brings me hot lemon and brandy. He buys me new clothes and cooks dinner when I am tired. He never yells at me and he is proud when I do something well.

But eventually I tell him that I want us to split up. We have been together for about two years and he has seen me through one of the worst parts of my life — the break-up with Rick.

Jurgen's family is sad. They love me and my children. And they love the fact that he has stopped using drugs. He has a job and a family.

'If you marry Jurgen,' they say, 'we will look after the children while you go on a honeymoon. If you marry Jurgen we will help with the wedding.'

I do not want to marry Jurgen. I love him, but I know he is not someone I want to marry. I am not ready for another marriage. I have to have my teenage years yet, and sometimes I feel that Jurgen is another child I have to care for. Sometimes the children come home crying when he has taken them to the park because he won't let them win, and I can't talk to him about my thoughts.

'I'm not interested in intellectual shit,' he says.

He still likes to wear my clothes and that makes me feel insecure. He talks about heroin as if it were a person — his real love — and says how much he misses it, and when he does that I feel apprehensive about our future.

'Do you love me?' I say to him as he brings me breakfast in bed on Saturday morning.

'Well, I fuck you, don't I?' he answers, leaning leisurely against the door, smiling, as if that's all there is to it. He tells me that he has lasted longer with me than with any other woman.

'It usually lasts only six months,' he says. 'I can make all the sexual techniques I know last till then, but I run out after that and they get bored with me and dump me.'

Before I met Jurgen I only knew the missionary position so I guess with me he had an open go.

He says he always knew the break-up was coming, but could we still live in the same house and I tell him we can — for the moment.

So now that Jurgen and I have split up, I am having an affair with Lutz.

'Did you know,' Jacob tells him, 'that once Robbi has had one glass of wine, she will tell you anything you want to know?'

'Is that right?' says Lutz, smiling as he fills my glass. And that is how he finds out that I want to have an affair with him.

Lutz is German too and he believes in fun. If something isn't fun, you don't do it. If it is fun, you do it until it isn't. I don't think Lutz would know how to say the word 'commitment' let alone spell it. He is the perfect partner for an affair. Lutz has great parties at his house, gets up and has gin for breakfast and he is the best cook. Lutz is a successful businessman. Lutz tells me that his partner understands his need to have affairs.

I figure his relationship with his partner is his problem, not mine.

He takes me to the beach, we make love in his van, drink liqueur and then we talk and talk. He comes to my house in his coffee break and we make love in my kitchen. We make love on the Westgate Bridge and on my dining-room table. We make love when he is on his way home from work and in the bathroom at his parties. He gives me the soundtrack to *Dirty Dancing* and says, 'I think of you whenever I hear this.'

'Why do you have to save lost dogs?' asks Lutz.

'What do you mean?'

'Christopher and Jurgen, they both need saving.'

I am also having an affair with Christopher. He and I share an art studio. I can never go for long before I start painting again. It is a part of who I am. Christopher is separated from his wife and is living in a flat. I have known him for ten years and he is part of Westgate Community. We have always been in the same Small Group. Christopher takes me to pubs for lunch and tells me that he has always loved me. He tells me that for ten years he has been yearning for me and that when we used to shop at the market together for our Small Group, he could hardly keep his hands off me. He is tall and spindly and needy and I hate to say no to someone who needs me.

Jurgen and I still make love too. He always says it's for old times' sake — which I know he hopes will lead to new times — but it is always pleasurable so I don't mind.

What I do mind is that none of these men gives me an orgasm. It seems unfair that it is so easy for men to have an orgasm: it just happens, very little effort is required and basically they can't get it wrong. But I'm dependent on the man touching the right spot in the right way, or it simply doesn't happen. I get the right spot touched and then he stops, or it's too hard, or he never gets the right spot and I feel angry about depending on him or having to tell him about the right spot, which I never feel okay about doing. Men don't have to say, 'No, up a bit; up a bit, my penis is up a bit; no, softer, move a little bit softer'. Men can get orgasms hard, soft, gentle, slow, fast and they don't depend on my doing it the right way.

I walk away from these lovely rendezvous happy, but so frustrated that, seriously, if I ever meet a man who can give me orgasms, I will marry him on the spot.

One day I meet Lutz for breakfast, Christopher for lunch and Jurgen for dinner and I still don't get an orgasm — but between them, they have five.

34

My settlement from Rick comes through after two years of wrangling and arguing. I get a cheque from the lawyer. She takes a hefty chunk to help pay her private nanny's wages and Jurgen talks about all the things he would like to do with the rest of it.

'I've always wanted a boat,' he says. 'Imagine the amount of dope you could buy!'

So I throw the kids in the car and drive to Daylesford, without him. I don't know really why I am driving to Daylesford or what I will do when I get there. Maybe I am going because my grandparents took me there so often, or because I have yearned for the country since I left Canaan College.

I walk into a real-estate agent's office and a man in his late thirties is sitting behind a desk poring over a newspaper and listening to the races. A stubby of beer sits open beside the radio. He motions for me to wait until the race has finished and then he turns the radio down and looks at me.

'Have you got anything for sale? I've got thirty thousand dollars.'

His eyes light up. 'I've got one block and that is exactly what they want for it. It has electricity and a shed you can stay in.'

'A shed?'

'Yep, all lined. It's a hut really — you know, a cabin.'

'It's sounding better all the time,' I say. So the children and I pile back into our car and follow his car out to the five-acre block. I fall in love with it and wander around, knee-deep in bracken, breathing in the scent of the peppermint gums. The boys are already creating cubbies in the scrub.

'Kangaroos out here?' I ask.

'More than you're gonna want.'

'I can give you cash.'

'I'm sure that by tomorrow morning it's gonna be yours,' he says happily.

I think that maybe the children and I could be happy here. If I move, of course, I will have to give up my dream of being a minister. I am closer to that dream than I have ever been before, but I am feeling worn down by the white middle-class boys' club of the church. I have seen women friends worn down by the church. Intelligent women, whose skills are not wanted because they come out of the wrong body.

If you are gay the church says no to you. If you are female the church says no to you. If you are divorced the church says no. The church excludes where it should include and welcome.

It seems to me that Jesus was an expert at saying yes; he was also an expert at breaking down barriers and creating new rules. He treated people who were marginalised with respect and dignity and empowered the powerless. Jesus was ahead of his time. It is this that enables me to preach at all and to speak about God in a way that is real.

How can I take my daughter into this environment? What has the church got to offer her? What has the church got to offer my boys for that matter? They don't want to be dragged out of bed at nine-thirty on a Sunday morning. What a ridiculous time to meet. They don't want to sit in a cold stone building singing weak ineffectual songs. The church is dying and in fifty years will probably be gone because it has not been able to be tolerant, because it has been corrupted by wealth, because it always protects the powerful when it should protect the powerless, because it has ignored the treasures within its very walls, for the Bible says that 'a good woman is worth more than rubies'. The church will die because instead of leading the world in change as Jesus did, it lags fifty years behind social changes.

The church talks about caring for the poor, but the poor could never afford to send their children to one of the church's schools or to be treated in one of the church's hospitals. They are for the richest in the country. Can you imagine Mary, a single mum on social security with her kid, Jesus, trying to get him into Carey Grammar?

I no longer love the church. Working at Port Melbourne has got it out of my system and even though the Uniting Church is saying yes to me, I am not sure that I want to walk this path any longer. I cannot have my dream and stay true to my own integrity. And I am not sure that I even have the dream any longer.

I no longer find God in church. Instead I find God in life.

Nor can I stay in the church and give my children the life that I want to give them. If I stay I will be stuck in the city for at least three more years while I complete my study and I detest the city.

Daylesford seems to be the right move for me. It will give me space from Rick and the life we had together. It will help me leave Jurgen.

I need to see who I am, without the church and without a man. I want the children and myself to be a family.

So I decide to resign from Port Melbourne Baptist and Fitzroy Uniting Church. I am leaving the church, but I am not necessarily leaving God.

* * *

I will wait until Rick gets back from his overseas trip before I tell him I am going. He has gone overseas for six months on a Churchill Fellowship to study housing options.

Indea thinks that Rick has gone to heaven in an aeroplane and is never coming back. If I ask her where Rick is, she points to the sky and says, 'Gone to heaven.'

Before he left he offered to let me stay in our old house for $110 a week, which I can't possibly afford, so he let it to a nice uni student, a single mother, for quite a bit less. Now his mother is frantic because it turns out the nice single mother is a front for a drug gang and the police have raided the house and smashed up everything with axes.

I am trying not to look pleased but I think it is divine justice.

The phone rings ominously at six in the morning and a woman says, 'Are you Robbi?'

'Yes.'

'Your gran has passed away in her sleep.'

Gone to be with Derek, I think.

I write a funeral service for her and my father comes with his sister and one of her children. We have it at Port Melbourne Baptist and Norma plays the organ. There are not many of us at the service, but I hope that Grandma Lyne likes what I say about her and already I am missing her. I really love her and I hope she is happier.

I have not seen my father since my mother left and ran off to Queensland. I haven't heard from my mother either. I hoped and expected to, but the children's birthdays came and went and not even a card. Then it dawned on me that she didn't want to remember either us or our birthdays, and I felt jealous of Rick with his family looking after him at court.

I am nervous about seeing my father because the last time I saw him he yelled at me for leaving Rick, but I invite everyone from the funeral over for a cuppa, including my father, and he surprises me by liking Jurgen — even with his long hair.

'Never liked that rich kid husband of yours,' my father grumps. I remember the angry words he yelled at me when I left Rick, but I just let it be.

He sits at my kitchen table, up the end where a head would be if we had one, the place where he has always sat, and he reads my grandmother's will. She has left him three thousand dollars.

'Tell you what,' says my father, when everyone else has gone, 'I'm lending this to you. You need it more than I do.'

I just about fall off my chair. My father has never done anything for me since he got rid of Rodney Burlington. Nothing, ever! I haven't even seen him and now out of the blue here he is lending me money.

'Thanks, Dad,' I stammer. 'Thanks.'

Maybe, I think, he is changing and cares about me. Maybe he wants to be a grandfather. No — that's not it. He has ignored the children completely, but at least he hasn't yelled at them and that in itself is an improvement.

As he walks to his car to leave, I am struck by the fact that he looks so defeated. His limp from the polio he had as a kid is definitely worse, his shoulders are decidedly slumped. He looks washed out. But at least he seems to be mellowing. I remember how differently he talked when my mother was in hospital for three weeks. Perhaps ageing and being away from my mother is taking the fight out of him.

Rick arrives back from overseas and comes to collect the children.

'Why is their hair so long?' he yells at me before he has even got to the front yard.

I look at Jacob and Seth, and they look like two little hippie kids. Indea's hair has hardly grown much at all, but there are the three of them, dressed in old nappies as loin cloths, running around with sticks for sceptres, because the game is Ancient Greece. They look like happy, well-balanced, grubby little Vegemites.

'Because that's how they like it,' I retort, starting to tremble as I always do when I am confronted by Rick.

'Robbi, you are so irresponsible.'

'It's *their* hair,' I say. 'Kids don't get to decide much about life so they can at least decide how they want their hair!'

Jacob and Seth bounce over to hug the father they haven't seen for six months and Seth blurts out, 'We're moving to Daylesford.'

'Is this true?' Rick turns abruptly from the children and glares at me. I can feel the volcano start to rumble.

'Yes. I want the children to grow up in the country.'

'But Daylesford is hours away! You can't take my children away from me!' he yells.

I feel guilty. I would hate the children to be further than two rooms away from me. But I say, 'It's an hour and a quarter away actually, and if I moved to the other side of the city — say to Hampton — it would take you longer to get to them there. I don't have any life here.'

Living here is all about Rick. When I walk down the street I bump into someone who says, 'How is Rick? What are you and Rick doing? I saw Rick and his girlfriend or Rick said this or Rick said that.' I want to build a life without having to think about Rick, with people who don't even know him.

'I won't let you do this!' he says angrily.

'I'm going to do it. It's not that big a deal,' I say. 'You've just spent six months away from them anyway. I'll bring them down to you every weekend.'

So, fuming and frustrated, Rick puts the children in the car and I go and plonk on the couch and wonder whether things will ever be reasonable between us. Will we ever be able to talk without having our swords already drawn, ready to strike?

Jurgen knows that I am always a mess after I see Rick so he has the kettle on to make me a cuppa. I am sitting on the couch reading *Monkey Grip* when the phone interrupts me again.

'Can you get that?' Jurgen yells from the kitchen.

Aunt Tonia says hello and since I haven't heard from her since I left Rick, I am surprised to hear her voice. 'I have cancer,' she tells me, getting right to the point. 'And there's nothing the doctors can do. I have to clear my conscience.'

I am feeling sick in my stomach: sick for my dying aunt, whom I love, and sick because I don't know what she could possibly have to confess to me. 'Are you sure there is nothing they can do?' I hear my voice say, breaking with emotion.

'I'm not having any treatment. I am trusting the Lord to heal me, if it is his will. I'm ringing because I have to confess something I have done. Something I shouldn't have done,' she says.

'Yes?' I grip the phone.

'I told Rick after you split up that I didn't think you deserved him. I said that he was far too good for you. I still think it, but I shouldn't have said it to him.'

'You still think it?' I say.

'Yes, but I shouldn't have told him. That was wrong of me.'

'It doesn't matter.'

'So will you forgive me for saying it to him?'

'Yes, of course,' I mutter to the phone. 'Bye,' I say quickly, because I feel too wounded to talk anymore. My own aunt loved my ex-husband more than she loved me and now she is going to die. I put the phone down and sit; feeling as if someone has whacked me with a spade.

Jurgen looks at me. 'Who was that?' he asks.

'My aunt,' I say, 'clearing her conscience.'

I resign from Port Melbourne Baptist and they tell me they will give me a year to change my mind and that they will officially put me on leave of absence instead of accepting my resignation. They give me lovely presents: tie-dyed stockings and money, because they know I can do with money more than gifts, and we drink mulled wine together.

I will miss them dreadfully.

I take the children to visit my father. He has a girlfriend now and the children pile out of the car, glad to be in the country after a long drive.

'You can call me Granddad,' he says to the children. He has actually spoken to them! This is a good sign. They are bemused. They don't really know who he is.

'This is Vic,' I say. But they are fairly unimpressed and the boys scamper off to play in the trimaran, the same one, still sitting there without its ends. The paint is peeling and the wood is cracked. He may have lost us over the years, but he has kept his boat, I think resentfully. Everywhere he has gone, and in each house he has gone to, he has made room for that boat. The sky blue that never got painted has deepened with age to the colour of storm.

'Watch out for spiders,' I call to the boys, but they are gone, absorbed in their own world. I take Indea and heft her onto my hip as I follow Dad and his girlfriend inside. In the lounge room I melt into one of the vinyl armchairs that were bought from Myer for the house in Parkdale. The vinyl is cracking now and I wriggle to get comfortable and Indea nestles into my arm. She likes to stay close to home. The girlfriend makes tea and sandwiches for lunch but Dad doesn't get up to help. He puts on his Mozart.

'Do you want a hand?' I call out.

'No, I'm right,' she answers. 'I always make your father's lunch for him, don't I, Vic?'

'Oh, yes. She's a good cook, aren't you, love?' he calls out to her.

'Listen, Dad,' I say after I have helped his girlfriend clean up after lunch. 'Did Mum leave all the photos, home movies and slides of us kids growing up with you? I'd really like to look at a few. The boys want to see what their mother looked like as a little girl.'

'I threw them down the tip,' he says gruffly.

'Sorry?' I am sure I have not heard right. I have photos of my children and I treasure them. If there was a fire the first thing I would make a dash for, after ourselves of course, would be the photos of the children. They are irreplaceable.

'I threw them down the tip,' he says again. 'I didn't want them.'

But didn't he think we might? How can a parent throw out photos of his children growing up — photos of a time that can never be recaptured? I sit there stunned.

I don't say anything and he is unaware of my reaction, but as I sit there I realise that he really doesn't have any fatherly feelings towards us. He isn't protective or proud of us. We are just these beings he has produced. The feelings I have for my children are comparable only to the lack of feeling my parents have for me.

We go and sit outside in the sun to watch Jacob and Seth running around.

They start to chase each other, squealing and laughing as they enjoy the space the country offers. Seth runs into my father's chair.

'Watch it!' screams my father, suddenly snapping.

Seth stops dead in his tracks, shocked by the menace in my father's voice.

He looks to me and I try to reassure him with an expression and gaze that says it's okay and I'll look after him. So the boys continue to play and shriek, laugh and tumble.

Soon my father is yelling again. 'Shit, you kids! Bloody kids! Christ!'

Jacob is only seven going on eight and Seth is two years younger and they have never been spoken to like this. They are shocked and frightened. I stand close to my chicks and I keep Indea on my hip.

Then it happens. Seth spills his fruit juice and my father's arm reaches out to swipe him. 'Bloody useless twit! Look what you've done!' he yells.

I step between my father and Seth, just in time. 'You are never to hit my children. Never!' I say in a low, deep and controlled voice. 'These are *my* children and they do not get screamed at, and they most definitely do not get hit.'

My father gets up from his chair, hitches his trousers and storms off to his bedroom, swearing, 'Bloody useless daughter. Bloody useless kids I've got! The bloody lota ya!'

'You've really hurt your father's feelings, you and your brothers and sister,' says his girlfriend. 'That's why he threw the photos down the tip. He didn't want to see any more of you.'

'He isn't half as hurt as we are,' I retort. I put the children in the car, drive home and decide that I won't see my father again.

Part Three

Love

35

The children and I are living in our ten by eighteen foot tin shed on our own bushy five acres in Daylesford. Indea is digging for frogs which she catches by the dozen. She caresses them, whispers secrets to them and sets them free. I am sitting in a camp chair, rugged up in a scarf, hat and japara, my knees jiggling with the cold. I am watching the boys playing war with the bracken. The rules are so intricate, I can never follow them and they seem to change constantly, but at least the two boys are on the same side. Merlin, our dog, bounds around after them. Jurgen gave us the dog. He is a pure-bred bearded collie and he is a gracious gift; I know Jurgen paid a lot for him.

I will have to shower the children tonight, because they will be filthy. I will boil up water on the pot-bellied stove that sits in one corner of the shed. This is our heating and where I do all the cooking. Then I'll fill up the camp shower with the warmed water, which is like a plastic bag with a shower nozzle hanging out of it, and because it will be evening the kangaroos will come and watch us as we stand naked under the gum trees showering. I'll have to wash the children's hair very quickly or they will end up with a head full of slimy conditioner. But the kangaroos stand there and gaze at us, their heads tilted quizzically as I race to clean the children's hair before the water runs out. I'll have to do my hair in the morning.

I wander inside to set up beds for the night. Every morning we pack up foam mattresses and sleeping bags to make living space — there isn't any living space unless the beds are packed up.

Tomorrow is pension day and I'll drive over to Ballarat and line up behind the senior citizens. Then I'll buy the children a roast dinner in the shopping complex. They only need one meal between them and they always finish off with trifle, reassuring me all the time it's okay that I don't know how to cook meat very well.

I don't go to church on Sunday mornings; instead I have a cup of tea and read a book. I keep feeling like I must be ill to miss church, but I remind myself there is one reason I don't go and that is I don't want to. And there are quite a few reasons for *that*. The children are just excited that they have an extra morning to play.

On Monday we go into town to wash our clothes at the laundromat. The man who runs the local tyre shop comes out of the supermarket with a bottle of red in his hand. For tonight's dinner, no doubt. He nods at me with that understated nod country blokes have, such a slight movement of the head in your direction that if you didn't know you'd easily miss it, and he starts to walk away but changes his mind and comes over.

'Those tyres need replacing,' he says gruffly.

I look at him. I don't know what to say. I can't afford new tyres. Besides, they look okay to me.

He sizes me up, then adds, 'Look, you can't drive children around on those tyres. See? The metal's poking through.'

I look and he's right: there are sharp silver threads sticking out of the rubber.

'Bring the car round now. I'll change the tyres while you

wait for your washing and you can pay me off as you can afford it.'

'You sure?' I say.

'Sure? Of course I'm sure. I just said so, didn't I?' he barks and he's off to the garage with the bottle tucked under his arm.

So I drive the car around to John Savage Tyre Repair and a man I've never met before is kind to me.

We have to leave our car, an old EJ Holden that is a beautiful blue Mato would have loved, up the front of the block or it becomes bogged in the mud. Then we tramp down the driveway to the shed in our gumboots, japaras, hats and gloves, lugging our washing and groceries in drizzly, grey weather. We've bought some cheap outdoor paint, so we dump the shopping and washing without even sorting through it and we start to cover the shed in pictures. We each take a wall and soon our Sistine shed has flowers and portraits that make it truly ours. As we sing and slap on the paint, gentle wet flakes start to fall.

'What's falling from the sky?' asks Indea.

'I think it's snow,' I tell her and the children start to squeal with excitement.

I thought Daylesford seemed bloody cold!

The children are absolutely sodden from dancing in the snow and I drag them into the shed to peel off their clothing and get them warm and we snuggle into our sleeping bags with toast and tea and I read them *The Once and Future King* until they fall asleep. Outside it is quiet and still.

On Wednesday night I take Jacob to ballet in Ballarat, where they are terribly excited to have a boy in the school. Friday morning Lutz comes to visit me, laden with wine and liqueur.

'Life is so safe in the country,' I tell him. 'The children can't get hurt here. I don't have to watch them the entire time, worried that they might get run over, or kidnapped or hurt in some other way.'

He and I are lying intertwined on one of the mattresses that I have propped up against the wall. I have to keep moving his hands from where they keep delving in case one of the children walks in. They've already caught us once. But I don't want to move his hands too vehemently because I don't really want him to stop. Between Lutz and me it must be a chemical thing, because neither of us seems able to control it. Two seconds in the same room and we are all over each other, if possible. If not possible, then we have sex with our eyes.

'I think,' he says as he kisses my neck, 'that Christopher,' and his mouth moves onto mine and we become lost in each other, 'really loves you,' he finishes.

'Do you think so?' I ask between kisses.

'Mmmmm,' he says and we entwine ourselves around each other again.

I reach for the Cointreau he has brought and quickly disentangle myself from his body as Jacob walks into the shed.

'See?' I say, pointing at Jacob. 'An example of healthy country childhood.' Jacob is covered in clean, healthy mud.

'I think I've got something in my leg,' Jacob says and he looks down at the same time we do. He goes white and, despite my light Cointreau-filled head, I bounce up and catch him just in time as he faints into my arms. The biggest rusty nail you ever saw is poking through his jeans like a dinosaur tooth and is embedded firmly in his leg.

Lutz picks him up in his arms and carries him to his van and lays him on the mattress where we have made love many times.

He drives Jacob to the hospital and I follow with Seth and Indea in the EJ.

The doctor introduces himself without fuss — 'I'm Fred'

— and he promptly pulls out the nail, gives Jacob a tetanus injection and tells me to keep him off his leg for a week, so that the infection doesn't spread.

Of course all this attention suddenly focused on my son sends the childless Lutz scurrying home — and leaves both of us discontented, our lust unfulfilled.

The local pharmacy lends me a wheelchair so I can take Jacob out. Keeping a nine year old from boredom in a shed for a week isn't fun.

With the school holidays over and Jacob and Seth back as two of twelve at their local country school, life is simple and sweet. Christopher comes to visit me almost daily between nine and three, until I ring him from the public phone and he tells me that he isn't really separated at all. I find out that his flat was some elaborate ploy to get me to have an affair with him and fulfil some ten-year-old fantasy he had.

I feel devastated at having been deceived so thoroughly. I trusted him. He had been my friend for so long that I thought he really cared about me, and now I have lost not only a lover but a close friend as well. I would have been quite happy to only ever have him as a friend. I didn't need him as a lover. I already had one of those.

When I next deliver the children to Rick he yells at me for having an affair with Christopher, because he is friendly with Christopher's wife, who of course hates me more now than she ever did. Before she had just hated me for leaving her friend Rick.

The children didn't like Christopher anyway. Jacob thought he was wimpy and Seth thought he was weird and they are glad he is out of the picture.

They are breathing the sleeping breath of angels, snuggled up next to me in their sleeping bags, and I start to doze off myself when a vision of my aunt fills my head and she is waving at me from the other side of a river. The river is glorious, surrounded by lush, soft grass and wise verdant trees. I know now that she has died. The cancer has been swift and cruel.

Her funeral is, of course, a joyous occasion, despite the fact that she is leaving behind her fatherless son, who is now a young teenager. My uncle says that even in her last moments alive she was singing praises to the Lord and looking forward to joining him in His kingdom. He plays a tape of her singing:

I am trusting Thee, Lord Jesus, trusting only Thee.
Trusting Thee for full salvation, great and free.
I am trusting Thee for pardon; at Thy feet I bow,
For Thy grace and tender mercy, trusting now.

I have tears streaming down my face again. I loved my aunt. She was creative and generous and kind to me until I left Rick.

At the house, which was my home with Mato, we have tea and cake after the service. My cousins from India, who are now university graduates, are here with their parents, as are many of my other twenty-six cousins, my aunts and uncles. I wonder what they make of Jurgen who has come with me to give me some support. He is back on drugs and back to beads and feathers in his hair. When he speaks he puts his face inches from yours, as if he is having trouble focusing both his eyes and his mind. His jeans are torn in just the right places around his bum and on his knees and he is wearing striped leggings underneath them. He is having an affair with Christopher's sister-in-law.

As I am standing among my relatives, feeling as if I don't belong and never want to go to another funeral in my life, the minister from Hampton Baptist comes up to me, carefully balancing his tea cup on its saucer as he moves through the crowd.

'Hi, Robbi! Remember me from theology classes?'

'Yeah, I do. Are you the minister here now?' I say.

'Yeah, I just started.' He leans close to me, lowers his voice and asks, 'Do you mind if I ask you what you thought of the funeral service?'

'I thought it failed to deal in any real sense with anyone's true pain or loss,' I say. 'I thought it denied the fact that my aunt is gone. We have lost her and that is painful and not something to rejoice over.'

'Phew,' he says. 'I'm glad I'm not alone.'

My cousin from India looks over her shoulder and says, 'Sshhh! Don't offend anyone.'

36

In Daylesford I am just another single, hippie mother looking for a nice bloke who has a job, a house and no drug problem, except I don't want the nice bloke with the house, the job and with or without the drug problem. I enjoy being alone with the children and having lovers at a safe distance.

But I'm not enjoying the poverty. I am on the single parent's pension and it's tough. I know it is all relative, but I can only afford one pair of shoes for the children. So if they get that pair wet — as they do — then they have no shoes. We definitely can't afford meat or ice cream. I can live without the meat, but the boys are little carnivores.

There is absolutely no chance of going to the movies in the holidays. We don't have a television, and that's great, but once again I am without music and I miss it.

Because I really want them to do ballet and piano I just have to go without other things that are not as important, but which the children want or need or miss.

Rick's family will take them to the movies in the holidays and I feel bitter that I am providing them with school, clothes and food out of my meagre funds and then along comes Rick's mother with all her money and she gets to do all the fun things with them.

Because the children go to such a small country school they spend their days making cubby houses with branches in the playground and they take last night's dinner and microwave it for lunch. They love their life here and through the school I make new friends. Because there are a lot of single mothers in Daylesford I feel supported and part of a community again. We feed our children avocado and bean sprout sandwiches and make miso and tofu soup for lunch and we talk about the available men, their drug problems, their lack of ambition and drive and how many women they are sleeping with at the same time. Most of the single men in Daylesford are feral and need to be taken home and given a good scrub.

'By the time you've been here five years you'll have been through every available guy and be back with the one you started with. That's what happens to every unattached person in this town. You just keep doing the loop,' Angie, one of the other mothers, tells me.

I will have to make sure that doesn't happen to me, I think. God, I hope I never get that desperate and lonely. But I can see that it could happen. I could become a frustrated single mother.

But I am strongly aware that as a single woman in a small country town, I need to be careful not to show any of the husbands too much attention or the wives will get angry and ostracise me. Because I am not yet carrying any good country weight to see me through the harsh winters and because of my mini-skirts the wives already mistrust me, and it has been reported around town that I am having an affair with the husband of a friend of mine.

I am experimenting with spirituality and so far I have had an astrology chart drawn up, a shaman healing and a reading by a clairvoyant. I want to find out whether these things are really as evil as I have been taught. At this stage I don't think they're satanic — just expensive. And when it comes down to it, not all that helpful. Some of the things these people ask me to believe are just as far-fetched as the virgin birth. So far I have a spirit guide that is a turtle, I was an Egyptian princess and Jacob and Seth were my two pet panthers, and I am very old and on my last life cycle. I hope this is true, because I don't want to do it again. But it seems to me that all this is no more than superstition.

I bought an *I Ching* book and found out that two people I know asked the *I Ching* if I and this guy were having an affair and the *I Ching* apparently said yes. Then word spread through town until finally my friend said to me, 'Are you having an affair with my husband?' I was shocked. I wasn't having an affair with him. I still had Lutz. She was so upset and all because after doing their dolphin meditation Leo and Jill thought they would finish off with a bit of the *I Ching*. That's Daylesford for you.

I have a friend named Ian, who is tall and skinny. His skin doesn't fit on him, as if he was washed on a heavy cycle instead of gentle and has lost his shape. He is a home father who is married and his little girl is the same age as Indea. Every day he comes to see me and the girls frolic naked together while we make herbal tea and chat about life. I tell him about Lutz, Jurgen and Christopher, about leaving Rick and how it was the most difficult and distressing thing I have ever done. But, I tell him, I'm glad I did it because I don't want my children growing up with our relationship as their model of married life.

He says it's pretty obvious that we won't survive the coming summer heat in our little shed. And before I know it, Ian has arranged for us to rent a lovely mud-brick house. I sell the block with the shed and buy a block of land on the school bus run. Maybe one day I can build on it.

The house is open plan and the top level becomes an island, complete with pirate ship, treasure and chilling seas that the children have built out of sheets, boxes and their beds. So they lie in bed with me at night because there is no room for them in their bedrooms and I read to them while bats come out of their daytime hiding holes and fly around our heads, chirping and singing to each other.

The centre of community life in Daylesford is the café and at the centre of the café is Sebastian. I have worked out a wonderful routine. During the week and every other weekend I belong totally to the children. It is such a relief not to have to juggle their needs with the needs of a man. But every other weekend I drive them to Melbourne to spend the weekend with their father and Saturday and Sunday are mine. I buy satay tofu and vegies from the Chinese shop and spin it out for lunch and dinner on Saturday. The reason I don't cook for myself is that it is so boring to cook for yourself, but as well I spend all Saturday painting. I set up my easel in the lounge room and I paint and paint. I paint on paper because I can afford it and I paint about Lutz and Jurgen and single motherhood. I use a mixture of paint and pastels. They are soft and create a beautiful matt texture on the paper. I can get the vibrant colours that I want and, just as with paint, I can pile colour on top of colour and create layers.

On Sunday morning I go to the market and buy my vegies. Then I hit the café for breakfast. Sebastian the beautiful, Sebastian the desire of most girls' hearts — well, maybe not their hearts but their hormones — waltzes towards me, smiling. He looks like a Ken doll: perfect, faultless skin, just right baby-blue eyes, supermodel physique, thick tousled hair. He balances my eggs, mushrooms and spinach and my pot of tea and blueberry smoothie on a tray on one arm.

Unlike a Ken doll, Sebastian's parts all work. My friend Sylvie asked him to father a child, but everyone knows she is in line behind Kate. Every girl in town is in love with him but me. I don't like perfect movie star looks. I like looks that are real and earthy. My ideal man has long black hair, dark brooding eyes and a solid body that can protect you if you are threatened by wild beasts.

Sebastian places my food in front of me and I fold up *The Age* to make room for it. As he leaves he gives me the smallest wink. I am sure he does this to all the girls.

The waitress who is working this morning has swollen red eyes. She places food down on tables with a thump and I notice that she starts crying and blubbering whenever Sebastian comes near her. Neil Young is singing 'A Man Needs a Maid' and Annette can take it no longer. She drops a tray of coffee cups that shatter on the ground. I look up from my breakfast along with everyone else in the café.

Someone weakly calls out 'Taxi' and Annette stomps out of the café an emotional mess, tears streaming down her blotchy face.

Sebastian shrugs. 'Anyone wanting coffee?' Felix does and people go back to their meals and gossip. I ask someone what is going on and learn in two seconds flat what everyone else already seems to know. Apparently Sebastian's ex-girlfriend is three months pregnant and he has been going out with Annette now for six months. If you're a half decent bloke in Daylesford you can get away with this sort of thing because the demand is pretty high.

After painting all Saturday it is time to get ready for the party Sally and Paul are having. Thank goodness the children are at Rick's this weekend and I can go. When I was married I never got a break from them and the best thing about Daylesford is the parties. They are regular, fun and outrageous, with plenty of dope and oodles of alcohol. I wear my short burgundy dress with my fishnet stockings and an old-fashioned garter. Sometimes I wear my black tunic that looks like a school uniform and the men are toast. I don't care what the wives think of me at parties. I am here for my lost teenage years.

I soon realise that it doesn't matter: the wives here are trying to forget they are married.

'Come on, Robbi, dance with us,' Trish insists.

I shake my head.

'Come on.'

'No, I can't, really,' I say.

And they grab my arm and pull me off my seat to dance with them.

'Listen, guys, I mean it. I can't dance.'

'What do you mean you can't dance?' asks Trish.

'I can't dance. I've never really done it.' I don't think that flailing wildly around a lounge room with Franciscan priests constitutes dancing. It's not the sort of dancing you can do at a party where you want to impress men.

'Everyone has danced,' they persist.

'Not me. I was brought up a good Baptist.'

'Well, girl, you're about to learn!' They pull me up onto the dance floor and even though I feel so self-conscious, I try to move like they do, but I know I look rigid and silly. A few more drinks and pretty soon I don't care whether I look okay or not. I am having such a good time. I am Baptist and I am dancing. I can't wait for the next party.

On Monday I deliver the boys to school and collect the mail from the letterbox as I arrive back home. Ian will be over any minute to have a cuppa. I have to clean away the children's dirty clothes that lie all over the floor like scatter rugs before he arrives. I open the envelope as I walk through the door. Inside is a note. It says, 'Thought you could use this for the children' and there is a cheque. Jurgen has sent us some money. Totally out of the blue. It just arrives in the post, a bank cheque for three thousand dollars.

I pay what I still owe to John Savage, the tyre repair man, buy a few things for the house like a television and video, and I book us into a caravan in Robe.

We sing all the way there. Mostly we sing along with the Mamas and Papas but our family song is 'Stand By Me', so John Lennon gets a good look in too. We sing it at the top of our lungs and not one of us can sing in key.

At Robe the boys body-surf, we eat fish and chips and we go for long walks on the beach. We have to walk slowly so little Indea can keep up. She is happy to be on the beach. The beach seems to her the most appropriate place for showing off her developing fashion sense and she has taken to wearing star-shaped sunglasses everywhere.

As we walk along, kicking up the sand, Jacob says to me, 'I love you, I think you are the best mum in the whole world.'

'Me too,' adds Seth.

'Why, thank you, boys,' I say and give them a curtsey.

'We want it to be always just you and us,' says Jacob.

'But what if I meet a nice man?' I ask, knowing there is potential trouble here that needs to be dealt with sooner rather than later.

'We don't want you to,' they say.

Surprise, surprise.

'Where would he sleep?' asks Seth.

'In bed with me.'

'But we sleep in bed with you,' he says.

'But, boys,' I say, 'one day you will grow up and meet someone nice and you will want to leave me and live with them. And that is what should happen. So don't you think it's only fair that if I meet someone nice I should be able to live with them now, so that when you leave home I won't be left alone?'

'I s'pose that's fair,' says Seth agreeably.

'Yeah, okay,' says Jacob. 'I s'pose it is. So we'll move over and make room for him in the bed.'

I laugh and we wander back to the caravan to cook sausages. Anyone can cook sausages and they always smell irresistible in caravan parks.

The children and I have such fun in Robe, but at night, when they are asleep, the solitariness of being a single mother hits me like a sledgehammer. There is no one to bounce things off. No one to share the slow, night hours.

When we get home Ian is waiting. I am surprised because it isn't the sort of time I would expect him. His wife isn't at work on weekends. He helps me get our bags out of the car and makes me a cup of tea. The boys are on the phone and within five minutes have arranged for friends to pick them up and take them to their houses. So much for continuing any family time! I put Indea to bed because she is exhausted from the trip and coming out of the bedroom I start to empty out some of the luggage, sorting dirty clothes from clean.

'Where is your wife?' I say to Ian.

'I've left her,' he says as if he were talking about grocery shopping.

I stop emptying bags, stand there and look at him. I can see he means it.

'I want you,' he says in the same monotone, matter-of-fact way.

I sigh. I like being a thirty-year-old woman in the prime of my sexuality; I can feel it tingling in my bones. It is never going to be better than it is now. I am single and old enough to enjoy it. But I want to have sex with men I am attracted to and inspired by, not just any man who comes along. The trouble is there don't seem to be any inspiring men around. I certainly don't get enough sex and sometimes ordinary — even bland — sex seems better than no sex at all. I can tell that this is what I am going to get from Ian, because there is friendship between us but no spark. But I decide to make the most of what is available. 'I don't want a relationship with you,' I say, 'but sex would be okay.'

He looks pretty happy with that. 'Would you draw me?' he asks. 'I've always wanted someone to draw me.'

'You mean naked? A life drawing?'

He has already started to strip off, but I have hardly put pencil to paper when the phone interrupts us.

'Hello, I am ringing from the Castlemaine Artists' Group,' says an unknown voice. 'You sent in a membership form.'

'Yes,' I say, waiting.

'Well, we were wondering if you would like to hold an exhibition as part of this year's fringe festival.'

'Yes, I'd love to,' I say eagerly.

'I'm going to have an exhibition!' I say as I hang up the phone and jump around the room. 'I have to get my paintings ready.'

At the exhibition in Castlemaine I hang a painting of Lutz and me drinking champagne in the bath. He has an erection and I call it 'My lover says he loves me for my mind'. I also have a painting of me in bed having erotic dreams about the work of Michael Leunig. The exhibition is hung in a Catholic church hall that has been hired by the fringe festival. I sit and wait for people to come and see my paintings.

A woman from the church stomps around my exhibition with her nose in the air and her high heels clopping noisily on the floorboards. 'Disgusting,' she mutters. She brings back the priest who seems more annoyed with her than with my paintings.

'It has to be taken down! It is offensive! This is a church hall!'

'This is an art space,' I say. 'I'm not taking anything down.'

'This is distasteful!' they say.

I answer, 'This is a celebration of life.'

After more discussion it turns out they object to the male nudity. They don't mind the female nudity though. But anything with a naked male in it has to be removed. I offer a compromise. I will put newspaper over my paintings with a sign saying 'censored' and if people want to, they can lift up the newspaper and look. The church accepts.

The press find out about the censorship and I am in the newspapers. 'EX BAPTIST PASTOR PAINTS PORNOGRAPHY.' Front page.

I am on the radio. 'We hear there are erections in your paintings?' the interviewer asks.

'Yes, but only little ones,' I say.

'Do you think your paintings are offensive?'

'Children going hungry is offensive; children with no shoes to wear. That's offensive. The naked body has been in art for hundreds of years. The naked body is not offensive. The church doesn't mind female nakedness; they just can't cope with male nakedness. Don't you think that's strange?' I say.

The TV people arrive with their Bollé sunglasses in Castlemaine, a town of eight thousand, in a helicopter with equipment that looks like machine-gun cases.

'What do you think of the pornographic paintings?' they ask the taxi driver.

'I can't see there's a problem,' he says into the mike. 'Weeell — art's art ain't it?'

They ask the same question of the local gallery owner. 'I think Robbi's paintings are fun and whimsical,' he says. 'She's playing with her sexuality. It's healthy.'

'Did you set out to be controversial?' they ask me.

'God, no!' I say. 'I've got three kids. I don't have time to be anything.'

Mary Delahunty on the '7.30 Report' says, 'Oh, oh, oh, I like that line. "I haven't got time to be controversial. I've got kids." Yes, well, I can relate to that.'

* * *

As I am sitting bored, squiggling on paper, babysitting my exhibition while people come to look at the censored paintings, a group of about ten elderly women visit and bring their own cask of wine and some plastic cups.

'Hope you don't mind, dear,' they say. 'We like your paintings. They make us laugh. Thought we might just have a little party here. Would you like some vino?' And they sit down and chat and laugh about men they have had and tell me that the older you get the better life becomes.

The gallery owner is soon visiting my house. He is a really nice man and I like him, but Ian gets in his way.

37

My landlord keeps coming into my house when I am out. He eats my food, uses my crockery and sleeps in my bed.

I ring up the tenants' tribunal and they suggest I move out. 'You could take him to the tribunal,' they say, 'and you would win, but he would make life unbearable for you afterwards. You would still have to move.'

So the kids and I move house yet again. We love this new house. It is two blocks from the shops and we can walk everywhere.

I don't have enough money to buy a house. I don't have enough money to build a house and I can see that living in rented accommodation is going to become a constant series of moves. I have too much money to apply for a ministry house and I don't want to fritter the settlement away on living expenses, because I know it is my only chance to secure a home for my children.

While I am thinking about these things the postman's bike goes past and I wander out into the morning sun and get the mail. I flick through the envelopes and moan because they are all bills. But one has 'John Konteck' written on the left-hand corner of the envelope. He is the real-estate agent we are renting through. I tear open the letter, curious to know why they are writing to me. Why wouldn't the agent just pop around the corner and see me? I read the letter as I wander back up the driveway. 'We are writing to inform you that the house you are currently renting has been sold and the new owners wish you to vacate within the next four weeks.'

I can't believe this has happened. We have only been in this house for eight weeks. Now I have to pack us up and move yet again. The shock of what I have done hits me. I have left my secure marriage, my community, my home and now I am alone with the full responsibility for three small lives and I can't even provide them with a house to live in for longer than six months. I do the only thing I can in the circumstances. I weep and sob, collapse to the floor and give in totally and selfishly to my sorrow and fear. I cannot bear the thought of another upheaval. And then the front door bell rings. It is Ian and I hand him the letter.

'You can all move in with me,' he says kindly. And he goes to the kitchen to put on my kettle.

A shiver runs through me. I am not ready to live with a man, especially a man who has children. I am enjoying my life with my three kids too much and we have such a good time together. We cook and dance around the kitchen to loud rock music that we play on Jacob's plastic cassette player. We sit in bed and read. Every Tuesday night is video night and we clamber under blankets on the couch and watch wholesome movies like *Anne of Green Gables.* We laugh together and one boyfriend says to me, 'You're not like a normal single mother. Most single mothers and their kids act as if something is missing in their lives, but you guys seem so happy together, just like a normal family.'

I don't want to move in with Ian. I don't like his son. He is the sort of child whose fist just suddenly flies out of nowhere and hits another unsuspecting child in the face. He will throw a ball into Indea's face at close range, even though she is four years younger than him, and Ian's response is always, 'Yep, that's my boy.' My sons are gentle and kind.

Ian lives in a tiny house. I can't imagine him, me and five kids crammed in together.

'Thanks for such a kind offer. I'll see what I can find first,' I say.

'Sure,' he says. He is offended.

I traipse backwards and forwards between the three real-estate agents, all of whom assure me there is nothing to rent in Daylesford anymore because every available house is being turned into a Bed and Breakfast.

'Are you sure you have nothing coming up? I'm desperate,' I say.

'Okay, go and look at this house down the bottom of Hospital Street,' says Heather with the long red nails and the power suit, and she gives me a real-estate agent smile.

I drive eagerly to Hospital Street and the house is an old double-fronted Victorian cottage. Great! Just what I love. I put the tarnished gold key into the front door, push it open and I am hit with the most awful stench. It is so bad I have to turn away and gasp for some fresh air. Finally I think I can brave it and I walk over the waves of the distorted floorboards and look in the first room. It is hard to see because the house is so dark, but my eyes adjust and I can make out that the curtains are torn, the walls are covered in mould and they are brown with dirt. From there it just gets worse, like a French movie. Frustrated and disappointed I decide to go back to the agent.

'I can't take that house,' I say.

'Why not?' Heather snaps. 'I thought you were desperate.'

'I can't take my children to live there. It's not fit for anyone to live in.'

'Well,' she says, tossing her hair around, 'if you want to be that fussy, we can't help you any further.'

'Would you let *your* children live in that house?' I say as I walk out the door.

Behind me I can hear her muttering about single mothers.

I put the children in the car and drive them to the house in Hospital Street. I get them out and we walk around the house and I lift them up so they can peer through the windows.

'Why are we here?' the boys ask.

'Where do you want to live, boys? Here, or with Ian?'

They take one look at the house. 'With Ian,' they say unhappily and together. The children don't like him. They don't like his son.

Seth is crying. 'I hate them,' he says. 'They don't even call spaghetti "spaghetti", they call it plaster.'

'He's mean to us when you're not around,' says Jacob.

'Listen, boys, I promise that as soon as I can find us somewhere of our own to live, I will. I promise.'

Living with Ian, I feel that I have lost all sense of myself. I am not moving forward. I'm stuck, but I am at least giving my children a roof over their heads without uprooting them once again from their community and friends.

However, my relationship with Ian is one of constant splitting up and getting back together — just like it was with the boyfriends I didn't really like when I was younger.

I tell him I want to split up with him and he says, 'Come to Uluru with me first.'

Next time I tell him he asks me to go overseas just as a friend, because he doesn't want to travel alone. In Thailand he gets angry every time I give money to the beggars. But I have to give money to them so that I can live with myself; it's the Westgate community still in me.

Ian yells at Rick when he comes to get the children and says he is disgusted that Rick could let his children have nowhere to live. Rick yells back that we could move out of

Daylesford and soon have somewhere to live. They pull back and forth on Seth's arms and I yell at them both to stop right now and I take Seth inside. I cuddle him all night while he whimpers and I sink into depression.

Ian decides to take control of the situation and writes letters to my ex in-laws to say how disgusted he is that they don't care about the circumstances that their grandchildren are living in. How can they have so much money and yet not provide for their own grandchildren? he says. I can feel myself slipping into a deep, dark hole. It is all getting too hard. I do not want to move from Daylesford, because it's our home now, but the poverty is grinding me down. I feed the children a lot of noodles and rice to make ends meet, but I don't know what to do about finding somewhere to live. My car is falling apart and I can't afford to have it fixed. I apply for jobs in cafés and they tell me I am not café material, but there are no other jobs to be had and, besides, I have now been at home for too long with the children. I am out of touch. The months slip by and the clouds settle right over my head.

I go to collect the mail and there is a letter from Rick's mother. Inside is a cheque for five thousand dollars.

I can now get a loan from the bank for a relocated house to put on our block of land.

38

We love our house but Ian has paid for the excavation of my block and our dam. I don't know how I will ever pay him back. He says he grew up in a family with a single mother and he can't stand the struggle single-parent families go through.

Though we have a phone we have no septic system, water or power, but the house is ours. The children can't do their homework because by the time they get home from school it is too dark inside to be able to see properly and the gas lantern casts too many shadows. I don't know how my great-gran ever coped. I guess in those days people just went blind.

I am experimenting with Wicca and doing pagan meditations. I light candles and cast spells. I've been inspired by reading *The Mists of Avalon.* I want to see if paganism is a valid form of spirituality. I have always been taught it is evil but so far it seems little more than superstition.

The spells and meditations are not giving me hope.

I am painting again but my work is dreadful and uninspired. Thank goodness for the dam though. I wash in it, even though it is cold, and Ian watches from his window next door. I cart up buckets to do the dishes and flush the toilet and to paint with. I do have bottle gas, so I can cook.

I read to the children and we all sleep together in my bed because we only have the one gas lantern. We go to sleep gazing at the stars through our bare windows and listening to the kangaroos thump around in the night outside. They are often down by our dam.

When we awake, it's to the noisy squawking of the tribe of cockatoos that perch in the old gum tree, gossiping and squabbling, and to the sun streaming in through the bedroom window clothing us in its warmth.

What a way to start each day!

39

It is the middle of the night and something warm and sticky wakes me. I gaze out at the quarter moon and the stars and the night ghosts of the massive gum trees. Slowly I become aware that Indea is whimpering beside me in the bed and then the odour of vomit hits me. I crawl over her and grab the torch. She has vomited all over the bed and the floor. Her pyjamas are saturated with it. I moan with my whole body, *shit, shit, shit!*

I have no water and no power to help clean up the mess.

I put on some slippers, because there is nothing for it but to make my way to the dam for some water. I tread carefully down the slope and when I reach the dam I try not to sink into the muddy bank. I throw the bucket out into the water and try to scoop up as much as I can. The dam water is muddy and brown and it slops down my legs as I heave the bucket up to the house. As I get closer the torch is starting to dim. *Shit! Shit! Shit!* I make it to the bedroom and the torch gasps its last breath and dies. *Shit!*

I fumble around for the matches that I know are somewhere on the bedside table and finally get the gas lantern lit, trying not to gag on the odour of the vomit.

I mop up some of the vomit with a flannel, but already I need another bucket of clean water.

I reach over and rock the children. 'Guys, come on, guys. You have to wake up. Indea has been sick everywhere. Come on, wake up!'

Seth half opens his eyes and peers out at me.

'Come on, hop up, honey. I have to clean everything up,' I say.

I shake Jacob gently but not even an earthquake would wake him from his sleep.

Seth crawls out of bed and on his way knocks the gas lantern, which smashes to the ground and splinters of glass go everywhere. Thankfully, and by some miracle, nothing catches fire, but the lantern has had it.

'Quick, Seth,' I tell him. 'Hop back into bed before you cut yourself.'

Now we are in total darkness. The torch has died. The lantern is smashed, there is glass and vomit everywhere and all we have is a bucket of water mixed with vomit.

A dark, wet cloud slips into my soul. I sit on the side of the bed, the children fall back into sleep and I slide down into depression as the tears roll down my cheeks while I wait for morning and light. I cannot bear the thought of climbing back into the vomit-covered bed, so I just sit and wait for the day and cry.

40

Ian is sleeping with another woman on weekends and with me during the week — and I am not too pleased about it. When he is with her, he acts as if I don't exist, and when he is with me he lies to her about it and says we are friends and that we just have baths together, like skinny-dipping. And she believes him.

Still, I deserve it. I had an affair with Lutz and acted as though his partner didn't exist, and now another woman is doing the same to me. One part of me is really upset about it, but another part doesn't care, because I know deep inside that Ian is not the man I want to spend my life with. So it is wrong to hang on to him. I should let him go and be with this other woman.

I am being selfish, but I am lonely too, and beginning to wonder whether I will ever find a man I do want to live with. Where is he? Does he really exist? I mean, I was quite happy to be on my own and have lovers, but I didn't expect to be on my own for this long. I am tired of being alone now. I don't want a lover anymore; I want a partner. Someone who will be there through thick and thin. I feel so miserable I can't do anything during the days and I have nightmares in the dark.

I make the children breakfast and lunch and see them off on the bus. Then I collapse on the lounge-room floor and that is where I stay until they come home. I have lost heaps of weight, as I can't even eat. I am truly starting to believe that the children would have a better life if I were not part of it. This thought is starting to take over. If I were to die, Rick's family would take the children under their wing and care for them properly.

I don't know why my life is like this. Why it is always so hard? I know that my parents have never loved me, so if even my own parents can't love me, then I must be pretty bloody unworthy of love!

The children love me, but perhaps as they grow up they will find out what I am really like and hate me. Thoughts like these consume me.

I walk to the kitchen and fossick in the drawer until I find the new kitchen knife that Ian bought for me because he thought the ones I had were useless. 'Couldn't cut an onion with those useless knives if you had all day,' he said.

I take hold of the new knife. It is so sharp that I gave myself a nasty cut just removing it from its plastic cover the first time I used it. I run the point up the vein in my arm. I know how to do it properly. I know to go up the vein and not across. It is for the children's sake that I am doing this. I can't keep them here with me when I can't provide adequately for them. How can I expect to be worthy of being a mother when I am not even worthy of my own parents' love? I haven't seen or heard from my own mother since she left for Queensland. Neither she nor my father even knows my children's birthdays or what their favourite foods are, and my mother has not seen Indea since she was born. That is how important I am to them. I have no one and nothing to give to my children and I press the blade against my arm and a trickle of blood forms on my skin. Then I throw the knife down on the ground in shock and my body heaves with the tears I am crying. I can't even kill myself properly.

I light a candle and do a Wicca spell, but I fall asleep and am woken by the piercing shrill of the fire alarm to find my square of carpet is smouldering happily and thinking of becoming a grown-up fire. I throw a bucket of water over the fire. I am not ready to risk the lives of others by letting my house in the bush catch alight.

When the children come home I force myself to act as if nothing is wrong with me. I make cauliflower and cheese soup with them and we dance around the kitchen, laughing and joking together. We have such a great time! I am so lucky to have such beautiful, articulate, gentle children. I read to them and ask them the questions I ask every night. 'What was the worst thing that happened to you today? What was the best thing that happened?'

Then they ask me and I say, 'The worst thing was that I felt lonely and the best thing was that you all came home.'

And I put them to bed where they are safe.

I go and sit in the dam. Perhaps if I can't kill myself with a blade, I can give myself pneumonia instead. The water is freezing and the cold creeps into my heart. I remember what I always tell people when I am counselling them: if you need help, ask for it, and if you don't get it from the first person you ask, then keep asking until you find what you need. I make my way back up to the house, not caring that I am dripping water onto the floor. The first person I ring for help says, 'Go to the doctor. Get happy pills.'

But pills are not the answer. They won't help me deal with what is happening to me.

I ring my friend Jenny. 'Jenny,' I sob. I am crying again.

'What is it? Robbi, what is it?'

'I think I'm trying to kill myself.'

'Where is Ian?'

'With another woman.'

'I'll fucking kill him,' she says. 'Okay, don't do anything. Promise me you won't do anything and I will be there in an hour and a half. I'm bringing Shirley. Sit in the lounge room and make a cup of tea.'

'I'm out of drinking water. I have to get it in town,' I say mournfully.

'I'll bring a thermos. Just stay put and don't do anything until I get there.'

I rock back and forth on the lounge-room chair and Jenny and Shirley arrive and Jenny puts a blanket around me while Shirley goes and makes hot tea. 'I just can't cope on my own anymore,' I say to Jenny. 'It's so hard with no water, no electricity, no sewerage and no money to get any of them. I paid the electrician up front and he ran away with my money and all my lovely old Bakelite fittings and the plumber won't fix the plumbing he did that isn't up to council standard. Jacob and Seth are supposed to go on school camp — how am I meant to find money for that? And education is supposed to be free! They are all supposed to have insoles for their flat feet — well, you can just forget about that! Seth needs a piano and he rang and asked Rick's family if they'd buy him one and they said only if he kept it at Rick's, but he only goes to Rick's occasionally. He needs it here to practise on and Indea needs glasses and they are another two hundred dollars and the neighbours took our bearded collie to the lost dogs' home, because he started chasing sheep with Ian's Rottweilers and the lost dogs have sold him and my parents hate me! Why is life so hard?' I moan.

'Remember *The Road Less Traveled*,' says Jenny. 'What's the first line?'

I smile at her. 'Life is difficult.' I say. 'This is one of the great truths.' And we both start to laugh. Because it's true.

In the morning I sit with Ian by the dam. I am drawing in the dirt with a stick, the kids are at school and Jenny and Shirley have gone back to Melbourne.

Ian says, 'I think we should marry. I would like to marry you.'

I say 'No' straightaway.

He stands up, his face is red and he is angry. 'You could at least have pretended that you need to think it over!' he says scathingly and stomps off.

I didn't realise he was so serious and he goes off with the other woman for good.

He rings me up and says, 'Can we still be friends?'

And, meanly, I tell him no.

41

I walk up to the end of the drive with the children to see them off on the morning school bus and collect the mail. There is an envelope with my mother's writing on it. She has found me.

My heart starts to pound as I gingerly tear it open. There are four typed pages and as I read through them my heart lurches and I feel ill.

She writes that I am a disappointment to her. That I have 'backslidden' from the Lord and I am on my way to hell. She writes that my life will never amount to anything while I am living in such a state of sin for I will never receive His blessing on any venture that I undertake. She writes, 'What has happened to your faith in the Lord?' She asks why I have been such a terrible daughter to her. She writes that I have not supported her in her leaving my father.

I fold it up carefully and put it back in the envelope. Then in a haze I walk to my bedroom and tuck the letter beneath my undies in the top drawer. I feel numb. I am so utterly alone and worthless so I take out the box of Phenergan and the bottle of Temazepam that is also in my top drawer and throw a couple of each into my mouth. I swallow them without water.

I lie down on my bed, expecting not to wake up.

42

When I open my eyes the world looks different. I have had a really good sleep. I look around my room: at the pictures on my wall, the photo of Mato with the boys and me. I see Jacob's ballet clothes scattered on the floor and through the door I see Indea's plastic horses cluttering the hallway where she has made a corral for them. I can see the bag of dope lying on my bedside table that a hopeful man gave me as a gift and when I look outside the window the clouds are gone and the sky is bluer than it was before. The dark night has passed. Just like that. All I needed was a really good sleep and everything is different. A miracle.

I can hear the children's voices. They have come home from school and are playing in the lounge room. They will be building spaceships with Lego, so I throw my legs over the side of the bed and get up. I wander into the lounge room and the children look up at me.

'Guys, I don't care if we have no money, we're going to the pub for dinner. We're celebrating,' I say.

'Are the brothers coming?' Indea asks.

'Of course,' I say. She always calls Seth and Jacob 'the brothers'.

'What are we sbrating?' asks Indea.

'The grey clouds have gone and we have each other,' I say.

The children like this answer because their faces light up. We play Franciscus Henri, for Indea, and dance around the lounge room, holding hands, giggling and singing.

And then as our dancing gets more raucous, we play Midnight Oil as loudly as we can on Jacob's cassette player. I don't even care that we are using up all the batteries.

Next morning I wake again feeling alive, refreshed and nourished from the pub meal. It is a shiny, sunny Wednesday, so I get the children off to school and decide to go and see the bank manager. He is a lovely man named Kelvin Putt.

'I need more money to finish electrical work and to put the sewerage on,' I say politely. I am trying not to sound too needy, as if I don't really care whether I get sewerage or electricity.

'Not a problem,' he says. 'You've always paid your mortgage. I know you're an honest person and the amount you want to borrow is within my jurisdiction. I find women hardly ever default on loans. It's the men who are the problem. You just go and organise what you need done and I'll fix up the paperwork.'

Just like that! What has seemed so hard for so long is really so easy and I couldn't see it. Just like that, life has taken a sharp twist and improved. I feel as if nothing bad can ever happen to me again. My life will only get better. Instead of things happening to me, I am back in control of my direction. And I am going forward.

I walk down the steps of the bank basking in the sunlight and see Mandy with her bright orange coat and henna'd hair waving at me from the other side of the street. I wait for her to cross.

'Hi, Mandy. Guess what! Kelvin just gave me more money. I can get my house fixed.'

'Well, let's go to the café and celebrate. I'll shout you coffee,' she says.

‘I don’t drink coffee.’

‘Okay, tea then,’ she says, rolling her eyes.

We plonk ourselves down at a table and Susan, one of the chefs, rushes out of the kitchen and sits beside me. Soon there is a crowd of us sitting around the table and Alice says, ‘Listen, you’re all coming to our party on the weekend, aren’t you?’

‘Yeah, I can come. I haven’t got the kids,’ I say. A party is just what I need now that I am back in life.

‘Great! Nine o’clock, okay? BYO drinks. It’s Sebastian’s farewell.’

‘What’s happening to Sebastian?’ I ask. I have really been out of touch.

‘Oh, he’s going to London,’ Susan says.

Sitting nearby is a man with long dark hair, thick and black, tied back in a loose ponytail that reaches to his elbows. He seems so at ease chatting to everyone, but he is taking little notice of me, so I touch him on the arm and say, ‘Will you be at the party?’

‘Sure,’ he says, giving me his full attention. ‘I guess I’ll see you there.’ And for that split second it is as if we are at the table alone.

From nowhere, Susan’s hand seems to have landed on my thigh and is moving upwards. She leans towards me and whispers, ‘Have you ever tried a woman?’

I look at her. She is handsome and I am honoured. ‘I’m sorry,’ I say. ‘But I don’t have a gay bone in my body.’

You have to expect these things in Daylesford, but I love men. I love the smell of them, especially when you put your head into the crook of a man’s neck; it smells so good in there. I love their arms and shoulders, but I especially love their hands.

I have finished my tea and I want to move away from Susan before she tries harder to convert me or I insult her, so I say, ‘Hey, Mandy, I have to go. Want to come?’

'Have you got any green stuff?' she asks hopefully.

'Yeah, a guy gave me some a while back. You can have it.'

'Oh, no, I couldn't!' she says, as if she's been offered my most treasured possession.

'Not a problem,' I say.

As we drive past St Vincent's, I make an instant decision and pull over. I go in and ask to see the person in charge of emergency relief. A man comes out and kindly ushers me into a small room. I explain to him my financial situation. It is the most embarrassing thing I have ever done, but it is worth the humiliation. The man is nice and gives me a one hundred dollar food voucher and a big box of groceries. He is especially happy when I tell him I am sending my children to the Catholic school. The Catholic school is fantastic; they give the children free uniforms and tell me that I don't have to pay camp fees. Just like that. Another problem gone. They are so kind to me, even though I am not Catholic.

With my box of groceries and my voucher I hop back in the car and take Mandy to my place, where we open a bottle of cheap pink champagne and sit down by the dam, under the gums in the afternoon sun, and talk about men's penises.

'They've got to be big,' says Mandy as she sucks seductively on her joint and passes it to me. 'I only want big. Big — with dirty talk.'

'No, no, no — small is fine if they're kind and interesting lovers. Sometimes big means they don't think they need to put in any effort,' I tell her. I suck on the joint and she laughs.

'You idiot! You really don't know how to smoke, do you? He's got to take control. I like a man who is in control of the sex,' says Mandy. 'I like to be spanked too.'

'No way,' I say, 'too kinky for me.'

'Yeah, but *every*thing's too kinky for you, you little Christian! You,' she says looking at me seriously and pointing her finger at me, 'you would have a lot more fun if you went out there and took whatever man you wanted. Take the initiative, girl!'

'Like you did with Sebastian?'

'I took home Tommy Roberts the other night.'

'You what?' I say gasping. 'The old rock star?'

'I did! I took home Tommy Roberts and he's not so old! He was at the Palais and I took him home. I didn't give him sex though. Just a blow job. I never have sex on the first night. I just give them head.'

'Mandy, if the men in Daylesford knew that, you'd have every last one of them lined up asking for a first date with you. And as for Tommy, you should sell your story to *New Idea*. God knows you need the money! I can see the headlines now: 'I gave Tommy a blow job'. My gran would've loved to read that story. What about Sebastian? What happened there?'

'You can't win every race,' she says. 'Sebastian has every second woman in Daylesford lining up.'

'Not me, sugar,' I say.

'And,' says Mandy, leaning back into the grass as she sucks on the joint, 'if you can't get a man there are always candles, a hot bath, Frankie Sinatra on the stereo, some champagne and a good-sized zucchini.'

'Mandy!' I say, shocked but laughing.

'Don't tell me you've never masturbated. Never made love to yourself?'

'Absolutely not. Tis too sinful to even think about,' I say mockingly. 'No, really, I just have no interest. I want a warm, testosterone-filled body muttering sweet nothings in my ear on the end of my zucchini. I do know one thing though. Sex is better if you fantasise while you're doing it. Lutz told me that. He reckons women short change themselves because they don't. They think of what they're going to cook for dinner that night instead, and then wonder why they don't come easily. Lutz says while you're having sex you have to fantasise about some other time you had really good sex.'

'Der!' Mandy makes a face.

'Speaking of men, who is the guy with the long black hair?' I ask, trying not to sound too interested.

'Ahh, you like Petie-pie, do you?' she drawls, sitting up and sniffing gossip.

'No,' I lie. 'I'm just interested. I've seen him around, but not often.'

'Ahh, you *do* like him! You like Christian Pete.'

'Christian Pete?'

'He is a seriously nice guy, has three kids — they live with him. But he's a Christian. Hey, you two might suit each other.'

'No way. My fundamentalist Christian days are over,' I say defiantly. 'Well, I'm still a Christian in that I believe in God, in that sacred part of each of us. But you know, I'm not interested in church anymore. I have better things to do with my Sunday mornings — like have cups of tea in bed.'

I have also thrown out my Wicca book and I am wasting no more money on clairvoyants. My life is in my hands. Tarot is okay though. It's a good way of meditating on what's happening in your life.

The babbling noise of happy children tumbles down the slope towards us, followed by Jacob, Seth and Indea home from school. I get up from the grassy bank, stretch and follow them up to the kitchen.

The children spot the box of groceries from St Vincent's on the kitchen table and yelp with delight. Inside are six cartons of Chocolate Chip Crunchy breakfast cereal. I never let them have sugary breakfast cereal and now they have a six-month supply.

'It's so great being poor!' they say and dance around the kitchen, organising bowls and spoons. There is no way they are going to wait till morning for chocolate breakfast cereal. Who knows when I might decide it is too appallingly unhealthy and just chuck the whole lot out? They don't want to run the risk of waiting the whole night only to find it gone when they wake up.

It is Jacob's birthday so I drag out the Visa card and buy tickets to take him to see Graeme Murphy's 'King Roger'. Mandy minds Seth and Indea for me. On Thursday night Jacob and I get dressed in our best clothes and go off and join all the men in their dinner suits and ladies in their evening dresses. The two of us stand out like Hare Krishnas at a Christian prayer meeting and I am surprised that we have really good seats. We are in the fourth row.

It is the first ballet I have ever seen and it is so stunning that it makes me cry with its beauty. For the first time I can see why Jacob loves ballet. I can see its magic. This ballet isn't prissy. It's strong and vibrant. Visually splendid.

Soon he is digging me in the ribs and I drag my eyes from the stage to look where he is pointing.

'Look,' he says excitedly. 'Look who's sitting next to me.'

It's the great man, Graeme Murphy himself. Sitting there with his curly hair pulled back in a ponytail right next to Jacob, with *his* curly hair pulled back into a ponytail.

Now, I've had erotic daydreams about Graeme Murphy ever since I read a feature article about him in *The Age*. He was asked what he liked to do most of all and he said making love in the afternoon sun.

How can you not have erotic dreams about a man who says that? I am tempted to tell him that I am in my prime and he can spend any afternoon with me.

'Well, say hello,' I tell Jacob.

He does and, before I know it, Graeme Murphy is actually speaking to me. Unfortunately he doesn't ask what I am doing with my afternoons.

'Do you mind if I take your son backstage and show him the set being changed?' he says.

I cannot get my mouth to speak to him so I just sort of nod stupidly.

Jacob trots off, looking like a mini Graeme Murphy, and he has the best birthday ever.

On Friday I drive the children to Rick's and on Saturday I get ready for Alice's party and off I go with a bottle of wine and in a light summer dress that Jurgen always loved on me.

Sebastian is getting ready to drive off to Melbourne. He is saying goodbye and the women are hanging around him like moths at a flame. I stand back, leaning against a car, watching all of this, when suddenly Sebastian looks over at me. He changes his mind about hopping in his car, shuts the door, walks across with that confident swagger of his, and in just seconds he has put a hand on either side of my face, drawn my face up to his and now he is kissing me deeply and his tongue has found its way into my mouth. It feels as if he is never going to stop. I'm not sure I ever want him to. His mouth is delicious and soft. Then as he slowly pulls away he says goodbye.

I am dumbstruck. He just gets in the car and drives off without a further word to anyone and I can't wipe the grin off my face. Life is definitely getting better.

Mandy is suddenly beside me. 'God, what did you do to deserve that?' she says.

'I don't know,' I say, but I remember the talks Sebastian and I had about religion and how there was a bond there because his mother was a Uniting Church minister. Maybe that is why he kissed me.

We go into the backyard and sit around the fire. Backyards in Daylesford are beautiful and Alice's backs onto state forest, so you never really feel like you're in a backyard at all. Christian Pete is looking at me from the other side of the fire and I can feel the magnet between us that makes it seem we are the only two at this party. After Ian I don't want to get involved with a guy who has kids, but the attraction is so palpable that I know I will change my mind. I can feel him watching me as I get another glass of wine. I can feel him watching as I stop briefly to talk to Dave on my way back to the fire. I wait, play it cool, and another woman squeezes herself down beside Pete. I watch as she smiles at him with her face open and inviting and still I wait, sitting in a corner. An observer on the edges: I am always like this at parties. I always feel more alone when I am surrounded by people than I do on my own at home. I sit and wonder why I am here, but then I know why. I am waiting for Pete.

And sure enough he is soon sitting beside me.

'Listen, I've heard you're a Christian,' I say as he sits down, 'and I just want to say up front that if you're into any fundamental or Pentecostal stuff, I think it is a load of superstitious bollocks.'

'Well, I am a Pentecostal, but I'd really like to hear what you've got to say,' he says, completely undaunted.

'You don't seem like much of a Pentecostal with a stubby in one hand and a smoke in the other. My grandmother would have thought you were on the slippery road to hell, giving into the temptations of Satan. Your body is the temple of the Lord and not to be defiled with drugs. Don't you know that?'

'Boy! You don't mess around, do you?' he says, smiling.

'I'm sorry. I guess the church has messed around with me.'

'What do you mean?'

'Well, if there is something that can be done I've done it — the whole gamut. So I'm warning you, don't try to convert me to anything because I've been there already and I have been learning Bible verses from the moment I started to speak. I've spoken in tongues. I've been slain in the spirit. I've heard God's voice — in fact it told me to get married. I've meditated and gone places and I've contemplated.'

'You speak in tongues. Can you still do it?' He sounds excited.

'Yeah.'

'Go on, do it.'

'No way!'

'Please.'

'Absolutely not! I will never speak in tongues again. So please, don't keep asking. I don't know what it is, but it *ain't* speaking to God. Maybe it's just releasing the ability to speak the gobbledegook we spoke when we were children. But all that Holy Spirit stuff is superstitious mumbo jumbo. "Lord, please give me a car park" when you're at the supermarket. I mean, really! Children are starving and what are Pentecostal Christians doing? Praying for good car parks when they go shopping. And what about spirits?'

I am on a roll now.

'Someone stays up too late and the next morning they have a spirit of sleep upon them or they get a cold and it's a spirit of blowing noses. Or they are just plain lazy, but no — it's a spirit of indecision. No, I never speak in tongues and I stay well away from Pentecostalism!'

I tell him about The Church of the Open Door and Pastor Greenslade.

'Hey, I've heard of him. I think that old guy's still alive.'

I laugh. 'Well, there you go. Maybe he's going to live forever, after all.'

'What do you believe?' Pete asks, genuinely interested.

'You really want to know?'

'Yeah.'

'I believe that true spirituality is acting responsibly towards others and to the world we live in. I believe that God isn't found in miracles and spirits, but in the little things of everyday life, like my children wanting to hug me every morning because they love me. God is in each and every human soul and if we look to humanity we find God. If we look to the "gods", we find superstition.'

'You're remarkable. I don't think I have ever been to a party and had this kind of conversation before,' he says.

This guy is really attractive and he has a lilting, intelligent voice. He is tall, about five foot eleven. But I really don't want to get mixed up with a fundo Christian who has kids. Still, I tell myself, if he is intelligent he will soon realise what rubbish it is and dump it. And he really is gorgeous with that stunning long dark hair — hair that he obviously takes care of, because it is so well groomed and shines in the firelight.

Mandy's words ring in my ears: 'Take the initiative, Robbi.'

I take a deep breath and brace myself. As nervous as I am I manage to say, 'Would you like to quit this party and come back to my place?'

'Yeah, where are your kids?' he says.

'At their father's this weekend. Yours?'

'Oh, they're older. They're scattered around the town at different friends' houses.'

'Okay, so we're free to go,' I say. I can tell from the way his eyes light up that he thinks he has it made for the night.

We drive to my place and all the way I am thinking this guy could be a rapist or a murderer and I am stuffed. I've invited him back and that is an open invitation for sex. I could never prove rape. This could be date rape. What if he has seen *The Texas Chainsaw Massacre*, which I know about because it was the favourite movie of one of the kids who came to live with me and Rick. What if he has an axe under his jacket?

When we pull up outside my house he gets out of the car and immediately picks up my axe, which is leaning against the wall of the house. It is lucky he can't see the white fear on my face in the dark. I don't know whether to run or scream. I quickly gauge the distance to the two neighbours' houses and decide the one on the left is closer, even if it is uphill.

'I'll just chop a bit of wood for your fire.'

'It's already lit,' I stammer.

'If you don't mind my saying, I am yet to see a fire that has been properly lit by a girl. There are three things girls can't do. They can't read maps — never take directions from a girl. They can't tune radios and they can't light fires.'

'Yeah, well, men can't do more than one thing at a time. Men never put their children before themselves. If it's "Mmm I'm hungry and the kids are hungry, who do I feed first?" the mother feeds the kids first, but the father feeds himself.'

'That's right,' he says. 'Dads are for playing games, having fun. You have to have energy for that. Besides, it doesn't matter how much a bloke tries to be a good dad, when the kids are hurt they only want their mum. Kids always side with their mums. Mums nurture. Dads play.'

'That is so politically incorrect.' I frown.

'So it might be, but it's true,' he says and starts to chop some wood.

Soon, instead of merely smouldering away in a pathetic, limp manner, my fire is roaring.

We sit in front of it and talk about our children. They are pretty evenly spread in age. His youngest is a year older than Jacob. We decide that their names all fit together nicely. It would be strange if my children had names like Willow Tree Song and his had names like Bruce. So maybe we have similar tastes.

I give him my old theological texts to take home and read, a huge bundle of them.

'I won't go out with you,' I tell him, 'unless you read these and then I want to know what you think.'

He brushes my hair and massages my head and shoulders. He tells me he has been searching for spiritual truth and that he joined Raja Yoga, but he couldn't take the celibacy. Then he joined the Pentecostals. He says he is sure that Pentecostalism is just part of the journey, because he is already having problems with it.

‘For a start,’ he says, ‘I am separated and there is no way I’m getting back with my ex-wife. She has ruined too much of my life already. But the first, biggest and most obvious problem for me with fundamentalist beliefs is their insistence in believing in Adam and Eve and the idea that the world was created in seven days, five or six thousand years ago. This is such arrant nonsense. I have never stopped believing in evolutionary theory. The evidence in favour of a world teeming with life for billions of years is overwhelming.’

Now he is challenging me and, even though I know he is right, I cannot get rid of that old feeling that evolution is evil.

I glance at my watch and see that it’s four in the morning. ‘Listen,’ I say, ‘I know I invited you back here and I had every intention of, you know, us going to bed for the night. But to be honest, I have never had a one-night stand in my life and I don’t think I can start with you. You have to go home.’

‘Sure,’ he says. ‘How about dinner on Sunday night?’

‘Sure.’ The children don’t come back till Monday night because it’s a long weekend.

His car has broken down so I pick him up and he introduces me to one of his daughters. She is a bouncy, friendly girl who is swamped with friends who flutter around her. Red Hot Chili Peppers are pounding out from her bedroom.

‘Blossom, I won’t be home tonight,’ he tells her.

Such impertinence I think to myself, to assume he is spending the night with me. But a thrill runs through me anyway.

He pulls a tray out of the oven. He has made spinach and feta filos to add to our meal. I have made vegetable laksa. We talk easily over dinner and wine and soon we are taking off our clothes.

The phone rings while we are eating breakfast.

‘Hi, Mandy,’ I say.

'So is he a good kisser? Did he go down on you? Did you have an orgasm?' she asks.

Normally I would answer all these questions, but this time the experience seems too personal to talk about with anyone but Pete. But I tell her later, when Pete has gone, that he is the first man who didn't yak, yak, yak all night about himself. I tell her that he said I was beautiful.

'God, Robbi!' she says. 'I was interested in him for a bit and he never said those things to me.'

Straightaway I hear about every other woman in Daylesford Pete has slept with.

'He was with Lara only two weeks ago,' says Maggie.

'Yeah, well, that was two weeks ago. He's not with her now,' I say, grateful that no one knows who I was with two weeks ago — except Mandy and she won't tell.

'Don't worry,' I say to my kids, when they come home from their father's. 'Pete won't be around for long. He'll be gone in six weeks. It's just a fling.'

43

I am trying to eat cheese, tomato and zucchini jaffles without getting the tomato everywhere. It squeezes out the sides when you bite in and tomato seeds go *slop, slop, slop* down your front. When you are a kid you think you will be able to handle difficult food when you grow up, food like spaghetti bolognaise and real hamburgers, but nothing ever changes. Your body gets older, but it is the same person peering out from within and messy food is just as difficult.

Pete has made me these jaffles for breakfast. Claire, his sixteen-year-old daughter says to me, 'He's trying to make you fat. He likes his women that way. All his girlfriends are fat.'

'So is it true?' I ask him. 'Are you trying to make me fat?'

Pete is leaning against a tree in that languid way men do, having a smoke, and I am sitting on the couch on the front porch eating his jaffle.

'Rubenesque,' he says. 'That's how I like my women.'

I take another clumsy bite.

'I'm going to marry you. You know that, don't you?' he says.

'We've only been going out a week,' I say between mouthfuls. 'This is a bit Mills and Boon, isn't it?' But really I am a sucker for Mills and Boon moments in movies. I could fall in love with him for saying that alone.

'I'm going to marry you and have a baby with you.'

I almost choke on my jaffle.

'I'm not marrying anyone who smokes or drinks heavily,' I say defiantly.

'Oh, I see. We can take the girl out of the Baptist Church, but we can't take the Baptist out of the girl.'

'Don't you know the joke?' I say. 'Anglicans do it by candlelight. Catholics do it en masse. Uniting Church do it by common consent. Baptists don't do it — it might lead to dancing.'

'I'll give up,' he says nonchalantly.

'What?'

'I'll give up. If it's that much of an issue to you, I'll give up smoking and drinking.'

'I'll wait and see if you do,' I say quietly. I know deep down that this thing with Pete has to end now, or it will be forever.

'Will you come to my brother's wedding in a few weeks?' I ask.

'Of course,' he says.

My brother Davie is marrying Wendy, the girl who lived next door. They have been best friends since they were about eight and he is part of her family. This is their second wedding, because we dressed them up and married them when they were little. I haven't seen my brother in years. He and Wendy drove up to Daylesford and hand-delivered the invitation.

'I love you,' Davie and I said to each other.

'But it's just too hurtful staying in our family. I have Wendy's family now,' he added.

'I understand exactly,' I said. I know that he too has had letters from my mother and his fights with my father were just awful. I know that he has found more love in Wendy's family than he ever found in ours.

We are sitting at a huge round table with white wedding flowers forming a horseshoe in the middle: the children, my mother, whom I haven't seen for years, in a bright aqua dress, Pete and me. My other brother, Wayne, is best man and I haven't seen him in a long, long time either. Karyn is not here. She is overseas getting married herself. So we have all fled from our origins. Davie has invited my father, but he won't come. He says he doesn't want to go to a wedding where he hasn't even met his daughter-in-law — which is stupid, because he knows Wendy very well. He has known her since she was eight.

Davie looks as if he has found a home. He and Wendy are content.

We are eating wedding food. My children, who are used to lentil casseroles, aren't sure if you are meant to eat this food or play with it. When they were babies I used to play, 'This little piggy went to market, This little piggy stayed home, This little piggy had lentils,' because they had no idea what roast beef was, until I took them to Ballarat for roast on pension day.

Then the three of them decide the wedding food is great! It's special because it is so different from what we eat at home. A disc jockey is playing love songs. At the moment it is 'I Celebrate My Love' and my mother leans over to Pete, whom she has only just met, right across me. I'm sitting in the middle to keep them separate and she says as if I'm not there, 'Robbi thinks her father sexually molested her as a child. She's got a very over-active imagination, that girl.'

'Mum!' I say, putting down my cutlery. 'I don't think we need to discuss this. We're at Davie's wedding, remember.'

She opens her mouth to continue her story when Wayne announces the bridal waltz.

'Please,' I say to Pete, 'don't listen to her.'

On the way home I cannot bring myself to speak to him about what my mother said. I am too afraid to find out what he thinks of me now. He will realise that my own mother thinks me a liar and I wonder whether Davie's wedding will be the end of us.

Pete leaves a love song on my answering machine. It is 'Catch the Wind' by Donovan. I guess my mother isn't the end of us after all.

My children already adore Pete. He tells them silly bum jokes and they roar with laughter and tease him back.

'Robbi likes George better than you,' they say to him.

'We saw Robbi kissing George the other day,' Indea adds, grinning from ear to ear.

'What's this?' says Pete, looking at me, and I shrug and the children giggle and run off.

Pete pulls me onto his knee and kisses me. He has won the children's everlasting admiration with his bad jokes. I would love to be able to win his children over as easily. Just tell them a few slimy anal jokes and bingo — you're a hero.

Falling in love when you have six children in tow requires some flexibility. Not for us the long, intimate meals over candles, then languidly falling into bed and into each other. For us it's the scramble and rush of feeding them all at once, of endless dishes and dirty clothes, of school notices and lunch boxes that accumulate unrecognisable growths and smells.

But it is only because we are both on the supporting parent's benefit that we get any time alone together at all. This is when the children are all at school and we treasure it. Pete and I are together nearly every minute; it seems natural.

In the morning we make six lots of salad sandwiches and take the children to school, then hide out in one of our houses. I think we have spent at least eight weeks in bed and I wonder how many times we are allowed to have sex before we have to tell Social Security about it. How many times can a man make love to you before you are to inform him that the government now expects him to support you and your children?

During our days in bed the world disappears, but come three o'clock the demands of parenting are upon us again.

We pick the children up from school in the afternoon and head to Pete's house, where he cooks a massive pot of dhal, though dragging my children over to his house all the time is making them very unsettled. His children are older and simply won't be moved. So we are the ones who always go to him. Now Indea is crying a lot. This is the price of true love.

We have just clambered into his mattress on the floor after dinner and started to snuggle when a head pokes round the door.

We look up over the doona to see who it is.

'Dad, I need a tea towel. I'm sure there is one in your bedroom cupboard. I saw one there once.'

'Tea towels are in the kitchen,' says Pete and he leans over to kiss me again.

But almost instantly the door opens again.

'Robbi, I have an itch. It just started and I've had it for ages and it won't go away.'

Pete and I smile at each other. Most children have not had to watch their parents fall in love, so we understand that they are curious.

We kiss in the kitchen while we make their lunches and it's, 'Gross, oh disgusting, I can't possibly eat that sandwich now you've done that over it!'

So we laugh and do it again and they stick their fingers in their mouths and pretend to vomit.

Jacob, Seth and Indea don't like having to bunk down in Pete's lounge room all the time just so he and I can spend our nights together. But the boys don't complain because I let them stay up later than I would in our own home. Indea, though, continues to cry.

I am not sure how long we can keep doing this.

44

It is Thursday and I tell Pete I want us to split up. I don't want to be with someone who smokes so heavily. 'I can't cope with worrying about you all the time,' I say. 'I am frightened every morning when you wake up coughing, spluttering and gasping for breath.'

'Okay,' he says and — just like that — we split up. After six months of being together this is the end. Six months of the children saying 'gross' and 'disgusting' and 'do you have to?' and 'this is *sooo* embarrassing!' Six months of squashing all the children into my little Nissan Prairie after school. In six months we have already developed a history. Our favourite foods, routines, secret jokes.

I am devastated and forlorn. I knew I cared about Pete, but now I realise just how completely and I do what all sensible women do in this situation. I look for a shoulder to cry on and I find that shoulder in Stuart, a guy I have spent occasional nights with before.

Stuart and I go on a date with Mandy and her boyfriend. Trouble is my date really wants Mandy and can't take his eyes off her. And I really want Pete. So I go home early and cry and all weekend watch soppy romantic movies in which everyone finds their one true love — and I wait for the phone to ring.

It does. On Monday morning.

'I don't want to live without you,' says Pete.

'Me neither,' I say.

'I've given up smoking.'

He has also given up Pentecostalism and he devoured every theological book that I have on my shelf.

I jump in my car and drive over.

'I have more news for you,' he says, coming out to meet me before I get out of the car. 'I can move in with you. The real-estate agent called on the weekend and the landlord wants his house back. The children have decided to move in with their mother. It's all just kind of happened. Now that we are going to be together,' he says, 'I want to go to church.'

So reluctantly I agree to go to the Uniting Church with him on the weekends when we don't have my children. When Geoff the minister finds out that I was a pastor he asks me to preach. On Mothers' Day of course and I am keen to get behind a pulpit again.

'This will really turn me on, seeing you behind a pulpit. I can't wait,' says Pete. 'There is nothing more sexy than a woman in authority. But what will you preach about? You don't believe in the virgin birth. Do you believe in the resurrection?'

'I don't think I do, but I do believe that Jesus gave us a life-changing example of how we can live. I think the Bible teaches us truths about life, not facts. And although I don't believe in the fact of the virgin birth or the fact of the resurrection, I do believe in the truth of those events: that Jesus was so special that those who wrote about him wanted to write in a way that pointed out clearly how he impacted upon their lives in a miraculous way. I can still preach about those truths,' I say.

Pete's parents come to hear me. They are the sweetest elderly couple you could hope to meet. I can tell that Pete has never had one unstable minute in his childhood and he knows his parents are devoted to him.

I preach on the motherhood of God again and as I stand at the door after the service, shaking everyone's hand, an old lady who must be ninety-five shouts in my ear, 'That was the best sermon I've ever heard, dear.' Though I'm not sure how much of it she did actually hear.

An old man shakes my hand firmly and says, 'It's so lovely to see a woman in the pulpit; I've never seen that before.'

But Glen, a local Pentecostal, snaps at me, 'It would take me two hours to tell you what was wrong with that sermon,' and he stomps off down the steps of the church.

Another woman says, 'We must have you back, dear.'

Pete's parents are proud of me. His father walks around saying in a loud voice, 'That's my future daughter-in-law. She's been to university.' And I feel like I have real parents at last.

I am in absolute panic. I have been alone for about seven years now. He has been alone for seven years too and I don't know if I can live with another adult. I panic over silly little things like what if he wants to put his crappy, cheap old saucepans in the cupboard with my nice new expensive ones that I bought out of the settlement? What if he spends too much money and we can't pay our bills? Because I am on social security, I am now dependent on him.

Just like that.

I will have to make space for his clothes and other belongings in my cupboards. What if he is really messy or has disgusting personal habits that I haven't discovered yet? What if our parenting techniques are totally incompatible? His children are so different from mine. His house is noisy and busy and his children are fiery and stunning. Our house is quiet, peaceful and my children avoid confrontation like they avoid their father's chilli bean burgers. What if Pete's children desert him and, down the track, he blames me for it?

I am so full of 'what ifs' but when I moan to my girlfriends they look at me, their mouths open with astonishment.

'What are you complaining about saucepans for? You've got a man, haven't you? A nice one at that!' says Mandy. 'What I'd give for a man in bed with me each night.'

'What I'd give for a man for *one* night,' Maggie moans.

'Geez, Robbi, you're so lucky. Don't you know how hard it is to find a nice man who is prepared to commit to you?' says Janice.

'Not to mention the fact that he doesn't have a drug problem,' adds Mandy. 'Unlike the other men around here.' And she drains her champagne glass and promptly refills it.

'He doesn't even mind that you've got kids,' says Maggie.

'Yeah, well, he's got kids too and I don't mind,' I say. I quickly pile bean sprouts on top of my avocado sandwich and take a good sip of champagne. But they just roll their eyes at me. All is silent for a few minutes and I continue to worry.

'Look,' says Mandy, 'he's kind and he even likes your children and they like him?' I nod.

'Right!' she says. 'So what's the problem? There's plenty of women who'd die to have a man wanting to move in with them and their kids.'

But Mandy doesn't understand that I would rather be alone and happy, than with a man and miserable.

'I'll never find a man,' she moans. 'All I want is one who has a house and a job, a man with a bit of oomph.'

'You'll find someone,' I assure her. 'A lot of men like single mothers. Jurgen always said that single mothers make better lovers.'

'I'd like to meet this Jurgen,' she says, smiling.

I tell my children that nothing in life ever stays the same, that families can change too and the change can be good. That families can be made up of all sorts of different people in all sorts of different structures. I assure them that having Pete and his children in their lives could be fun. 'It will bring the love of four new people into your lives,' I tell them. I am so politically correct.

I take them to the pub and when they have chosen their meals I say to them, 'Pete is moving in to live with us. It won't change anything at all.'

I draw circles on the placemat. 'See, the inside circle is us, but Pete is joining our inner circle. The next circle is all the other people close to you who you love. Your father, your grandparents and Pete's children are joining that circle.'

Kelly, the waitress, puts our meals in front of us and when she has moved away, I add, 'It won't change how I feel about you three. You know that. You will always be my children and you will always be special. It won't change anything.'

'Can we have dessert?' asks Seth. And all three of them look at me hopefully.

'Of course,' I say and that seems to be the end of our in-depth discussion about Pete.

Pete is arriving any minute with his battered old ute and I am pacing. I have been pacing all morning. Waiting for the moment when my life will change.

I see the cloud of dust roll down the driveway as he arrives. He pulls up outside the house and the ute is loaded to the hilt. Mainly with his drum kit. I hug him and he unwraps another Soother. He has been sucking them ever since he gave up smoking. We unload everything into the lounge room, all his boy stuff: his drum kit, his footy records, his sixties and seventies record albums, his cricket ball that he has had forever and his love letters from old girlfriends. I make a mental note that *they* have to go!

And I was wrong when I said to my children that nothing would change. From the moment he puts his drum kit in the lounge room, everything changes. The drum kit is in the place I've had my easel and paints, but there is nowhere else for it to go. His books are where the special Lego spot was.

Well, I think, I'll just have to remind the children that they promised to move over and make room. And that is exactly what Jacob and Seth do. Immediately they make space for Pete in their lives and in their hearts and I am so proud of them.

He is here and it seems as if he always has been. He doesn't seem like an intruder at all.

But I can see the pain, etched just beneath the surface too. The pain of leaving his children, the fear of losing them, and it seems to me that it is a terrible shame that step-families bring with them the pain of the past. There is no clean slate upon which to start. Yet my grandparents made theirs work.

For the first time I have help getting the children ready for school in the morning. Pete makes them porridge and calls them to the table.

'Can you make our sandwiches? You know — big fat salad ones like you make for Claire and Rhiannon and Ariel? We love your sandwiches,' Jacob says through mouthfuls of porridge.

'Sure,' says Pete and he starts to grate carrot. 'Indea, can you pass me the bread?' he says.

Silence. She just keeps spooning the porridge in.

'Indea, what would you like on your school lunch?'

Silence. In goes more porridge.

I stop making a pot of tea to watch this exchange.

'Indea, do you want some Vegemite or cheese or salad like the brothers?'

Silence. More porridge.

He is a pane of glass.

Indea won't talk to Pete now that he has moved in.

Suddenly, Pete is up from the table, he throws his arms around me and says, 'She is my Robbi. I found her first.'

'No!' says Indea adamantly. 'I was in her tummy!'

'No, she's mine,' he persists.

'Uh-uh! I knew her before you.' And Indea grabs my other arm.

'No, she loves me best,' says Pete.

'No, me! She loves me more than chocolate.'

'Well, she loves me more than — more than frog's legs dipped in chocolate.' And before too long they are laughing and outdoing each other and I am forgotten and go on making that pot of tea.

Pete wins her over with games. Every morning he plays 'She's my Robbi' until one morning Indea grabs hold of him and says, 'I love you almost as much as I love Robbi.'

'I love you too, Indea,' he says as he gives her a big hug.

But I don't have a clue how to bond with his teenagers. How do you play games with teenagers? They come over, but our home isn't their home. We don't have an aerial on the television and they can't watch their favourite programs. They don't have rooms or beds here.

I don't know if we are going to be able to forge a road ahead here and form an identity as a family that takes everyone's needs into account. There is no map for Pete and me to follow. We are not a blended family! I hate that term! We have not been thrown into a food processor and blended so that we become one mushy mess, with our individual origins and qualities now indiscernible. I don't want to invalidate the family life that we have each experienced until now, but I do want to embrace the family life that we'll share from now on.

The bottom line is that because Pete and I have fallen in love, we are all thrown together and so we might as well just get on and make the best of it. And I hope that the two of us survive.

45

I can't make small decisions in life. If Pete asks me whether I'd like Earl Grey or Prince of Wales tea, I have no idea. Honestly. Indian or Thai for dinner? Do I want to go for a walk or watch a movie? No idea. But if he asks me whether I want to marry him, I know straightaway. The answer is YES.

'We are older,' he says, as we lie in bed wrapped up in each other, 'certainly not getting younger. I am forty-two, you are thirty-five. I want to try for a baby straightaway. And we've been together for nearly a year now. I think we should get married as well.'

It feels so right to be marrying Pete and, as it happens, the children (all of them) seem to take it in their stride and are happy that there will be a wedding. It's an excuse for new clothes. So we start to look for a church minister to marry us because we want a Christian ceremony. It is our heritage. Our attendance at the Uniting Church is becoming spasmodic. The building is cold and empty and the services meaningless to us, but we persevere, so we ask Geoff if he can marry us, but he is pretty booked up. So we try the other protestant minister in town, who is Anglican.

'I can't marry you,' he says, sitting on a chair that is higher than ours so that he is looking down on us. 'You are both divorced. I can't marry a divorced person. Robbi could have grounds for getting her first marriage annulled, but not you, Pete. I'm sorry.'

'But,' says Pete, 'this church was started because Henry wanted to divorce his wives instead of chopping their heads off.'

I know Pete'd be quite happy to chop his ex-wife's head off sometimes.

The Anglican priest looks towards the door and the meeting is over. So we go back to Geoff.

'If you're not worried about the date I can squeeze you in,' he says, as he ushers us into an office that doubles as his lounge room. We sigh with relief. 'But I can only fit you in on 11 February after four. It's a busy year,' he says.

'Yeah, sure. We don't mind what date,' we tell him.

'The sooner the better, before I look too pregnant,' I add.

'Why are you getting married?' Lutz is on the phone. 'It is so conventional.'

'Not at all,' I say. 'No one gets married anymore. We are the unconventional ones. We're the revolutionaries.'

'No, really — why?' he persists.

'I can't explain it. It's just the type of relationship we want. It's the type of relationship we have. This is the right thing to do. We really couldn't do anything else.'

'I still remember that day on the beach,' Lutz says, trying to keep the old connection.

'Bye, Lutz. See you at the wedding,' I say.

Jurgen rings too. 'What's he got that I haven't?' he asks.

I don't answer. I don't want to hurt his feelings.

'Well, there's still time. You could change your mind and marry me instead.'

'No, I can't, Jurgen,' I say warmly.

'Oh, well,' he says. 'Never mind. I gave it a shot. And who knows? Maybe it won't work out for you and Pete, then I can come back on the scene.'

* * *

In between vomiting, I lie in bed, propped up on pillows, an ice-cream bucket nearby, and I write our ceremony while Pete paints the lounge room.

'Don't worry about a thing,' says my friend Jeanette. 'You just lie there and I'll organise everything.'

So I do and the days blur into each other with illness, until I crawl out of bed on 11 February. I am going to get married. I hope I don't vomit in the middle of it.

Leaving the dirty dishes, we all pile into the car and go off to get married at the Cosy Corner café. The two of us and our six children, plus one that is being nurtured inside me. We are nearly at Hepburn and I realise though I have written the ceremony we haven't chosen any vows.

'What will we do? We haven't written any,' I say to Pete. 'Everyone writes their own vows these days.'

I grab the list Geoff gave us from where it lies crumpled on the floor of the car and smooth out the paper. I read out the one I like best.

'Yeah,' says Pete. 'That's what I want to say. That'll do.'

As we pull up, the guests are standing under the veranda, sipping champagne, chatting and smiling and you can feel the air of expectancy. As I step out of the car in my wedding dress, my mother grabs me by the arm and drags me inside, away from our guests, and she is fussing. She has come down from Queensland and Wendy and Davie have come too. My mother has decorated a cake that Shirley made for us to a design I've chosen. I insisted.

My mother hasn't shrunk with age — mind you, she is only fifty-nine. She is still five foot eleven and a solid build. She always seems to me so concrete and imposing, like a castle keep. Life's battles just bounce off her — broken relationships, whatever, hardly dent her surface — she carries on through everything.

'I've worked so hard at this cake and it's not on the right tablecloth. You need to get a different tablecloth,' she growls. 'You don't appreciate how much trouble I've gone to for you. I need a better knife; this knife will make a mess of the cake when you cut it. Go and get me a sharper knife.'

I haven't seen her for so long. But it is my wedding and this is what she says to me.

'Mum,' I say, 'the tablecloth is fine, the knife is fine, it has a bow on it, for goodness sake. I am the bride. I'm pregnant and I am barefoot; I'm not doing any rearranging.'

I look around the café, the place I am to be married. It is such a stark contrast to The Church of the Open Door. Jeanette has made the café look so sweet: she has tied stunning ivory-coloured flowers and ribbons to the seats, the walls and put some in vases on the tables.

I leave my mother, who is still grumbling at me, and go outside to the guests.

Geoff calls everyone to come in for the ceremony. I am shocked because he is wearing ministerial robes. Baptists don't wear them. They seem so outdated to me, such a symbol of how far in the past the church is stuck and I know they are ridiculously expensive. But I shrug. It's a wedding. I don't care what people wear, as long as they have a good time.

'Now have you got the rings?' he jokes.

'Of course we have. Seth has them.' I laugh.

'Seth, where are you?' we call out, trying to peer through eighty people squashed into a small café to find him.

'He just went out with his friend. I think they've gone to play in the park,' says one of the guests.

'I'll go and find him,' says Pete. And off he goes.

Soon Seth, Pete and Seth's friend are back. I look at Pete and he explains, smiling, 'It turns out he and his friends were on the Hepburn Reserve Bridge, spitting over it, if you please, trying to hit a Coke bottle lying in the mud way, way down on the mushy ground. All this in his good clothes and with our wedding rings loose in his pocket!'

We start the ceremony and I know it might look strange, the bride standing up and giving the wedding sermon, but after what Pastor Greenslade did at my first wedding I don't want to take any chances. This wedding is going to be warm and friendly. I want it to be a party and after I explained what my first wedding was like, Geoff has been very kind and understanding.

Everyone at this wedding has vows to say: we do, Pete's parents, the children and our guests. It is a real communal affair. I say the vow we chose on the way to the wedding and I don't promise to obey Pete. Then as Geoff says, 'I now pronounce you husband and wife,' the moment is so profound that it touches me somewhere deep in my soul and I feel something shift and the tears well in my eyes. I gaze at Pete and see that he is crying too. We are both silly sooks, I think, and I look out at our guests and see that many of them are dabbing their eyes with tissues too.

Because we are too poor to be able to afford a reception, we've asked all our guests to pay for their meal instead of bringing a gift and everyone says that the curries are great. I am pleased about that, but I feel too ill to eat any of them.

Pete and I dance together, he in his black suit and white T-shirt and me in my wedding dress, a new white one that is embroidered with silver daisies, while a friend serenades us on his guitar. He sings 'The Way You Look Tonight' and I could live in this moment forever. The wedding is perfect and the party that is our wedding continues well into the early hours of the morning and it is the best wedding I've ever been to.

46

I have decided to have my fourth baby at home. There are no birth centres in Daylesford and I can't stand the thought of going to a hospital. Even if it is just a small local one. Even though they don't shave you anymore — because you never know, they might just change their minds. Besides, I want the children to be there, they want to be there and can you just imagine six children dash teenagers, Pete's parents and us all squashed into a hospital labour ward?

Of course everyone says, 'You're having it at home? But what if something goes wrong?'

When people say this to Pete he gives them the lecture. He is an avid home birth advocate. The lecture goes: 'Well, now, I have had three children born at home and it was a wonderful experience for everyone. What I don't understand about the feminist movement is why they haven't struggled to get more options for women giving birth. After all, most women give birth at some time in their lives.'

I say to him, 'Yes, but the feminist movement isn't interested in anything to do with stereotypical women's lives, because they see that as part of the oppression of women. Having babies is stereotypical. However, most women still have babies. And the feminist movement has failed women in the home and in birthing.'

If I go to Daylesford Hospital and something goes wrong, I have to travel forty minutes to Ballarat anyway, so what is the difference?

I am not stupid. I am getting a doctor to deliver the baby. I ring up an old doctor named John Stevenson and he is happy to deliver my baby at home. In fact he has done well over a thousand home births. When someone says to him, 'But what if something goes wrong?' he says, in his slow, gentle voice, 'I have delivered many babies at home and of all those births, only twice has something gone wrong — and it would have gone just as wrong in the hospital. When I started delivering babies at home I did it because I could see how much more closely home birth babies bonded with their mothers and families and how rare postnatal depression became.'

It is midnight and the first contraction ricochets through my body. Twelve hours later I am swearing at the top of my lungs. There is pain the whole time. No breaks. John is worried and he pushes down on my stomach to try and get this baby born: he is just too big.

'Get him out, get him out.' I am frantic. I've had enough of this labour stuff and I just want a nice meal in a café. Anything but pain and discomfort.

'I'm never having sex again!' I yell at Pete.

The next peak comes and I feel John's hand reach up inside me, then I scream with the most excruciating pain I have ever experienced as John pushes open my cervix with one hand and pushes down on my belly with the other. Finally out comes Zane into Pete's waiting hands. He is born in front of his brothers and sisters and Pete's parents and they are all ecstatic.

We name him Zane after Pete's father, John, because Zane means 'John' in Gaelic.

He weighs nine pounds, nine ounces.

Zane bruised me from the inside out with his kicking,

twisting and turning, and would only settle down inside when we play Jimmy Hendrix full blast.

He is chubby and beautiful and even though he is only minutes old, his eyes are alert and questioning, and as I hold him to my body he peers at me and asks, 'Who are you?'

Pete's mother, Thelma, wipes my brow and hugs me and tells me how wonderful I am. Zane is passed from sister to brother and from brother to sister and I say, 'I want some champagne and some Panadeine Forte!'

Pete looks to Dr John for approval.

'Give a new mother anything she wants is my motto,' the doctor says.

And I gulp down the champagne and Panadeine Forte and start to feel a whole lot better. Pete also brings me flowers and a card thanking me for our baby and a silver bracelet.

When I tell the local doctor about the birth he says, 'Well, if you had been in hospital you would have had a caesarean. That John Stevenson is a remarkable man.'

I have put Zane in his best clothes because today is his dedication. All my children have been dedicated. Baptists have dedication ceremonies instead of infant baptism. No promises are made on behalf of the baby that he will grow up to be a good Christian, because the child needs to decide that for himself, when he is old enough. The only vows that are made in a dedication ceremony are those made by the parents, who dedicate themselves to the role of parenting and thank God for the gift of the child.

Pete and I have given up going to the Uniting Church, where we felt we didn't fit in and where the services were taking on a Pentecostal tone due to the recent experiences of the minister. I am missing ceremony in my life and because I think our Christian heritage should not be thrown out altogether and because having a baby is such a special event that it needs to be consecrated, we have taken tables, food and wine down to the dam. We stand in a circle with our children and our friends. I hold Zane in my arms and he squirms and wriggles and doesn't know he is the centre of attention. Peter and I make our vows to him and we both voice our wishes for his future. Then we drink and eat together and celebrate new life.

We are still on social security, so it is pretty tough. The car is about to die, the house is disintegrating and we can't afford a holiday.

'I think we should make pottery,' I say to Pete out of the blue.

'But we don't know how.'

'It can't be that hard,' I say. 'We can sell it. You can make it and I'll paint it. I don't want to stay on social security and there are no jobs in Daylesford. Anyway, hand-painted pottery is in.'

I can see by the spark in his eyes that he thinks it might be a good idea and he finally says, 'What the heck! I'll give it a go.'

He rings every clay company in Victoria to find out how to slip-cast pottery. He makes an absolute nuisance of himself, but he gets the information. He sands the first piece smooth and passes it through to me at the kitchen table, surrounded by small tubs of underglaze, ready to paint it while Zane crawls around my feet.

'What are you going to paint on it, blossom?' Pete says.

'Aha, wait and see! A true artist never reveals her work until it is finished.'

The first piece is a large bowl. I paint it and I call Pete to come and look.

'Naked people? Oh, blossom, I don't think anyone is going to want to buy a bowl with two naked people frolicking all over it!'

'But they're not doing anything offensive,' I protest. 'It's a celebration of life.'

The next piece he prepares for me I cover in nice safe roses. Soon our house is filled with pottery; it's stacked in every corner, in various states of production. Poor Zane has only the kitchen to play in. Pete spends his days on the back veranda making mugs, vases and bowls, dressed in his thermals for an Arctic expedition while he puddles in cold clay and icy water.

We fire the pottery in a little kiln on the veranda. It was a huge decision to buy this because it meant taking out a loan on our Visa card. Pete's parents paid for the rest of it, to get us started. When we have our first load from the kiln we carefully pack it into the car to hoof it around to the shopkeepers to try and sell it. The first shopkeeper we approach buys all of it, three hundred dollars worth at wholesale price, and before we know it we are selling to forty or so shops.

We are making pottery seven days a week, often until eleven at night, and in between we are dealing with the ongoing demands of being parents: the meals that need to be prepared despite the fact that there is always one person who won't like it, the doctor's visits for ear aches and stitches for cuts; the school visits about the kids being bullied on the bus; and of course the driving to friends' houses and piano and ballet classes. If we go to Melbourne to sell pottery we have to be back in time for the children, so we never stop to eat until we are home. Then, after all this, we fall into bed exhausted.

We do it in the hope that one day we will be able to pay our bills without having to go, 'Oh, who can we put off this week? Who's screaming the loudest?'

47

'You need to put Zane in a crèche,' says the local doctor, Fred. 'He'll respond well to the structure and you need a break.' Zane is trying to take apart Fred's computer.

'Okay, I might try it,' I say.

On the days Zane is in crèche we try to get as much done as possible. We go flat out at the pottery, try to do the shopping and we try to cook a meal that will do for a couple of days. And we try not to feel guilty about Zane being in crèche.

We have managed to buy a shed so we can move all the pottery out of the house and we now have three kilns operating: two large kilns and the baby one we started with. Our days together in the shed making pottery are blissful. Some couples might hate being stuck together all the time, but Pete and I love it. We talk and talk and when we're not talking, we listen to Radio National and Lucky Oceans and talkback shows with elderly male callers ringing up to berate parents who have their children in crèche. When we have a backlog of orders for pots we are stressed because we are flat out trying to get the orders through as quickly as possible. An outgoing order means incoming money. And when the number of orders drops off we are stressed because there is no money coming in to pay the bills. We work as hard as we can to get off social security payments.

The naked frolicking design is called 'Naughty People' and we paint it on plates, vases — anything — and we can't keep up with the demand. We have a business name, Red Hot Parrot, and pots with that name on it become collectors' items. But there is only so much of it we can make and it's never enough.

When I ring retailers to ask for payment they are never there. They always seem to be away on holidays although we never get one ourselves. Then in frustration we work out that even though our mugs sell for $24.95 each, we are making only about $1.50 an hour each for our labour.

Pete starts to make me large platters and vases. 'Now these are not for the shops,' he says. 'They're for you to paint whatever you want on them.'

So when I feel that I've had enough of production work and that I am going to start having nightmares about being stuck in a little tin shed, with the sun beating relentlessly on its roof, baking me to a crisp while all I get to do is paint the same design over and over and over, I get one of these special pieces Pete has made for me and paint in the same way I would paint if it were canvas. Then I sell these pieces for a lot more through the local gallery.

Pete is washing the dishes. It is a hot, dry January day. If you look out the windows you can see the heat haze. The birds are quiet but the skinks slither quickly over our back steps in a frantic effort to hide in a crack. The spiders and snakes are out. It is their time and often a tiger or black snake will sunbake on our driveway, as if it has every right in the world to be there and we are the intruders.

I am hanging out the washing under the gum trees when I hear Pete call me through the kitchen louvres. I wander over. I hate the heat and just want to hide until summer is over.

‘Phone, blossom,’ he says.

I pick up the phone and it’s Miss Pam, Jacob’s ballet teacher. I am driving Jacob to ballet twice a week now, but I’m not a good ballet mother. I never show up for rehearsals. I don’t do his make-up or hair. I don’t sew costumes. I just deliver him to the door and he is whisked away by a flock of ballet mothers, who fuss over him because he is still the only boy. When I collect him he is covered in make-up.

‘Look, I’ve just been contacted by the director of a private ballet school in Melbourne. He spotted Jacob in the end-of-year concert and wants to offer him a scholarship,’ she says enthusiastically.

‘Wow, that’s great. He’ll be so pleased.’

‘Yes, but there’s more,’ she explains. ‘Ballet school is six days a week from eight-thirty till five-thirty, sometimes later. He’ll have to move to Melbourne to start school next February.’

‘But he’s only fourteen! That’s only two months or so away!’ My heart lurches at the thought.

‘Think about it. It’s a wonderful opportunity,’ she says.

After talking to her I flop into a chair and tell Pete what she said. This is definitely a proper pot of tea time.

He and I wait for Jacob to get home from his friend’s house and we sit him at the table, with another pot of tea, and tell him about the school.

‘What do you want to do?’ we ask.

‘I want to go. Definitely,’ he says without a moment’s thought. I knew he would say that.

‘Is Jacob going away?’ Seth and Indea ask.

‘I’m afraid so. It will be sad for us, but Jacob needs to do this if he wants to be a dancer,’ I say, also wanting to be sure myself that this is in Jacob’s best interests.

Seth and Indea both look shocked, as if someone has whisked something precious away from them without warning.

'I also want to change to my middle name. I want you to call me Asher,' Jacob tells us.

'Okay,' I say. 'I think I've always liked it better anyway.' Seth, Indea and Pete agree and immediately it seems natural to call him Asher. The changeover takes no time at all.

When Asher isn't looking I curl up in Pete's arms and cry. My baby is leaving home and he is only fourteen years old. But I know it is what he has wanted since he was three. So I try not to be an absolutely sooky mother about it and I fail dreadfully.

Asher moves to Melbourne and he goes to live with a friend of ours, who assures him she will treat him like a grown-up. I ring him every night and I worry because he sounds lost and he isn't a grown-up at all.

48

Sometimes I feel like I have spent my life vomiting.

In fact I have worked out that by the time this new baby is born I will have spent three years and nine months of my life vomiting and that doesn't count for bouts of the flu and other illnesses.

So far I have spent about eight years breastfeeding and too many years wondering when I will get back into shape.

'You put on two kilos with every pregnancy, you know,' a friend's mother told me once. I was horrified. How does it help the species if the good breeders become less attractive with each production? What sort of incentive is that? It would be much better for the survival of the species if with each new pregnancy a woman became thinner, younger and her body firmer.

I am struggling down the street to get groceries in my nauseous state, making a mental note of the nearest public toilets in case I need to get there in a hurry. I wander into the health food shop, easing my body down the skinny aisle.

The aromas of coffee and samosas are overtaking me and I struggle to fight them off. I have tried ginger, travel pills, bicarb — everything for morning sickness — and the only thing that helps is acupuncture. And even that only takes the edge off it.

'You need a rebalancing,' Kate says as I put my bags of muesli on the counter. I smile and nod.

'If you had your aura cleansed it would stop the morning sickness,' says Maggie leaning over her basket full of fresh bread, tofu and muesli.

I try not to look at the food and I escape the shop as quickly as I can and step out into the street. It can take two hours to walk the length of the shops in Daylesford, because you need to stop and talk to everyone you know. It's wonderful, as long as you don't feel like you are going to puke.

Alex approaches me, pats my belly and says, 'You're a goddess with your pregnant belly, a goddess.' I gaze at Alex with her dreadlocks and nose ring. She has never been pregnant.

I head into the vegetable shop and run straight into Lyn.

'You're just not accepting this pregnancy. You need to welcome it,' she says.

'I need to have the baby!' I snap back, suddenly sick to death of new age Daylesford advice.

At three in the morning I wake with the first pain. I ring up Rick's house and he very kindly brings back Asher, Seth and Indea so they can be here. Pete rings our friend Aileen, who says she will pick up his children, but she can't wake anyone at their house and turns up without them. We think it's too late for Pete to go for them. By six I am swearing.

'Fuck!' I yell.

'Fuck!' yells Zane, who is twenty-one months.

But the baby doesn't get stuck and Maia is born in a few hours. She is named after Pete's lovely mother, whose second name is May.

Maia is so quiet and still and delicious. I cuddle her close to me and whisper in her ear, 'You will always be my baby.'

Indea crawls into bed beside her newborn sister and cuddles her too.

'I'll make your favourite brekky — eggs, spinach and hollandaise sauce,' says Pete.

'I'll make you a pot of tea,' offers Aileen.

'I need more,' I say. 'Can we open the champagne?'

'She knows what she needs,' says Dr John. He really is the loveliest man.

And I drink three glasses, down the Panadeine Forte and I feel a whole lot better once more. John holds Maia in his arms tenderly. She is his 1032nd home birth. He gazes at her, his eyes brimming with tears. 'I never get immune to the miracle of birth,' he says.

Pete brings me breakfast and jewellery, cards and flowers and tells me how thrilled he is and I love him.

49

So here I am in Ballarat, in the hectic, crowded city, on a busy Saturday, shopping with my five beautiful children. The older ones all need supplies for school. Material for Seth, pens and paper for Indea and a tracksuit for Asher. I feel fulfilled and delighted as a mother. Becoming a mother to these five souls has been the most healing and liberating experience I have had in my life.

First we do the boring stuff and go to the supermarket to get it out of the way. Zane is so dynamic that, even with Seth and Asher helping me, we cannot keep tabs on him. We think we have him and, as soon as one of us is distracted by some product, he is off. He disappears so often that my voice is hoarse from calling to him. I find him under the lolly aisle looking for defecting strays. I find him in the staffroom chatting to the staff. I find him in the vegetable section stuffing grapes down his mouth by the handful. And then I can't find him at all. So eventually I walk up to the checkout and say to the girl in her uniform and long fingernails, 'Excuse me.'

I lean over and take hold of her microphone. 'Zane Elijah Neal,' I say in my cross-mother voice and it booms out over the entire supermarket.

Shoppers stop in their tracks and all the people lined up at the checkouts turn to look at me.

They recognise the voice of a frustrated mother on the edge.

'Zane Neal, you have until I count to three to get to the front of the shop!'

There is dead silence in the supermarket while every single person waits.

'One...' I say.

'Two...

'Three...' And the pattering of a child's feet is heard as Zane appears and every mother in the place laughs and claps. He thinks they are clapping him and he smiles at them all. But still we spend more time looking for him than shopping.

I dump the shopping in the hall and quickly throw on a suit, brush my hair and tear out the door. I am a civil celebrant and I'm late for a wedding. I applied to become a celebrant for a few reasons. We need the money and it makes me feel like I am offering the community the skills I have gained. Skills I would have used in the church. But it is strange work with some strange requests. I have even been asked to show photographs of myself to see if I am photogenic enough for the wedding shoot.

Today's wedding is a lesbian couple and when I arrive one of them is in tears because, even though they have lived in a committed relationship for eight years, her parents won't come to their wedding. I try to be as supportive as I can and wait for her to compose herself. When the ceremony begins the atmosphere is full of the love and care of their friends and it is a really moving wedding.

I marry people on top of mountains and the bride is two hours late. I do pagan weddings and the grooms do not want to pledge fidelity. I marry people who I don't think I should marry, but if I don't someone else will.

But I also marry couples who are devoted to one another,

happy and comfortable in each other's company, and then I think being a celebrant is the best job in the world.

It is Sunday and my sister and her husband are in Australia. They have come up for the day and brought my mother with them. She fusses over the children, but the younger ones keep their distance because they don't really know her, and the older ones have hardly ever seen her and think she is old and strange.

'Do we have to call her anything?' they ask.

'Just call her Rowena,' I say. And they disappear to their bedrooms.

'I love you all so much,' she says as we sit around the table.

I look at her and don't say what I know I should — that I love her too. I don't say anything. It's as if my voice has shrivelled up inside me.

'So what are you going to do with your future,' she says to Pete and me.

'We're going to open a shop. We can't make any money out of the wholesaling,' I explain.

'Well, I will pray to the Lord to bless your venture,' she says.

I want to argue with everything my mother says and I think the best way to handle the situation is probably to have a drink, because I can feel my insides curling up into a tight, tangled ball.

'Mum, would you like a gin and tonic?' I ask. 'I'm having one.'

She looks over at my sister's husband and says, 'No, you know the Lord doesn't approve of alcohol.'

'How about you guys?' I ask my sister and her husband.

'Thanks, but we're just going to go and have a look at the children's bedrooms. Besides, we're driving,' my sister says and the two of them trot off down the hall.

As soon as they have left the kitchen my mother says, 'Perhaps I will have a gin after all.'

We tell Pete's dad we are opening a shop and he says, 'Oh, oh, oh, oh, people open shops and they go bankrupt. Oh dear me, you'll be bankrupt in no time.' And he rubs his beard with worry.

'Well, Dad, we have to take that risk. I'm too old to get a job, even if there were any around here, we don't want to stay on social security and wholesaling just isn't getting us anywhere,' Pete says.

Our shop opens in Daylesford, with a thousand dollars worth of stock. That is all we can rake together. We also have some stock that an old customer lends us to help out, and we split the profits from that and fill the rest of the shelves with our pottery. But we take more in our first week than we ever do in a month of making pottery and wholesaling it. We still have to work long hours as the shop is open seven days and often we are up to eleven-thirty pricing and displaying stock. Word seems to spread that we are open and people drive from the edges of Victoria to get our pottery. We start to make enough money to move house and get a new car and to spend a week holidaying in the Grampians.

In one week we sell our house, buy another and move into the township of Daylesford. It was nice being out in the bush with the crimson rosellas, the cockies and the wallabies, but the driving has been unbearable and the older the children are getting the more driving they need. One day I added the time up and I had spent two and a half hours driving in and out of town.

Now in Daylesford there are the born-and-bred locals, families that have been in the town for four generations and of course there are the local houses with local addresses. If you want to send a card to my friend Jeanette, you address it, 'the house opposite the park'. And it gets there. We move into Jamieson Street and I am duly stopped and asked where I have moved to.

'Number Ten Jamieson Street,' I say proudly, as I love my new home. It has become mine from the moment I found the kettle and made my first cuppa. But when I say number ten, I get a blank look as people try to place the house.

'You know, the one with the big tree out the front.'

Blank.

'You know, white weatherboard.'

Blank.

'You know, Cammo's old house.'

'Oh! *Cammo's* old house. Oh, you're in Cammo's house.' And there are smiles of recognition. 'Yeah, that's a good house. How much did you pay for it? More than Cammo did, I'll bet!'

Now Cammo hasn't lived in the house for five years, but it's always going to be his house. He and Nicho and Savvo renovated it and it was going to be his ever after. 'Well, it'll never be your house until someone in your family has died in it, you know,' someone says to me and I quickly touch wood and think, it can stay Cammo's, I don't want anyone dying.

So now we are only two blocks from the shops and I love being able to walk there. It feels so healthy, so less wasteful of resources than driving. Zane and Maia scoot along on their bikes and the sun warms us.

As we get home from wandering down the street we see Pete's parents pull up in their car that is twenty years old and so well looked after that it's almost like new. Apart from the design, of course.

Pete's dad loves to ask people, 'How old do you think this car is? Go on. How old?'

‘Oh, five, six years,’ they guess.

‘Nope,’ he says proudly. ‘Twenty-two years old, this car is. That’s what happens when you look after your car. It can last you a lifetime.’

‘Nana, Nana, Nana,’ squeal Zane and Maia as they tear past me.

I go to help John and Thelma with their luggage and throw my arms around Thelma to hug her. As always, she feels so tiny and frail. Zane and Maia bounce around us full of delight.

‘This is for you,’ Thelma says, putting a framed drawing in my hands.

It is my favourite drawing — one she has done herself — it is of an old lady named Daisy.

‘Why are you giving me this?’ I ask and study her expression. Thelma pulls a funny face, but I know. I can tell that she thinks she is going to die, and seeing that I know she thinks this she nods her head, telling me not to say a word.

We have a birthday party for Maia’s third birthday. The table is laid with her favourite food: pesto pasta. All of us will be together. Eight kids, Pete and me and his parents. Thelma and I slam tequila down with lemon and salt, while Pete and his dad chat and the kids play. Thelma and I marvel that till now we have been ignorant of such a wondrous concoction. We are already giggling and telling silly jokes and Maia comes and sits on her nana’s knee while Zane tries to nick food from John’s plate. And the house is bedlam.

Thelma and I move on to champagne cocktails and before too long I drag the Baptist Hymnal off the bookshelf and starting at the first hymn Thelma and I sing our way through, hymn by hymn, in loud sloppy voices. We sing at the top of our lungs and declare our undying love for each other in between hymns. Neither of us sings in tune, but I am so happy to have a mother-in-law who loves me as Mato loved me, a husband who loves me and five gorgeous children who love me and three beautiful step-children, who might one day love me. I couldn't be luckier.

The teenagers head off to visit friends and Pete and I wander back inside after seeing them off. Our arms around each other, proud and satisfied with our family, and I say to Pete, 'Cup of tea wouldn't be bad.'

'Coming up, blossom,' he says.

Pete's mother died. She is seventy-four. Three score years and ten, the Bible says. She had a good life.

'I have had the most wonderful life,' she would tell me. 'I don't mind if I die now.'

But we all mind. It has been coming for the last two weeks and still it is a shock when it happens and Zane can't stop crying. He adores his grandmother, but then everyone adores her. She knew what she was doing when she gave me that drawing and she was right. We go to her funeral and nurse our loss. We sing Thelma's favourite hymns. I look at Zane and Maia. They want their nana back. I look at Pete's older kids who are sitting with his dad and his brother. I can only see their backs. There is a hollow space that is left in my heart with Thelma gone.

50

There are some things in life that only a man can do, like chopping loads of wood for the fire when you have forgotten and it's freezing cold. Or getting the leaves out of the gutter when it's storming and the rain is so heavy it is starting to drip through the ceiling. Or dealing with spiders: they are all big, all evil, all related. They are the spider mafia and they come in gangs.

Now I am a feminist. That is, I believe in the rights of women. I believe in the rights of all people. And let's face it, if the things that still happen to women in some parts of the world today were happening to a group of men, there would be public outrage, sanctions imposed, media attention. It is amazing how thoroughly you can oppress a group of humans if you do it in the name of religion or culture. Worse still, instead of fighting injustice we allow the oppression in the name of political correctness and multicultural and cross-religion tolerance. That said, though, I am a flexible feminist. I find it very useful to cook Pete a good hot meal, in a nice warm kitchen, sipping a glass of wine while he is facing the tempest and the wild beasts.

I have some skills and he has others. Besides, there is nothing as sexy as a man doing things around the house.

Pete's involvement in keeping our household running has more impact on me than any number of red roses.

I am beginning to think that life can only get better and better. I have my prince and five beautiful heirs. Asher is settled in Melbourne studying ballet and is now in tertiary. Seth is doing year eleven at high school, Indea is in grade five, Zane is in kinder and Maia has curls and looks like Shirley Temple. And they are all happy.

Once, before Claire moved, she said to me, 'You're my family now and I don't let anyone hurt my family.' I sat there too stunned to say anything back. Then the moment passed and I could have kicked myself, because I wanted to say, 'You're one of my daughters now and I won't let anyone hurt you either.'

'Come on, come down, come to Melbourne,' Claire, Rhi and Ariel say on the phone. 'Bring the children.' But it is not that easy. It is hard to travel with little children who vomit from car sickness for most of the journey. The shop is a bind too. Despite its initial boom, it doesn't make enough money for us to employ regular staff; it makes just enough to pay the bills, and travelling with little children is still not easy. We are both on social security payments.

Pete and I are happy: exhausted, but blissful. I am watching a movie with the children and he has made me a cup of tea. Then the phone rings, I grab my cup of tea and answer it. I think I could live quite happily on Earl Grey and Frangelico, my latest discovery. I say hello and recognise instantly my sister's voice. She is living in Queensland. My mother is in New South Wales and I don't know where my father is.

My sister sounds desperate.

'Mum has cancer. Ovarian. They think it runs in the family and I'm trying to get her to do genetic tests so I can see if I have it too,' she says. 'She refuses to have chemo, so she probably hasn't got long.'

'Do you think you have it, this gene?' I ask.

'Good chance. Fifty-fifty, actually, the geneticist said, but I'm trusting the Lord and we'll see what happens. If we have got it, we need to have preventative surgery, but we need some results first.'

'What sort of preventative surgery?'

'Get our breasts removed; total hysterectomy.'

Oh, is that all? I think to myself.

'I want to fly to Sydney and visit my mother,' I tell Pete while we sit in the coffee shop.

'Sure. Go,' he says. 'That's what we have Visa for.' So I go, and take Maia with me. I figure if my mother is dying I should end our relationship with grace and dignity.

We have a pleasant time together and, as I am leaving, she tells me she is moving to Melbourne to live with Wayne. 'I've only ever wanted to be a doting grandmother,' she says. 'So if I move to Melbourne I will be able to help you all.'

She decides to have chemotherapy after all and I ring her at the hospital.

'Sorry, your mother doesn't want to talk to you. She will only talk to her sons,' says the nurse apologetically.

My sister rings me in tears. 'She won't talk to me.'

'Me neither,' I say.

'It's boys, boys, boys with her!' says my sister.

I decide to wait until my mother feel likes talking to me and soon enough there's a phone call.

'I thought I might come over for a few weeks. Wayne needs a break from me. Mind you,' she adds, 'he's not too happy about me coming to see you. He thinks you won't look after me properly.'

'Sure, come over,' I say.

'What!' says Pete. 'Your mother is coming here? But you're always in tears after talking to her. Just look what happened at Davie's wedding and when she visited us that time in Daylesford!'

'She has cancer. I have to look after her.'

An hour later and her car pulls up.

'Mum, hi,' I call out as I go to greet her. She has huge bald patches on her head and long tufts of hair sticking out in other places. She looks medieval.

'Oh, I had a terrible drive over here. I was stuck behind a slow driver. Forty kilometres an hour I had to do the whole way. I've been in the car driving for two and a half hours.'

'But, Mum, I was talking to you only an hour ago.'

'No, it was at least three hours ago that I spoke to you. Your watch must be faulty,' she says.

I take her inside and sit her at the kitchen table. 'First thing we are going to do,' I tell her, 'is shave your head. Then I'll make you a cuppa.'

'Do you think it would look better shaved?'

'Absolutely. At the moment you look like you have some sort of terrible disease. At least if we shave you, you'll only look like a Buddhist nun.'

I get out the shaver I bought when the boys were desperate to have undercuts and I get to work.

'Oh, I can't look like a Buddhist nun,' she exclaims.

'Good heavens, of course you can. It's a religion that deserves our respect.'

She starts muttering in tongues to keep evil Buddhist spirits away and then she says, 'There is only one path to the Lord our God.'

'That's much better,' I say as I step back to look at her. 'I'll make you that cuppa now.'

'Oh, that would be lovely. Where are the children?'

'Outside playing. Oh — well, Seth is in his room listening to some head-banging music.'

‘They’ll be glad to see their gran,’ she says. ‘I love them so much. I’ve always wanted nothing more than to be a wonderful grandmother.’

‘Do you want some cheesecake? There is some left over from Indea and Maia’s birthdays.’

‘Did they have their birthdays? And I missed them? Goodness, what dates are their birthdays?’

‘Maia’s was on the eleventh and Indea’s was on the fourteenth.’

‘And I’ve left their presents sitting on the bench. I was going to grab them on my way out the door and I forgot. Do you think they’ll forgive me?’

‘I’m sure they won’t mind. Cheesecake?’

‘No. No, I’m not eating any cheesecake. No dairy. Dairy is very bad for cancer. I only eat vegetables now. But I can have coffee. Coffee is very good for people with cancer. My homeopath said that,’ she says.

I go and tell the children she is here and when I get back she is eating a huge slice of cheesecake and I see she has also found the cream and has smothered the cake with it.

Seth walks in. ‘Hey, Robbi, can’t I have a TV in my room so I can play Playstation and watch stuff you guys don’t like having on?’

‘Honey, we’ve had no TV on and off for years and it’s been great. Now we’ve got one again for the first time in years and I really think one is enough.’

‘Do you know that my television,’ my mother says to Seth, ‘was the first colour television in Australia? Your grandfather made it and there weren’t any colour TVs in Australia except the one I have.’

‘Do you mean it’s like thirty years old?’ Seth asks her, astonished.

‘Oh, it’s much older than that,’ she tells him.

Seth raises his eyebrows at me and I shake my head.

He smiles at my mother. ‘How are you, Ena?’ he says.

The children still won't call her Gran or Nana because they hardly know her. I know she doesn't like them calling her by her first name, but it's that or nothing.

'I'm good,' she says. 'The Lord is healing me. The doctors are absolutely amazed.'

'Are you having genetic testing done?' I ask her.

'I know Karyn wants me to, but I don't want to at all. It isn't necessary. You only need to trust in the Lord to look after you. Karyn should place more faith in her Lord. Mind you, Karyn isn't too happy with you. She thinks that you don't respect her beliefs.'

I lean over to get some peanut butter out of the pantry and I bump my head. 'Shit!' I cry.

In a flash my mother is over and her hand is on my head. 'Thank you, Jesus. Praise you, Lord. Hallelujah, Jesus,' she is murmuring.

'Mum, what are you doing?'

'If you put your hand on an injury and pray to the Lord within three minutes, you will feel no pain.'

'Cheap medicine for the free world,' I whisper to myself.

I once questioned everything she said and made her angry. Now, I realise happily, I must be finally maturing a bit because I enjoy her company and I can ignore the things that she says, the statements that I once would have challenged.

'Mum,' I say when the children have gone outside to play, 'tell me about when you were thirteen. You mentioned it when I was sixteen, but I want to hear again now that I am an adult.'

She is very forthcoming. 'I got pregnant to a man who was twenty-eight. He was living in our house. Your grandparents took him in to help him. He was a minister and he had a wife and children back in Czechoslovakia, but we didn't find that out till later. He wanted to bring them to Australia too. My parents said I had seduced him away from following the Lord. I had a year off school. I really failed the Lord then. I don't think Mato and Granddad ever got over it.'

'Mum,' I say to her, 'you were thirteen years old. Whatever happened, it wasn't your fault. He was twenty-eight and you were thirteen. That's a pretty uneven age spread!' I am glad to be able to say this to her, because when I was sixteen I wasn't old enough to know.

'Oh, I nearly ruined your grandfather's work for the Lord. I nearly took him from his calling,' she says.

'Mum, if Indea got pregnant to a twenty-eight-year-old guy I would fucking kill him! I don't care what anyone says — a thirteen year old is a child. After I had killed him my next thought would be how to support Indea. It sounds like you got no support at all. How can you have seduced him? You might have had a woman's body, but inside you were a child.'

My mother starts to cry soft, quiet tears.

'Your grandparents moved him out for a while, but six months later they had him back,' she says sadly.

'They had him back? Mum, they were wonderful grandparents to me,' I say to her. 'But lousy parents to you.'

My mother is crying, so I pour her another cuppa. 'Mum, it wasn't your fault,' I say to her, putting my hand on hers.

'I have a hard time believing that,' she says, 'but I guess you're right.'

51

There is one thing you can say about my mother: she is a survivor. She has rallied and I feel really pleased for her. It is a year now since she was first diagnosed and her hair has grown back, and it's so curly now she won't have to get it permed.

She is very pleased about this and gives thanks to the Lord for her curls.

I go to the gynaecologist to get checked because I am a bit worried. So far, two of my aunts, two of my uncles and one of my cousins have died of cancer. And now there's Mum. It turns out that my great-grandmother also died of cancer in her forties and my other great-grandmother had cancer too. That's a lot of people in one family and it would be just my luck to get it too. Just as my life is becoming so wonderful.

The gyny says there is nothing at all to worry about. He has a good prod around and there are no lumps. I know this gynaecologist quite well. I went to see him after I had Maia.

'I want to get my tubes done,' I say, sitting in his office. He is not much older than I am. But he feels older.

'Ah well,' he says, looking over his glasses. 'Now, does your husband want you to do this?'

'God, no!' I say. 'He wants another baby, but I don't.'

It's got to where I panic if Pete even stands in the bedroom door. I'm, 'No, go away, don't look at me or I'll get pregnant.'

'Well, we have a policy,' he says. 'We don't like to do anything permanent unless both people in the partnership agree. How many children have you got, Robbi?' he asks absently as he starts to write notes.

'Five.'

His glasses fall off his nose, 'When would you like to be booked in?'

Pete and I are gearing up to celebrate our seventh wedding anniversary. It is Saturday night and we have a day off on Wednesday, so we are going to Ballarat to have lunch together.

I am sitting down watching *Mary Poppins* with the children. It is one of my favourite movies. When I was little my parents took me to see it at the drive-in and afterwards I tried to go down the banister just like Mary did, and broke my leg. But now my favourite line is when the mother sings about men as a group being rather difficult, but individually adored.

Slowly, my watching is interrupted by a burning sensation in my breast. I put down my cup of tea and my Tim Tam and put my hand there. It is hot to touch and there is a rash. I get a sick feeling in my stomach that starts scratching viciously at my insides and I press harder — sure enough, there is a hard lump.

I race into the kitchen. 'Pete, Pete! There's a lump in my breast. I am only forty-one and I've got a lump!' The fear has reached my throat.

'Well, don't worry. The doctor checked just two weeks ago and there was nothing there, so it can't be cancer. Cancer doesn't grow that quick. It doesn't just pop up. Go round to the hospital and get Greg or Fred to have a look,' he says, trying to reassure me and control my mounting hysteria.

The hospital is just around the corner and Greg is on duty. We have been seeing him or Fred ever since we moved to Daylesford twelve years ago and they know each one of us. Fred is warm, experienced, sensible, funny and good-looking. Fred and I swap jokes. Greg is our age and is kind and gentle and often turns up at the same parties.

'I've got this lump, Greg, in my breast,' I say as he ushers me into the casualty room. His face turns white.

'Let's have a look. Mmm, I'm going to put you on antibiotics. I think it is probably mastitis. I had a woman in her fifties had it just last week. But I think you should have a mammogram to make sure.'

Walking home, I am relieved that it is just mastitis, but underneath the worry is there because I have been feeling ill and tired all summer. I've been falling asleep in the afternoons and I have sat and watched the children play instead of chasing them.

'It's just mastitis,' I tell Pete.

'Don't worry, blossom,' he says on our way to the mammogram that we are having instead of the anniversary lunch. 'It's just mastitis. Antibiotics don't work so well these days.'

I get into the cold, starched gown and they do a mammogram.

'Wait here, please, Mrs Neal and we'll get your husband for you,' the nurse says without looking at me.

I stare at her vacantly. No one calls me 'Mrs Neal'. No one in a hospital has offered to get my husband before.

When Pete comes in, the woman with a cardboard face asks me to follow her and takes me through to ultrasound, where they do one of those as well and I am starting to really panic.

'When are you seeing your doctor?' asks the ultrasound doctor, who not long ago was showing me pictures of Maia.

'I haven't got an appointment,' I mumble through the sick wall of fear that is building brick by brick around me.

'We will contact him and get him to ring you this afternoon. We're ninety-nine per cent sure it's cancer.'

We go home in a complete blur.

'We won't tell the children anything until it's definite, will we?' I say to Pete. It's all I can manage to say.

'No. I don't think there's any need to upset them unnecessarily. Besides, there is nothing certain yet, blossom. Doctors do make mistakes. Ultrasounds make mistakes too.'

He rings Fred. 'We need a referral and an appointment, Fred. It looks like Robbi has cancer.'

'No, she won't have cancer,' says Fred hopefully.

'Fred, please!' Pete insists. 'Get us in to see someone good tomorrow.'

The next day we see the surgeon. He prods the lump that I have in my breast and says, 'There is a rather large one under your arm as well. It's cancer, all right, an aggressive one. I'm arranging tests for this afternoon and an appointment with an oncologist for five-thirty. We'll have the results by then,' he says and shows us his door.

Somehow I stumble out of his office and down his bluestone path. The tears are flooding down my face and the world has disappeared. I think my heart is going to split, it hurts so much. I am inconsolable. I have been thrown into the deepest, darkest pit and there is no way out.

Pete rings Aileen to get her to pick the children up from school.

I go for tests. I cry as they stick huge needles into me. I cry even more when I can see from their faces that they know, from what they are drawing out, that it is cancer. I cry as the oncologist tells me that I have aggressive, locally advanced cancer that has got into my lymph nodes.

'What do you want to do?' he asks me — as if I would know.

'I want whatever you've got that can make this go away.'

'We can start you on Monday,' he says and starts writing prescriptions. He is a kind man, our age. I can see he finds it hard telling people that they have cancer.

'Will I lose my hair?'

'Absolutely.'

'My beautiful long frizzy hair.'

'I'm afraid so.'

'I want you to treat me in the same way you would want your wife to be treated,' I say to him. 'My baby is only three years old. She can't live without me. I have a lot to do yet. I am only halfway through my life.'

'I will do my best,' he says. 'We're going for a cure here,' he adds kindly.

I believe him. I trust him. I put my life — what I have left of it — into his hands.

'What do you see that is different in people that survive this to people who generally don't? If you could see one difference, what would you say it was?' asks Pete.

The doctor is silent and finally, after some thought, he says, 'People who survive educate themselves. Now,' he goes on, 'we have to do more tests and see where the cancer has gone.'

Pete and I drive the forty-five kilometres home in silence. It is Valentine's Day tomorrow. We are in too much pain to talk and I cry all the way home.

I get there and we tell the children straightaway. Indea crawls into bed beside me and we cry together. I hold her, but I cannot take away her pain. Seth just looks like someone has kicked him in the guts and Maia and Zane know that I am sick.

I want my Mato, I want Thelma. I call Aileen, but I get the answering machine.

I cannot stop crying. My world has just crumbled and I didn't even do anything bad to make it happen.

I call the phone number on the pamphlet that we grabbed on our way out the door and a lady named Lyn who we have never met drives for an hour from Maryborough to be with us.

I am quite hysterical now and I cannot stop sobbing. I can't get out of bed. I want to wake from this nightmare and she puts her arms around me. She is bald and when I think I will soon be that way too, I cry some more.

'I've had cancer for twenty-three years,' she says and that makes me stop crying.

'How long?' I say.

'Twenty-three years. And you know how long they gave me? Three months. Three months and here I am twenty-two years and nine months later. They have no bedside manner, doctors. They just tell you and kick you out the door. They don't explain to you that you're not going to die in a month. They just dump it on you and off you go,' she tells me in a soothing voice.

Greg comes around and drops off some pills to sedate me and in the morning, after no sleep, I go for more tests to see how much of my body has been attacked.

I cry as they tell me to drink some gunk that tastes like I imagine urine tastes and they put me through a CAT scan. I cry when they stick more needles into me.

I cry as they take blood and scan my bones. I am so distraught that the medic scanning my bones says quietly to us on our way out, 'I'm not supposed to tell you this. You're supposed to wait for the doctor. But there is nothing wrong with your bones.'

And I think to myself that I will remember this man's kindness forever. He has given us one tiny speck of hope.

Pete and I wander around the shopping centre in a daze and while we are wandering he grabs a book about breast cancer from a book shop. We go and park the car near the lake and start to read straightaway. It is a book by a woman named Jane Plant, who had breast cancer and was given three months to live, five years ago. As I am reading this I begin to feel a tiny, microscopic bit better. I begin to see that I might be able to do something to aid my recovery and that gives me enough of a sense of power and enough direction for my pain that I stop crying for a moment and Pete and I make a list of all the things she recommends we do.

The oncologist, Phillip, rings us on our mobile as he gets the results for each test and gives us the news that, as far as they can tell, the cancer has spread no farther than my lymph nodes.

I am still scared. So scared. Nothing I have ever been through in my life compares with this. 'I would swap a million bad marriages and hard childhoods not to have cancer,' I say to Pete.

'Oh, blossom, this thing hasn't beaten us yet,' he says, hugging me while I cry.

I wake the next morning, it is only five and everyone else is asleep. I go to the computer and start to write. I start to write about how afraid I am and then I write about who I am, because if I am going to die I want my children to know who their mother was. I want them to know why I don't hit them. Why they call me 'Robbi' instead of 'Mum'. I write with my grandfather's Bible in front of me. It is inscribed with 'Padre J.G. Langton 79th Squadron RAAF'.

When I can write no more and Pete has woken up, I say, 'We're going to see Pam at the health food shop. We're getting flaxseed, carrots, apples and this stuff called co-enzyme Q10.'

'I'll ring around and see if someone can lend us a juicer,' says Pete.

'I'm going off dairy, meat, alcohol and sugar until I'm better too.'

Next I ring Julie at the crèche. 'Julie, I have cancer,' I say and I start to cry into her ear.

'Hey,' she says, 'listen, I'll arrange it so Maia can come every day and there won't be any fees. Also I'll organise a casserole roster. You're going to need food.'

Pam organises organic fruit for us and Aileen gives us her juicer and Pete immediately starts juicing. The kids are soon lining up for juice and they love it.

Sunday night I do our bookwork and Pete says, 'You're going to have to show me how to do that.'

I burst into tears. 'That's because you think I'm going to die. Already we have to plan how life will be without me in it. Already I am becoming dispensable. I don't want to die!' I sob.

His arms are around me. 'I'm not going to let you die,' he says. 'I've not spent my whole life looking for you so I can lose you now. We all need you here and we're going to read every book and find out and do everything possible to make sure you won't die. We won't put all our eggs in the one basket. We'll let the doctors do what they can and we'll do everything else as well.'

52

I am in hospital, sitting in a Jason recliner. I have had massive doses of Dexamethasone and there is a drip running into my arm. It carries the chemotherapy. It is so toxic that the nurses are covered from head to foot in protective gear. If I go to the toilet I have to flush it twice because my wee will be toxic. They are poisoning me. I am sure one day we will look back on chemotherapy in the same way we look at leeching. As the chemo runs through my veins, my arms and legs start to burn and ache. It is an ache that is deep in my bones and I hit the Panadeine Forte. Every day for ten days I am going to have to inject myself with stuff to keep up my blood count. What if I can't do it? I'm a wimp. I can't stick a needle into myself.

The man in the chair next to me says, 'I've got lung cancer. What've you got?'

I don't want to talk about it. I can't say it yet, but I have to be polite so I mumble, 'Breast.' I can't say 'cancer'.

'Still it ain't changing my life,' he says. 'I ain't givin up my beer an smokes for nothing.'

I look at him. I can see that is true. He looks ravaged.

The chemo takes two hours to drip into my body and then they wheel me to the hospital ward. I don't want Pete to leave me, but he has to go home to the children and I clutch the photo of them that I have brought with me. They are my future, my hope.

The registrar on duty comes in and picks up the clipboard. There is a nurse with him.

'Well, you're a real life-or-death case,' he says.

I burst into uncontrollable sobs and the nurse puts her arm around me as the registrar walks off and she says, 'Are you all right? Are you all right, dear?'

'No, I'm not,' I blubber.

'Perhaps we could get the social worker for you.'

'No, I don't want any social worker. Why should I be all right? I might die. How can I be all right about that?' I tell her between sobs.

I can see the poor woman doesn't know what to do so I force a small smile and say, 'I'm sure I'll be okay. I just need some time.' But I don't mean it in the slightest, because time is something I may not have.

The next evening after work, Pete takes me home and I fall into bed. I cannot move. Even sipping water is a struggle. Every bone hurts dreadfully. I feel nauseous. My body is a dead weight. I can see the panic on the children's faces at seeing their mother so ill. Even the little ones are frightened now.

The phone rings and its shrill hurts my ears and head. Pete answers. He hands me the phone but I am too weak to hold it. 'Just a moment,' he says into the mouthpiece. 'It's your sister,' he says to me and puts the phone to my ear.

'Hello,' I moan, barely audible. It is the best I can get my voice to do.

She launches straight into it. 'You have to go down to Melbourne. Tomorrow! It has to be done straightaway. I need blood from you before the cancer is gone,' she says, talking at what seems to me like a hundred miles an hour. 'That way I can see if I've got the gene too. You have to do it straightaway before the chemo has a chance to work.' She is in a real panic.

'Okay,' I mutter and Pete puts the phone back.

* * *

But I cannot move. Pete is at work, the children are at school and crèche. I am alone in the house and I am too ill to even get a cup of tea. Going to the toilet is a marathon and the pain is unbearable. It is far worse than labour. When I walk the bottom of my feet feel as though I am treading on broken glass. I lie in the empty house, desolate and sad.

'I cannot come and look after you or the children,' my mother says on the phone, 'because I have to give out the hymn books at church on Sundays.'

A friend comes in, dragging her eleven-year-old daughter with her. I sigh, I do not want other people's children seeing me in this state, but I am too ill to do anything about it.

They sit on the end of the bed.

'It's all karma,' says Michelle. 'Everything in life is karma. There is a reason for everything. There is something you need to learn and that is why you are going through this. There is good in this. It is karma.'

I want to punch her but I can hardly lift my arm.

Jean, Pete's aunt, writes me a long, encouraging letter and I lie in bed and cling to it.

I lie there absolutely helpless and cry like a child afraid, in pain in the empty house. I am forty-one and I want a mother, someone who will make me feel like it will all be okay. I am so terribly alone because no one, not even Pete, can go through this for me. He has his fear in this and I have mine. We are separated by our different experience and I hate the cancer. I hate the threat it has put on my physical life, but I also hate the way it has threatened my relationships. I can't look after my family. I can't work. I can't go for coffee with friends. I can't be a wife. I can't do anything except lie here. The cancer has put a huge gulf in my life and separated me from those I love. I wonder if Pete and I can survive this.

On the third day I am back in our small local hospital that is just around the corner. I have a fever and I am hysterical again. I cannot cope with the aches, the diarrhoea and the nausea a moment longer. I am pacing the room, round and round in circles I go, trying to escape the pain, but there is no way out.

'What can we give you?' asks Greg.

'Everything!' I say, grabbing my abdomen as the pain cuts through me as if I have swallowed razor blades.

He writes madly on his pad and gives me prescriptions for Valium, more Panadeine Forte, stuff for diarrhoea and sleeping pills. I have stuff for nausea that only specialists can order and I take everything.

'Now isn't the time to be a hero,' says Pete, who knows my aversion to drugs, and then he has to leave me and go to work.

Fred comes in and sits on the end of my bed. 'I'm sorry I haven't spoken to you earlier,' he says, patting my hand.

I look at him blearily through the wet haze of my tears.

'You know, my mum had cancer when I was eighteen. Forty years ago. I didn't understand at the time what she was going through,' Fred says quietly and he goes on, 'She says to me now, you lot were bloody selfish buggers when I had cancer, and she's right.'

'Forty years ago?' At last there is a glimmer of light.

'Yep, forty years ago,' he says. 'She got over it. She's been right as rain ever since. But mothers don't always get the support they need.' I love Fred and I want to kiss his handsome face for telling me this.

Ursula the nurse comes in and says, 'You know, Robbi, I had cancer seven years ago. That's why I've got one boob twice the size of the other. You'll get through this.'

And I am so grateful for the care that I am getting in our little hospital. I am so grateful for the slivers of hope these people have given me.

The ten days crawl by and on the eleventh I can manage to get out of bed and slowly climb back into life. By day thirteen I am creeping down the street to get a few groceries.

I lean on the trolley for support as I push it around the supermarket. Zane and Maia usually tear up and down the aisles, but now they stay close by, hanging near me in case I disappear. I hope I am invisible. I don't have the strength to talk to people.

Jess spots me. 'Robbi, oh, we're so sorry to hear you're not well. What are the doctors saying? What are your chances?'

I glance at the children as if to say, Please, not in front of them. But she continues.

'My mother had breast cancer. She only lasted three months after the diagnosis.'

Ah, just what I need to hear. 'Did she have chemo?' I ask.

'Yeah, but it didn't work.'

I look at Zane and his big brown eyes are wide with fear. He takes in everything.

I say, 'Well, I've got to do some shopping,' and I push off and in the next aisle I am stopped by Miranda.

'Oh, Robbi, you poor thing. Listen, what you need is wheatgrass; if you have wheatgrass I'm sure you'll be right. Wheatgrass is so wonderful.'

By the freezer department, Freda tells me, 'You need to meditate. You should go to the ashram and meditate. And have you heard of Ian Gawler?'

At the checkout Jill says, 'I know just how you feel. My father, he's ninety-eight and he has cancer, so I just know exactly how you feel.'

I smile weakly and say nothing. I feel so frail and small and vulnerable.

‘We are praying for you,’ says Carol from the Pentecostal Church.

‘Thank you,’ I say.

I will take anything, whether or not I believe in it. I don’t think God goes around answering individual prayers. Like going shopping. ‘Oh, God, can I have this? Oh, dear God, please give me that! Oh, dear God, please cure me.’ If God was up there answering shopping list prayers, she would provide food for all the hungry children, she would stop oppression and war and rape. Because if that was what God was, if this being we call ‘God’ had the power to do that and didn’t, but spent her time helping middle-class western Christians with their petty worries, then she could hardly be anything but cruel and have a very warped sense of humour. So I do not expect God to miraculously cure me. I expect to fight my way through this and come out the other side one way or another.

‘Would you like to come to our service for a laying-on of hands?’ Carol asks earnestly.

‘Ah, no, thanks. I don’t think I can.’

‘Oh, well, we’ll pray for you anyway.’

Everyone says, keep positive! But how can you be positive about having cancer? I am angry. I have breastfed all my children. That’s a total of ten years of breastfeeding. I have only smoked half a cigarette in my entire life and probably five joints. I don’t drink — well, not that much, not every day — and the number of times I have been truly drunk can also be counted on one hand. I have taken the pill for a total of three weeks *and* I have breast cancer. *It isn’t fair!*

Never again will I be able to say, ‘When I am old I will do such and such,’ because I don’t know if I will get to be old. I can no longer take life for granted.

Everyone says, keep positive! And I realise that what they need is for me to be positive for them, to make them feel better about me having cancer. It is too much for other people to be able to handle.

'Keep your spirits up,' says Pete.

Yes, yes, I think. I must find my spirit in this and try to keep it alive. I must not give up hope.

So on day fourteen, I take out my easel and I start to paint. Before I got cancer I had started a series of paintings of middle-aged, normal women who were beautiful. I asked women I loved and thought were stunning to model for me, women who had never modelled naked before. I painted Thelma before she died. I had been painting these women on large platters, on paper and on canvas. And as sick as I am, I decide to keep going because I do not want cancer to ruin my life.

On day twenty I am having Dexamethasone and getting ready for the next treatment.

My hair is falling out in clumps. It's gross! I feel like a freak! I crawl out of bed, get the shaver out of the cupboard and hand it to Pete, who is sitting at the kitchen table eating sardines on toast for breakfast.

'Do it,' I say. 'I can't take it like this. I would rather take control and just get rid of it all.'

'You're sure?'

'Well, it's going to happen anyway.'

He puts his toast down and shaves off the rest of my hair. The kids think it is a great joke and start laughing.

'Hey, you look really sexy with a bald head,' says Pete, smiling.

'Yeah, right! You're just trying to make me feel better. It's kind of you, but I can take the truth. I look bloody hideous.'

'No, really. You have a nice head.'

'Things are looking good,' says the doctor after the second treatment. 'This is a remarkable response to the chemotherapy.

There is no evidence of any lump left under your arm or in your breast. This is remarkable.'

I don't tell him that I am also taking Cassie tea, Noni tea and purieh tea and antioxidants by the bucketful, not to mention ming gold, wheatgrass, colloidal minerals and gallons of carrot, fennel and apple juice. Also co-enzyme Q10, and then there are the things I am not taking. No fat, dairy or protein. No alcohol or sugar or meat. But I fair dinkum rattle with all the pills I am taking and when I am well enough I continue my paintings of beautiful women.

I am talking about quitting; I am up to the fourth treatment. There are two more to go. I don't think I can take anymore. I don't think I can go through another ten days of injecting myself. I want to give up, but Pete doesn't let me. The only thing I can eat when I am going through the treatment is a bit of fried tempeh or fried tofu, but because of the drugs I am not even getting thin.

'How are you feeling?' everyone asks.

'I'm feeling okay,' I say, regardless.

Once I actually said how I really felt and the person asking was shocked.

I feel like saying, 'Go home and thank whoever you believe in that this is happening to me and not you, because someone might as well experience some good out of this and it ain't going to be me. One in ten women gets breast cancer, I'm obviously the one, so you are probably one of the nine. Be glad!'

'You're so brave,' says Maggie in the supermarket. 'I don't know how you get through it.'

'I'm not brave,' I say. 'You don't see me screaming and crying in utter despair when I'm at home. I just have to get through it. What choice do I have? It's happening whether I like it or not. People are only courageous when they choose to be. I don't have a choice.'

'You're so spiritual,' says Janice, 'suffering like this.'

'No, I'm not,' I say. 'If this is the road to spiritual enlightenment, just leave me in the dark.'

'Some good will be in this,' says Karen.

'There is no good in cancer,' I say back. 'Nothing. It's a shit! Good things are happening to me while I have cancer, but not because of it.'

'I hear you have cancer,' says Rick's mum. 'Tough luck.'

Zane cries at school whenever I go to hospital. We know this because another parent told us that he stands in the corner of the room and cries for hours. She told the teacher he was crying and the teacher dismissed her with, 'Yes, well, his family is going through a hard time at the moment.'

We take him out of school.

Maia seems to know something is wrong and goes off to crèche every day without a whimper. When she gets home she snuggles into bed with me and lies still and close. She says, 'I will massage your little bald head and make the hair grow.'

Indea has just started high school and is growing her own breasts. I wonder how she feels growing breasts when her mother's are the source of disease and are going to be chopped off.

Seth has just started year twelve and is doing his exams. He is in shock.

Asher says he is going to stop school to come home and I lie and say, 'No, you don't need to. I'm fine. I'm cured.' He is in his final year. He loves ballet because he gets to spend all day with scantily clad girls and he gets to place his hands all over their beautiful slim bodies as they do *pas de deux*. He is going out with a lovely girl who is studying law, so his father needn't have worried after all. He comes and visits me, lies beside me and holds my hand. He massages my head too.

* * *

We realise pretty quickly that when you are going through something like this it takes all your energy just to survive. We surround ourselves with people who support us and stay away from those who don't. Support comes from unexpected places. People who we don't even know well bring around food. Even Pete's ex-wife's mother writes to me, sending her thoughts, and Jack and Fiona, a couple we hardly know, take Zane for weekends. Ariel, Pete's son, has grown into a gentle and kind young man and he comes and stays overnight just to be with us. He takes me to lunch when I am well enough to eat. He rings every week to see how I am. He plays with the children. He tells me he loves me.

David, Zane's piano teacher, offers to come and give him lessons in our home.

Pete's dad comes to visit and offers us money if we need it for doctors.

My friend Renate visits me every time I go to hospital and sits and chats about her horses and Mandy comes and cooks roast lamb for us as soon as I am well enough to eat something other than soy. And even though I am not eating meat, I treat myself and have a nibble and hope I will still live.

My sister sends me flowers and cards telling me that I will make it. I want to believe her. I am inundated with beautiful flowers and cards from people who care. We are overwhelmed with the love and support we receive from unexpected places.

We drive down to Melbourne to the Peter MacCallum Cancer Hospital to get a second opinion. As we sit in the cold, harsh waiting room, I am distressed by all the miserable, hopeless women waiting to see the doctor. The waiting room is thick with despair.

Finally we are ushered in and I say, 'We are just here for a second opinion.'

'What treatment are you on?' asks the young blonde oncologist.

'Taxotere,' I say.

'No, you can't be on that,' she says. She is a breast cancer specialist. I try to decide how old she might be and settle on twenty-six. I don't want to think about her income. She says, 'Taxotere is still on trial and you don't fit the trial guidelines.'

'No, that's what I'm on,' I assure her.

'Well, then you're very lucky. Your doctor must have told a fib to get you on that. You wouldn't be on such new treatment here. We couldn't give you that. We won't have it for another six months.'

The mobile phone rings and Pete excuses himself and goes outside to answer it.

While he is outside I say, 'What are my chances of survival?'

'Well, we can only give you a statistic.' She is very forthright. I can tell she answers this question a lot. 'But, with the sort of cancer you have, the stage it has reached, you have a twenty per cent chance of surviving the next three years.'

I think I am going to die. I am not ready.

'This isn't fair,' I wail to Pete on the way home. 'Haven't I been through enough in my life? Why should this happen when I have just found you, when I have found happiness?'

'Life isn't fair, blossom,' he says kindly.

53

I have finished the chemo treatment. It lasted for six months. It was hardest when the children were on school holidays and ran around the house, feral with no one to care for them. I would lie in bed racked with guilt.

I have been thrown into early menopause by the chemo and I feel like my body has aged fifteen years. I have lost my vitality. I am only just forty-two and I am old and now I have to have my breasts removed. My doctor said I had to have the breast with the lump removed. I have chosen to have both of them removed because I read an article about women with genetic breast cancer reducing their chance of getting it by ninety per cent if they had both their breasts removed.

And I have calcification in the other breast.

'I want them both off at once,' I tell the surgeon, who has been kind to me and has tried to give me hope.

'Oh, I don't think I want to spend that long in surgery,' he says.

'I can't do this twice,' I tell him. 'I've only got the strength and resolve to face it once.'

He shakes his head, but then comes back and tells me he has got a colleague to help with the surgery and I can have both breasts done at once.

* * *

Before it is done Pete and I go away for two nights and Seth and Asher mind the younger children for us while we drink wine and sit in a spa bath. A friend comes and gives us massages. And Pete holds me tight in bed and I cry. Normally you cannot feel your organs, but I can feel my heart and it is cracked and chipped from the pain and I cry whenever Pete holds me. I am not the woman he married. That person has died. Does he love the new one?

I don't.

I cannot think about getting my breasts amputated. It is too hard. I am too scared of how I will feel when I wake up, because breasts are our most physical symbol of our womanhood. All else is hidden away, but our breasts, whether they are small or big, are out there proclaiming our gender. A man always looks at a woman's breasts before his eyes move to take in her face. Even the sensitive ones do it, they just do it more subtly. Will a man ever look appreciatively at me again? Will Pete? Will I feel that I am no longer a woman?

I feel okay.

I realise now I have woken that I am still me. I look disgusting but I am still myself.

'Hey,' says Pete, 'we don't care if you have no breasts. We just want you alive. If you say to the kids you can have no mother or you can have a mother but she won't have breasts, what do *you* think they would say?'

I try to concentrate on that: the fact that I am alive.

'I'll get reconstruction,' I say. 'I'll get pert twenty-year-old breasts with sticking-up nipples that have never been stretched by breastfeeding.'

The nurses at the Daylesford Hospital spoil me and sneak in fish and chips and Cointreau.

Next I am off to Geelong for radiation treatment, which only lasts for fifteen minutes but I have to have it every day.

I am staying in a hospital flat and I am bringing one of the children to stay with me each week. On my first day of radiation I walk out of the changing cubicle and there, waiting for her first dose, is Lucille who was my closest friend when I lived in Yarraville. She lived two doors down and her daughter, Michelle, was Asher's friend. We throw our arms around each other and go through the radiation together.

I am burnt red raw, my chest is weeping from the radiation and I am back in hospital with septicaemia. Every time Fred tries to put the antibiotic drip into my arm it pops out because my veins are so ravaged from the chemo. Then he has to go searching for another vein and I don't have many left. I look like a junkie. It hurts and I cry again. I feel like I have been in pain for too long.

Pete and I are sitting in the room of a plastic surgeon. It is a small, stifling room and so uncomfortable.

I have put my name down on the public waiting list while I am having radiation, but the nurse says, 'Don't hold your breath! The list is at least two years long.'

'Two years?'

'Might be up to five,' she shrugs, 'and of course you have to take whichever plastic surgeon is on.'

Two years without breasts!

I read women's magazines: I know there are plastic surgeons and plastic surgeons.

So I start shopping.

The surgeon sits staring at me and we are waiting for him to speak. Finally he says, 'Silicone.'

'Pardon?'

'You'll have to have silicone. Not enough weight on you for anything else.'

'Can I have nipples?' I ask.

'What do you want them for?' he says scathingly. 'Only your husband is going to see you.'

'Why do you want breasts?' says the next plastic surgeon. 'Is it so you can look nice in dresses?'

'Why do you want balls?' I ask him.

I am sitting in the waiting room of another plastic surgeon. Her waiting room is large and luxurious. Finally she calls for me and tells me to take off my top.

She looks at my back and says, 'I can give you size A, a small A. It's long surgery. Very dangerous. You have to be fit and you have to exercise. You will lose some of the use of your arms.'

She talks non-stop about how dangerous the surgery is and totally freaks me out.

I ring another office. 'Is he nice?' I ask the receptionist.

'He's lovely. We'll see you on Tuesday.'

I wait in another luxurious waiting room and finally I am called. If only they gave you gin and tonics all this waiting for doctors would be bearable.

The plastic surgeon has a friendly, warm, round face. He's pretty cute with a few freckles and lots of wild curls. I'm totally at home with hair like this, since I now have the chemo curl.

He shakes my hand solidly and says, 'Ian Holten. What can I do for you?'

'I want my husband to chase me around the house again,' I blurt out. 'I want him to gaze at me and get that look in his eye. I feel so ugly. I want to feel okay about my body as my children grow up. I want to stop hiding behind a locked bathroom door and avoiding mirrors.'

'We can fix all of that,' he says kindly.

'Can you give me nipples?' I ask.

'Of course. Wouldn't be a finished job without them. Are you on private health cover?'

'No, I'm not,' I say.

The reality is that we borrowed forty thousand dollars from the bank to move our shop to a better location and we spent the money getting the new shop habitable. Even though it is rented we still had to put the electricity and the phone through it, build a storeroom and paint the whole thing. And because I am so sick we had to pay people to do it. There was also signage, stock and shelving — and that was the end of forty thousand dollars! The rent was exorbitant but we took the chance and for the first three months it paid off. But then September 11 happened, everything died and we are up shit creek.

Pete's father was right. Open a business and you go bankrupt. And all we wanted to do was get off social security.

I tell Ian that my father-in-law has given us four thousand dollars towards the costs.

'Okay,' he says, without a moment's hesitation. 'I'll charge you a flat rate of one thousand dollars. You'll have to pay for the room, which will come to eighteen hundred, and I'll get a friend to help, which will be a thousand for him too. The other two hundred you will need for a girdle. We're going to chop up your tummy, give you a tummy tuck; then you'll have to have a surgical girdle.'

Even though I love Pete, I want to kiss this man deeply and passionately. I can see that he is going to change my life, put me on a new path and give me hope.

I walk away on a cloud. He is an angel sent from God.

My hair is starting to grow back, thank God! And with relish I throw all my beanies and scarves in the bin. I look like I have shaved it to make a statement and lesbians give me the eye: the you're-one-of-us-so-I'll-give-you-a-bigger-slice-of-cake-with-your-tea look in cafés.

Men in banks glare at me as if I am making a statement about their dicks and I want to shout, 'I just had cancer, okay. I don't have an attitude. I'm not a militant dyke!'

My friends won't believe me when I tell them this is what it is like.

54

My mother is on the phone to me and she is crying.

'Why are you crying?' I ask.

'I'm not crying!' she snaps.

'Okaaaay — more denial,' I mutter.

'I don't cry,' she says vehemently.

I remember that it is a sin to show your feelings. Feelings are self-centred. 'Tell me,' I persist, 'what is making you cry.'

'I'm just concerned because of your big operation tomorrow. Will you let me come and visit you?'

Now this is the twelfth time I've been in hospital in the last twelve months and not only has she not been terribly concerned before, she has never wanted to visit. And now it's will-you-let-me-visit in a pleading, helpless voice.

'Of course you can visit,' I say. 'Why wouldn't I let you? Hospital is so boring I want all the visitors I can get. Especially if you sneak me in a Cointreau!'

'Are you sure you'll let me come and visit you?' she asks in her little girl voice.

'We've talked about how you're going to visit each day already, remember?'

The problem here, I realise, is that when she was in hospital not only wouldn't she let my sister or me visit her, she wouldn't take our phone calls either. She would only see her sons. She's worried that I'll retaliate.

'I'll leave straightaway if Pete shows up,' she says.

This is another dig at my husband. She thinks he doesn't like her but I ignore it.

'Pete can't come, remember? The hospital is a one-and-a-half-hour drive from here and Pete has the shop and the kids to look after. We can't afford staff at the moment.'

She starts crying again and finally I cotton on. What really started this off is the email I fired off asking her to stop sending me religious propaganda and threatening to return it in kind with left-wing socialist propaganda if she didn't.

Suddenly she stops crying and says, 'Wayne just gave me a new computer screen.'

'Really, that's great,' I say.

'He's wonderful. I'm so lucky to have a son like him. Fancy giving me a new computer screen.'

'Where did he get it?' I ask.

'Oh, they were throwing it out at his work so he grabbed it and gave it to me. Well, the picture jumps all the time, but if I sit really still when I'm using it it's not too bad.'

'The picture jumps around when you use it?'

'Yeah, but it's okay if I sit really still. It only has one little thing wrong with it, but Wayne will be able to fix it in no time.'

Well, I think, obviously! Wayne always was her favourite child. He is a much better offspring than I am. Not only is he a boy, but he gives her computer screens and I only send her cross emails.

I am scared of this operation. I will be under an anaesthetic for at least eight hours. It will be painful and of course there is always the possibility that I could die. I am so sick of staring death in the face. I just want it to go away so I can get on with my beautiful life, with my beautiful children and my beautiful husband.

I have just had my ovaries, cervix and uterus removed. Anything that can get cancer is gone and menopause has set in with a vengeance. Most days I feel lousy, no energy, in tears, anxious that the cancer has come back to ruin my life.

'You'll be okay,' Pete assures me.

'You'll be fine,' my sister says.

One last visit with Ian before the surgery and he asks, 'What size boobs would you like?'

I tell him 'A'.

But Pete says 'C' at the same time and Ian laughs.

I will be in hospital for a week and I have written a will. As I am rolled into theatre I am scared, but glad that when I wake up I will have a flat stomach and breasts.

I'm awake and I want to die. I'm in agony and they have put me in a room that has its temperature set at forty-two degrees. I have a blanket over me with hot air pumping through it and that must be forty-two degrees too. Altogether that makes eighty-four degrees and I am a winter girl. I cannot move and when I need to go to the toilet they call two men to lift me. You cannot go to hospital and retain any inkling of dignity.

I feel like I want to die for four days and then I start to feel better; in fact I feel well enough to get out of bed and slide the temperature control on the room down degree by degree, so the nurse doesn't notice.

My mother comes to visit me and I say, 'I hope Karyn won't have to go through this. It is horrendous.'

'She won't!' snaps my mother.

'Why do you say that?'

'Because she got her testing done. She hasn't got it. She hasn't got the gene. She won't get it and neither will her kids.'

I feel like someone has kicked me while I am down and for a split second I wish once more that I were my sister. It seems so cruelly unfair. Why me and not her? It would seem so much fairer if it were both of us, or neither. She probably thinks the Lord has protected her because she is faithful! I think bitterly. Already my heart lurches sometimes as I gaze at Maia and Indea. She will never have to worry about her kids getting it. And why didn't she tell me herself? Why did I have to hear like this?

'Don't go down that path, blossom,' Pete says to me on the phone. 'It won't lead you anywhere useful.'

I know he is right and I know it is not my sister's fault that she won the gene Tattslotto. I try to be happy for her because I wouldn't wish cancer on anyone, but I do a terrible thing and take my hurt and anger out on her. I yell down the phone about all sorts of things that have nothing to do with my real hurt.

The fifth day, my friend Lucille comes to visit me and brings me sushi.

My friend Renate comes. She has shaved her head for leukaemia day. 'It's terrible,' she complains. 'Men glare at me like I am a dyke and dykes try to chat me up.'

'Ahh-ha!' I say. 'I told you and you wouldn't believe me.'

And then the next day I go home to bed.

Eleven and a half hours I was in surgery. I feel rotten. I can't stand up straight, but I have bumps on my chest. I have a scar across my belly and Pete says, 'Don't worry about it. I've seen women with worse stretch marks than that scar.'

The bandages come off my breasts, bit by bit, week by week, and even though my new breasts are nothing like the ones I had, they give me new hope. During the day I forget that I had my breasts removed. It is only when I look in the mirror at night that I am reminded.

With new hope I get excited about my next exhibition. Painting these women has taken on new meaning. As my body is being destroyed and chopped up, it seems right to be painting pictures that celebrate the beauty of women's bodies. It seems to say, I am alive and I am still a woman!

'I've started to paint,' says my mother. 'I've always been an artist. Perhaps I could put some of my paintings in the exhibition too.'

'Sure, Mum,' I say.

All the women who have modelled for me are nervous about appearing in my exhibition, but I promised to make them look four kilos lighter and to show how fine-looking they are and I hope they are happy with the results. This exhibition is in Daylesford because I want it to remain in the community and I am holding it in a café-gallery because I want it to be intimate so the women involved don't feel exposed.

I am wearing some gorgeous pants that Pete bought for me. After the surgery he insisted on taking me clothes shopping on our Visa card. It was a celebration that I was alive.

Pete's father has come to Daylesford for opening night, and so have Seth and Asher, so we pile the children in the car and off we go. I am nervous. But as Pete pulls up outside the café I am amazed. 'It's packed!' I shout.

Just about everyone in Daylesford has turned out for opening night.

Between wine and cheese and noise and laughter John Savage looks at a painting of Maggie's rear and says in a loud voice, 'I wouldn't mind seeing the front.'

I sell about twenty-six pieces and the gallery owner declares the exhibition a huge success.

Our shop, though, is not as successful. We need a new school for Zane and we need to get rid of some of our debt. Our business is going broke and we are not paying retailers on time. We realise we just have to wear the forty thousand we borrowed, even though we can see nothing in return for it. Mind you, our landlord has done all right out of our loan. We try to sell the lease, but all the potential buyers back away when they hear the ridiculous amount we are paying in rent.

So we sell the house I love and we move to Buninyong, a little hamlet out of Ballarat that reminds us of Daylesford when we first moved there. Buninyong is threatened by inappropriate development, but for the moment it is picturesque.

My boys are nineteen and twenty-one now and when they have girlfriend problems they talk to me and every girl is brought over for my approval. Some poor girl somewhere is saying, 'What is it with boys and their mothers?'

When I take my children out, all five of them, I truly do feel like a goddess. We make an impact as we float into a café. Me, surrounded by my five glorious children. I am so proud of them — not because of what they might achieve, but because of who they are. Because when I really needed them to give me hope, they did. They stood by me and urged me on. They have courage and kindness. They welcomed Pete into their lives and they love him. They are my future. I feel like I have more goodness in my life than any woman could wish for.

I have finished experimenting with spirituality. One day Pete's brother Geoff says to me, 'New age is nothing but superstition. You might as well say black cats bring bad luck.' And I think he is right!

People have thrown out Christianity and some of it needs throwing out, but what they have adopted in its place is just as unbelievable. I haven't found true spirituality, but when I do find it, it will have to be real, grounded, human and it will have to lead to justice. It will also have to lead into life, not out of it. Life is messy. You can't avoid it and if your life isn't messy then perhaps you're not really living.

Take relationships. Relationships are messy. Every time you take the risk of allowing someone into your life, whether it be a lover, friend or stepchild, you can be assured there will be misunderstanding, hurt and arguments. But there will also be incredible joy, laughter and fun.

The messiest experiences in life have to be falling in love and having children. When you fall in love everything is thrown into chaos while you combine your life with that of the person you love. But falling in love has to be one of the most joyous, broadening experiences you could hope for. It is the miracle of allowing another person to change who you are. In our case our love also threw into disruption the lives of our six children.

And you can't get messier than children. From the moment they are born they vomit, wee, poo and burp on you. Then they splatter your clothes and your house in paint, toys and bits of food that you find six months later, down the back of the couch, green, with life forms growing out of them. Children mess up your life with demands and needs. If you plan anything special you can bet your last dollar one of them will come down with chickenpox half an hour before the special event. Our children, all eight of them, made our falling in love a messy business indeed. Would I choose to have done it without them? Never! So where would I look to find true spirituality? I would have to say in the messiness of life.

Just as I get home after picking the children up from school in the afternoon, the phone rings. Therese, a friend from Daylesford, is in tears. Her beautiful twenty-one-year-old daughter has been killed in a car accident. How do people live with such pain? I think to myself. How can I help her?

'How can I help you, Therese?' I say, wishing I could take away some of her pain.

'Can you do the funeral?'

'Of course,' I say, wondering how I can write a funeral for a beautiful girl lost at the beginning of her journey. And again I feel so lucky. What right do I have to whinge that my life has been threatened when a child like Jasmine has her life cut swiftly from under her? What right do I have to complain about life when I have never had to face the sort of pain Therese is facing, the horror all parents fear of losing their child.

I knew Jasmine. She was sweet, stunning.

'I had a crush on Jasmine,' says Asher when I tell him the news.

'So did I,' says Seth. 'I think every boy in Daylesford had a crush on her.'

I try to write a ceremony that acknowledges the agony of their loss, that we all share. A ceremony that celebrates the life that Jasmine lived and the love people had for her. We have it down by the lake. It is sad but beautiful. The community of Daylesford stands there beside Therese and I feel honoured to have been asked to be a part of it.

55

Indea is eating muesli and reading the local paper with her dog on her knee.

'Did you know?' she says to me suddenly through her muesli, 'that *Winnie-the-Pooh* is filled with minority groups?'

'Sorry?'

'Think about it. *Winnie-the-Pooh*, the book. It's about minority groups. Winnie-the-Pooh is intellectually challenged. Anyone can see that. Even he calls himself a bear of very little brain. Piglet is a male who always wears pink. No further explanation needed. Tigger has ADHD: he never stops bouncing. Kanga is a single mother, Rabbit is obsessive compulsive, Owl has senile dementia setting in and Eeyore is a manic depressive. It's, like, totally politically correct.'

She doesn't say much, Indea, but when she does it is a well-thought-out gem.

'Oops, gotta catch the bus. See ya!' And she is out the door, leaving a half-eaten bowl of muesli on the kitchen table.

Zane and Maia go to a Steiner school, which brings us another new community and people welcome us into their lives. I have found a few good cafés and lovely women who I can drag along to them for a good gossip.

You cannot live in isolation.

* * *

When Zane is not at school he is practising or composing on his battered old piano.

David, Zane's piano teacher, is gorgeous in that perfect way. His skin is clear and pure. His eyes are blue, his cheekbones are carved and he has a very pink jumper that he bought in Kings Cross. He has become our friend and comes to our parties, which invariably turn into impromptu concerts, and when we introduce him to our female friends they flutter and fuss.

'Such a lovely man,' they gush. 'Don't you think he is just the most perfect man?' They go on drooling and David turns red at the unwanted compliments.

They surround him and one friend who has had quite a bit to drink says to him, 'You know, David, I'm not really a woman at all. Just think of me as a man stuck in a woman's body.'

David looks to me for rescue, but I just shrug. He can look after himself.

Having cancer has changed me. I have toughened up a bit and I'm not very tolerant when people complain about colds or broken toes. Is it going to kill you? I think to myself. No? Well, then, don't complain!

I don't think that I have survived so far through anything more than luck. So much of life is just luck. I felt hurt to the core when Rick's mum said, 'Tough luck.' I wanted her to say how sorry she was that I had cancer, to offer me her support. But the other side of the coin is that she was right. It was just tough luck.

God isn't up there rewarding some of us with a nice life and punishing others of us with horrid lives. We are all at the mercy of luck. Sometimes it's good and sometimes it's bad and the way we respond to it is our responsibility. Like everyone, I've had both. But most of my life has been messy; it has been lived and in living it to the full I have found God.

It has been hard for me to leave the support, kindness and history we had in Daylesford and even though we opened a shop in Ballarat, George Bush Junior started to talk about war and people stopped buying our products. So we did just as badly. In fact we are bankrupt and have had to sell our home.

When, like everyone else, I dream of winning Tattslotto, this is what I dream of:

I dream of being able to pay our bills, without sweating over them.

I dream of having a holiday once a year.

I dream about being able to send my kids to private secondary colleges.

I fantasise about spending my days painting and writing without having to worry about the state of the house and the pile of dirty clothes that grows like a rampant plant spreading out from the bathroom.

I dream of owning a Chrysler PT Cruiser because I have always missed my car Hezekiah.

I dream of giving money to Amnesty International and Community Aid Abroad.

I dream of having a bearded collie, because I miss the one that Jurgen gave to us.

These are just basic material things and not so important.

The important dream is this: I dream of growing old enough to be a grandmother.

We are having a Christmas concert. I am tired from cooking curries for Christmas lunch and the rumpus room needs vacuuming. I drag the vacuum cleaner down the hall to the rumpus room. Pete is on the internet, dreaming about the stocks he would like to buy when we are rich. I plug in the cleaner and sigh. I hate carpet. Our old house, which I loved, was all polished floorboards. Easy. Just grab a mop and broom and off you go. Carpet is hard work and I can't wait to be rid of it.

'What's the matter?' asks Pete, his face glued to the computer screen.

'Nothing.'

'No, I heard you sigh. Come on. What is it?'

I laugh to hide my true feelings. 'I was just thinking how I used to watch my mother doing housework late at night when she was tired, while my dad watched telly. I swore it would never happen to me and here I am, nine-thirty at night, dragging out the vacuum cleaner.'

Pete gets up from the computer and points at the couch. 'Sit!' he says. 'Don't move till I get back.'

He comes back and places a mug of herbal tea on the coffee table. 'You sit and drink. I'm vacuuming.'

'No! You don't have to,' I say.

'Just sit. I don't mind. My mother never had to vacuum late at night.'

Pete is a perfectionist and takes two hours to vacuum just the rumpus room, but it sparkles for Christmas Day.

We open presents in the morning, slowly, so we can ooh and aahh and thank the people who gave them to us. Then we sit down to a Christmas meal of curries and salads.

'Let's say grace,' I suggest.

Pete looks at me and raises his eyebrows.

'Let's say grace. Everyone hold hands. We'll do our old Westgate grace,' I say.

Seth and Asher remember this well. We move our hands up and down as we all shout at the top of our lungs, 'We thank you, God, for good food and good friends. Amen!'

There are no closing eyes. There's no sombreness. Just fun and laughter.

'Let's do it again!' says Zane, who likes any excuse to be loud.

So we do.

After lunch, the highlight: our first family Christmas concert. We are all going to perform little pieces for each other.

Asher dances a *pas de deux* with Maia and lifts her high in the air. She grins with pride and spreads her little arms wide like a real ballerina. She is so thrilled to be dancing with her big brother and her face is alight.

Seth performs Shakespeare from the production of *A Midsummer Night's Dream* that he is in. He is playing the part of Puck. And we cheer and whistle and all agree he is going to be a major star one day.

'I want to be thanked when you get your Oscar,' I say. 'You have to tell them, "I couldn't have done this without my mum."'

Zane has been reading music since he was four and a half and he plays the piano for us. He likes to perform and when he is up to his sixth piece we laugh and tell him that it is time to give someone else a go, but we are proud of his talent.

Pete's dad, John, tells a story and we are a bit apprehensive because his stories can go on and on for hours, but it turns out his story is a joke. And — even better — it is funny.

When it is my turn, I say, 'I am writing a story,' and I read to them about Grandma Lyne and her Christmas gifts.

Then Pete gets out his drums and after his piece we all grab something that can be used as a percussion instrument — sticks, saucepans and blocks from the toy shelf — and we make the loudest noise possible.

I am laughing and trying not to get a stitch. We are nearly bankrupt, but the children are beautiful and two years have gone by and the cancer hasn't come back.

There are still days when Pete comes home to find me curled up in bed crying.

'Honey, what's wrong?' he asks, although he knows.

'I'm sure it's back,' I weep.

'Is it your big toe that hurts, or is it cancer of the nose?'

I laugh despite myself and he makes me tea. I wake nearly every night panicking that the cancer has come back. But it hasn't.

I finally got the genetic testing done and I have got BRAC1 gene mutation.

'But,' the geneticist says, 'if you have got rid of the cancer you had, then with all the surgery you have had, your chance of getting cancer again is only three per cent. That is less than the average woman, whose chance is ten per cent.'

Anyway, I am almost through the three years that I only had a twenty per cent chance of surviving. I worry about which of my children this horrid genetic mutation has been passed on to and hope that medical research jumps forward in leaps and bounds.

I watch the children thumping away on their instruments together with Pete, whom they all adore and think of as their father. Indea puts her arms around his neck and kisses him.

'You know that you're only going to last for three weeks,' Asher says to Pete.

'Yeah,' adds Seth. 'You're just a fling, Pete.'

Pete laughs and Indea says, 'Of course, she still likes George better.' Then she reads us her contribution to our concert. She has written a poem.

There is always a tomorrow, but when will it arrive?
I'll pray for tomorrow for the rest of my life.
I hope for tomorrow for it to be there.
And I fear.
It never will be.
It's you that keeps me here.
You've helped me through my fear.

Hold me close, hold me tight.
Tell me it will be okay; tell me it will be all right.

We all clap wildly and then she puts on her new CD that she got for Christmas and as the first note rings out of the stereo we all recognise what has become our family song. We sing and dance around the lounge room together. Only Pete and Zane can sing in tune, only Asher can really dance, but we dance and sing at the top of our lungs anyway while 'I Can See Clearly Now' booms out of the stereo.

I have half my life yet to live and I dance and sing with my husband and the children I adore. No one tells me to stop singing and I think how blessed I am by God to have such love in my life. For here is the real miracle, the real spirit of God. It is right here inside each one of us, in our ability to love and be messy.

Acknowledgments

My thanks to:

Linda Funnell — who chose me and gently encouraged me onwards.

Peter Bishop — who opened doors I didn't know were there.

The Eleanor Dark Foundation and Varuna — where I spent ten days in a dream as a winner of the Varuna HarperCollins Manuscript Award.

Bec, Grace, Sylvia and Glen — who shared many good glasses of red, and lots of laughter.

Alan Marr — who read a very rough draft and fine-tuned details and Lyn Tranter and Mark McLeod who ironed out crinkles.

Seth — who created a fantastic list of titles, of which *Sunday Best* was chosen.

Asher — who was the first to read the very first chapter and urged me to keep going.

Indea — for the use of her poem.

Vanessa Radnidge — who not only edits but makes me laugh.

Julia Stiles and Nicola O'Shea for their empathy and support.

John Neal — who provided genealogical info.

Asher, Seth, Indea, Zane and Maia — who put up with too many frozen meals.

Peter — who said, write whatever you want.